TRUST AND TREACHERY

TRUST AND TREACHERY

A Historical Novel of Roger Williams in America

LINDA KRAEGER AND JOE BARNHART

SMYTH&HELWYS
PUBLISHING, INCORPORATED   MACON, GEORGIA

Smyth & Helwys Publishing, Inc.
6316 Peake Road
Macon, Georgia 31210-3960
1-800-747-3016

Library of Congress Cataloging-in-Publication Data

Kraeger, Linda
Trust and treachery : a historical novel of
Roger Williams in America / by Linda Kraeger and Joe Barnhart.
p. cm.
The 1996 ed. has subtitle : An historical novel of
early seventeenth-century England and New England.
ISBN 978-1-57312-434-8
1. Williams, Roger, 1604?-1683—Fiction.
2. New England—History—Colonial period,
ca. 1600-1775—Fiction.
3. Great Britain—History—Early Stuarts, 1603-1649—Fiction.
4. Theologians—Fiction.
5. Puritans—Fiction.
6. Pioneers—Fiction.
I. Barnhart, Joe E., 1931-
II. Title.
PS3561.R119T78 2004
813'.54—dc22

2004017151

CONTENTS

Prologue: From England to Persia, 1588–1625 1

Cambridge, July 1626 6

Cambridge, Early December 1630 10

The Atlantic Ocean, January–February 1631 12

The New World, Massachusetts, February 1631 16

Boston and Along the Charles River, March 1631, A Month
    Following Roger and Mary's Arrival 33

Salem, Massachusetts, March 1631 43

Salem, Late March 1631 57

Boston and Salem, April 1631 60

Boston and Massachusetts Bay, April 1631 65

Massachusetts Bay, April 1631 70

Plymouth Colony, August 1631 78

Boston, August 1631 81

Plymouth Colony, August 1631 85

Long Island, November 1631 103

Boston Colony, November 1631 105

Plymouth Colony, November 1631 108

Boston and Plymouth Colony, November 1631 122

Boston and Plymouth Colony, December 1631 129

Wampanoag Village and Plymouth Colony, October 1633 137

Plymouth and the Wampanoag Village, November 1633 147

Boston, November 1633 156

Boston, Plymouth, and Salem, November 1633 161

Boston and Salem, Late November and December 1633 179

Boston and Salem, December 1633–Spring 1634 188

Salem and Boston, Summer–November 1634 191

Salem and Boston, January–Spring 1635 193

Boston and Salem, Spring–Summer 1635 197

Boston and Salem, Summer 1635 205

Boston, Summer 1635 211

Boston, September–October 1635 214

Salem and Boston, October 1635 218

Boston, October 1635 226

Aboard Ship and in Salem, October 1635 228

Boston and Salem, October 1635–January 1636 230

The Massachusetts Forest, January 1636 236

The Massachusetts Wilderness, January–February 1636 243

The Seekonk River, Spring 1636 246

Aquidneck Island, Late Spring–Summer 1636 254

Aquidneck Island, Summer 1636 258

Aquidneck Island and the Connecticut Territory, October 1636 261

Boston, October 1636 269

Providence and Boston, October 1636 270

Boston, March–Early Spring 1637 276

Providence, Rhode Island, March–April 1637 278

Narraganset Bay and Salem, April 1637 280

Providence, May 1637 285

Boston, May 1637 287

Providence, May 1637 290

Providence, August 1637 297

Boston, August 1637 307

Providence, Late September 1637 313

Study Hill and Providence, November 1637 321

Providence and the Narraganset Village, February–March 1638..............328

FROM ENGLAND TO PERSIA

1588–1625

In summer 1588, the day Spain's Invincible Armada set sail across the English Channel to seize the crown for the Catholic King Philip, my mother gave birth to her fourth son, Samuel Firebrook. As citizens of London in those turbulent days, my parents knew not whether he would be raised Catholic or Protestant.

Under Queen Elizabeth, who had rejected Philip's proposal of marriage, the Church of England remained officially Protestant; but a growing number of Puritans complained that their church was still more Romanist than the Creator intended. When the Archbishop of Canterbury learned that half of the dreaded Armada's ships had either fallen captive or sunk, he jumped out of bed, slipped into his cassock, and publicly decreed that church bells should ring with celebration and that prayers should ascend on behalf of Good Queen Bess.

When I, named Eric by my father, entered the world one year and a half later, no church bell rang to celebrate my arrival. Born prematurely and of the wrong gender, I displeased my mother immediately. With four sons already and no daughter in her brood, she had petitioned heaven with the request that I, the child of her womb, emerge as Abigail, the darling daughter of her heart's desire. But when the midwife informed her that the newborn was not the answer to her prayers, she turned her head to the wall and cried out, "Take it away!"

In truth and fairness, I should add that eventually my mother forgave me for arriving ahead of little Abigail. At the age of fifteen, I bade farewell to my good parents and my only sister after informing them of my intention to seek both position and fortune in the world.

Three years later, two Islamic Turks from Constantinople invited me to join them in a promising shipping venture. To my surprise, wealth came quickly. But when I prepared to return to England, the Turks turned against me, selling me into slavery.

Abbass Hakim, a Persian merchant who spoke five languages, became my master. From him, I learned three languages and the art of buying and selling for profit. Abbass's only son, Hamza, proved so ungrateful and lazy that he brought more shame than pride to the family.

Abbass and I soon discovered that we inspired the best in each other. I resolved to learn all I could from him while he relished serving as my patient teacher. He became more my master of instruction than my owner.

One spring day he said, "If Hamza is the son of my loins, you, Eric, are the son of my heart and head."

I remember not when I began calling him Abba, an ancient Aramaic word meaning "gentle father." But it pleased him and drew us closer together. Abba had many friends in cities and ports from India to the land of the Danes. As we sailed together over many seas, his friends became my friends.

He had three wives and many daughters, some of whom had their father's gift of selling and bartering. Through their own ingenuity and hard work, two of the daughters made a modest fortune by shipping their exquisite knotted silk rugs to European capitals.

As a follower of the Islamic faith, Abba was allowed four wives. One morning as we sailed through the Strait of Bonifacio, I asked, "Abba, why have you never taken a fourth wife?"

"Why have you never taken even one?" he replied.

In truth, my mate was the sea; I could not at the age of nineteen imagine taking another.

From the beginning, Abba had urged me to keep detailed journals about our friends and their customs in every land. "When you are much older," he often said, "your journals and diary will prove useful."

Over the years, I compiled several journals, including my interviews with a Buddhist priest in Bangkok and a French Jesuit who sometimes talked for hours with Abba when we were in Paris.

When I turned twenty-one, Abba said, "Eric, my son, I wish to see one of your journals."

"They are for no eyes but mine," I protested.

He frowned, paused for a long period, and nodded. "That is good. They are your property. Use them as you wish."

The saddest day of my life came in my mid-twenties. Near ten of the clock in the morning, like angry Zeus from the Greek mountains, a storm descended and snapped Abba's ship as if it were a dry twig. The waters of the Aegean Sea, which had carried us to numerous friendly ports, turned into taunting waves threatening to become our grave.

"Abba, where are you?" I cried out when he vanished from my sight. The wind had no mercy. The thunder clapped in my ears as darkness covered the waters like midnight. The relentless hail mocked my frantic efforts to find and rescue him. Only when the lightning flashed its teeth could I see. I prayed and shouted, hoping Abba had found wood on which to float. I heard men scream for help, but the wind's howling carried their voices in every direction.

"Abba!" I shouted until my voice weakened to a hoarse whisper. My arms ached from swimming the stormy waters, but the pain could not compare to my fear that Abba had suffocated beneath a mountainous wave.

Minutes became hours. My aching arms felt as if flames burned inside them. Refusing to give up hope and clinging now to bits of wreckage, I prayed that Providence would disperse the storm and send the sun's rays to shine upon us. *Abba, you must not die!*

When I at last washed ashore, I forced my exhausted frame to comb the beach in search of him. At sunset, my hope still burned inside as I thought that perhaps Providence had cast him like Jonah on the shore of some hospitable Nineveh.

Very early the following morning, Greek fishermen rolled me over in the sand, fed me, and informed me they had found two other survivors. Neither proved to be Abba.

Two months later, I ended my search, having gone to the ports on the Aegean that Abba would most likely visit. None of our friends had news of his survival.

I returned to Persia to meet with his three wives and daughters. An imam in a gray beard and black turban approached me. He spoke slowly, doubtless thinking my Persian inadequate. "Eric Firebrook, you are requested to attend the reading of Abbass Hakim's last testament."

The three wives, their many daughters, Abbass's son Hamza, and I sat before the imam. An exceedingly tall man whom I knew to be Abba's keeper of records accompanied the imam. Because of his accuracy and honesty, Abba had rewarded him handsomely over the years.

The keeper of records looked at me with his shiny black eyes. "Eric Firebrook, you have fallen heir to a considerable portion of Abbass Hakim's wealth."

Listening carefully, I learned that I had inherited a generous portion of Abba's money. The wives received his land, his houses, and the remainder of his money. To my surprise, the keeper of records disclosed that Abbass's larger ship, the *Nahda* (meaning renewal or renaissance), now belonged to me. It was docked on Persia's southern coast.

A deep sorrow shadowed me. If Abba had taken the magnificent *Nahda* instead of his older ship, we might have weathered the Aegean storm and Abba would still be among the living.

I heard the imam say solemnly to Hamza, "Your father has left you one camel and the hope that with your own mind and hands you will succeed in all your ventures."

Hamza looked around as if he had heard a disembodied voice. "An outrageous mistake has been made!" His face flushed crimson and his forehead dripped with sweat.

Speaking calmly, the imam told Hamza the story of a beloved prince who hired a carpenter to build a fine house.

"I must journey to another land but will return in three months," the prince said and departed.

In the prince's absence, the carpenter cheated by using cheap and shoddy materials in building the house. "The prince will never know," he told himself daily, grinning with triumph as he concealed his inferior workmanship.

After three months, the prince returned as promised and asked to see the new house. The carpenter took him to the site and stood at his side, considering himself exceedingly clever in the way he had disguised the many flaws behind the structure's facade.

"Ah," said the prince, as he stepped back to admire the house. "I trust its walls are solid and its roof is sturdy, for I wish to give it to you as a present. From this day forward, it shall be your house and the house of your wife and children."

Hamza hung his head in shame and left with his camel. He knew he had squandered his father's love over the years. That was the last time I saw him.

For the next eight years, hard work became my close companion. My heart spoke its gratitude every day to Abba for the knowledge he had given me during my years as his apprentice. My ship *Nahda* and I were always welcomed to the ports of many seas. As if he had known that someday I would become the captain of his ship and the heir of his enterprise, Abba left me a letter commending me as his true successor.

On the eighth year of my position as captain and at the peak of my success, I became strangely restless. Alone in my cabin during the nights, I often read books by candlelight and studied the journals Abba had urged me to compile.

One summer night, I left my cabin and stood alone on deck under the bright stars. The North Star caught my attention, and soon perplexing thoughts washed over me like waves. Abba had followed the way of Islam, and I the way of Christ and the Church of England. The Buddhists and Hindus, equally fervent in their faith, believed the North Star guided their journey. A Hindu merchant had once told Abba that in their separate religions all human beings followed the same Polar Star under different names; but Abba had disagreed in his polite, yet firm Islamic way.

Standing on the ship's deck nightly while glancing up now and then at the heavens, I often reflected on the dispute between Abba and the Hindu merchant. Disturbing thoughts kept invading my mind. Perhaps in religion there is no Polar Star. Perhaps we are all deluded. Perhaps none of our ships of faith has a destiny. Are we all wandering aimlessly, pretending to follow a star of our own invention?

My restlessness grew fierce, like the monsoons in the Bay of Bengal. Nothing would calm the storm. For a full year, my thoughts churned with questions and roared with doubts until at last I resolved to return to England. Two and a half years had elapsed since my ship had last crossed the channel, and I was now eager to see my relations and my good friend, the London lawyer John Winthrop.

Abba had often told me that I was a man of action who would in time become also a man of reflection. He prophesied that eventually I would take up the pen as readily as some men had taken up the sword. If my memory is correct, the time of reflection began in full earnest when I witnessed the execution of a woman in the sands of Arabia. I will not dwell on that grim incident. Perhaps it was only the last grain on my mental scale, for only a month earlier a Danish captain had informed me of an Anabaptist seized by the crew of Lutherans and thrown overboard.

It was as if my North Star had disappeared from the sky.

In June 1625, I anchored the *Nahda* off the coast of Portsmouth, less than thirty-four leagues south of London. As soon as I arrived in London, my friend John Winthrop dismissed everyone from his law office and insisted that I sit down and explain the words I had written him two months earlier.

Born in the year of the Spanish Armada's humiliation, Winthrop was now thirty-seven, tall, lean, and gifted with the special Puritan sense of humor that saw the irony of Providence in everything. He was thoroughly English: thrifty, fond of poetical expressions, and quite confident the English were heaven's chosen people. Like most

Englishmen of his class, he believed that since danger and chaos loomed only steps away, every citizen stood duty-bound to contribute to the moral seawall that prevented chilling waves of anarchy from turning the jeweled island into a hellish swamp.

Winthrop and I talked far into the night. I had long admired his integrity in a profession familiar with corruption. Like many Puritans, he kept what he called his spiritual diary, which he had begun shortly after turning nineteen and a week before the birth of his first son.

A few days after my return to London, Winthrop, understanding my deep need to find my North Star again, said, "Captain, you must put your soul in harbor. It has been too long at sea."

"Have you a particular suggestion?" I asked.

"I know you to be an adventurer. But I sense in you some intense change. Although you have sailed far and wide, you seem restless to . . . ." He paused, stared at me, and tapped the tip of his finger against his temple. "Could it be that you now long to travel on the seas of the mind, to journey back in search of the wisdom of the Greeks and Romans, to comb the ancient Scriptures of our Lord?"

Although I knew Winthrop had attended Cambridge University, nothing had prepared me for his proposal that I seek entrance to the university, where I might sail the high seas of time, dropping my anchor with Homer, Plato, Virgil, Matthew, Mark, Luke, and John.

"Your brain has overheated," I said. "Like yourself, I am in my mid-thirties."

He laughed. "So much the better."

"I am glad you find me amusing, John. But—"

"You have a gift for languages, do you not?"

"Yes, but—"

"That is half the battle at Cambridge."

Again, I protested; but my thoughts sped to the university. I recalled my visit there with my father to see my cousin, who was then twenty and I only eleven.

Winthrop urged me to ponder his suggestion and promised to use his influence to open the way for my entrance.

Events moved swiftly. When a Scotsman with his burring "r" asked to purchase my ship, I grew angry. "Sell *Nahda?!*" I shouted.

"I quite understand, Captain Firebrook." The Scotsman stared at me with his one good eye, which looked like a shining emerald set in a face of hard oak.

"You understand nothing. Selling *Nahda* is like selling . . . why, sir, it is like selling a wife."

As the Scotsman remained stone-faced, I realized he had often dealt with the likes of me. Captains become sorely attached to their ships.

He clamped his broad hand on my shoulder. "I will take proper care of your *Nahda.*"

In time, I relented; yet I could not easily rid myself of the feeling that I had deserted a good and faithful friend.

On the night before selling her, I had a dream. Old Abba appeared and stood with me on some distant shore. Together we watched *Nahda* sail away without us. Sometime thereafter, I packed my belongings, loaded my chest of journals onto a carriage, and departed north to Cambridge.

Soon I discovered that Winthrop had failed to reveal one fact about Cambridge, a crucial fact that descended upon me only after I became a student among new friends. The university was a hotbed of Puritans who possessed an intensity rivaled only by their contradictions!

My story begins in that hotbed. Of all the journals I kept over many years, I prize none above those depicting the winsome Roger Williams, a daring Puritan whose heart gushed forth as if from underground springs of a mysterious source. His adventure I am compelled to disclose.

Perhaps you will forgive me if like a playwright I frequently appear on stage alongside Roger, Winthrop, John Milton, and the other characters. I beg you not to think me vain. I long only to be accurate; and in fulfilling this longing, I must not yield to the false modesty of pretending I was nothing in their lives. I was present sometimes as a substantial person, other times as an attentive shadow. On still other occasions, I was present only vicariously through witnesses who proved to be most reliable sources.

In many ways, the adventure with those Puritans compares only to sailing around the hazardous tip of Africa—not a journey for the faint of heart.

CAMBRIDGE

July 1626

To my surprise, I thought I saw England's most renowned jurist hurry from a carriage and slip inside a home on the outskirts of Cambridge. When visiting London's greatest library, I had seen Sir Edward Coke's portrait, his learned eyes peering down at the readers as if to admonish them to apply themselves with diligence. A friend in London had once told me that another famous English jurist, Sir Francis Bacon, had despised Sir Edward and engineered his dismissal from his position as chief justice of the king's bench. I still remembered my friends saying to me, "Do not underestimate Sir Edward. His knowledge of the law supercedes that of anyone in England, and he has won favor with many in high places." I did not underestimate him and had joined many others who cheered his election to Parliament despite King James's connivance to ruin him.

I turned to my fellow student. "Was that not Chief Justice Edward Coke?"

"'Twas indeed, Captain. But does it not seem strange to you that he should be in Cambridge?"

"Aye, on this day in particular! I have no doubt our new chancellor would take displeasure in seeing his old enemy so near at hand. But tell me, who was that self-assured gentleman with him? Perhaps he holds the key to our mystery."

"You have not met Roger Williams? He is a vigorous student here."

"But did you not tell me that you had introduced me to all the gentry at Cambridge?"

"I did, but Williams is not of the gentry. His father was a London merchant tailor."

"Then, pray tell, what is this Roger Williams to Sir Edward?"

"His stenographer and protégé. Some say he is like a son to the judge, and I hear that he is no one to tangle with in debate. As far as I can judge, he is pleasant, straightforward, and speaks in a winsome, baritone voice. He also listens well, I have observed."

Why, I wondered, would the judge arrive on the day of the Duke of Buckingham's inauguration as chancellor of Cambridge University? All England knew of the animosity between the duke and the judge. Sensing intrigue, I resolved to meet Roger Williams soon.

Inside the house that Sir Edward Coke and Roger had entered, the drapes quickly closed, but not before the owner of the house, the judge's old friend, had taken a discreet peek out his parlor window. He turned to the judge and nodded silently.

The two guests then walked down a long, shadowy corridor and entered the library. A frail, stooped-shouldered man appeared a moment later, handed the judge the library key, and left without saying a word. Roger Williams took the key and locked the library from the inside.

The judge sat down at a table lighted with candles. As Roger closed the drapes to the three windows, twilight turned to darkness. The judge whispered, "I presume you heard the new Cambridge chancellor's speech today. Give me the full report."

"Crafty Buckingham has yet to make a formal speech. I overheard useful conversations that may nevertheless interest you."

"Formal speeches often reveal little. Did you gain access to talk in small circles?"

"Aye." Roger let his eyes search every corner of the library.

Coke's brow furrowed as he removed his coat. "Who observed you listening?"

"No one." Roger casually took the judge's hat and coat to hang on a hook. "No one so far as I could tell."

"Give me the gist."

Still standing, Roger took three pages of notes from his pocket, laid them on the table, smoothed out the creases, and moved quickly to the heart of the matter. "First, the king appointed the Duke of Buckingham to serve as watchdog over opinions permitted to thrive at the university. Second, Buckingham knows he has opposition. But he has the king's approval to use stern measures. It bodes not well for our university. Third, Buckingham assures us that the king will sweeten the pudding by building a new library." Roger paused, knowing that Sir Edward Coke would speak.

"A library? Bah! A museum for yet more of the king's lavish portraits!"

Roger knew to ignore the judge's irascibility and to treat his notorious temper as a great gust of wind that would quickly wane. Recently Roger had learned of King Charles's secret promise of gold for certain men if they could find solid evidence to undermine England's most influential judge. Charles still fumed because of Coke's boldness in leading the attack to impeach the Duke of Buckingham, the king's closest advisor in matters both military and civil. Fully aware of Coke's fondness for Cambridge University, King Charles had vindictively placed the duke at its helm.

Thus far, only John Milton Sr. and Roger knew Coke had published the documents that exposed the practice of extracting confessions by torture. Even now, when knocks came at his door, Roger stiffened, wondering if at last the spies had uncovered the truth about Coke.

Sitting now at the table across from Roger, Sir Edward Coke shook his head. "I could believe that Charles would richly reward and even promote his former jester and attendant in clandestine trysts. But to install him as the chancellor of our distinguished university is beyond the pale of rationality."

"George Villiers Buckingham had only to ask for the position," Roger reminded the judge. "You know better than anyone how this schemer has clawed his way up to become now the unrivalled power behind the throne." Roger said no more, for he could see he had added to his mentor's dismay.

Growing at last weary of raising public money to finance Buckingham's military adventures and elegant masques for his political partisans, Judge Coke had led Parliament to impeach the duke after his disastrous expedition to the Spanish seaport of Cádiz. George Buckingham, however, had come back undaunted, proclaiming his natural right to membership inside the royal circle. Unabashedly he spread the story that King James himself had once said, "Christ had his John the Beloved, and I have my George." Buckingham professed to believe unequivocally in Charles's claim that as king he owed account of his action, not to Parliament or English law, but to God alone.

The judge now closed his eyes tightly and rubbed his creased brow. "Take up your quill, Roger. The words I am about to give you are only my disjointed thoughts for the present. When the time comes, however, we will stitch them together and call them the Petition of Right."

Roger fought against the taut muscles in his shoulder. Loosening his large, white collar, he set his chin firm. Sensing that this would be no ordinary night, he dipped his quill into the ink and waited anxiously for Sir Edward to deliver his first sentence. He had an overpowering conviction that he would remember this night for the rest of his life.

As the candle flames flickered, Roger took down Parliament's complaints against the king: illegal forced loans (with imprisonment of refusers), arbitrary taxes without Parliament's consent, compulsory quartering of soldiers in private homes, capricious imprisonment of decent and law-abiding citizens, and unjustified marshal law.

Cold chills ran down Roger's spine. He understood why the judge spoke in a near whisper. The far-reaching import of the petition made Roger's thoughts reel.

Five years before assuming the throne, Charles's father James, clad in a pale blue satin suit with silver lace, had laid aside his large, white-feathered hat and picked up the royal quill to sign his name to the long treatise he had written in defense of monarchy by divine right. A week later, still wearing the feathered hat, James had picked up the royal quill again to argue his defense of the monarchy's absoluteness. "Kings are breathing images of God upon Earth."

Chief Justice Coke never concealed from Roger the peril of his mission to oppose the doctrine of absoluteness. Roger, by now a confirmed student of English history, agreed with his mentor that the divine right of kingship violated the ancient and sacred tradition of English law. James had written, "Before there was law, there was the king." But Coke dared to advance the opposite maxim. The law came first and then the king, who must himself remain subject to the law.

As Roger transcribed his notes into longhand, he felt perspiration on his face and flicked back the unruly lock that habitually curled on his forehead.

Sir Edward paused. Roger looked up and noticed the hugeness of his mentor's shadow on the wall. How appropriate! As a Puritan with passion for both freedom and reform, Roger could no longer stand in awe of any human mortal. Still he felt that for whatever reason, Providence had cast him on stage alongside a towering man whose shadow would fall across England for centuries.

Allowing himself the pleasure of reminiscing, he could scarcely believe it had been only a decade since as a lad of thirteen he had learned shorthand. Yet in some ways, it seemed a lifetime ago that the judge had happened to see him taking notes at St. Sepulchre. How odd that they would even chance to cross paths inside one of London's largest and oldest churches! Or was it chance? He could still picture the judge leaning over to look at what he—a mere boy—had written. And on the following day, Sir Edward Coke had sent for him, complimenting him on grasping the importance of accuracy. How mysterious—how difficult to comprehend—how wondrous! Coke had instantly taken him under his wing. *Ten years ago*, Roger mused, and now they sat across the table from one another in a house scarcely a stone's throw from Cambridge University. He lit a fresh candle, put it in the holder for Sir Edward, and handed him the transcribed notes to read with his keen, critical eye.

While the judge read silently, Roger's thoughts again returned to the past. It had been almost six years since his father had died. He would never forget how the judge had become a second father to him, gently nurturing him, using his influence to help him gain entrance to the Charterhouse School. It was Sir Edward Coke who had taught him to dream of distinguishing himself at Charterhouse in preparation for eventual ascendancy to Cambridge University. Sir Edward had so filled him with the love of learning that he had earned a scholarship for three rigorous but promising years at Cambridge.

Returning from his reminiscence, he pushed a candle closer to the judge and was careful not to interrupt the silent reading. Moments later, Sir Edward nodded with vigorous approval and stood up. "Roger, speak to no one about this. It may take two years before the time is ripe to lay this before the king. Guard yourself against treachery!"

"I understand." He quietly tore his shorthand notes into small bits. He would burn them later.

During the following two years, he did not forget Sir Edward's warning. Yet despite his caution and keen understanding of political intrigue in England, the hounds of betrayal and treachery became increasingly relentless at his heels. Far from winning favor with either the king or most members of Parliament, his new thoughts of liberty of conscience rendered his life in England precarious at best. Were his days there numbered?

CAMBRIDGE

Early December 1630

Four years after first meeting Roger at Cambridge, I heard the courageous young woman he married say, "Roger, I have no longing for widowhood."

As brave as anyone I have met, Mary had grown up in a clergyman's house and had listened to her father speak in subdued tones of Bishop Laud, a man who had the king's ear and sufficient power to send opponents to London's infamous Tower.

Years after meeting Mary, she confided in me as a friend that her kind husband had taken her hand in his and looked into her eyes. "Are you willing, Mary, to sail a thousand leagues across the icy Atlantic?"

"Only if we sail together," she had replied. "Your friend John Winthrop has already departed England's shores, leaving *his* wife behind."

Mary spoke the truth. After convincing King Charles to appoint him the Massachusetts Bay Company's governor, the adroit London lawyer Winthrop had sailed for New England to begin a new life.

While expecting John Winthrop's departure, I confess that I was not prepared for Roger and Mary's decision to leave England. When I saw that a letter had come from Roger, I read it quickly. The contents hit me like a thunderbolt at my feet.

Good Friend Eric,

I left for Bristol without saying farewell. At this moment, I wait in expectation that my Mary will join me. She is en route from Lincoln to Bristol and should arrive on the morrow. When you read this epistle, if all goes well, my loving Mary and I will be aboard ship on the Atlantic. I make no pretense to comprehend all the intricate ways of Providence in preparing us to sail for the New World.

I know that our friend John Milton Jr. has no desire to leave England, save for a brief journey to Italy or Geneva. It is good he has friends in high places. As for yourself, I confess that I already feel a hole in my heart, knowing Mary and I might never again see our friend Captain Firebrook. Or is it possible that heaven will someday guide you to join us in the New World?

I will write to Milton to feed his courage and resolution to serve heaven with the beauty of poetry and the high calling of religion undefiled by the tyranny that forces men and women to mask their true beliefs. When you see him, let him know that though my heart aches at leaving behind family and friends, I face the new horizon ahead without flinching. Joy rings in my heart, for the New World offers the opportunity to sow the seeds of true liberty of conscience. Though the arrogant Bishop Laud and his ruthless commission schemed to bring about suppression throughout all England, heaven works always to bring about good ends. I pray that the seeds of soul liberty will take firm root in New England. Before heaven, I vow to expose and oppose those apostles of tyranny who would force many to play the hypocrite rather than suffer persecution.

Give my kindest regards to the Reverend John Cotton. Would that we had found more time to explore our thoughts together. I pray that heaven will move him to heed our warning concerning his danger. Perhaps he will see the wisdom of joining us in the New World. . . .

I could not finish reading Roger's letter without sitting down to recover from the thunderbolt. As if he knew that dark clouds would collect over my head, he closed his letter with words of ringing cheer and hope. When I folded it and put it away, I found myself both weeping and laughing. I had not shed tears since losing my dear Muslim friend Abba in the cruel sea. Yet despite my sorrow and my anger at the High Commission that had hounded Roger, I could not help laughing at his undaunted hope in the face of what some might regard as irrevocable defeat.

On the next dawn, the bright red sun reflecting off the river brought a strange and wondrous peace to me. Roger had escaped both Laud's hounds and the fate of the Tower. The joy in my friend's epistle rang like bells inside me. I had no doubt that he possessed a new dream and that both King Charles and Bishop Laud had unwittingly served to give strong wind for Roger's sails. Courageous Mary and he would carry their dream to New England. Down deep, I knew that because of them the New World would be new in a way that few in England scarcely imagined. Remembering that Roger and I had solemnly promised to share our journals and notes with each other for many years, I took heart. If fortune smiled on me, some of my account of Roger's adventures would come from his perspective. Though I had never disclosed to Mary the precise plan of my book, she too had vowed to record memories and someday share them with me. Only later would I comprehend the true value of her observations and reflections.

THE ATLANTIC OCEAN

January–February 1631

The sounds of lowing cattle, squealing swine, and groaning passengers sick below deck mingled discordantly with the howling, swirling wind. After a relentless twelve-hour rain, the stalking twin storms found a new way to torment the passengers aboard the *Lyon*. The wind yielded to an Atlantic fog so thick that Captain William Peirce could see no more than thirty feet ahead.

A putrid stench stirred the captain to order a search for its cause.

"No search is required," a burly crew member said, leading him to the quarters of the four landsmen.

"Pigs put you to shame!" the captain roared. "Take buckets of water and scrub the filth from this floor."

The landsmen grumbled mildly, but the captain's withering eyes put a stop to their complaints. "You endanger the health of us all. If you should fall overboard with the dirt caked like scales on your skin, the cod would take you for their kind." Upon promising to inspect their progress soon, he left.

A day later a whale followed alongside the ship. The spouting creature delighted the English children, who jumped up and down while competing for a suitable name to call their new, magnificent friend.

The soupy fog, now far behind, had succumbed to a handsome gale that filled the sails. The weather and moods changed frequently during that week, mirth replacing despair or fear replacing contentment, all according to the weather and shifting circumstances.

The Sabbath came, and many passengers called upon Roger Williams again to expound the Scriptures. He selected texts from the Epistle to the Galatians that bespoke his favorite subject, divine grace. Puritans of every stripe held that justification before God came not through works or deeds, but through trust or faith in divine grace and kindness. Puritans abhorred the notion that sinners *earned* their way to heaven by payment of indulgences or prolonged deeds of penance.

Almost two months after leaving England, the ship suddenly lay a-hull, drifting without sail for lack of wind. After the people suffered forty hours without progress in the sea, a nerve-fraying restlessness rose like a vapor among them.

An old woman lifted her voice, wailing in prayer so that all could hear her accusations against Captain Peirce. Before heaven and the people, she charged him with leading them, like Moses, to wander aimlessly in the wilderness.

On the third day with lack of wind for the sails, men began to wonder aloud if among them stood on deck a Jonah who had disobeyed God. "God is punishing us for Jonah's disobedience!" roared Simon, the huge, one-eyed blacksmith from Bath.

Another voice shouted, "Let us cast lots to determine who among us is the Jonah."

Roger feared that Simon and the others caught up in desperation would cast the supposed Jonah overboard. He recalled that when serving as chaplain at Masham Manor he had observed some Puritans magnifying their deeds beyond humility, imagining that every shift in the weather came by a moral flaw in themselves, their enemies, or a personal demonic force that had temporarily wrested control of events from the Creator.

Stepping beside the blacksmith, Roger faced Simon's audience. Without flinching, he looked into their bewitched faces, raised his palm, and held it facing them until there was silence. "Listen to me, brothers and sisters. Scripture is plain. Christ our Savior said, 'You shall not tempt the Lord your God.' This derangement of the mind, this invitation to tempt your God, will only turn you against one another. Does not the good Apostle himself in the Epistle to the Ephesians counsel a life of 'patience, forbearing one another in love, eager to maintain the unity of the spirit in the bond of peace'? Perhaps, brothers and sisters, we have embarked on this venture to refine our patience. If any one among us possesses excess of patience, let him step forward that I may learn of him."

When no one stepped forth, he gripped Simon's hand warmly. "Patience, good brother, and God will bless us both. It may be that before this severe journey ends, we will lose more than one of us overboard. Let us not stain our hands with blood by making human sacrifice in the manner of the ancient Canaanites."

When no one seemed offended by this gentle appeal, Simon looked around as though to urge someone to challenge Roger.

At first, Roger took comfort when no one spoke. Then an alien feeling seized him as though he stood on some ancient mountain before people of a perverse religion whose god required human blood. *What is this? Have we reverted to the pagan Agamemnon?* Images of Agamemnon sacrificing his daughter to the goddess Artemis captured his mind. For the first time, he felt he understood the ancient Greek seamen who trembled before their whimsical gods and goddesses and placated them with blood and other morsels.

All at once, Simon broke out in wild, painful, uncontrollable but infectuous laughter void of mirth or joy. Soon, all on deck were laughing, throwing their heads back. Tears gushed out for some as though water had overflowed the kettle.

Then Roger began to laugh, not in pain, but in celebration that they were all yet alive, having escaped a moment of madness and murder aboard the *Lyon*.

Just as the sun began to sink below the watery horizon, two seamen fell at odds over food they had stolen. Fists flew and curses resounded. The short, stocky seaman kicked the tall one in the knee and grabbed him by his long, skinny neck. The tall man turned blue as if life were leaving him. Then a frightened cow broke loose and stepped on the assaulter's foot.

"Arrest those men!" the captain commanded.

Four crewmen pounced upon the assaulter and swiftly bound him despite his pig-like squealing. The tall man gasped for breath and for a moment appeared to have given up the ghost. When his breath and color returned, he too found himself bound with ropes.

On Monday night, the captain abruptly called out, "Lower the skysail!" Wind and icy rain struck the ship with such ferocity as to sling passengers across the top deck. Converging twin storms had turned into one mighty force.

Time itself vanished in the whirling chaos. Fear invaded every cell of Roger's body. Before his eyes, the sea turned into rolling mountains. "Get below deck!" he shouted and frantically shoved men, women, children, and even animals into the ship's belly lest the waves snatch them away as fodder for the chaos.

Below deck the swaying lanterns cast grotesque shadows upon the wall. Screaming children, cracking thunder, bleating sheep, roaring sea, and shouting sailors made it seem as if he were in a cave of horrors. Men pushed, women yelled in search of their children, and the ship cried with creaking anguish. Amid all this, a woman gave birth.

Then tranquility came with such suddenness that men and women looked at one another as if to ask, "Have we in truth passed from Earth to eternity? Have we passed so quickly through the straits of death into the tranquility of the life to come?" Others trembled as if half expecting the Great Judge to appear to inform them as to whether they would now enter heaven or descend to hell.

But the calm slowly overcame their suspicion. Smiles broke out on a few faces and spread quickly from face to face. Had they survived the storm? Soon, Roger, Mary, and a handful of other passengers dared to venture out on deck.

"It has passed! It has passed!" some of the crew shouted back to those below.

Thanksgiving erupted from the lips of even the children, who no longer cried. With his arm around Mary, Roger relished the relief. Thank God, none had perished. The ship had not become their casket.

But the tranquility proved ephemeral. The storm circled back like hungry fangs. The ship trembled until the passengers, again below deck, feared the mighty vessel would pop open like a ripe melon.

A young man with a large Adam's apple went berserk like the sea until Simon the blacksmith slapped him with one blow to the floor. Everyone began to shake. An unbearable chill filled the air. "A blizzard!" trumpeted a woman's shrill voice.

A frantic scramble for blankets and cover ensued. Then as the ship rose up on a swelling wave, some passengers fell down from vertigo while others fought to keep their stomachs from rolling like the sea.

"Our watery doom! Our watery doom, Lord!" an old man cried out until his daughter pulled him into a corner and sang to soothe him. Yet her voice cracked and dissolved in tears.

Thinking Captain Peirce might need him on top deck, Roger threw a blanket around his shoulders and ventured up the steps. But the icy rain pelting his face forced him to turn his back to walk against the wind. When he reached the helm, he thought he saw the captain ahead.

Suddenly, Roger's feet slipped and he crashed to the icy deck. In vain, he struggled to get to his feet. *What is happening?* He felt himself sliding uncontrollably on his side toward the stern. As he clawed at the deck, the blanket whipped off his shoulders and sailed overboard like a leaf. *Do not panic!* Sensing that he could be instantly hurled overboard, he grabbed a hatch rope and clung desperately. A full minute passed before he realized he had grown rigid in fear.

He fought to recover his lucidity. He had to think. How could he assure himself the captain still commanded the ship? His doubts drove him to the cliff of temporary madness. If only he could claw his way forward away from the stern. He had to find the captain! With all the strength in his quivering muscles and chilled bones, he grabbed, clawed, and pulled his way until he saw the captain tied stoically to the post at the helm, his eyes transfixed. Clearly, Captain Peirce resolutely faced westward as if some celestial dispensation had granted him momentary power to see the shores of the New World stretched out like welcoming arms beckoning him.

"We can ride her out, Master Williams. A praying man at my side—'tis good you have come."

The wind played with the ship like a cat using its paws to molest a mouse. But the captain kept uttering encouraging messages. "We will wear out this beast, Master Williams. Hold fast! Our hour will come if we do not faint!"

He took new heart upon witnessing the captain's courage.

To the evident surprise of everyone except the captain, the wolfish storm abruptly veered its course, hunkering and cringing in retreat. The captain and his crew had triumphed! The ship became vital again like a wounded caribou struggling at last to her feet, swishing her tail, and proudly dashing away, wounded but unconquered.

On the fourth day of February, a bird lighted upon the ship's deck. Soon a spontaneous, joyous shout of many voices exploded across the water.

Roger lifted Mary off her feet, whirled her around with him like children at play, and began singing a psalm. The others aboard joined in, singing to the top of their voices.

Early the next morning, Mary and Roger stood arm in arm near the ship's bow and eagerly scanned the horizon in search of land. They shivered as blocks of ice floated past the ship.

A prolonged hush fell across the deck, everyone seemingly listening for the seagulls. As the morning sun transformed from red to orange, Mary whispered, "Listen."

Then older children began to shout, "Seagulls! Yes, yes, seagulls!"

With his keen eyes, Roger saw dots fluttering in the sky. Soon, they became flapping wings. Feeling elated, he hugged his wife tightly and thought the squawking gulls made music.

From the crow's nest above, a husky voice rang out, "Land ho!"

Men and women appeared a few at a time from below. Some came with frowns of skepticism. Others squinted, shielding their eyes with their hands. Fathers held their children on their shoulders.

Roger and Mary helped two widows gather their possessions. Mary seemed to take particular interest in the children who had lost their father at sea.

Simon the blacksmith stood with his chin dropped, looking like a statue. Some scurried about, gathering their belongings while mothers gathered up their children. Others seemed unable to believe that Massachusetts Bay lay only a few miles before them.

Roger felt a hand clutch his. He looked down to see a boy whose fever had long passed. The boy's grandfather smiled at them both, and Mary bent down to kiss the child's cheek.

Grown men wept, some in grief, knowing they would never again see England. Others, men and women, shed tears of joy, knowing they could now turn a new page in their hard lives. A few stared in utter amazement. Others perhaps felt the uncanny trickle of memories from years gone by in Old England.

Roger felt the martyred Bartholomew Legate smile from heaven and nod with approval. He could almost see himself and Sir Edward Coke sitting down at the flickering candle, composing the Petition of Right. He heard auburn-haired John Milton read musical poetry. Yes, he sensed that he stood on their shoulders and that without them his dream of a better way would have been impossible. Gazing up into the glistening sky, he thought of the great cloud of unseen witnesses who had lived before him. Then he looked into the moist, luminous eyes of the woman he loved with all his heart and heard her say triumphantly, "A thousand leagues across the Atlantic! Our journey has ended."

Yes, it had ended. But a new journey in a new world now beckoned.

THE NEW WORLD, MASSACHUSETTS

February 1631

Days earlier the passengers had seen only clouds hovering low in the far distance. Now blue hills appeared on the horizon as if surfacing from the ocean floor. "Could those hills be mere figments of the mind?" some wondered aloud. Roger rubbed his eyes to dispel all disbelief.

Mary's voice rang with joy. "Heaven has brought us safely to our new home."

Roger threw his arms around her and heard the captain tell the crewmen they would drop anchor off the shore of Nantasket.

The captain called Roger to his side. "Despite these unforgiving waters, we have made our way with speed. Still the ice will not permit us to enter Boston Harbor for perhaps three days. Let me ask you yet again to use your calm authority to spread patience throughout my ship. You see how the sight of land stirs their blood. If we sink in this ice, their blood will soon chill."

Roger saw the inhospitable drifts of ice; and although he too longed to set foot on Boston's dock, he left to carry out the captain's request.

When the people grew disgruntled on the third day, he gathered them and playfully recast the story of the children of Israel wandering forty years in the desert. "If Providence requires of us a fortnight's delay with Boston in our sight, what is that beside forty years? From Mount Pisgah, Moses gazed across the Jordan to see the Promised Land, which Providence forbad him to enter. From this deck, we see our Promised Land; and if we are patient and do not murmur against our captain, this sea will be not our tomb, but our highway to carry us safely through the ice."

Simon the blacksmith stood beside Roger and raised his mighty voice. "Though this wind be cold, I feel the warmth of this good minister's heart; and I am sure that in God's good time, it will melt this ice sufficient for us to pass."

Before sunset, a loud cheer resounded throughout the ship.

"Governor Winthrop!" the captain shouted and then urged his men to bring the honored guest aboard.

After greeting the captain along with Roger and Mary, the governor lifted his welcoming voice. "I have sailed from the warmer waters of Long Island Sound to greet you one and all."

The governor seemed near exhaustion. As soon as Winthrop welcomed everyone and praised heaven for their safety, Roger said to the people, "Let us not prevail on Master Winthrop's hospitality. On the morrow, we shall hear more from our good friend and governor. Sleep soundly tonight. Let this ship rock you peacefully like baby Moses afloat in his basket by the river's bank."

When the people laughed, he laughed too, understanding the humor of his counsel. He shrugged teasingly. "If we cannot sleep like baby Moses, then we have no choice but to lie with one eye open—Romeo awaiting his Juliet, or Rachel pining for her Jacob."

As they walked toward the place where Winthrop would sleep, Roger and the captain heard Winthrop speak scarcely above a whisper. "There has been much travail in our colony . . . ." His voice trailed off, but Roger, perceiving the governor's weariness, had not the heart to probe for particulars.

On the next day, the crew laughing with joy weighed anchor and hoisted the sails. The ship moved precariously, the sails popped in the wind, and the menacing blocks of ice begrudgingly made way for the *Lyon*.

Standing on deck and watching Boston Harbor move closer, Mary frowned and pointed leeward to the humble mortals' dwellings ashore. "The tents? What purpose have they in this frigid land?"

Hoping for an answer to Mary's question, Roger turned to the captain, who focused on nothing but the ominous ice.

Roger turned back to Mary. "I thought I saw Masham Manor ashore."

She grimaced. "I have heard that men at sea oft behold scenes not there save on the stage of the mind."

"Mary, someday Boston will sprout into a prominent city of merchants, whalers, midwives, and shipbuilders."

She drew her woolen shawl tightly around her shoulders. "I too see this vision: carpenters following the trade of our Lord, farmers, and every manner of enterprise."

Holding hands and laughing nervously, they defied the bitter cold and talked excitedly. "Will Sir Isaac and Lady Arbella take us in until we build our house?" Mary asked dreamily.

"They are of generous heart, but we will quickly make ourselves of service." Roger knew the Johnsons would not ask for payment in shillings. Generosity required leeway. No one could accuse him of lacking generosity, and he felt no compunction about receiving help from those who could afford from their bounty.

Mary looked into his eyes. "You have received much from others, dear, and given much in return, wishing to spawn still more generosity." She laughed merrily. "You do not keep miserly accounts of generosity's flow."

"I remember the day when Lady Arbella whispered into my ear, 'New England has need of strong-minded women such as your Mary.'"

He then paused, turned his palms up, and looked at them. "Although Sir Isaac will be surprised at our arrival, I have no doubt he will welcome these hands to help him in this new land."

Mary grinned. "With your strong hands and my strong mind, we will do well in this new world." Children aboard ship ran up to Roger and Mary. He lifted two in his arms so that they could see their new home.

She took a third child in her arms and, looking at Roger, said, "Our children will love this land. I believe it with all my heart."

His hair blew like a flag in the wind. "Let New England flow with good will and the milk and honey of our labor."

"We will plant daffodils." Mary handed the happy child back to her mother.

Immense chunks of ice broke apart as though preparing a highway for the ship. Roger set the two boys down on the deck and watched them scamper away like squirrels, one chasing the other.

"Daffodils?" Roger deliberately projected a half-moon eyebrow. "Love, 'tis strong faith indeed to look this ice in the face and pronounce *spring daffodils*."

She laughed, closing her eyes. "I still see the jonquils of Masham Manor and Old Polonius gathering three or four of them for the table."

"Mary, we left behind good friends. But let us dream of a new world free of the bishop's threats. Breathe deeply, and relish this air of freedom a thousand leagues away from King Charles's tentacles. I can almost hear liberty of conscience ring clear and sound."

Dropping anchor, the ship's crew cheered while the passengers crowded together, tiptoeing to peer over each other's heads. A mother mildly scolded her children. "Be still lest the governor think we are animals stampeding."

Picking up a child and putting him on his shoulder to let him see the shore, Roger said, "This little raccoon can go home with Mary and me."

Governor Winthrop appeared from his quarters. "I have prayed for this day, Master Williams."

"Thanks be to God's mercy and the famed skill of our good captain," Roger replied, welcoming the governor's embrace and warm words.

"The captain informs me your journey proved severe and hazardous."

Mary and Roger glanced at each other. "It would have been more hazardous had we not been in the sure hands of Captain Peirce."

Two boys tugged at the governor's sleeve and boasted of their triumph over sleet, squall, and blizzard.

Winthrop handed Mary his brown woolen scarf. "Take this. Your teeth chatter." Then he chuckled. "You arrive on the warmest day of this icy month."

Captain Peirce, leaning his head back and looking up to admire the vast sails of his ship, smiled. "She's a sturdy one, she is."

Roger said to Winthrop, "Our kind captain brings your people an abundant store of lemon juice."

"You do read my thoughts," Winthrop replied. "The scurvy has taken its toll. But you, Master Williams, will bring sunshine to cold New England."

In his husky voice, the captain ordered three of his men to unload the store of lemon juice. While the passengers prepared to leave their ark, the governor signed documents.

"The total goods," Captain Peirce explained to the governor, "are more than 200 tons."

The ship's crew and the townsmen lost little time in unloading the animals and the merchandise, including plows and seed from Lincolnshire. For a quick moment, Roger thought of his childhood, working at the side of his merchant father in London. He listened with pleasure to Governor Winthrop's kind words to Captain Peirce. "Take this cloak of beaver skins. The Dutch south of here gave it to me. Make it yours."

The captain threw the cloak over his shoulders. "My sincere thanks."

The new settlers, having left the Port of Bristol only two months earlier, spoke their earnest farewell to the captain as they departed his ship and stepped onto dry land. Governor Winthrop, Roger, and Mary escorted the woman whose husband had lost his mind before surrendering his life. On the dock, Roger found a carriage for her and her children.

Mary looked around, evidently hoping the radiant Lady Arbella and her husband, Sir Isaac Johnson, might have seen the ship enter the harbor. "How is Lady Arbella?" Mary asked the governor. "I hope she fares well. Are she and Sir Isaac living in Boston or—?"

"Or in Salem?" Roger rubbed his palms together with excitement, eager to talk with the Johnsons. But then he noted that the governor's mouth twitched and his eyes stared at the ground.

"The ways of Providence." Winthrop kept his eyes cast downward.

Mary gasped.

Fear streaked through Roger's body, and he gripped Winthrop by the arm. "What is your meaning?"

"Lady Arbella . . . died in August. Sir . . . Sir Isaac . . . ."

"Where is Sir Isaac?" Roger demanded.

"In Abraham's bosom. God took him from us."

Mary's face became almost translucent like the ice. "Both dead?"

Winthrop nodded. "Both. We must trust the ways of Providence. Come, I will take you to your quarters at my house until you find a more suitable place."

Unable to move, Roger remembered how both Sir Isaac and Lady Arbella had befriended him in England during treacherous times. Though evidently still dazed by the news of the deaths, Mary at last pointed to tents on a nearby hill.

"Some live in tents while building their houses," Winthrop said, pointing to a large tent. "Their house burned on the twenty-fifth day of December."

"Such misery," Mary said softly.

A forlorn look swept across Winthrop's face. "Misery indeed. Boston has suffered much hunger, scurvy, and consumption. The lemon juice you have brought will speedily attack the scurvy and disperse its grim specter of death . . . at least for a season."

Roger watched two men beg for food from the ship's crew.

"The taller one is Captain Welden's father," Winthrop said. "You remember the captain, do you not?"

"Yes. Did he not sail with his father? Where is—?"

"We buried the captain here in Boston. A military funeral."

"Died of what?"

"Consumption."

Roger shivered, realizing the brilliant young captain was his own age, twenty-seven. How could such high hopes and precarious events travel in such close company?

Roger and Mary went with Winthrop to his house. Then Winthrop left after instructing the servants to assist his guests with their possessions.

Before unpacking, Roger and Mary stood at the window of their room as his mind became a sea, wave upon wave, thought upon thought. Had they made a grievous mistake? What would happen to Mary in this land of ice and snow? *Would the Tower of London not have been better than this?* He looked into her eyes and at once knew the answer. He thought of the biblical passage warning against looking back after putting the hand to the plow. He thought also of the Apostle Paul and of the prophet Isaiah's counsel against growing fainthearted.

Earlier, the servants had told Roger of Governor Winthrop's sermon, "A Model of Christian Charity," delivered aboard the *Arbella*. In the sermon, Winthrop had set forth the model of the circumspect Puritan life.

Seven days after the *Lyon's* arrival in Boston, pleasant rumors and excitement spread among members of the Boston church.

"The new Cambridge man will speak to us tomorrow."

"I hear he expounds the sacred Scripture clearly."

"My brother and I heard him preach in England. Master Williams inspires hope where there is despair."

"We have urgent need of such a clergyman to teach us," one church member said, referring to the fact that the Reverend Wilson had returned to England. "They say his wife Mary has the wisdom and good counsel of one twice her years."

Perceiving that Roger had won the hearts of the people, Governor Winthrop began to form a plan. If he should recommend Roger as teaching elder of the church, the people would profit considerably as would the governor's reputation. He decided it both wise and expedient to present Roger before the synod of church leaders.

A few days later, Winthrop said to Roger, "The synod voted to call you as minister to the church, pending your answers to their specific questions."

Roger could not deny feeling tingling anticipation. At Masham Manor in England, he had made kind friends and believed he had served both his people and his calling well. Now, a new opportunity unfolded with startling quickness. Was it possible that heaven had allowed him to suffer leaving his fruitful work and caring friends at Masham Manor to prepare him for this rigorous New England church? He allowed himself to imagine his influence as minister of Boston's first church. Winthrop had arranged for the inquiry to take place within a week at his home less than a mile from the meetinghouse and Boston's marketplace.

Events both fair and foul moved swiftly that week. Mary watched widows and others board Captain Peirce's ship to return to England because they could no longer endure the savage winter. Two hundred settlers had died during the year. For the sake of her husband, Mary fought back the tears. But New England's primitive dwellings, severe cold, and meager means contrasted sharply with England's milder climate, elegant houses, ancient walls, manicured gardens, and towering cathedrals. Living now in a humble house, Mary tried not to think at night of her former life of comfort and pleasant routine.

In New England, every day ended for her in exhaustion. Never had she imagined having to grind corn in primitive mortars hollowed from a block of wood or a tree stump. She had *assumed* there would be mills for grinding. She had assumed so much that did not correspond with New World reality. Since scarcity was the rule, many settlers were reduced to using burning pine strips for lamps.

Each morning at the first streak of gray, Mary woke to the sound of Roger adding logs to the coals in the stone fireplace or striking metal against flint to kindle a new flame. She stepped onto a cold floor to prepare porridge and then served it in wooden bowls. Secretly she confessed she had not expected her new life to be so grueling.

With all her heart, she wanted to relish the new challenges and new friends the way Roger relished them. She knew that by becoming Boston's minister, her husband would demonstrate his goodness to the people. She let herself dream, not of an easy time as the minister's wife, but of an interesting life beyond drudgery. Like Roger, she had known work as her close companion from childhood. What she longed for was a life fit for human beings created in God's image. Each morning she talked to herself alone. *Soon I will recover from the shock of this New World.*

One day while the wind howled with fury, she realized that much of her brooding was not for herself, but for her husband. She had witnessed his zest and exuberance as chaplain to those at the manor. Having seen him at his best, she now prayed that heaven would give his talents another opportunity to flourish in the open.

For herself she longed for hard yet meaningful work, new friends, and the means to help those whose lives had become drudgery. *This is no time for brooding. New horizons do not appear before downcast eyes*, she said each morning as her ritual.

The time came for Roger's meeting with the synod at Winthrop's sturdy house. Sitting in a carriage outside the house, Roger could not help admiring the servants and workers. In the spring and summer, they had carved out a farm of six hundred acres on the fertile land up the Mystic River, allowing Winthrop to move into his new stone house before autumn.

From many people, Roger had heard the story of how Winthrop originally made his headquarters in New Towne on the north side of the Charles River. Because the New Towne water carried sickness, however, he had led a following to the peninsula of Boston, earlier called Trimountain and Shawmut. Although eleven of his servants had perished, Winthrop wrote to his wife, Margaret, in England that he had never felt better or slept more soundly in his life.

As soon as Roger entered the house, Winthrop revealed his talent for disclosing his connections with people in high positions. Beginning the meeting by introducing Roger to the synod, Winthrop moved quickly to explain, "My friend the Reverend Roger Williams served faithfully as chaplain in the household of another of my friends, Sir William Masham of Essex, whose wife is cousin to my former client, Sir Oliver Cromwell, who had once considered sailing to our New England."

Poignant questions about the candidate's conversion and calling to the ministry began at once with an intensity that surprised Roger. Far from feeling threatened, however, he availed himself of the opportunity to demonstrate to the synod that his heart and mind were one with theirs.

Deputy Governor Thomas Dudley cleared his throat loudly, evidently displeased that the waters had run too smoothly. A resolute man distinguished as a soldier and as a former steward to the Earl of Lincoln, he spoke with no formality or ceremony.

Taking Roger aback with his aggressiveness, Dudley said bluntly, "There are tales and rumors."

Roger waited, deliberately cocking a defensive eyebrow and folding his arms across his chest.

"Rumors? What rumors?" a synod member asked.

Dudley jerked his head back. "Why, rumors of Antinomianism, the cursed disease our Governor Winthrop fearlessly denounces daily. What do you say, Master Williams?"

Roger felt the jolt. He wondered if Dudley had some sinister reason to deny him his opportunity to serve as minister. *Why the invective tone? Has some subterranean rivalry flourished between Winthrop and Dudley?* Roger wondered, looking at one and then the other.

Dudley opened his mouth and pointed his finger as if to hurl a charge at Roger, but Winthrop interrupted. "Deputy Governor Dudley, I think the question could be raised more precisely."

Again Roger could not help conjecturing that some jealousy passed between the governor and the deputy. Apprehension seized Roger. *Have I become a pawn between these two men of politics? Does Dudley think that by harpooning my ministry, he will thereby harpoon Winthrop?*

Dudley flattened his palms on the table and leaned in Roger's face. "Have you acquaintance with this Antinomianism, which permits private revelations and plays loose with morality?"

"Acquaintance, but no truck with it," Roger answered.

Evidently dissatisfied with the answer, Dudley exhaled loudly. "Have you received personal revelations from heaven?"

Roger tapped his fingers on the Bible. "What need have I with further revelations when we have a plenitude in this book?"

A large, approving grin curled on Winthrop's lips. Dudley's brow furrowed and his eyes narrowed as he stared menacingly into the face of the candidate for an inordinately long time.

"Your eyes," said Roger at last, "probe without benefit of your voice." Though the gift of patience came to him at this moment, he found himself unable to fathom Dudley's hostility.

"I hear that like the Antinomians, you have private interviews with heaven," Dudley accused.

"It is you who hears voices. I do not know the source of rumor-bearing voices," Roger said calmly.

"Your tongue is too sharp for one who professes to be a minister of the gospel," Dudley retorted.

Having had his fill of Dudley and his dull wit, Roger turned to Winthrop, who called for more questions "pertaining to our purpose." A flood of questions from the synod came, all of which Roger answered forthrightly.

Dudley, twisting in his chair with unmasked dissatisfaction, suggested they meet a second time. "Let us give the good Reverend Williams more time and freedom to probe this synod."

Roger said nothing but understood Dudley's words to mean, *Let us give this younger man more rope with which to tie himself in knots.* Roger did in fact have many questions he wished to ask, particularly about the ties, if any, between the Boston church and the Church of England. During his past two months at sea, he had thought deeply about his future alliances. He had resolved to have no part in any national church, which always received special favors from the state and made all other churches the state's stepchildren at best. Any church using the state's power to enforce its doctrine, he had concluded, possessed the spirit of the antichrist rather than of the Christ of Scripture.

Roger had not, however, deluded himself about the success of carrying still further the Reformation, which he, like Milton, believed had begun in England a century before Luther in Germany. With Winthrop, Roger longed to see the Reformation continue in the New World; but Roger insisted that no progress in pure religion could advance without liberty of conscience. Such freedom, he now knew, entailed the freedom to believe false doctrine as well as true doctrine. *If true doctrine prevails, it must do so through honest inquiry and not through compulsion.*

"I will gladly meet with you again," Roger said to the synod, "for I too have questions."

This pleased the men, and they all agreed to assemble again soon.

Half an hour later, Roger returned to the small, wooden dwelling that a merchant had lent Mary and him until they could know where they would live. Greeting him at the door, Mary insisted that they take a ride in the carriage a neighbor had left with her.

Roger blew on his cold, stiff fingers. "Where are we going?"

"Take this blanket." Mary teasingly rubbed his hands with it and threw it over his head. She laughed good-naturedly and said in a mysterious voice, "I desire to see the Charles River."

"After two months on the Atlantic, you long to see a *river?*"

"For a good reason. But while we travel, let me tell you an amusing though true story the women from near Boston told me about one of their pastors."

As soon as Roger hitched up the horse and they were in the carriage, Mary began. "Two months ago, the pastor announced from the pulpit that children born on the Sabbath would be denied the sacrament of holy baptism."

"Do not tell me—no one is permitted to labor on the Sabbath, not even a woman in labor."

Laughing, Mary shook her head. "No, not that—but something equally absurd. The pastor presumed that all children are *born* on the same day of the week in which they were *conceived.* The most amusing part is that last week the pastor's own wife birthed twins."

Roger smiled. "On what day?"

"On the Christian Sabbath. When asked about the hypocrisy of his wife's conceiving on the Sabbath, the pastor declared with somber countenance, 'At the time, I believed sincerely that the conception had taken place shortly *before* midnight on Saturday. I contend now, however, that Satan had slowed the clock to trick me into conceiving on the Christian Sabbath.'"

Roger grinned. "Some of our Puritans gag at gnats but gulp down camels whole."

"It seems the good pastor misread his own advice and for many days thereafter *conceived* of no sound ideas. But I recall no Scripture requiring our minds to abstain from thinking." Mary then gave Roger other reports from neighboring towns as they rode beyond the edge of Boston along a trail leading into a forest

Roger in turn spoke excitedly of reports about the natives and their customs.

"Move with caution," Mary warned. "I overheard some of the women refer to the natives as Canaanites having no good will toward us."

"I will heed your warning, Mary; but I still have in mind to meet some of them face to face. Today I learned of a certain prominent sachem among the Narragansets. I intend to approach him."

When they came upon a huge tree, larger than any Roger had seen in England, Mary pointed. "Stop the carriage at that oak tree. I know you possess a burning desire to learn from the natives. A small band of them gathers here every full moon for two days of feasting and celebration."

"How did you come by this knowledge?"

"From a beaver trapper. Ruth Blackstone introduced me to him this morning at the market."

Roger's heart raced. "Has the trapper seen the native celebration with his own eyes?"

"So he told me."

"Then I must talk with him soon."

Mary smiled with evident self-satisfaction. "He will be at the market tomorrow."

Roger jumped down from the carriage and tied the horse to one of the smaller trees. Then taking Mary by the hand, he ran to the huge oak. Together, they stretched their arms to embrace it, Mary on one side, Roger on the other. Two squirrels chattered over their heads. A wild turkey fluttered nearby and disappeared.

"Look, Roger. Through the mist, you can see the Charles River. The trapper said that sometimes the natives appear in canoes."

Despite the biting cold, they waited in the carriage for almost an hour in the hope of catching sight of one of the natives.

Later, as they rode back to Boston, Roger fancied he saw natives peeping from behind trees. He smiled, however, reminding himself that it was not the time of the celebration at the full moon.

Two days thereafter, Roger and Mary found themselves at Winthrop's dinner table. William and Ruth Blackstone, considered the two most generous people in all of Massachusetts, once again proved their neighborliness by volunteering to assist Winthrop in entertaining. Since Margaret remained in England to give birth to her child, Winthrop evidently needed the Blackstones' company. He explained to Roger, "Mr. Blackstone served as my guide to an excellent spring not half a mile from where we sit. Thanks to his knowledge of the terrain, the people elected to make Boston our prime city. As Christ said, 'A city set on a hill cannot be hid.'"

The English had never won prizes for their cookery, and New England had not improved over Old England. The peas at Winthrop's table seemed barely softer than pebbles and scarcely more succulent than scraps of leather. The hard bread, chewed first by the teeth and then by the stomach, had kept most of the new settlers from starving during the cruel winter. For that, Winthrop gave thanks. But to Roger's delight, the natives had taught the New Englanders to cook corn, which the guests now savored at Winthrop's table.

Mary ate gratefully, remembering the stark meals aboard the *Lyon*. But she remembered also Polonius's wondrous cooking at Masham Manor. Polonius, having learned his art from the French rather than from his English mother, justly took pride in his varied repertoire before the large manor stove. Mary vowed that one day she would own an oven and bake Roger an apple pie to equal Polonius's.

As she ate, Mary admired the furniture in Winthrop's house. The chairs had doubtless come from England, but the long table had likely been made recently by carpenters who had sailed on the *Arbella* with Winthrop. Yes, when the governor's wife arrived the furniture would please her.

It pleased Roger to learn that Blackstone had attended Cambridge with Isaac Johnson. When tempted to feel sorry for himself, Roger thought of Isaac and Arbella, who had left their magnificent Tattershall Castle and sailed bravely to Massachusetts only to die. Having felt a special kinship with them, Roger now wished to help make the New World better in their honor. They had become a part of him; and his work would be their work too.

Winthrop handed him a plate of mutton. "Have some more, Master Williams."

Roger politely declined. He now wished to enjoy the conversation as food for the mind. He admired the ease with which Mary, though the youngest at the table, talked with the Blackstones and Winthrop. Her conversation was thoughtful, her wit keen. Roger noticed that Winthrop, seemingly unaware of his actions, made subtle moves to belittle her contributions. Her forthrightness nevertheless encouraged Ruth to speak her mind more explicitly. Observing this interchange, Roger smiled to himself.

Shifting in his chair halfway through the meal, the governor expounded his dream for what he called "a city set on a hill." Mary's eyes brightened; and Roger listened with infinite care, caught up in the lawyer's words, which rose up like pollen floating from blossom to blossom. "We shall be a city set on a hill, a beacon light to the Gentiles. In this new Promised Land, God has set the captives free from the tyranny of Egypt so that they may pursue justice, walk humbly, and show mercy."

"Yes," Roger joined in. "Where tyranny has no hold, true religion will flow from the heart, and confession will come unrestrained."

Winthrop resumed, his voice shaking. "In England, I saw corruption in high places, thievery, deceit, treachery, and greed beyond compare. But in this good land, severe and cold though it be, we shall sow the seeds of honesty, hard work, truth, and loyalty. A Christian's yes will be yes, and his no will be no."

A quiet knock at the back door interrupted the governor's eloquence. Winthrop did not seem surprised. Rising quickly, he scooped up a dish of kidney beans, a pot of porridge, some succotash, a loaf of bread, a bowl of mutton, and other portions of food and placed them in the bucket in his hand. Taking the food with him, he opened the back door only enough for a hand to take the bucket.

Roger heard only a whisper: "God bless you, Governor. God bless you."

Mary broke out in words that were almost in song. "Oh, to think that we now live in a land where kindness and gentle mercy are blessed and not scorned. In Essex I saw decent men whipped and charity berated."

Blackstone, a quiet man who listened but seldom spoke unless addressed directly, burst out in praise of Winthrop's indomitable spirit and capacity for inspiring people with his vision. Ruth Blackstone laughed with mirth and then grew serious. "Around Mr. Winthrop, it is impossible to be lazy."

"God has not given us a sloth's nature," Winthrop said. "If Satan marshals to fight, we shall unfurl the flag."

The governor's sincere eloquence plucked the cords of Roger's heart. Under the table, he pressed his hand against Mary's, looked into her eyes, and thought he saw dreams of children skipping rope and laughing in a land where decency and acts of kindness prevailed. He remembered moments in England when Winthrop and he had bemoaned the debauchery that stained their native soil, rendering it an unfit place for youngsters to romp and play at will.

Roger decided to broach a most delicate subject. No one could have accused him of crossing the line blindly at this precarious moment. Though Mary had begged him to wait at least a month, he had told himself that while there were times to keep counsel to oneself, there were also moments to step out of the shadows.

For the past year, he had wrestled with the memory of witnessing Bartholomew Legate's execution. London's bishop had ordered him burned alive for the crime of embracing Anabaptist beliefs. Roger wrestled also with the looming thought that his Church of England had chained itself irrevocably to Rome's hoary tradition of persecution and superstition. He now believed that where the mind and heart live in bondage, they soon succumb to superstition and to the mask of hypocrisy worn for escaping the inquisitor's torch. He remembered the account of the two Separatists hanged by Queen Bess and her loyal bishops. He thought of the scheming Cardinal Richelieu, whose hands still dripped red with Huguenot blood. And he remembered the Anabaptists drowned by German Lutherans who had forsaken Rome's tyranny only to become another tyranny under another name.

"Governor Winthrop, we mortals delude ourselves more than we care to admit," Roger began softly, scarcely above a whisper. "I fear that if we think we will reform our Church of England in our lifetime, we have drunk too deeply from the cup of delusions. We must leave Babylon to her own devices."

Ruth Blackstone quickly moved away from the table to serve the stewed blackberries. When she set a bowl before Winthrop, he pushed it away. Roger felt a chill enter the room and saw Mary shiver. A servant entered at Winthrop's request and laid two large logs on the hot coals inside the fireplace. Valiant Ruth worked hard to smile, but the look of pain prevailed. The servant left. As the moments slipped away, Roger realized that the turn in the conversation now drove itself.

"No, no, my friend," the governor said to Roger. "We must reform the Church of England from within. The church is our mother. When you were young, did you not feed upon the milk of this good but wayward church?"

"This I cannot deny. But what shall we do with a mother who persists in playing the harlot? She sleeps with tyrants and sells herself back to Rome, that brothel of all brothels."

"But you must concede," Winthrop retorted, "even Bishop Laud, cruel though he be, turned his back on the pope's red hat, refusing to take the cardinal's oath of loyalty to the pope."

"What need had Laud for a cardinal's hat when his ambition would lead him to declare himself the pope of England, Scotland, and Ireland?" Roger gave no voice to another question that fleeted through his mind. *How can a man like Winthrop avoid severe self-contradiction and shattered integrity by pledging public loyalty to a church he vows to undo and remake?*

The women tried to soften the rift between Winthrop and Roger, but each passing moment raised the possibility that en route to their separate goals the two reformers might never come to an agreement.

Roger had seen the authorities in England tighten their rein month by month. London's powerful Bishop Laud had sworn on the altar that all of England's churches, without exception, would conform to the same ritual of worship. The king and archbishop would lock arm in arm atop one hierarchical pyramid. Such an alliance Roger judged unholy, ruthless, and malignant.

"You misread the signs," Winthrop told his younger friend. "You lack the patience to strengthen your resolve. Your zeal is like sails without wind. If we have Bishop Laud as our nemesis on our right hand, we have Lord Chaos looming at our left. Consider the king's mind. If we go the way of the Separatists, King Charles will send troops to shackle us and carry us back in shame as prisoners to England."

"If we do not separate, Governor, the king will have no need to shackle us. We will have shackled ourselves and engineered our own shame."

"You do forget the charter of our colony. If we follow your course, Master Williams, the king will revoke with his left hand what he bestowed with his right."

Roger opened his mouth to speak, but Winthrop glanced twice over his shoulder as if looking for the kitchen servant. When Roger then looked into Mary's eyes, they seemed to say to him, *You have made the governor squirm so that he must pretend he did not hear you.* Roger paused to rehearse what he wished to say to the governor. *What right had Charles to give his subjects land not his to give?* He wished to explain that in claiming the land belonging to the natives, the king was a thief no more virtuous than a roguish highwayman. But he said nothing, partly because he did not have Winthrop's full attention and partly because he knew his novel thoughts required still more time to grow. Until then, wisdom would counsel silence.

Sitting now quietly at the table with the governor, Roger strove to perceive him not as an evil man conniving to feed his ambition, but as an earnest Puritan longing for righteousness and tranquility. He believed that Winthrop, in turn, saw him as earnest in his desire for reform though perhaps deluded on certain particulars.

"On Thursday," Winthrop said, "you will have opportunity to persuade the synod of your recent ideas."

When Roger and Mary stood up to leave, Ruth spoke kind words as if to moderate the flashes of lightning that had cracked between Roger and the governor.

As soon as they were out in the cold wind and on their way to their little house, Roger said, "Mary, the governor is a good man and my friend. Between us stands a question of degree and of substance. But when he said that I will have opportunity to persuade the synod, he used lawyer talk to say his real meaning."

"That the synod will have opportunity to bring you over to the governor's opinion?" she asked.

He nodded, and they continued to traverse the gentle hills of Boston. Then all at once, they saw a disturbing sight in the distance: three men taking one man captive.

"Is that not the town jail?" she asked.

Roger picked up his step, taking Mary by the arm. Passing the meetinghouse, they headed west toward the jail.

"You vultures!" the man under arrest shouted at his captors.

"You want to rail, do you? Then rail at prison walls," said the jailor evidently in charge.

As Roger and Mary approached, the second jailer looked up. "Reverend Williams, this is an evil one. Could you speak to him and help him see the error of his way?"

Roger looked at the man from head to foot. "Sir, I would speak with you but only with your free consent."

Inside the jail, the prisoner and the minister spoke in confidence. Minutes later, when Roger walked out, Mary said, "Roger, your face is bloodless!"

Impatient to protest the injustice he had seen at the jail, Roger set out to arrive early at the meetinghouse where the synod of nine men would soon gather. Since no one was at the meetinghouse when he arrived, he ignored the cold and walked a few paces to the marketplace in the hope of seeing the beaver trapper. Instead, he caught sight of a native who seemed in a rush.

Abruptly, the native stopped before a horse to study it as a farmer might examine a plot of land for sale. Then he turned, saw Roger staring at him, and walked up to him. An awkward silence followed.

Not knowing the native languages, he hesitated until the native at last said, "English. I speak English."

Believing that God had made all people of the same blood, Roger longed to learn what sort of society the natives had cultivated. As they stumbled in their conversation, he asked how he might learn to speak the Narraganset tongue. But the native left without answering.

Puzzled, Roger stood motionless until the native disappeared. *Did I inadvertently offend the man?* He returned to the meetinghouse.

The first person he met inside was Thomas Dudley, who invited him to sit near the crackling fire. Roger heard the other men talking and gave close attention to their glances, gestures, and tones to discern whether they possessed information about the recent conversation at Winthrop's table. *No, they have not heard,* he concluded. Scarcely had he made a decision to aim straight at his target than the meeting began. He sensed that the men were eager to ask probing questions. But before answering any, he had to reveal what lay foremost on his mind.

"I have need to speak briefly of persecution and of those who in the name of our Lord sought converts by threat of sword and torch. I refer above all to the Inquisitor General, Tomás de Torquemada. During his eighteen years of terror, one hundred and fourteen thousand victims came under the official charge of heresy. Of those, he incinerated more than ten thousand. More than ninety-seven thousand suffered either life imprisonment or perpetual humiliation through forced acts of public penance."

Roger, no less a master of persuasion than Winthrop, so drew the men into his speech that they joined him in denouncing the Roman hierarchy's persecution of Protestants. But when Roger disclosed the persecution and threats issuing from such Protestants as Luther, Zwingli, Calvin, and Queen Bess herself, Winthrop grew noticeably uncomfortable.

Then Roger fired the cannon that visibly shook Winthrop and the others. "I speak only for myself, but I say here and now I wish no longer to give my small voice to a church that turns plowshares into swords for persecution or that hammers its pruning hooks into inquisitorial spears. Recently I investigated an incident that moved me deeply. I want to believe that the event came more by misguided zeal for righteousness than by sober policy."

"What incident?" a synod member asked.

Reminding himself that Winthrop was a lawyer, Roger cautioned himself against yielding to the heat of indignation. Sir Edward Coke had taught him the importance of transforming his rage over injustice into a tactic for action. He softened his tone. "A certain servant among you named Phillip Ratcliffe was whipped, forbidden to speak his thoughts, condemned to banishment, and severed from his ears."

"He was convicted justly in our court!" Dudley fired.

"If so, it reflects policy, not hot zeal alone," Roger said.

"If your right eye offend thee, pluck it out," a synod member said.

"And his offence?"

"Invectives," Dudley answered heatedly.

"Invectives? Not murder, not rape, not brutal pillage?" Roger asked. "In brief, then, the man delivered mere words against the churches and the government. Did he wound your flesh? No? Did he invade your homes by force? No? Steal your cattle? No? Then his crime—ah, yes, hurling words of air that displeased your ears. But the court and you, instead of either heeding his words or ignoring them, sliced off his ears."

"If your right eye offend thee, pluck it out," the synod member repeated.

"In which Gospel did Christ admonish Peter, James, or John to pluck out their neighbors' eyes or slice off their ears?"

Winthrop interrupted, taking charge as was his manner. "If we permit dissent, the whole commonwealth crumbles."

"If you do not permit dissent," Roger replied, "you cut the heart from the commonwealth and bind every conscience in a cage."

When he then told the governor and the deputy governor that the state should presume no right to enforce the First through Fifth Commandments of Moses, Dudley sprang to his feet and denounced Roger as a Separatist: "I will not sit here and listen to this . . . this false doctrine," he roared.

Roger looked at the ceiling and lowered his voice. "What, Brother Thomas? You say I am a Separatist, and now you make yourself a separatist by desiring to separate from me?"

"You make sport of holy matters," Dudley charged.

After urging Dudley to sit down, Winthrop said, "Brother Roger, the cloud of zeal has darkened your wisdom."

Roger held his tongue and waited. Although he did not think his zeal had clouded his mind, he did not refer to Winthrop's metaphor. Instead, he addressed the other men, including Deputy Governor Dudley. "The worship of power is false worship. I will kiss the ring of neither pope nor king unless he kisses mine also in brotherly and scriptural affection, not in submission. I will bend my knee neither to bishop nor prelate, and I ask none to bend the knee to me even though I serve as teacher and evangel of our faith."

"Give thought to the path you would take," Winthrop warned. "We Puritans offer the Church of England a purgative, but the Separatists would kill the body whole with their cup of poison."

"We bandy mere metaphors and ignore substance," Roger replied. "If the question is about where to draw the line in our Reformation, I say draw it with the substance of Scripture and conscience, not with the sword."

"You speak with a *false* conscience," Dudley said, slapping the table.

"Ah, then persuade my conscience with the power of reason and Scripture, not with the force of the sword. The threat of the blade makes not converts, but hypocrites who profess with their lips in the hope of saving their necks. I read in Scripture that Christ preached on the mount and the Apostle Paul on Mars Hill, yet nowhere do I read that Christ took either sinners or disciples to the whipping post. I do not read that the apostles bound their rivals and enemies in chains. Did either Christ or the apostles call for the pillory? Did Christ send Peter to the dunking stool when he foully cursed and denied him thrice?"

"Anarchy! Anarchy! You preach damnable Antinomian chaos and call it freedom!" Dudley threw up his hands and walked to face the window behind him. "False freedom in matters of religion sinks into libertine morality. You would fiddle with our common-wealth until it goes out of tune."

"I have no craving for chaos," Roger replied. "I speak rather of an unholy yoking of state and church that strangles tender conscience."

Dudley whirled around like a tornado. His eyes flashed. "I perceive that you are beside yourself."

Roger became aware that he was stroking his chin the way Coke had stroked his when attacked by another lawyer or judge in court. "Is any man more beside himself than when he plays the hypocrite? Would you use the state to enforce creed and doctrine, thereby herding many to play roles foreign to their conscience? The hypocrite divides himself in twain; and when his *concealed* self comes round to meet his *public* self, he cannot tell which he is. You would institute self-alienation, inviting a citizen to believe one thing but practice and speak another. If that is not counterfeit worship, then counterfeit has no meaning."

A heavy cloud of gloom settled over Roger as he sensed that he could not persuade the synod to go the way of the Separatists. He remembered a story his brother Sydrach had told him regarding four men captured and made to serve ten years in chains on a Spanish ship. When the ship fell captive to an English crew, the chains of the enslaved men were broken. But the men sat frozen as if still bound. They could not move, for they could not believe they had gained freedom. As Roger looked at the men around the table, he thought he saw men chained in their minds to the bloody past of tyranny and intolerance.

Vowing in his heart to be rid of the gloomy cloud hanging over him, he spoke to the synod softly but earnestly, looking each man in the eye. "I stand with grateful humility for your kind and generous offer. I beg you not to think me lacking in warmth and gratitude toward you. But each must follow his own light, however dim it may be. I cannot in good conscience lend either my voice or my name to a church too much in love with persecution." After pausing, he looked at the deputy governor and at Governor Winthrop and then added calmly, "If one foot stands in liberty of conscience and the other in Rome's ancient slough of persecution, then someday you must choose to lift one foot and place it with the other. Which foot will it be?"

BOSTON AND ALONG THE CHARLES RIVER

March 1631, A Month Following Roger and Mary's Arrival

"Captain Eric Firebrook!"

I had scarcely set foot in Massachusetts when I heard the voice I did not recognize. I heard it a second time. Then a long hand shot up in the air over the heads of my fellow passengers, who also had just left the ship. A wiry, freckled young man ran up to me. "I have come from Governor Winthrop. He described you, sir, as a tall gentleman with red hair."

"Did he tell you I might have a few threads of silver among the red?"

Far from succumbing to my humor, the youth seemed so awed by my presence that I surmised Winthrop had built me up to be one of the mighty warriors of the sea.

"Please, follow me, Captain Firebrook. The governor has reserved a room for you. He urged me to apologize for his absence."

The look on the youth's face warned me of something askew. "What is wrong, son?"

"It is beyond me, Captain. I must not meddle where forbidden to tread."

Two burly men were already unloading my chest of books, journals, and manuscripts from the ship. "There," I said to the men, "heave them gently onto that large carriage."

A second and then a third youth appeared from town, one having only a stump for a hand. Yet he made good use of himself as did the others in helping to load my belongings.

Upon learning that Governor Winthrop would not be at liberty for perhaps three hours, I urged the freckled youth to take me first to see Master Roger Williams and his good wife Mary.

"They are away," he said, climbing into the carriage with me. "I heard them speak oft of you, Captain. They would be here greeting you had they not been compelled to leave."

"Compelled?"

"The governor will explain. Ahead, sir, is where you will stay."

After guiding me to my temporary room, the youth bade me farewell and quickly rode away. While I unpacked, I could not help wondering what he had meant by "compelled." I counseled patience for myself and took satisfaction in observing that the contents of my wooden chest of manuscripts and journals had survived both thieves and foul weather. Carefully I picked up a copy of John Milton's glorious new poem *On the Morning of Christ's Nativity*, an image-rich accomplishment of controlled artistry and joy. Before leaving Cambridge, I had gladly promised John that I would place the poem in Roger's hands. I held it in mine as though it were the crown jewels.

Wishing to discover for myself the nature of both the people and the New World's terrain, I hired a horse and carriage and an old man to guide me. Before we departed, he showed me a crude map he had drawn. On our way, he told me that four hundred men, women, and children had arrived on the *Arbella* and that six hundred had followed shortly thereafter.

I could see for myself that though a delight to the eye, this cruel land gave its bounty grudgingly. Nevertheless, the bay provided a natural fortress. By commanding the channel at Nantasket, Governor Winthrop and his men could defend the whole place against attack by Spain or France. Still I wondered about the settlers' marksmanship.

Driving west, I stopped to buy a deerskin cloak for the old man and urged him to keep it drawn tightly around him. I pointed at a nearby hillside. "What are those?"

"Caves, Captain, dug by human hands."

This sight shook me. Living like bears did not suit the manner of proud English settlers. Later I learned that since there were but a few axe men and sawyers among them, most people had little means to build themselves fine homes. On ship, however, I had met five men who boasted of being among the finest of English sawyers. Perhaps within a year, the roofed-over cellars to the north of me would become suitable houses.

The old man pointed south. "Those are wigwams."

Smoke curled out of the tops of the wigwams. Only the hardiest souls could survive such sparse dwellings. A few settlers had erected board houses, most of which had gaps between the boards, gaps wide enough to accommodate an enterprising snake. I had seen sturdier versions of the same house in Europe's Westphalia. The caves, the tents, the wigwams, and even the board houses contrasted sharply with the few stone houses I had seen since coming ashore.

Soon the old man and I came upon a gathering of twelve people who had killed two wolves. Pointing twenty feet ahead, the old man said in his wheezing voice, "Behold, Captain, a dead cow and two swine. The wolves must have slain them."

Stepping out of my carriage, I asked the old man to tie the horse.

A stooped-shouldered man with a knife in his hand was carving on the swine. Even though the wolves had made the kill, the settlers claimed the flesh. The two men butchering the cow turned to me and inquired whether I had recently arrived from England.

"Within two hours," I answered. Then I asked whether the wolves had found their stock to be easier prey than were the deer of the forest.

"A wolf is like a Spaniard," one of them answered. "Turn your back, and he will . . . ." He threw his hand up as if to say, *We all know how Spaniards are.*

"What do you know of the governor of Massachusetts?" I asked, concealing that I had more than once engaged Winthrop as my lawyer in England.

A short, stocky man with a woolen scarf around his head looked up from kneeling beside one of the wolves. He wiped the blood slowly from his hands as he talked. "The governor is a man of many talents. I have never witnessed him breathe the air of despair. He walks among us like an officer in battle, exhorting us to give our foremost."

I had oft observed how virtue in mere mortals rose or fell according to the shift of circumstances. I had known good seamen who after promotion became cruel taskmasters with stone hearts. It pleased me to learn that in his position as governor, Winthrop had taken to his high calling with courage and wisdom. Yet the word "compelled" continued to plague my brain. What had happened to my good friends Roger and Mary?

Overhearing our conversation, a third man added, "Governor Winthrop is Joshua, anointed by God to lead the children of Israel into this savage land of promise."

Then I heard the women complain that they lacked fresh fruit for their children, ate dried meat only, and longed for window glass to let in the sun's rays. I stuck my chest out and boasted that the ship on which I had arrived had brought saws, axes, kettles, and, yes, many rolls of cloth.

"Did you bring gunpowder?" a toothless man boomed in my ear.

I told him that his voice resounded enough for gunpowder, which made them all laugh. He showed relief when I revealed that the ship had indeed brought both guns and gunpowder. I asked about furs, fish, and sassafras. Some women gave me a stern look, and only later did I learn that the Old World had used sassafras as a cure for the disease the English Puritans called the French pox.

Four or five others joined us, and I asked if they perchance knew a clergyman named Roger Williams.

The man carving up the swine stopped and looked up at me. "The whole village has heard of the good reverend though he arrived only recently."

"Can you tell me how I might find him?"

"Not here. He has sailed to Salem," said a voice behind me.

"Much to our discredit," said a gray-haired woman who then sought to explain that a rift had formed between Roger and Governor Winthrop. The more she explained, the more confused I became.

Others joined in, and soon I sensed that many shared my confusion. Roger had without doubt made a powerful impression upon them, but I failed to discern its nature. Although all agreed he was a most godly and winsome person, they divided over what they called his Congregationalism. Some sided with Roger that each congregation should run its own affairs without benefit of governing presbytery. All agreed that of bishops and archbishops, they had had their fill.

"We did not come to this new world to separate ourselves from the Church of England. We are all Anglicans," said a short man with a resonant voice that told me he came from Lincolnshire.

I asked, "How can you deny having separated from the Church of England when you are a thousand leagues away?"

"The Church of Christ Jesus," he replied without hesitating, "is confined to no nation."

I could not resist asking, "Then why do we call ourselves the Church of England and not the Church Universal?" It soon occurred to me that only Puritan men and women would stand in such cold weather to discuss ecclesiology.

An hour or so later, Ruth and William Blackstone greeted me warmly and invited me into their large stone house while the servants carried my belongings into the spacious room on the east side, my first home in New England.

"Because there has been a fire in the village, Governor Winthrop cannot dine with us," Ruth said apologetically

When the three of us began eating in the dining room, William said, "My wife and I are pleased that you consented to live in our house."

I felt the sincerity of their welcome as we talked of Cambridge, where William had once lived.

A messenger arriving at the back door cut our conversation short. He spoke in such whispers that I could not overhear him. A moment later, both the Blackstones hurriedly put on their coats and apologized for having to depart so abruptly. On her way out, Mrs. Blackstone commended me to the care of their maid, Lydia. I had no time to thank them. They left in a rush without explanation.

The other maids and servants kept themselves busy mending garments and cleaning the house.

While Lydia attended her infant in a crib in the dining room, she revealed to me why the Blackstones had left so abruptly. "They have no children," she said. "But they have a fine mare whose time for foaling has come. A healthy workhorse in this hard land is a treasure."

After ending my meal, I went over to Lydia's baby and let him grip my finger.

"Pick him up, if you are a mind to. He's a friendly child. We call him Seth."

I recalled meeting a man in London who had told me he was William Blackstone's servant. I turned to Lydia. "Have you knowledge of a man named Barnabas?"

Lydia directed me to the parlor. "I know him."

"I met him in London," I said, stroking the infant's forehead. "Barnabas told me he had returned from New England to London to visit his ailing mother."

Lydia spoke without looking up from her work. "The poor ailing woman died only a week after Barnabas's return to England. A dear soul she was."

"You knew her also?"

"Somewhat. She was my mother-in-law." Lydia kept sweeping the floor.

"Your . . . then you are . . . you are Barnabas's wife!"

Lydia leaned on her broom and looked up at me. Her eyes laughed. Then a mysterious smile formed on her thin, red lips. "I have been his wife for twenty odd years, though at times it seems a hundred and more odd than not. Still, all in all, never would I have found a man more companionable. Barnabas is a cup of life overflowing, the wit of three men. He more oft makes me laugh than cry."

As I cradled little Seth in my arms and walked him around the room, a strange thought occurred to me. Of all species on the Earth, human infants suffer the most prolonged dependency on parents. "What is the world like for you, little Seth?" I asked aloud. *You do not interpret the world through Catholic eyes. Your blood is not Islamic or Lutheran. In countenance, you appear no more Anglican than Anabaptist.* I remembered Abba's granddaughter and how I had held her. Then I thought about something Abba once said to me:

"If you had been born in Persia, Eric, you would be Islamic and not Christian."

"If you had been born English," I answered, "you would have been baptized a Christian."

"Of what stripe?" Abba had asked with a grin.

I did not know the answer.

A cold chill passed through me. Imagining Little Seth in my arms as my son, I desired to look Doctor Diodati in the eye and ask, *Did the Creator predestine Seth for salvation? Or for endless damnation?* A confirmed Calvinist, Doctor Diodati had told our mutual friend John Milton that while little Jacob and Esau lay yet in their mother's womb, "God loved Jacob, but hated Esau."

Lydia's cheerful return to the room interrupted my morbid thoughts. "You have made inquiries about the Reverend Roger Williams?"

"We are good friends. But I hear he resides in Salem."

Again, Lydia kept her eyes on her sewing. "He would reside neither there nor here if Governor Winthrop had his way."

I heard a door open.

"That will be my Barnabas. He'll join us shortly." Lydia then resumed talking about the church in Salem.

To gain more particulars about Roger's departure to Salem, I asked, "Have the governor and the Reverend Williams . . . ?" I stumbled over my words and added with chagrin, "What of their friendship?"

"For some, friendship is like an animal's fur that sheds with a change of weather."

"Do not speak of the weather but of my two friends."

"The governor thinks a commonwealth can be trimmed and dressed as neatly as the hedges of English gardens."

Believing that she had again chosen to speak evasively, I asked, "Have Masters Winthrop and Williams spoiled their friendship?"

Lydia set her sewing aside. "I am not a person who will judge our esteemed governor lightly. Still, the devil and the governor deserve their due."

I could not suppress a grin. "You cushion your words."

She laughed. "A servant learns early to cushion her words, but my Barnabas tells me I cushion mine with more flint than wool."

"Then speak to me with flint."

"I'll speak in the language of flowers and gardens. The governor is a master gardener—neat and orderly, nothing too much out of place. But while the Reverend

Williams is also a gardener of no mean stature, he fears less the encroaching wildflowers and fears more the gardener who knows not when to lay down his axe and hoe."

I heard a man in the hallway clear his throat. Thinking he was Barnabas, I turned toward the parlor doorway and heard Lydia gasp at the sight. From her lips two words escaped in a shriek: "Governor Winthrop!"

Removing his hat, John Winthrop shrugged his shoulders and tried too hard, I thought, to give the appearance of one who had overheard nothing of our conversation. He grabbed my hand. "Captain Firebrook! Welcome to New England."

He cut his eyes sharply to Lydia, but then he looked back at me. I felt heat in my face and observed his prominent nose turn red. Recovering quickly, Winthrop apologized for failing to greet me at the dock and told me how happy my arrival in Massachusetts made him.

"I was a fool not to have left earlier with you," I said as Lydia escaped the room.

Winthrop now spoke jubilantly. "I desire to hear the full tidings about yourself and our England. But first you must be fed."

"I ate a quarter of an hour ago. I will give you the news. But above all, Governor, I must bring regards from your gracious wife. When I departed, she and your offspring enjoyed good health."

Winthrop's whole appearance changed as if for one wondrous moment Margaret stood in his presence and flooded him with the special warmth only she could provide him.

Despite my thirst to know the precise substance of the schism between Roger and Winthrop, I dared not broach the subject. Instead, I indulged his relentless desire to learn more about affairs in England. When he inquired of Milton, I informed him of William Chillingworth's plan to publish Milton's defense of free will in a book designed to build a bridge between the Calvinists and the Arminians. "We have some hope that Chillingworth will solicit Bishop Laud's help. He is the bishop's godson."

"I know the Chillingworth family. The father did business with me," Winthrop said.

The more I talked about Chillingworth's scheme to publish a book containing all our arguments pro and con under the title *Dialogue on Predestination and Free Will,* the more Winthrop pressed for the particulars. His eyes flashed, his words tripped rapidly off his tongue, and he grabbed my arm with such intensity that I felt the need to constrain him. His thoughts seemed to whirl. Yet the more we talked, the less could I tolerate the unnatural absence of Roger's name from our conversation. Resolving to unlock the mystery of the schism, I inhaled deeply. "What news of our friends Roger and Mary?"

"They are in Salem," Winthrop answered but volunteered nothing.

I asked other questions as to their health and status, but he answered stingily and soon changed the direction of our conversation to probe still more deeply into my knowledge regarding Chillingworth's meeting with Bishop Laud in London. I had the puzzling sensation that all my answers came like heavy blows to him. He ran his long fingers through his hair, muttered unintelligible words, and then suggested that we take his coach to his office.

We hurried to the coach as the wind shook the tall, barren trees at the front of the house. The coach horses snorted, blew billows of frosted breath, and bobbed their heads as if to pay their respects to the governor. As soon as we boarded the coach, the driver cracked the whip.

With the coach wheels rolling, the governor seemed oblivious to everything except his thoughts of Chillingworth's visit with Bishop Laud.

I explained that Chillingworth himself had suffered most. "The bishop threatened to imprison him, his own godson, unless he revealed the names behind the book's several pseudonyms."

"Did reprisals fall upon you?" Winthrop asked.

"No, I had alliances, which gave me the feeling of temporary security."

"Why temporary?"

"My security was limited to the boundaries of Cambridge. But I had no wish to seclude myself in one town or permanently depend upon the bishop's whims. Nor had I any longing to become caught between the assaults that the Puritans and Laud's Arminian Anglicans made on one another. I said farewell to Cambridge, leaving in haste early in January."

"Milton? What move did the bishop make against him?"

"Milton has key connections in London, including Ben Jonson." I remembered with pleasure that Jonson had commissioned Milton to compose a poem in honor of the second folio of Master Shakespeare's plays.

"Doctor Diodati?" Winthrop asked. "We Puritans hold him in high esteem. What was his fate?"

"He returned swiftly to the safety of Calvin's Geneva."

"Were there other Cambridge fellows?"

"Sir Edward King. He has the fortune of being a favorite of King Charles. He suffered only reprimand."

"No reprisals?"

"None, so long as he remains a friend to the king," I answered, adding that Milton in particular had urged me to give Roger a copy of the dialogue on free will and predestination. When again Winthrop ignored my reference to Roger, I resolved to probe the mystery.

But evidently sensing my intent, the governor stroked his beard slowly. This time, I could not blame my imagination. I saw pain etch itself like a signature across Winthrop's face and heard him say, "A misfortune has befallen your . . . our friend."

With my heart pounding like horse hooves, I blurted out, "You lead me into a fog. Speak plainly, man."

"I do not know how to describe the recent turn in him." Winthrop paused, frowning as if his thoughts had fallen into mud.

"His health?" I demanded.

"He has the stamina of a horse but the disposition of a mule."

My patience gave way to the anger surging inside me. I laughed sardonically. "Roger has the disposition of ten mules, but . . . ."

Winthrop turned up the collar of his coat and pulled down the rim of his hat as if he feared recognition. I had never seen him act in so mysterious a fashion. "A wedge has come between you!" I charged.

"I will explain. Indulge me."

As the coach made its way up a hill, the governor gave vent to his sadness. "Master Williams has outdone the Separatists themselves."

"How so?"

"He proclaims the foolish doctrine that the state should have no jurisdiction in matters of religious belief."

"But your face and manner tell me there is much more!"

"More?" Winthrop asked in disbelief. "Did you not hear my words? The man has become a double Separatist!"

I stared into the governor's face and saw a stage across which swept a score of violent emotions. "I will not yield until I know the whole truth."

Winthrop drew in a deep breath; his voice shook with conspicuous and disarming grief. "Captain, there was a second reason for my failure to greet you at the dock. At the time, I was meeting with certain key men of our colony and the church regarding both Master Williams's charges and our duties toward him."

"Has Roger offended you or the church?"

"Since you will learn the details from others soon enough, I will tell you now. Master Williams declined our generous offer to install him as teaching elder to our Boston church. Recently I learned that the church members in Salem desire him as their teacher."

"Is there some harm or danger in that?"

Winthrop clenched his fist. "We cannot permit him to spread the error of Separatism."

"We?"

"The synod and the magistrates of Massachusetts. I am sure you understand fully, Captain. False teaching is contagious. If it breaks out in Salem, it will spread like the plague across our colony."

Having learned long ago in England that Winthrop was an honorable man free of corruption, I listened to learn all I could regarding his interpretation of the gulf between himself and our friend Roger. As we drove around the village, I heard him tell me of his calling to serve as governor of a city where corruption and fraud would never prevail. I had never heard him talk more earnestly. When he spoke of Roger, I felt that his heart had become a battleground where anger fought with anguish.

Winthrop soon convinced me that the Massachusetts magistrates must appease King Charles, lest the colony's charter be revoked, leaving the *city set on a hill* to remain a dream unfulfilled, a soap bubble to sparkle only for a moment and then to vanish as if it had never existed.

I understood my friend Roger well enough to know that he too had weighed this heavy matter on his scale. But I did not know what else he had weighed on the opposing scale. I had two good and strong friends between whom I did not wish to choose.

As though reading my thoughts, Winthrop said, "Perhaps Providence has sent you to us for this very time. If Roger pulls west and I east, then you must pull us back together."

"Have I the strength of Samson to yoke such mules together?"

"Roger is a mule, but a sweet-tempered one. He will give ear to you, Captain. You do not speak with the fury of a waterfall, but with the calm of a smooth-running river."

"You wish me to sail to Salem to be your advocate?"

"If you were Winthrop and I were Firebrook, I would serve as your advocate. I entreat you in the name of friendship. Take my interpretation to Salem and present it before Roger as though he were a jury. Plead my case as you see fit. Then return to plead Roger's before my jury."

Winthrop's position in London had been that of a court lawyer traveling back and forth as an advocate and mediator between disputants in Parliament and in commerce. Now, he wished me to play the mediator.

"I will go to Salem if you give your word on two matters. Lay out your case plain and clean, not painted up like the face of a French whore. Then upon my return, lend both keen ear and thought to Roger's interpretation as I present it."

When Winthrop gave his word, I vowed to represent him as accurately as my talents permitted. He then ordered his coachman to turn the horses toward his house, not his office.

When we entered his new stone house, he instructed his servant to interrupt us for nothing except disaster. True to his word, upon entering his library, Winthrop forsook all flowery eloquence and plainly spoke the interpretation he wished me to deliver in Salem. The simplicity of his doctrine glowed with its own eloquence. Deeply moved by his self-revealing earnestness, I took notes on all the details of his argument.

Even before going to Cambridge University, I had observed no society that could live without doctrines circulating among its members, like the blood circulating, according to Dr. Harvey, through the body's veins and arteries. Despite all my resolve to look with dispassion upon the dispute of doctrines between Winthrop and Roger, I discovered I was no aloof Plato. At Cambridge I had learned that the Greeks could not imagine their divinity Zeus looking down with pure indifference from his Olympian splendor at struggling mortals. I confess that I felt moved when I heard Winthrop expound his Puritan doctrine, making his case for order against the wild winds of chaos.

I had heard some students at Cambridge swear, *We live free of all doctrines.* Of course they might more readily have said that they lived without breath or blood. They merely gave their doctrines another name. In my travels with wise Abba, I discovered no societies without doctrines. None proved more dogmatic than those professing to live free of all dogmas. No nations have shown more belligerence than those who could not see their doctrines as *interpretations.*

After a quarter of an hour, I interrupted Winthrop. "If I detect what appears to be a contradiction in your interpretation, then Roger will detect it without fail."

"What contradiction?" The governor's tone made me impatient.

"John, if probing a flaw in your argument is like probing your skin with my dagger's point, I will probe no more. Flattery is for sale, but not by me."

Without murmur, Winthrop took my rebuke and said, "A wise man heeds his advocate's council. Adam's curse weakens every man's reason; but at points where mine is flawed, let yours fill the gap with sound advice."

"You say the Antinomians confuse themselves with God and think their lips are God's lips speaking?"

"Aye, and they imagine their inner twitches to be heaven's undistorted messages. When their stomachs growl, they fancy they hear angels whispering into their ears."

"But Roger will ask you, John, 'What divides you from the Antinomians when you take your interpretations of Scripture as infallible messages whispered in your ear by the Holy Ghost?'"

Winthrop's sullen eyes gave me a withering stare.

I spoke no more about the matter and asked instead, "What one message above all do you wish me to carry to our friend in Salem?"

"Tell Master Williams that our common mission in this new Promised Land is eyed by all Europe as well as by heaven. If we spoil our holy experiment, we make the Reformation not a model, but a target of scorn throughout the world."

Suddenly, as I continued to write down the governor's words, my legs felt numb. The boldness of the man in my presence astounded me. In my years of travel, I had known many daring adventurers to take risks beyond belief, exude raw courage, and perform blood-chilling deeds of valor. Yet only in John Winthrop did I encounter a human mortal whose boldness would cast both Achilles and Hector in his shadow. The truth about Winthrop came to me in a flash: He intended to *found a new nation. A holy empire!*

My thoughts spun like a thousand tops inside my head. I felt I had come upon a new world of the mind. Winthrop's vision astonished me. Like Moses, Winthrop had led his people to the other side of the sea. Like Abraham, he had forsaken his native soil to travel to a land prepared by God. I could not escape the conclusion that Winthrop looked upon both himself and his fellow believers in Massachusetts as the true heirs of the Reformation born in England more than a century earlier. He had little doubt that heaven had foreordained Massachusetts to become the supreme commonwealth and the Protestant model of Christianity throughout the world. *If Constantinople stood as Eastern Orthodoxy's capital and Rome as the Catholic citadel, then in Winthrop's mind, Massachusetts stood foreordained as the New Israel and capital city of the Reformation.*

Before the morning of my journey to Salem, I suffered strange and hellish nightmares. The earth shook, oak trees split, unnatural shrieks tore from the bowels of the planet, clouds turned to fire, immense ships vanished under watery mountains, and heaven itself seemed only one step from civil war.

Waking late in a foul mood, I washed myself in cold water and left in a rush, meeting my ship only minutes before the towering sails caught the wind. Once aboard, I quickly gained my sea legs, drew in the salt air, and dared to think of myself as the merchant of good news. Still, the alien air of my nightmares followed me like an albatross.

SALEM, MASSACHUSETTS

March 1631

Salem's population exceeded Boston's. The intrepid Captain John Endecott had governed Salem and the Massachusetts Bay area until Winthrop arrived armed with the Royal Charter that designated him the new governor.

After stepping off the ship at Salem, I soon learned that Endecott, a burly man with a large forehead and a short temper who jealously guarded his honor, had succumbed quickly to Roger's natural charm and earnestness. Roger also won the hearts of the busy citizens of Salem. Though perhaps saintly, he never appeared sanctimonious. He had once joked, "Some people think religion is worthless unless it has the taste of vinegar."

Even when the object of Roger's anger, I never felt demeaned or spurned. Like sunshine, he radiated good will rooted in the soil of genuine respect for the infinite dignity of every person he met. Hence, the news that the Salem church members and their pastor had invited him to become their teacher gave me no surprise.

As was my custom, I headed toward the highest point in the village to gain an overview. On my way, I saw in the distance a dozen or so fishermen ashore working on their nets a few feet from their ship. They seemed engaged in vigorous conversation with a man, whom I recognized immediately. Eager to see Roger, but not wanting to interrupt his intense conversation, I walked up behind him and stopped to listen.

A fisherman named Ezra Welch boasted at length, "Reverend Williams, I possess the power to command the devil himself and to cast out the lesser demons. I can give you this power too."

"I know a way to shame the devil, good brother," Roger said.

Ezra dropped his net and stood straight with a puzzled look on his ruddy, weather-beaten face.

Roger laughed good-naturedly. "Why, 'tis easy. You shame the devil, who is the father of lies, by telling the *truth*! Now, if you possess power to command the devil to appear, we all possess power to make him disappear by speaking the truth. So, my good brother, let us dismiss the devil by being truthful."

I covered my mouth to prevent my laughter from being heard. Has ever a man called another a liar in a more artful manner? All the fishermen understood Roger's meaning at once.

Far from taking offense, Ezra shook Roger's hand vigorously. "Pray for me, for I perceive you are a prophet of truth."

"As are you," Roger replied, "if only you do it naturally, like breathing. Breathe out the truth, and the devil will choke upon it."

When Roger turned around and saw me, he jumped like a surprised boy and threw his arms around me as if we were Italian brothers. His excitement made me laugh and feel welcome. In Roger, Merry Old England had come to New England.

He presented me to the fishermen. Then we headed north for a short walk. The cold, swift wind shifted, driving away the milder air from the south.

After rubbing his face with a piece of fur he carried on his belt, he suggested that we head for the house where Mary and he now lodged, the hospitable home of Captain Endecott.

While we walked, I kept remembering a comment Winthrop had recently made. *Roger is a mirror to my conscience.* Although still uncertain of its full meaning, I felt the comment as a reminder of my heavy promise to the governor.

Mary greeted us at the door, looking like springtime itself. "Captain Firebrook!" she exclaimed as she pulled us in from the cold.

For a moment, I felt that my heart would not contain all its joy.

While Roger carried in wood for the fire, she made me sit in the kitchen and tell her about my plans. Because the Endecotts in Cape Ann were away to see friends and conduct business, she felt free to cook what she pleased. I told her of my relief in knowing that she, not Roger, would cook during my visit.

Puritans often boiled their meat and vegetables relentlessly as if trying to boil away original sin. Governor Winthrop ordinarily viewed eating not as an occasion for pleasure, but as replenishing the stomach as if it were a fireplace. His provincialism, not his Puritanism, made him view shellfish with suspicion and use such a gourmet's delight as shad roe for fertilizer.

Fortune befriended me. Mary took much pleasure in creating an abundance of flavorful foods. In the corner of the Endecott kitchen, an old brick fireplace roared and crackled, emitting the tantalizing aromas of turkey, cornbread, apple scones, and what the Narragansets called *askútasquash.*

"Not since my visit at Polonius's table at Masham Manor," I said to my hostess, "have I felt such fervid anticipation of dinner."

The next day, Roger invited me to travel a few miles into the forest, where he expected to meet a small party of natives. "They are teaching me their language and customs." We rode off on horseback a mile or two into the forest.

A sound suddenly turned our blood to ice.

Roger held up his hand, signaling me to pull rein on my horse. He spoke scarcely above a whisper. "Listen. Never have I heard anyone, man or woman, sob with such melancholy."

I heard the deep, hoarse wail wafting through the trees. It seemed to fill the whole forest with gloom.

"From whence comes the voice?" Roger asked as we dismounted and tied our horses.

After I pointed, he in his long, confident stride moved toward the source of the sound. I followed until we stopped perhaps two hundred feet farther. In the distance, we could see a man resting his forehead on his forearm and leaning against a tree. The wails were the saddest sounds I had ever heard.

"Do you recognize the man?" I asked.

After nodding his assent, Roger walked toward him and his horse, taking care not to startle either. I lingered behind.

"Why do you weep, pilgrim?" Roger asked.

So enveloped was the man in his sorrow that he seemed scarcely to have heard the question.

"Have you lost someone you love?" Roger spoke, his voice soft and direct.

Catching his breath, the man replied, "It is too late."

I braced myself against a tree and tried not to move.

Roger asked, "Perhaps I could take you to your abode or to your good father's house? He could help lift you from this pit of melancholy."

"No, Reverend Williams, I will not inflict this malady on my father. There is no hope." He was a big man with broad shoulders and a chest that housed lungs worthy of his horse.

Roger spoke patiently. "Then let me bear some of your burden on my shoulders."

"Would that I could, but it is too late. I have lost my soul forever." The man seemed to struggle to suppress his loud, deep sobbing that sounded like a lonely voice emerging from a bottomless well.

"You claim your soul is lost, but can it not be redeemed?" Roger asked.

"My name is written in the Book of the Damned."

"Have you discussed this with Pastor Skelton?" Roger asked.

"Yes, but he too saw that all hope was lost. My thoughts would not leave their bog."

"Did he read the Scriptures with you?"

"He did, but the Scriptures only confirm my damnation."

I knew at once that whoever this man was, he had rejected taking his own life. If he truly believed he was among the doomed unelect, he would not rush into hell by means of suicide.

"Do not condemn Pastor Skelton," he said to Roger. "It is not of his doing. My condition was sealed before the world began. In his eternal chambers, the Creator fore-ordained me to damnation. What can a creature like myself do to change heaven's decree?"

Suddenly I heard my own voice ask, "Sir, why should God wish to condemn you and not your neighbors to damnation?" I do not know what prompted me to reveal my presence or to ask the question. Yet I had felt compelled.

He ceased sobbing and turned away from the tree to face me. "It is God's secret will. Sir, I know the Reverend Williams, but you—"

"Firebrook," I said. "Eric Firebrook."

He paused and then said, "I am Henry Winthrop."

I was stunned. When I recovered my power of speech, I asked, "You . . . you are John Winthrop's son?"

"His wayward son, I regret to say." He then turned to Roger. "I had no wish to disturb anyone and came here alone with my soul's sorrow."

Roger seemed consumed with compassion for this bereft mortal. "Perhaps heaven has made this hour possible for the three of us. If you consent, I will speak with you about the claim that your name is inscribed in the Book of the Damned."

We sat down on soft pine needles. Above us the puffy white clouds floated while the wind singing in the pine trees calmed our spirits.

"Until now," Henry said, "I have spoken of this matter to no one, save Pastor Skelton."

After quickly building a small fire to warm our bones, I listened as the two men spoke for half an hour of salvation and damnation. It occurred to me that if we Puritans had left men and women not only sensing their helplessness, but also without hint of divine intent to redeem them, our doctrine would debilitate us all. Our theologians had fortunately divided the process of salvation into stages so that the earnest soul might determine its progress. In truth, this Puritan analysis had become something of a philosophical experiment of the soul confronting its Maker. Roger had already written *Experiments of Spiritual Life and Health* to encourage himself and his wife in their Christian progress.

"Put your supposition to the test," Roger said to Henry. "First, have you heard the preaching of the Word and found some comprehension of it?"

"I have heard it from childhood, and I understand fully that salvation is not earned by deeds of righteousness, but comes as heaven's unmerited grace."

"Second," Roger asked, "have you experienced remorse and regret?"

"Day and night, I have known little more for the past month."

"Is this remorse because you do not wish to suffer torment in hell, or because you regret having caused your parents grief and having sinned against heaven?"

"Both, I confess. But I understand the distinction between mere remorse and true guilt."

"Third, having confessed your guilt, you appear submerged in contrition."

"My contrition is sincere," Henry said. When Roger made no reply, Henry added hesitantly, "But . . . I know that neither sincerity nor any good deed can earn the salvation I so desperately seek."

Roger inhaled deeply, his gentle smile conveying infinite warmth. "Henry, you are not far from the kingdom. True, our good deeds never earn us salvation; but your confessed guilt, sincere remorse, and understanding of God's free grace shine as signs of salvation yet to come."

Henry bit his lip and shook his head. "But are there not sinners in hell who have this remorse? Did not rich Dives in hell lift his voice in remorse?" Again, Henry's grief struck without warning.

Roger's eyes grew wide with apprehension. Appearing to calm himself, he touched Henry's shoulder as a mother might reassure a child in sorrow.

At last, Henry looked up. "Did not Dives love his five brothers even when he was in hell?"

The question took Roger by conspicuous surprise. It clearly posed a wide discrepancy for him. He frowned, looking away as if he wished to consult another scholar. Our ministers had told us there could be no love in hell, yet this dismayed sinner sitting before us found Scripture to contradict them. I could not help thinking of a passage from the Apostle Paul: *And now abides faith, hope and love, these three; but the greatest of these is love.*

"I cannot refute what you say," Roger said. "Scripture does in truth show us that love so welled up in Dives' heart that he begged Abraham to send Lazarus to warn his brothers lest they come also to the place of endless torment."

A native appeared at a distance. Roger stood up and walked to meet him. After they had spoken briefly, Roger returned.

For perhaps another half an hour, Henry and Roger talked further. I marveled at the change that came about in Henry's countenance. For the first time since our arrival, he smiled, not with mirth, but with warm gratitude. Roger made no practice of giving false hope, yet I felt the promise of tomorrow.

Roger stood up and pulled Henry to his feet. "I have kept my native friends waiting long enough. Henry, you have no reason to suspect that God has closed the door against you. Heaven's special gift of salvation comes not according to our human clocks, but according to divine wisdom."

Henry threw his arms around Roger and wept, not with agony, but with hope that beamed like sun rays streaming through the tall pines.

"Can it be?" Henry shouted, causing the birds above us to flap their wings and the playful squirrels to dash out of sight. Then, shaking Roger's hand, he asked calmly, "Can it truly be that heaven has increased my grief now to enhance my joy when I am truly forgiven of all my sins?"

On the following day, the sun lay hidden behind huge piles of gray, cotton clouds shifting and taking on diverse forms. The strong wind from the north gave Roger a push, making him walk faster on his way from the church to the Endecott house. From the corner of his eye, he saw a man walking in a hurry toward him.

Suddenly a strange sensation washed over Roger. *Is it possible?* The man in the heavy fur coat turned sharply to enter a small house nearby. Roger's heart raced, his insides feeling as if they might leap out of his skin.

Isaac Johnson! Roger stopped in his tracks and stared in disbelief. Just as he was about to run to catch the man, he abruptly realized that the man in the fur coat could not be Isaac Johnson. *He is dead. Isaac is dead.* A weight of sadness formed in Roger's chest as he turned to head again toward the Endecott house.

Only a week after landing in Boston, he had made a similar mistake for a fleeting moment, thinking he had seen Milton walking in the rain. Though he had corrected his mistake quickly, the feelings had lingered. He had heard of men who, losing their arms or legs, nevertheless felt them as phantom limbs.

Roger's pace slowed, but his thoughts raced. He reflected on the human mind's proclivity for indulging the heart. At Cambridge he had read Plato, who desired to transcend the heart, to leave it behind like a wild alien from which to escape. Roger had rejected Plato, or that one aspect of the elusive Athenian, and had found himself more at home with Aristotle and the Scriptures.

Keep the heart, Roger told himself. *Better to keep it and correct its errors than to cut it out.* He laughed aloud as the March wind pushed harder at his back. *Only the dead make no new blunders or have no misadventures. The living venture out. And to venture is to risk mistakes.*

For the past year, Roger had relentlessly pursued the thesis that when governments make mistakes, the consequences spread to everyone. The rulers' errors and misadventures become our misadventures. *We* pay the price.

During the year, Roger had begun to formulate the vague but persistent principle that each individual must be free to make his own mistakes. Mary's mistakes must not be his unless he chooses to partake. His delusions must not be hers unless she elects to partake. He felt compelled to think about his duty to Mary and eventually the children they might raise. From his own childhood, he remembered a friend's mother, void of a life of her own, had labeled herself as "the slave."

Upon landing in the New World, Roger's Puritan conscience had arrived with him. It spoke as unyielding inner voices that carried on debates. In fleeing Bishop Laud's hounds and arriving in New England, he had gained his freedom. Yet he made himself face the question of whether he had unwittingly turned his own dear wife into "a slave of his vision."

The moment Roger returned to the Endecott house and greeted Mary, she opened the door, bundled up to face the harsh wind, and stepped outside.

"Where are you going, Mary?"

"To the Widow Thornton's house. Her neighbors asked me to speak with her." She lowered her voice. "John Winthrop's son Henry awaits you in the parlor."

"Did he come alone?"

"Yes. I fear he is more alone than any mortal should be. I will return within two hours. According to her neighbors, Widow Thornton claims to have wrestled with an angel during the night."

"Angels do not always wrestle according to the rules. Pay Widow Thornton my respects." Roger kissed Mary's cheek.

In the parlor, Henry, though haggard, rose to his feet. He looked as though he had wrestled ten angels all night and had lost every match. His voice cracked. "Brother Roger, at dawn I saw a huge whale swim to the beach and lie in the sand as though offering itself up as a sacrifice. Two hours or so later, a crew of fishermen came near and made haste to kill it."

"Yes, I have seen two whales beach themselves and die."

"Do you think whales can contemplate suicide?"

"I do not know." Roger removed his coat and hat. "Perhaps they lose their bearings but cannot imagine they have taken the wrong course."

"I know whales to be intelligent," Henry said. "I think they do not lose their way but find their routine of eating fish and swimming no longer sufficient."

"Are you speaking of boredom?"

"Unbearable boredom. If some whales possess our intelligence somewhat but lack our hands and our considerable power of speech, they may come to feel like prisoners doomed to chase fish and to copulate. Beyond that, nothing. What would your life be, Brother Roger, without hands to write and build and without a language of vast repertoire at your command?"

He took Henry to the kitchen, where they threw a log on the fire and sipped the broth the natives had given Roger.

"Why would God create the great whales to suffer?" Henry asked. "Have they original sin? Was there some primordial Adam Whale whose sin brought some or all whales under the curse, or is damnation reserved solely for fallen angels and human mortals whose names appear in the Book of the Damned?"

Roger listened carefully and asked himself one question: If the Creator had elected Henry for damnation, would he have then generated great compassion in him? Some Puritans, Roger knew, believed that all men and women were depraved in every way and to the fullest except those elected to new birth and salvation. Such Puritans believed with Martin Luther that the image of God no longer existed in "the natural man."

"Brother Roger, if the whales may beach themselves because they suffer misery, is there no way for a human mortal in misery to beach himself forever? Have I no choice to blow out the candle, to empty the cup? Why must I suffer in full consciousness in hell forever? Will my suffering atone for some evil? Infinite suffering for infinite evil? You preach liberty of conscience. I have heard you. Nonetheless, if God foreordained me for hell while I was yet in my mother's womb, where is my liberty of conscience? I am convinced my father does not believe in liberty of conscience. More than once I have heard him say that even those in hell will praise heaven for their damnation. It seems my father's God cannot rest content with praise from the good angels and the saints but must also have the praise of those suffering torment forever."

"I lack the power of mind to solve these problems," Roger confessed, "though I possess sufficient power to understand that no other among our preachers and theologians has solved them. I see a wide canyon. High on one ledge stands Arminius; high on the opposite stands Calvin. Each leaps in the hope of landing on the other side to make converts. But each ends by plunging to the bottom of the wide chasm. Still, I do not doubt heaven's mercy."

"Then where is mercy for me?"

"There is mercy overflowing if you believe and repent by accepting heaven's grace."

"I have repented. I have seen the grievous waste of my years. Though I have opened my heart, no grace enters." The expression on Henry's face changed radically. It was as if a lighted lamp had entered a dark room. "I must face the truth: my father has never really loved me." Henry came to his feet, "Yes, I will go to him and admit that I became an unloving son, a drunkard, a vessel filled with hatred and rebellion. Go with me, Roger."

"I will go." Warmth spread throughout his body. "Your father wants to love you. Yes, we will go. Embrace him and he will embrace you. If he has never truly loved you, then you must teach him how."

"Who could measure the grief I have brought him? Reckless, caring for none but my own pleasure. Brother Roger, I confess I have burned with hatred for him. No, do not attempt to dissuade me. I know hatred. But it was born of fear. How much I feared him as a child. How oft I would climb into his lap only to . . . but he had sired so many children, all like squealing piglets at the trough."

Roger listened with mixed feelings as Henry laughed with such evident anticipation that Roger felt it might be a prologue to the peace and happiness for which Henry had longed but had never known.

"If only my father will accept my repentance, then perhaps it will be a sign that the Heavenly Father has chosen me for salvation. Ah, Roger, promise you will accompany me to Boston. I am weak. You do not know how weak. Look at me. I have the strength of a bull in these shoulders while inside I tremble like a child."

"You have my promise. If you wish to leave on the next ship to—"

"First, I have duties to attend. In three days. . . Ah, Roger, what a man you are. Look, I am smiling and laughing. And you . . . you are as a brother to me. No, do not be too modest. You have been more than a brother. Heaven bless you. Why am I laughing?"

"Heaven has already blessed you. And blessed me in counting you as my friend."

"Yes, yes. Can it be? Well, shake my hand, Brother Roger. In three days on the noon ship to Boston."

"In three days." He walked Henry to the door, opened it, and Henry exclaimed, "See, the sun shines through the clouds, and I have work to do. Tomorrow you will speak to the people, and I will be there in the audience."

Watching Henry walk swiftly away, Roger laughed to himself at the bounce in Henry's step. Suddenly, a magnificent wave of emotion rose up inside Roger as he pictured Governor Winthrop embracing his prodigal son and showering him with kindness. Yes, the sun had indeed begun to disperse the gray clouds.

"We sail together three days hence," Henry called out, looking over his shoulder as he hurried away.

The next morning, Roger, Mary, and I rode to the meetinghouse where the congregation officially welcomed Roger as their new teacher. Before speaking, he eyed everyone inside the crowded room.

As I prepared to take notes, I too had a vague feeling of apprehension and tried to dismiss it as mere superstition, telling myself that Henry Winthrop would soon arrive with the handful of men rowing in from their work on the river and in the bay. Memories of yesterday's meeting between Roger and Henry in the forest flashed with disarming clarity. The more I thought of Henry's predestined doom, the more the arguments from our *Dialogue on Predestination and Free Will* ravaged my mind. I could hear myself asking my Calvinist friend Doctor Diodati, "Why would the Creator select Henry Winthrop for everlasting damnation?"

Mary's face glowed as members of the congregation rose to express their joy that Providence had sent Master Williams to serve as their teacher.

With quills, ink, and paper in hand, I quickly found a suitable place for taking notes. Mary had once labeled Roger and me as philosophers, referring to our habit of studying our own people as if they were an exotic tribe. Puritans met sometimes thrice weekly to expound the Scriptures. They made no secret of their goal to train everyone to read the Bible, and their literacy excelled that of all other large bodies of people in Europe. Upon observing children sitting beside their parents and reading the Bible along with them, I thought of Milton, who in England had already begun devising a pleasurable learning process for the very young. He believed that his process would assist those English Puritans who sought to bring their children under early instruction.

Roger once told me that by translating the Bible into the language of the people, Luther, Tyndale, and others had undermined the authority of priests poorly versed in the Scriptures. He referred to *reading* as currency, meaning that in becoming their own priests and ministering priests to one another, believers could go to the bank of Scripture to draw out deposits of grace without hierarchic control of the channels of grace.

At ease before his new congregation, he could speak jovially or so somberly as to bring tears. One of the old fishermen would later say, "What need have we for an organ? Our teacher can play the pipes better than angels strum their harps."

To my surprise, Roger began, not with the flurry of oratory, but with a voice so intimate as to make each woman feel that he spoke to her or each man to him. And he addressed the children by name.

"They call some of us Puritans," Roger said, "a name we may gladly embrace. Yet if our path leads to self-righteousness, then we must blaze another trail. I speak plainly so that you may plainly agree or disagree. I will not hide my meaning in a fog."

Puritan theologians took justifiable pride in the clarity of their expositions. They regarded rational discourse as not only an art, but also a moral duty. Often I had heard Puritan preachers sound more like plodding lawyers building a case than like inspired prophets proclaiming from the mountaintop.

"Two opinions prevail among us regarding the Church of England," Roger continued, warning again that he would not equivocate. "On the one side stand those who would have us cling to her. But I say, let us flee her as we would the company of murderers and tyrants; for such a company she has become. Scripture teaches, 'Do not follow a multitude to do evil.' I ask you, good parents, do you not instruct your children to make no partnership with thieves? You will hear others argue that our loyalty belongs to the Church of England. But I say this church has turned herself into Babylon. She forges a partnership with thieves who use the state's power to pick our pockets and turn them inside out. In return, the bishops would foist on us a scarcely literate clergy whom we neither request nor approve. The king's prelates insult our hearts and minds by sending us ignorant lackeys who know the Scriptures no better than do cackling hens or braying asses."

Once when Roger had said that tradition, not heaven, appointed kings to their thrones, I asked him if he preferred to throw all tradition overboard. He answered, "Tradition is like a large storage house. It accumulates both necessities that nurture us and rubbish that chokes us."

A man whose beard hung down to his belt stood up in the meetinghouse and challenged Roger to speak more clearly about the king and the people's duty to the throne.

Roger did not answer quickly, but stared at the ceiling. "I do not tell the king what garden of religion he must hoe. If king and bishop dislike my garden, let them offer their words as opinions, not as laws, least of all as edicts purporting to be from heaven."

To the surprise of everyone, a man from the rear walked slowly toward the front, took a stand beside Roger, and raised a voice of protest. I did not know this man; but when he opened his mouth and spoke, a secret rage seemed to underlie his words even though he tempered his tone. "I protest," he said. "Does not Scripture teach that we must obey our leaders? As offspring of Adam, we are not to be trusted with our own opinions free of authority. When every man does what is right in his own eyes and there is no king, each servant rises up to proclaim himself a monarch. Every bleating goat proclaims himself a *theologus*. Opinions run wild like insects at night, and society loses all control."

The man went on in this vein for at least ten minutes. I could not help wondering if Dudley or one of the other Massachusetts magistrates had sent him, for he represented those like Winthrop who professed allegiance to the Church of England. The people grew restless until a stocky fisherman stood up to say he had heard the story many times and wished now to listen to their teacher expound again.

I confess my admiration for the orderliness of Puritan meetings. Far from being half-drunken Englishmen wagging their heads, shaking fists at one another, and railing, Puritans gave each his turn and regarded it as a religious duty to listen.

Captain John Endecott, having recently returned from Cape Ann, stood up and in his gruff voice said, "Brothers and sisters, let everything be done in decency and in order." He then nodded his head toward Roger, who stood again before the congregation.

"What is Puritanism?" Roger resumed. "For some, a byword. For others, it is a most precious word, a flag under which they sail their doctrines. Above all we would *purify* ourselves of the hoary tradition of bloodletting. How deeply does the vein of killing run among us? While shouting 'Christ Jesus save you,' Protestants and Catholics slash their neighbors' throats and join hands to imprison heretics. Violence that once lurked like panthers in the shadows now breaks out publicly and without shame. Though professing to follow the Prince of Peace, the king's bishops would force their precepts upon us, violate our person, and spill our blood upon unholy altars. From one side of the mouth, they extol *free will.* From the other, they threaten to shackle us in iron if we disagree with their doctrine."

He kept looking at the door. Was he expecting someone? Since Henry Winthrop had told both of us he would attend this meeting, I expected him to enter at any moment. Roger soon became absorbed in responding to questions from the congregation. Evidently the members had stored up flaming brands of perplexity, which they now held up before their new teacher. The discourse among them stunned me with its intensity. The meetinghouse shook with a collective mental fever.

To a flood of questions about the Holy Eucharist, Roger suggested they consider the fact that the doctrine and practice had divided Christendom into warring kingdoms. "Those who control the Church of England would compel us to perpetuate the priestly class as if we were yet tied to Rome and the abominable Mass. I say 'abominable Mass' not because I abhor grand and beautiful ceremony, but because the Mass perpetuates the very notion of bloody sacrifice. Bishop Laud and the cardinals in Rome ignore those Scriptures telling us that Christ Jesus came as the Prince of Peace to shut down the entire enterprise of bloody sacrifice. Through the prophet Hosea, did not the Lord say to the people of Israel, 'I desired mercy, not sacrifice, and the knowledge of God more than burnt offerings'?"

Where have I been? I wondered almost aloud. I sat astonished at Roger's sweeping insight. Until this day, I had never heard him weave the strands of his doctrines into a whole fabric. I felt like someone watching weavers send their shuttle back and forth skillfully between the warp threads faster than the eye could see. With a transparency that shook me, I saw both the origin and the fruit of his philosophy. He had grown up during the reign of King James, notorious for giving to undeserving sycophants and gangs huge monopolies in the world of commerce and estates. Now James's son King Charles had set out to create an all-encompassing monopoly in the vast marketplace of religion.

Roger had given long, involved thought to Martin Luther's protest against Rome's merchandising of salvation. In his heart, he had declared his independence of all such merchandising and monopolizing of heaven's grace. He would neither bend his knee before the golden calf nor return to the fleshpots of Egypt. If he had to negotiate with the king's gangs to gain freedom, so be it. But no longer would he align himself with Charles's corruption and arbitrary wielding of power. Roger made known his belief that the king's gang had already carved the Reformation's heart out of the Church of England.

Suddenly, the door of the meetinghouse flew open. Roger's face grew strangely pale. An old man with bulging eyes burst into the meetinghouse and shouted, "We cannot find him!"

Roger's voice shook. "Come in."

The old man waved his cane wildly over his white head. "He disappeared! Vanished from sight!"

Two men from the audience, grasping the old man's meaning, jumped to their feet and dashed out into the cold March wind.

Rushing after them, Roger called back over his shoulder to Endecott, "Brother John, we will need your help."

Alarm spread throughout the meetinghouse. Children began to cry. I grabbed my coat and woolen steeple hat as Endecott and I ran out the door, following the others to the river.

The moment we arrived, we saw men in two small boats probing the river bottom. "Young Henry Winthrop!" a gray-bearded boatman shouted to Roger. "Carried overboard. There, where the river meets the bay."

Roger stopped in his tracks and grabbed a stocky, bald man as if to shake the desired answer from him. "You saw him come up, did you not?"

"No . . . no, Reverend."

Roger rushed toward the spot where Henry had been washed overboard. But seeing nothing, he called to the boatman, "How long? When was it?"

"Quarter of an hour, sir. Maybe longer."

My eyes kept scanning the surface as I tried to push away the thought that no one could survive long in this freezing water.

Roger ran along the shore, peering out into the bay. He pointed to an anchored ship and called back, "Our only hope, Eric!"

I agreed. If the undertow had carried Henry out to the bay, perhaps the crew had fished him out.

From the meetinghouse, more men and women came running and yelling, "Henry! Henry!" Some of the women wept. "Oh, the poor governor. To lose his wayward son before . . . ."

Roger ran into the water and looked right and left, searching and shouting for Henry, hoping he might have swum ashore. Roger fought back his anguish and gritted his teeth. Unbearable emptiness rushed in upon him like a storm from the sea. "Henry! Henry!" he cried out again and again, driven by thoughts of the grief that would consume his friend John Winthrop should the tow carry Henry's body beyond the bay and into the sea. Aware that the moment required action, he conquered all feelings. "The shallop!" he shouted, jumping into it and motioning for me to join him.

I read his intention to race against time before the open sea claimed the body.

"He has drowned! Henry has drowned!" a young woman screamed, rushing up to the water's edge.

"Dry your eyes quickly," Roger ordered, not looking at her but grabbing an oar. "Show me where you saw him last!"

"But I did not see him," she cried out.

"Then join the search," Roger barked angrily as I grabbed the second oar.

We rowed away from the bank; and Roger, his hair twisting in the wind, called to the young woman, "Use your voice! Cry out for him along the shore."

My heart raced, and I let my eyes scan the bay's surface in the hope that Henry would somehow appear. I knew in my heart that one question hammered without mercy inside Roger's mind: *Did Henry receive the gift of salvation?*

The anchored ship bounced with the waves, and our small shallop seemed helpless against the uncaring wind. Yet Roger's powerful arms at the oars never yielded to weariness.

"Henry! Henry!" Roger boomed out over the waves.

In desperation, we rowed toward the ship, now nearby. As soon as we climbed aboard, leather-faced Captain Jason asked roughly, "What is causing the commotion ashore?"

Roger pointed west toward the river. "Governor Winthrop's son was drawn overboard."

Though the ship's haughty captain growled that he had seen nothing, Roger persisted: "Would you be so good as to inquire of your men?"

"Is not my word sufficient?"

I stepped forward. "I am Captain Eric Firebrook. If words were needed, they would be sufficient. I speak of eyes. You have two only, sir."

The disdainful Captain Jason summoned his men. Peering through the first mate's spyglass, Roger scanned the horizon in vain. He felt deeply for Governor Winthrop, who had already suffered much because of Henry's waywardness in England. When the ship's crew stood before Roger, he looked at each man separately. Could at least one of them give a favorable report? With each shake of the head, cold futility crowded out hope. The eyes of the seamen told him they had seen Winthrop's son neither dead nor alive. One corner of Roger's mind could not bring himself to surrender all hope. In the other corners, hope drowned in grief.

Four days after Henry's disappearance, a one-armed captain sailing from Nova Scotia reported to Endecott that he had found a body floating near the coast of Gloucester.

Roger and I accompanied Governor Winthrop to the ship and approached the dreaded sight. When we stopped, Roger and I looked down, whereas Winthrop held his eyes tightly closed. We waited.

"Is it . . . ?" Winthrop asked.

Roger placed his hand on Winthrop's shoulder. "It is Henry."

Winthrop's whole body quivered. Though he opened his eyes, he could not bring himself to look down at the sight. "You are certain?" he asked Roger.

"Yes, your son Henry." Roger thought of his conversation with Henry and found it difficult to believe that he would never again look Henry in the face. Roger had to turn away for a moment when he tried to imagine the sense of loss and horror that passed through the father.

Winthrop lowered his eyes and seemed to shrivel into his own shadow. A groan came up from the shadow like a wailing sound from Hades. "My son, my son," he whispered as though addressing the uncomely corpse. "Would . . . would that I were lying there and you were standing here."

Sensing that the father meant those words, Roger felt an almost unbearable sorrow. Winthrop would never again see his son. Suddenly, Roger remembered the very day on which he had lost his twelve-year-old sister. In tears, his father and he had embraced as if to repel death's cold fingers closing around them.

Turning aside and speaking in a whisper, Roger said, "Eric, what thoughts have you on whether I should eventually tell the governor everything Henry told us in the forest?"

"My present thoughts bubble up and turn to vapor. On this matter, I fear my counsel stands in need of counsel."

Roger turned to face the governor and after swallowing tried to speak his sorrow. The governor seemed inconsolable as lines carved themselves into his grieving face. Though Roger intended well, he felt his words sounded hollow and powerless to heal Winthrop's spirit.

Endecott could only shake his head and confess to Roger his worry that the wound had cut too deeply into the governor's heart.

At last the governor emerged from his silence. "How shall I tell my Margaret?" he asked Roger again and again as he swung his head slowly from one side to the other like a chained animal. It was as if his grief had confined him to one spot until Roger helped him break the shackles. Then, together, they walked toward the ship named *Trial.*

On the stony loam shore, a lanky man with stunningly innocent eyes stepped in front of Winthrop, causing him to stop. "Do you remember me, Governor?"

Winthrop frowned but gave no answer.

"You should." The man's voice quaked. "I am Jeremiah Paynter. Two months ago, I criticized you openly when you refused to consider our petition for land at Marblehead Neck. A week afterward, my little one died. Do you remember what you said?"

Seeming not to comprehend, Winthrop tried to maneuver around Paynter.

"Her name was Naomi." Paynter breathed heavily into Winthrop's face. The guards who accompanied the governor put their hands on the intruder's shoulders. To their conspicuous surprise, they could not easily remove him.

Sensing violence in the offing, Roger stepped up and gently signaled the guards to give the man leeway. They backed away, and everyone around listened to Paynter speak, his lips trembling.

"Little Naomi, my only daughter—she died. But you, our righteous governor— you proclaimed her death to be God's judgment on me. In public you accused me of private sin. Do you hear; I accuse you! To your face, I accuse . . . ."

Paynter seemed so overwhelmed with his own grief in losing his daughter that he could not complete what he undoubtedly had rehearsed and longed to say to the governor, who had deeply offended him. An awkward silence followed, Paynter keeping his eyes fixed on Winthrop's face like a hawk circling its prey.

"You look pale, Governor. Quite pale!" Paynter's voice rose to a frantic pitch. "Has your iniquity at last come home to roost? My dear little Naomi has gone to heaven. Now your wayward Henry shrieks in hell, and . . . ." Paynter's voice trailed off into incoherent muttering as tears flooded his big, childlike eyes.

Roger walked up quietly and put his arm around Paynter's shoulders. "Walk with me, Jeremiah. Revenge wears poorly on your kind face."

Paynter obeyed, seeming to understand that Brother Roger had interceded on his behalf and defended his right to address the governor.

As they walked a few paces away from Winthrop, Roger said, "Go home to your wife and children, Jeremiah. I will call on you before sunset."

Roger then returned to Winthrop, who stared blankly and shivered as if a wave from the icy bay had washed over him.

"Come, good friend," Roger said. "It is time for you to set sail." Standing on the shore, he watched Winthrop board the ship. Soon, the *Trial* slowly disappeared over the horizon, carrying the tormented governor and his dead son south toward Boston.

SALEM

Late March 1631

Two days later, Mary, as hardy a soul as her husband, rode with him into the forest to meet a small party of natives southwest of Salem. About an hour into the forest, they came to a creek that danced over the rocks. The horses leaned forward with their long, powerful necks to drink the cold water. Dismounting, Mary and Roger walked upstream to cup their hands in the spring. Kneeling down at a spot on the bank where the water ran smoothly, Roger studied a school of minnows.

In the water, the reflection of a man appeared without warning. Roger's stomach tightened like a wound spring. After turning his head to face the intruder, he rose slowly to his feet. The two men searched each other's eyes.

Mary caught sight of a woman in a fringed deerskin dress who was kneeling down and braiding the hair of a little girl. Within minutes, ten other adults emerged from birch-bark canoes. Roger recognized two of them at once. They called to him their welcome, dispelling the tension.

The younger of the native men spoke English fluently while a second struggled. After observing protocol on this surprisingly mild day, they exchanged pleasantries and gifts. Then the natives sat down to instruct Roger in their Narraganset language.

One of the children spoke English so well that Mary and she soon became friends. Abiding by their custom, the Narraganset women talked in one group and the men in another.

Roger soon learned that this handful of Narragansets had traveled northeast for four days to trade with their Algonquian kin in whose camp they had slept.

For at least two hours, Roger copied down vocabulary and listened to the natives chuckle at his valiant efforts to pronounce each word and phrase precisely.

Comishoonhómmis? Came you by boat?

Kuttiakewushaùmis? Came you by land?

Mesh nomíshoon-hómmin. I came by boat.

Meshntiaukè wushem. I came by land.

Kukkowêtous. I will lodge with you.

Yò Cówish. Do lodge here.

Howúnsheck. Farewell.

Nétop tattà. My friend, I cannot tell.

Then for another hour, they talked of the Narraganset customs and beliefs. Roger overheard one of the natives, a Qunnihticut, address the esteemed Sachem Miantonomo. A short discussion followed. Sensing that their talk was about religion, Roger asked the sachem, "Does your Qunnihticut friend have a question for me?"

"He has a message for you and me," hawk-nosed Miantonomo answered. "He said, 'Souls go not up to heaven or down to hell, but to the southwest, as our forefathers have taught us.'"

"What did you say to that?" Roger asked Miantonomo.

"I said, 'But how do you know that your souls go to the southwest; have you seen a soul go thither?'"

Roger asked, "And the Qunnihticut replied?"

"He wanted to know whether you had seen a soul go to heaven or hell. And I answered that you have books and writings, one which God himself gave your people regarding your souls."

The little girl who had made friends with Mary said that her name was Matoax (*Little Snowfeather*) and that her mother braided her hair when she behaved well. Then Little Snowfeather grinned mischievously and said in clear English, "She braids it for me every day."

Near sunset, when the air turned abruptly cold again, Mary and Roger joined the Narragansets deeper in the forest, where they slept in oval frameworks of saplings covered with slabs of elm bark. The damp air and the smoke inside the wigwams made the night painfully long for Mary, who snuggled close to Roger.

"Are you awake?" she asked.

"Yes."

"I feel cold. Do your teeth chatter?"

"Yes," he answered. "The north wind has returned." He sat up and moved his hand in the dark until he found another animal skin to pull over them. Then, when they felt warm again, they fell each into a deep sleep as the fire burned low.

When morning came and they had eaten berries and fish, Roger persuaded the native who spoke English fluently to help him with the dictionary he had begun to compose. They worked steadily until the sun rose overhead.

The cold air gave Mary and Little Snowfeather reason to walk swiftly along the trails. After their brisk walk, they found Roger and his Narraganset friend, whose name was Many Tongues, sitting on a large rock near a pond.

Mary laughed aloud at Roger, who, wrapped in bearskins, gave the appearance of a bear with a human head. Though the wind had grown calm, the cold air seemed to have teeth.

"It has been a profitable time!" Roger exclaimed excitedly, looking up at Mary. While his face was that of a boy lost in wonder, his manner was that of a man resolved to accomplish a goal worthy of an intellectual Hercules.

Mary had heard William Blackstone say that Roger was perhaps the only person from England or Scotland capable of living with the natives and learning from them.

The slanting rays of the sun, the call of the eagle, and the movement of the little animals in the forest told Mary that they should begin to say good-bye. "Roger, is it not time to leave?" she asked.

He agreed, and the Sachem Miantonomo as well as others of the Narraganset party gave them more presents and most of all their good will.

Mounting their horses, Roger and Mary turned northeast toward Salem. But before they could leave, Little Snowfeather ran up to Mary and, looking up with glistening dark eyes, tugged at her foot. The two of them exchanged gifts; Little Snowfeather politely accepted Mary's blue silk handkerchief and tucked it into a woven bag where she kept other sacred and precious articles.

Later, just before arriving in Salem, Roger suddenly spoke the words *hactenus inculta*.

Teasingly, Mary replied, "Does not Scripture say that if you speak in tongues, you must have an interpreter?"

Roger shifted his body on his horse. "I was thinking in Latin. According to the *hactenus inculta* decree, European sovereigns take special liberties. They declare as empty land all territory unoccupied by Christian men. Literally, it means *until now, uncultivated or neglected*. In short, Mary, the Latin phrase blesses royal thievery and royal murder."

In all England or New England, no one burned with more zeal than Roger to evangelize the natives. Yet he knew that the European practice of converting masses by threat and means other than persuasion had produced a contemptible Christendom, harboring more hypocrites than true Christians acting in liberty of conscience.

In England, he had seen women compelled to marry men against their will. In the bone and marrow of his being, he equated love to sham and pretense unless it grew out of free choice and conscience. Christ had specified that the greatest of the commandments surpassed all burnt offerings and sacrifices: first, to love God with full heart, soul, mind, and strength; and, second, to love one's neighbor as oneself. Yet, without free consent, no mortal could truly love anyone. Roger believed this so strongly that he denounced conversion through force and intimidation as *soul rape.*

BOSTON AND SALEM

April 1631

As a ship captain in the turbulent Aegean Sea, I had sweat blood while navigating around deadly reefs and through narrow passes concealed in fogs that seemed eager to destroy my ship and crew. Navigating in Boston politics proved no less trying. How could I penetrate the thick fog of political schemes? In this fog, how could I discover the truth about Roger's fate? Each lead seemed designed to carry me deeper into the fog of rumors, lies, and mystifications. Above all, I needed to speak with the governor and present my favorable opinion of the man whose future rested in his hands. Had Winthrop withdrawn behind a rock wall instead of a fog, I might have scaled it. Contrived ignorance so prevailed that not even Barnabas, with his wily stratagems, could gain dependable information about the magistrates' decision regarding Roger Williams.

Knowing that Roger waited anxiously for my report, I went surreptitiously to a magistrate to lay before him my wish to learn of my friend's future in Salem.

Binding me to secrecy, the magistrate begrudgingly yielded only one morsel: "Early this morning, Governor Winthrop and most of the magistrates composed a letter to Endecott regarding Master Williams."

Upon learning this, I took the next boat from Boston to Salem. An hour after arriving in Salem, I entered the Endecotts' parlor. The downcast look on Mary's face told me Endecott had received the letter.

"Where is Roger?" I asked her.

"He went to chop wood; but through the window, you can see him trying to stop a skirmish between two boys."

I lowered my voice to a whisper. "I have reason to think a letter from Governor Winthrop—"

"Yes," Mary cut in before I had time to sit down. "The Endecotts left half an hour ago, so you need not whisper. The governor did write a letter to Captain Endecott to say that my husband is a dangerous man. You would think he had turned into a spotted leopard. You have known Roger and you—"

"You have read the letter yourself?"

"Yes, with Captain Endecott's permission."

"Has Roger?"

"No, he has not, and I am glad you are here. This wrathful letter burns so hot as to turn friendship to ashes. I cannot understand the governor, yet Roger loves him still."

She handed me the letter, which I read carefully. Though I wanted to tell her that Winthrop's flaming words were the fruit of his grief, I could not bring myself to believe it. Mary then gave me a treatise written recently by Winthrop. Upon reading it, I realized that I stood irrevocably between two mountains, Winthrop to the east and Roger to the west. Only hope gone mad could imagine a bridge spanning the immense distance between the two peaks.

Though Roger returned to the parlor, he did not yet see me. He was laughing while explaining that Little Freddy always arranged to have his fights in front of the home of someone who would rescue him if the other boy gained the advantage. "Now the boys are friends again," Roger told Mary cheerfully.

I could not help wishing my friend could as easily repair the rupture between himself and Winthrop. When I revealed my presence, Roger greeted me with enthusiasm and made me sit in his chair.

Mary wasted neither time nor words. She faced me. "Is it not naive to hope for reconciliation between the governor and my husband?"

I shrugged, disturbed at my own thoughts. Of late I had come to think the controversy between the governor and Roger portended an even more ominous rift, the New World itself tearing apart from top to bottom. I trembled to think this controversy would infect the New World for generations to come. For some unclear reason, I blurted out, "Mary, this land is like a woman in travail. In her womb stir two children yet unborn. Will they both live and thrive? Will one become the murderous Cain and the other the butchered Abel? I know not." My mind wandered in that vast chasm between Mt. Williams and Mt. Winthrop. The time had arrived for me to find my own answers and in so doing make some sense of my past and future.

Roger interrupted my thoughts. "Has the captain sailed off into his private world again without us?"

"I once spent a month at sea in anchor, having neither wind nor current to carry me," I said evasively and added that recently I had been training my spyglass on my past.

"For what do you search?" Mary asked politely, her kind eyes inviting me to share my troubled thoughts.

I laughed uneasily. "Sometimes I think I search for the wind." I secretly wondered what powerful gale had driven me to Cambridge. At times I felt as if my whole mind were vast stretches of land divided by seas and oceans. I had talked with Buddhists, with pilgrims to the Genghis in India, and with followers of Mohammed and Christ. I had talked with worshipers of Lord Money from Vienna and with spirit doctors from Africa's western coast. Perhaps I had gone to Cambridge to overcome the fear that I might turn into a mental chameleon. Was I destined to be an actor, to play the role of an Islamic believer when among the worshipers of Allah? A Mammon worshiper in Vienna? A Calvinist in Geneva and Cambridge? An Arminian in Oxford or the Royal Court?

After traversing diverse parts of the world and listening to expositions of sundry doctrines, perhaps I had entered Cambridge to explore my Christian heritage. At Cambridge I had found reason to doubt my faith but none that led me to abandon it. In Cambridge's scholarly climate, I could no longer feel content to walk in the murky Christianity of my youth. Yet when my haze lifted, I was shocked to see that my long-embraced Christianity had formed itself into bitter, hostile camps.

Mary and Roger held their eyes on me while I still held Winthrop's treatise in my hand. "The governor keeps hearing confusion and chaos hissing like vipers at the door," I said. "He cannot think of Separatism without conjuring images of vipers."

Mary stiffened as if she had discerned that Winthrop looked upon her husband as a dangerous spreader of chaos.

Roger said nothing. I felt uncomfortable. Opening the treatise to the tenth page, I began to read Winthrop's words aloud: *What demon has breathed on these Separatists? Are they incapable of understanding that our social order is not a natural phenomenon like rain or sunshine? Do they not see that the social arrangement must be cultivated by us perpetually?*

Roger interrupted. "Has he particular Separatists in mind?"

When I hesitated to answer, Mary insisted that I give my interpretation of why the governor had spoken so violently against the Separatists.

"You are right, Mary, to say his language grows more violent. I think he harbors a fathomless fear of Separatism."

"Why should he?"

"Let me reveal what the governor told me. I can still see the terror in his eyes when he said that years ago he had seen *Hamlet* on the stage and remembered the account of the king's death and how the usurper Claudius poured poison into the king's ear."

Roger stretched his hand out toward me. "Does this mean he believes Separatists would commit regicide? That they are usurpers who would pour poisonous—"

"No, it is far worse than regicide. He thinks the Separatist doctrines are poison poured into the people's ears. Or to shift the figure of our speech, the Separatists would chop the social order into tiny pieces and scatter them to the wind, like King Lear's divided kingdom. His most violent language, however, rails against what he thinks is the Separatists' dangerous trust in the *natural state* of the human race. In all earnestness, Winthrop believes that the natural state of our species is murder, deceit, and rape. We have no social order unless it be sent by divine revelation."

Roger's quick response took me by surprise. "I know nothing of a *natural state,* but only of human mortals in their social habitats."

"Still Winthrop hotly contends that Separatists would dismantle the seawall of society stone by stone and call it freedom."

Roger pushed back the lock of hair on his forehead. "Do you find yourself agreeing or disagreeing?"

The simple question caught me unready. In my mind I saw a sprawling savanna on which heroes and martyrs emerged from their graves to stand as my contemporaries.

My Christian heritage seemed not a horde of mute ghosts, but a vast army of witnesses divided into angry, threatening camps.

Evidently sensing that Roger's question had tangled the threads of my mind, Mary suggested we move to the kitchen.

"A warm proposal." Roger's eyes twinkled as she escorted us to the warmest room in the house and prepared three cups of tea.

"My knees are stiff with this New England cold," I complained as we took chairs before the large brick oven in the kitchen's corner.

Laying a fresh log on the hot coals, Roger again tossed me the question I had not answered.

"I need time to untangle my thoughts on these matters. At Cambridge I fought to stand on neutral ground; but the Isle of Neutrality between you and Winthrop shrinks daily."

Roger took a sip of hot broth. "Perhaps you stand on a foundation of fantasy. Nevertheless, if you have a third interpretation that sides with neither the governor nor me, describe it. I will listen."

He said this with such gentleness of spirit that I should have in no way felt pressed to the wall because of him. Still, I felt pressed, sensing a need to resolve matters in my mind.

"I confess I cannot stand neutral toward Laud's tyranny. Neither can I pretend neutrality toward the threat of chaos. I challenge you, Roger, to wrestle with a question put to me by the governor when I once warmed myself before his fireplace in Boston."

Roger clasped his palms together as if to crack walnuts. "Release now Winthrop's lion. Either it will send me up a tree, or I will take its hide."

I set my cup aside. "Winthrop thinks the Separatists' version is a manual for placing chaos on the throne. Does not freedom of conscience itself become the tyrant, creating confusion, fettering our *reason*, and scattering our *affections* so that we know neither who we are nor whom we truly love?"

Mary turned her blue eyes on Roger. In their sixteen months as husband and wife, she had learned he never ran from questions that bared the lion's teeth and claws. Puritans like her husband did not hide their doctrines in a cave, but brought them into the open to test them fiercely. In my years, I had seen physical courage that I admired. From Roger, however, I learned true moral and intellectual courage. I wondered if my intellectual courage could ever equal that of my Separatist friend.

Roger refilled his cup. "Winthrop's doctrine is inferior to the distinguished man himself."

Mary blinked with skepticism.

He explained, "Some people do not measure up to the doctrine they profess. Winthrop's doctrine, by contrast, fails to measure up to him. He towers over it like a giant pine over a thornbush. His doctrine is like a spyglass with a scratched lens. When he peers through his doctrine as through a spyglass, he thinks the scars are on the faces he sees rather than on the lens of his doctrine."

"What doctrine?" My own aggressiveness surprised me. Having promised to play the continuous mediator, I made careful notes for my next report to Winthrop.

"Why, the doctrine that the nation is a person and that widespread chaos prevails when this giant person entertains diverse opinions and doctrines. According to Winthrop's strange doctrine, the nation-person overcomes confusion and chaos by eliminating all opposing opinions. The governor then describes this repression as the *nation disciplining herself.* But he errs from the start in holding that the nation is a person. The opinions he would yank out like rotten teeth are not his own, but his neighbors' if they disagree with his interpretations."

"But I have never heard him declare a nation to be a person," I protested.

Roger set his cup down with uncharacteristic force. "Does he not teach that a nation makes a contract and covenant with God?"

"Yes, that I have heard him teach many times."

"Then tell me, Eric, do you yourself make two-way covenants with rocks?"

"I am not mad, but what has that—?"

"Aye, you make no such covenants because a rock has neither a *mind* for understanding the terms of the covenant nor a *will* for carrying them out."

"Then do you not imply that the nation has neither mind nor will?"

"With all my mind, I do imply it," Roger answered.

"King Charles calls himself England's mind in establishing our covenant with God."

"A feebler mind one could scarcely find," Roger quipped. "If a nation were a man or woman writ large, Charles would not be the upper part of the anatomy. But I use a misleading figure. Even if we agree to portray a nation as one vital creature, it still possesses no central brain. It resembles more a giant earthworm than a human person like you or Mary. The king and his bishop know that nations neither bleed nor suffer. People suffer. Mary suffers as do you and I. Thus, when Laud and Charles inflict punishment, they inflict it on real human beings, never on a fictitious person called England."

While Roger poked the hot coals and laid another log on the fire, I reflected on my doctrine and upon the rift between my two friends. Again, I saw that I had no credible middle way to mark off between the two.

In Cambridge I had learned a trick of debate called the middle way. Using the ploy, I would first select or create two doctrines and then arbitrarily position in the middle of them a third doctrine, the one my Cambridge teacher had called on me to defend. I would then refer to my doctrine as the middle way and dismiss the two rivals as the wild extremes. No longer in Cambridge trying to win a debate but in New England seeking truth, I now needed no such ruse.

Two days after my visit with Roger and Mary, I prepared to journey to Plymouth to learn for myself what manner of government prevailed on the southern border of Massachusetts. Though Governor Winthrop had criticized it, he had no jurisdiction over it since Plymouth Colony was not part of the Massachusetts Bay Colony. Before I could strike sail, however, Roger pulled me aside to show me another letter.

"At noon today . . . Endecott!" Roger tried to catch his breath, his words tripping over one another. Yet I had no trouble piecing together that at noon a second letter had arrived in Endecott's hands. Though I had never seen a ghost, Roger's face could have been that of a sea phantom. While I read the letter, the blood rushed back to his cheeks. Only with difficulty did he restrain himself.

As soon as I finished reading it, he looked me straight in the eye. "Do not go yet to Plymouth, friend. I implore you. Go first to Boston on my behalf!" He stared at the letter again and shook his head. "What possessed Winthrop to take such a drastic measure against me?"

BOSTON AND
MASSACHUSETTS BAY

April 1631

My doubled efforts in Boston went far less smoothly than I had hoped. My mission weighed so heavily on me that I felt like the Greek Olympic runner with weights attached to his limbs. When I first arrived at the governor's office, the attendant turned me away with the explanation that the General Court and the governor had convened for business.

The letter Endecott had received from Winthrop on the day of my departure from Salem left no room for guessing the meaning. After again labeling Master Roger Williams a dangerous man who taught a perilous doctrine, the governor warned Captain Endecott that the magistrates and the synod of Massachusetts clergymen strongly recommended that the Salem congregation dismiss Master Williams as teaching elder. The governor further instructed Captain Endecott to ensure that Master Williams cease all talk regarding the dangerous doctrines recently voiced before the Salem congregation.

The content of the letter evidently had in no way surprised Endecott, who had said before leaving Boston, "Captain Firebrook, I entreat you to persuade your friend and mine to acknowledge that he has sorely displeased Governor Winthrop and the synod."

Though Roger was eager to sail to Boston at once to settle matters, Winthrop had made it clear there would be no conversation between them until Roger removed himself from Salem.

In Boston I had a plan to uncover all the complaints that Winthrop and the magistrates kept raising against Roger. With patience and a measure of good fortune, I positioned myself in the shadows while overhearing a conversation at the Boston jail.

A town magistrate spoke in confidence, he thought, to his brother the jailer. "At the Salem church, Master Williams defended the right to utter blasphemy."

"To say it is a right is itself blasphemy," the jailer said.

"True," said the magistrate.

Not so! I wanted to say to them. Roger had not defended blasphemy, but charged the state guilty of blasphemy for presuming to be God in punishing all moral and religious sins.

"There is more," the magistrate said. "Master Williams charged that Martin Luther played the tyrant when he advocated death for the Anabaptist blasphemers."

"Did Luther so advocate?" the jailer asked.

"Aye, and more. He wrote that any heretic who taught that Christ Jesus did not belong to the Godhead should be hanged or committed to the flames."

"What did Master Williams say?"

"I will give you Master Williams's very words: 'Catholics from Rome or Spain would burn Luther for heresy while Luther would burn others for blasphemy.'"

The jailer winced. "Master Williams squanders no words, does he?"

"That, I give him," the magistrate said. "But there is more. He boldly asked how Luther's wickedness in persecution differed from the pope's."

"Does not Scripture itself forbid us to blaspheme sound doctrine? What did Master Williams say to that?" The jailer wagged his head in anger.

"Why, he said that any church may if it so chooses strike from its register any of its members who blasphemes. 'But the state,' said Master Williams, 'possesses no moral authority to discipline or punish either heretics or blasphemers so long as they use no force against their neighbors and commit no acts of thievery.'"

Standing in the shadows, I heard much more. Though a tickle kept playing like a feather in my throat, I neither coughed nor sneezed.

The magistrate again warned his brother to disclose their conversation to no one. Then as he turned to leave, he saw me.

"What? Is that . . . ? You there in the shadows," he said to me, "step forth."

I obeyed, my blood quickening at the sight of the anger on both men's faces.

"You!" the magistrate demanded. "Your name!"

I took in a deep breath. "My name?"

The magistrate scowled. "Be quick!"

I swallowed. "If I do not know *your* name, you will find it to your advantage."

"What do you mean by *it?*" the magistrate snapped.

On the jailer's forehead, a vein swelled until it turned blue. He pulled his brother aside and whispered in his ear. Then the magistrate returned to me. "What you heard or imagined you heard would best be locked inside you."

"Best for the three of us." I then walked away, hoping the jailer would forget my face but knowing he would not.

On the next day, my third attempt to see Winthrop succeeded somewhat. I arrived at his office in time to learn that the Massachusetts General Court had just reelected him as governor. He saw me and quickly pulled me aside.

Before he could speak, I said, "I have plans to visit Plymouth."

He looked puzzled and held me by the arm. "Stay until tomorrow. We have much to settle." He dropped his voice to a whisper. "Is Master Williams yet in Salem?"

"Why do you ask?"

Winthrop did not answer my question but said, "Tomorrow morning, we break the fast at seven. If you would do me the honor . . . ."

"At your house?"

"I will send my coach for you at a quarter before the hour or later if you prefer."

I accepted. Then Winthrop guided me into a smaller room and handed me what appeared to be a treatise of perhaps fifty pages. "Please, read it at your leisure." The first page bore his name.

Winthrop's coachman appeared. "Captain, may I drive you to your destination?"

The coach headed toward the Blackstone house. I had traveled scarcely half a mile when all at once the coachman cried out, "A fire ahead!"

"Crack the whip!" I ordered. The horses stretched their long legs to a gallop. I stuck my head out the coach window and saw the red flames shooting up like giant tongues.

"The Cheeseborough house!" The coachman pulled rein hard on the horses.

I leaped out and then dashed toward the house, but the frame seemed suddenly to vanish before my eyes as if it had melted.

"We are too late," a man with his shirt in his hand called to me. Four or five other men having come to give aid stood mute, their eyes bulging. Those of us who moved closer to the charred remains were forced to draw back because of the heat.

A woman came running up beside me. "The whole family is cooked!"

After attempting to console the Cheeseboroughs' neighbor, I arrived at the Blackstone house. Lydia greeted me as I stepped out of the carriage and made me take her to the Cheeseboroughs' ruins to see if she could be of service. Later that day, after retuning to the Blackstone house, she beamed while escorting me to my room. "See, Captain, it is cleaner than polished silver."

"'Tis true. This house of music is medicine to my spirit," I replied, referring to Lydia's habit of humming English ballads while she worked.

"I have reason to sing. My Barnabas will return soon from Nova Scotia."

"Barnabas? Is he—?"

At that moment, Barnabas entered the parlor. "Behold! You see before you King Arthur or Barnabas. Choose!"

"I choose King Barnabas." I gladly shook his big, friendly hand.

He snapped his fingers and merrily ordered one of the other servants to attend my every wish. The servant bowed low, carrying out Barnabas's good-humored drama. The other servants, crowding near the parlor doorway, laughed, apparently eager to enter Barnabas's drama.

With a flare, he waved his arms. "These fine mortals you see before you, noble captain, are the royal princes and princesses of Blackstone Palace." He introduced each by name and then took me aside. "Captain, they have planted seeds for a new garden outside your east window. If you wish, I will guide you to the spot."

But before going to the garden, Barnabas himself took my few belongings to my room while I carried Winthrop's treatise and a container of important notes I had written in Salem.

As Barnabas and I walked to the garden, he whispered, "Your friend Master Williams would be unwise to return to Boston."

"What news have you heard?"

"The moment I stepped off the boat, news flew to me from hither and thither. Seems our governor suffers much from Master Williams but knows not what can be done with him." Barnabas stopped at the garden mound. "Come the month of June," he added, looking down at the fertile dirt, "this mound will be so rich with the color of flowering vines that the honeybees will make bids for it." He lifted his head and pointed to a large oak perhaps two hundred feet away. "Under its shade will be my beehive. And we shall have ample honey for your biscuits, Captain."

As old Barnabas and I walked toward the future home of the hives, I inquired, "Has Mr. Blackstone any opinion about Master Williams's future?"

"He looks with genuine favor on Master Williams but knows not what counsel to send him except to avoid Boston. Our governor fears Master Williams. And I will venture a further opinion if—"

"Show no hesitation," I said, taking him aside.

A stern look from Barnabas quickly drove away one of the servants who had lingered to eavesdrop. Barnabas whispered to me, "Our governor must prove to England that he is more Church of England than is the Archbishop of Canterbury himself."

"Why?"

"Perhaps because he senses that it's a lie." Evidently startled at his own bold answer, Barnabas hurriedly added, " Our governor makes much of being Anglican. He repeats it daily as though to persuade himself."

"Your meaning plays in shadows."

"I mean the governor and his many admirers are Church of England in name only. I mean the governor, being a lawyer, sticks to the letter of the law but supplies his own special reading."

"Do you hold this against him?"

Barnabas laughed. "Against the man? Yes. Against the lawyer? No."

When Barnabas and I arrived at the oak tree, he pointed to the ground. "My beehive will stand there. Yes, yes, by autumn, there will be honey running over our pots unless there is excess of evil thoughts among my neighbors."

I closed one eye and looked at Barnabas. "What link holds between evil thoughts and the work of bees except by remote analogy?"

Old Barnabas shifted on his feet and rubbed his chin. "The governor tells us that if there is excess of evil among us, the flow of milk and honey will diminish by proportion."

"You speak in riddles."

"I will tell you outright the governor's meaning. If Master Blackstone's neighbors think evil thoughts, heaven will punish all New England, Mr. Blackstone's cows will dry up, and my swarming bees will grow lazy."

"That disregards the prophet Ezekiel's teaching that the soul who sins shall be the soul who pays for the sin," I protested.

"So 'tis with Ezekiel the prophet, but not with Winthrop the governor." Old Barnabas gazed up into the sky.

More than once had I heard Roger refer to the prophet Jeremiah: "They shall say no more, 'The fathers have eaten a sour grape, and the children's teeth are set on edge.' But everyone shall die for his own iniquity; everyone that eats the sour grapes, his teeth shall be set on edge."

I had heard Winthrop contend that while God punished the soul, the magistrates punished the flesh. Among the Arabs, I had seen men's hands severed for stealing. Before first going to Salem to visit Roger and Mary, I had witnessed the Boston trial of a man accused of adultery. After the court sentenced the man to die, Winthrop opened the Bible and read from the Book of Deuteronomy. Standing now with Barnabas under the oak, I asked about the carpenter convicted of adultery.

"Zachary Cole is his name," Barnabas said.

"Has the sentence been carried out?"

"He escaped."

When I inquired further, an enigmatic contortion formed on Barnabas's face, and he evaded my question, quoting the Golden Rule. Later I learned that Zachary Cole was Lydia's cousin.

An hour before sunset, a carriage rolled up at the Blackstone house. A young man jumped out and rushed to the door. "A letter for Captain Firebrook!"

Lydia took the letter herself and invited the driver inside in case a reply proved necessary. In the parlor, I opened the letter and saw that it was from Governor Winthrop. The letter said he could not meet with me to break the fast on the morrow but wished to meet with Roger Williams in secret. He requested that I discreetly arrange the meeting between them on a boat as soon as possible. His closing words were, "We have little time to lose."

MASSACHUSETTS BAY

April 1631

At sunrise the blue waters of the bay lay calm; the pink cotton clouds above gave no threat of a storm. If a storm should erupt, it would soon occur aboard the small ship *Rachel* anchored off the coast of Marblehead Neck east of Salem.

On the beach, I said a prayer and waited for Roger. My thoughts drifted despite the urgency of the hour. Had God predetermined all the consequences of the coming meeting between Winthrop and Roger? If so, why pray unless my prayers were also predetermined?

The red sun peeped over the water from the east, and the image of a one-horse carriage appeared on the western horizon. No doubt at this moment, Roger felt the surge of both trepidation and excitement. Shielding my eyes with my hands, I looked east to assure myself that the *Rachel* had not vanished. She sat serenely at the center of the magnificent red ball as the sun ascended like Osiris from water and into the sky.

When the carriage stopped near the beach, Roger and Captain Endecott jumped down. I hurried to greet them. "You are prompt," I said.

Tying the horse to a shrub, Endecott spoke gruffly. "In Salem only our wives and we know of this meeting. I see the governor has arrived."

"He slept well aboard ship," I replied.

Captain Endecott's foul mood meant little since it shifted many times in one day.

Facing east, Roger shielded his eyes with his hat as he searched for the *Rachel*. Then, in his long, swift stride, he walked toward the small shallop I had pulled upon the beach.

Endecott returned to his carriage and took the reins in his hand. "Pay my respects to the governor. I expect to be informed." Endecott had served as head magistrate in Massachusetts until Winthrop's arrival from England in spring 1630. Winthrop had assumed firm control from the start, leaving Endecott now in need of saving face.

To help him save face, I called back, "You will be fully informed, Captain."

Roger had already begun shoving the shallop toward the water. He seemed more than eager to meet John Winthrop face to face. I joined him, and together we began rowing toward the *Rachel*. Roger took the oar since I lacked his strength.

"A ball of energy so early in the morning?" I laughed. Evidently, he had prepared himself for the coming ordeal and now fought to hold rein on himself until the trumpet sounded.

When we latched our shallop to the *Rachel*, the two seamen with whom I had sailed from Boston reached down to help us aboard.

Winthrop came from below deck and greeted Roger. He seemed resolved to keep a cool composure befitting his position as chief magistrate. But when he saw Roger, his eyes lit as if Roger's warmth had flowed out to him. "Let us go inside," Winthrop said, leading the way to the cabin but leaving the two seamen outside.

Winthrop locked the cabin door behind him and invited us to be seated. Extraordinary politeness filled the air, for we were clearly aware that much depended on this moment. Both men had shared many of their thoughts with me and with my full consent had used me as their messenger. They would continue to use me for many years. I knew and they knew that each man represented a possible future for the New World. We knew also that they had separate visions for their new homeland, visions that had enticed them away from England and to this wilderness we called New England. Though each used the words "order" and "freedom," they lacked crucial agreement on their meaning. Winthrop was prone to speak of "true freedom," by which he meant devotion to the Puritan way as he envisioned it. Roger saw freedom, above all, as following one's own conscience rather than another's. Did Winthrop and Roger see themselves as people of destiny? Aye, they did. They had no patience with false humility or cheap flattery.

Never a man to waste time or to turn his back on negotiating, Roger started by praising John Winthrop for throwing open the General Court's first meeting to the whole body of settlers. "I mean this as sincere praise, John. If you recall, I know the details of the king's charter."

"I do not grasp your point." Winthrop's tone seemed surprisingly defensive.

Each seemed to have a strategy in mind, anticipating each other's moves as on the board or battlefield, straining to read the other's thoughts.

Roger had informed me that the Massachusetts Bay Charter gave sweeping powers to the governor and the Massachusetts Company. As governor, Winthrop now possessed the authority to make and ordain laws, statutes, and directions.

Roger offered his lawyer friend a sincere compliment. "A man bent on power for its own sake would not share his authority as you did with the settlers."

Instead of taking the compliment as such, Winthrop turned pale, which confused me. Why had the praise generated apprehension in the governor?

After an awkward pause, he cleared his throat and spoke in a voice louder than he doubtless intended. "Roger, you raise the question of the charter." Winthrop paused as though to remind himself that he was not dealing with one of his Boston magistrates. In England he had of course witnessed Roger's tenacity and skill in facing men of power. He lowered his voice. "You and I will not be the same after today, Roger. Nor will the future of New England. Let us not pretend otherwise. Do you agree?"

"I do."

"Then we must not distract ourselves with clever ploys. Shall we speak openly and directly?"

"Yes."

"Good. May I respectfully remind you that the king will deal severely with our colony if we declare ourselves to be Separatists? I . . . I confess to having suffered acute guilt upon leaving the shores of England for Massachusetts. Good English neighbors and friends I had known for years rebuked me, saying I showed ingratitude to think of abandoning my native soil and church. Even on the day of departure, I felt like a son forsaking his aging mother in her bed of sickness." Winthrop frowned as if perhaps he had opened his heart too quickly.

Roger replied that the governor's self-revelation had lifted a fog. "Let us now strike at the heart of the matter."

John Winthrop, the older and more experienced of the two, did not yield the floor. A well-trained lawyer, he had come prepared. For several relentless minutes, he greeted Roger with a platoon of well-calculated questions. "Roger, in becoming the spokesman of freedom do you propose to give rein to thieves all in the name of liberty of conscience?"

"No, a thief invades the freedom of others."

"Let us move to the particulars. If a thief enters your neighbor's house and steals his goods, do you say to your neighbor, 'Go find him and punish him as your private conscience dictates'?"

"No, that would lead to excesses and vendettas that would—"

"Ah, now *who* will catch the thief and bring him to justice?" Winthrop squinted his eyes and politely waited for an answer.

Roger flipped an unruly lock of hair from his forehead. "In this world, we settle for approximate justice."

"You fail to answer the point!" Winthrop said politely.

"I . . . I would have the magistrates and their appointed deputies find the thief and punish him."

"Ah! Then you admit that in saying this, you accept our *principle?*"

"Principle? What principle?"

"Why, it is clear. The magistrates alone must punish evildoers." The governor reached behind his back for the Bible on the shelf. Taking it in hand, he quickly turned the pages. "Roger, you have oft studied this very passage of Romans 13, which speaks plainly of the magistrate as God's minister to punish evil." Winthrop then drew in a deep breath and read carefully from the Epistle: "Rulers are a terror, not to good deeds, but to evil deeds. Would you have no fear of him who is in authority? For he is the minister of God to you for good. But if you do that which is evil, be afraid; for he wields not the sword in vain; for he is the minister of God, an avenger to execute wrath upon him who does evil. Wherefore you must be subject, not only for wrath, but also for conscience sake."

Roger gave no answer. A trickle of sweat flowed down his temple. Of all passages in Scripture, this one numbered among those that troubled him most. Far from instantly harmonizing with the four Gospels and the book of Acts, it seemed to be a squawking crow among nightingales.

As if knowing he had cornered Roger, the governor laid the Bible in front of Roger's eyes. "If you truly follow the Reformation and do not sail under a false flag, then you must, my friend, take all Scripture as divine revelation. Omit none or else you contradict your own belief about Scripture. Please do not look away. Answer me without equivocation!"

Wincing, Roger opened his mouth to speak; but the lawyer pointed to the biblical text with his long finger and requested a forthright answer. Although Roger again opened his mouth, the lawyer continued directing his attention to the text. "Is this Romans 13 divine revelation, or do we pick and choose from Scripture only what we fancy?"

Despite wincing from the sting of the question, Roger evidently saw clearly something Winthrop had perhaps overlooked. Could Winthrop no longer remember the history of tyrants and magistrates who had served as terror to *goodness*?

"I pose a counter-question," Roger said in a quiet voice. "Is it true that rulers are always a terror to evil deeds and never to good deeds? Do you believe that God ordained and approved the corrupt and sinister magistrates who made martyrs of Jews and Christians? Must we forget all we have read in Foxe's *Book of Martyrs*? Was Herod a magistrate for good deeds when he presented the head of John the Baptist on a platter?" Roger quickly flipped through the New Testament until he came to the story of Pontius Pilate. Looking the lawyer in the eye, he whispered, "Was cowardly Pilate a magistrate rewarding those who did good deeds? Pray tell, what evil deed did Christ our Savior perform that Pilate should turn him over to the executioners?"

Winthrop shook his head and held his ground, pointing again to chapter 13 of Romans.

I remembered Roger telling me he could not help believing that some obscure scribe, not the Apostle Paul, had much later penned and inserted the first half of this chapter. At Cambridge I had learned to my amazement that none of the Bible's original documents had survived. Not one! Why had God seen fit to preserve only corrupted copies of copies? How many gaps lay between the sundry Greek and Hebrew manuscripts? These questions had long puzzled scholars, and Roger knew that neither Catholic nor Protestant scholar had posed worthy answers.

Outside, the wind began to stir as the sun rose above the sea. Flushing red and feeling warm, Roger stood up and opened the door to let the April breeze pass through the cabin. Then his penetrating eyes fell on me.

I had seen that look before at Cambridge when we Protestants had dared to raise the question that haunted all Christendom. If the Scriptures were the supreme revelation and authority, why had Providence permitted the teeth of time to devour the originals one and all? Protestants like Roger and Winthrop never tired of challenging the Catholic scholars with one further agonizing question: If the Roman Church is the infallible authority, why had God allowed her to suffer perversity and her pontifical authority to accumulate corruption on top of corruption?

Roger closed the door, locked it again, and sat beside his friend. "John, you know that the authorized translation of the New Testament under King James depended upon a certain collection of Greek manuscripts."

"Yes, Stephanus's accepted text."

A heavy silence filled the room. At Cambridge I had learned that the primary collectors of those certain manuscripts were Stephanus and the noted Dutch scholar Erasmus, who had visited Cambridge before our time.

The exchange of glances between Winthrop and Roger sent a cold chill down my back. Roger seemed to want to say more, yet I sensed hesitancy when he beheld intense perplexity on Winthrop's face. Roger believed the meaning of Romans 13 flowed more naturally without the verses Winthrop had quoted.

"A scribe. I admit a scribe could have . . . ." Winthrop shook his had and left his sentence unfinished. He did not need to finish it. We knew what burned in his heart. Had a scribe added this troublesome first half of the chapter? Every Protestant and Catholic scholar knew that over the centuries various scribes had added, subtracted, and revised biblical texts according to their understanding of what the original texts would have been.

All at once Winthrop tapped the table with his fingers. He turned the pages of his Bible again to the first half of Romans 13. "This is my sword! The sword of the Lord."

"If we both wield *only* this sword of Scripture against all whom we brand as heretics, then you and I have no quarrel," Roger said. "But if we take up the sword of steel—"

Winthrop waived aside Roger's words as if they were a mere annoyance to him and made no reply. Roger sat silently, evidently fearing that unless the governor were at this moment successfully challenged regarding the limit of the magistrates' power, all New England would become Old England's twin.

I looked with apprehension. Was their good friendship teetering on the brink? I stood in the presence of Moses and the Apostle Paul of the New World. Eventually, would I or this new land be compelled to choose between them?

Suddenly Winthrop gathered new strength and unveiled another platoon of well-formed arguments, all asking Roger if his way would open the floodgates to anarchy and chaos in the name of liberty of conscience. Winthrop swept me up with his sincere eloquence. I was sitting in the presence of one of England's most trusted lawyers, who had composed arguments for Parliament and had more than once changed the thought of influential men.

Roger patiently noted each contention, drawing air deep into his lungs. Though not a lawyer, he had served under England's foremost judge and had worked closely with legal advocates from his youth. Like Winthrop he could quote Scripture as if citing legal precedent although he resisted thinking of religion as mere transactions. "John, I align myself with the whole New Testament rather than lean on this shaky text from Romans 13. Did not Peter and the apostles say to Jerusalem's magistrates, 'We ought to obey God rather than men'? Did not Peter and John in the book of Acts draw a line between right in heaven's eyes and right according to the magistrates?"

Winthrop interrupted, but then seeing that Roger had another point to make, invited him to make it.

Roger cast it in the form of two questions. "Would you agree, John, that idolatry sets in if we expand the power of magistrates beyond proper limits? Must we not leave room for each pilgrim to fight his own inner war and discuss his own religious thoughts with fellow pilgrims even though those thoughts disagree with the magistrates? I do not believe that you intend to bestow omniscience on mortal magistrates."

As Winthrop stared at Roger I could not help thinking that he would forget nothing of this unsettling day.

Roger in turn stared at Winthrop as if he saw two men: one, a magistrate on the brink of tyranny, a beast of power raging in the cellar; the other, a supremely rational man of conscience, deserving endless respect. But which would prevail, the dangerous beast or the man of reason? Tapping his finger lightly on the Bible, Roger smiled. "Tell me, good friend, what have you to say about the last book of the Bible? Do not we *Protest*ants join in its *protest* of magistrates who mistake themselves for divinities?"

The pain on Winthrop's face faded, giving way to hard resolution. He pointed his finger at Roger. "You yourself have freely admitted that I extended political rights to a larger portion of the people."

"I do so admit. Massachusetts Colony enjoys the extension far more than do Londoners under the crown."

"Then by what twist of fact do you insinuate that I confuse myself with God?" Winthrop rubbed the tip of his nose with his fist, stroked his beard, and grit his teeth. "Roger, I know not why; but no man cuts me like you."

Evidently remembering the man in Boston's jail whose ears had been cut by order of the magistrates, Roger said bitterly, "Better to cut a man's conscience than to sever his ears from his head." I remembered Milton's friend Alexander Gill Jr., who had suffered mutilation in England.

Winthrop's left eyelid twitched as he looked down at the table and ran the knuckle of his thumb twice across his teeth. He was doubtless struggling with his conscience, and Roger gave him time to struggle

When Winthrop did not look him in the eye, Roger chose his words with care. "John, I know you agree that some men play God step by step. With the first step, the magistrate becomes a *conscience* for all his subjects. Soon he presumes to be their *mind* and later their *heart*. By and by, the magistrate asks, 'What need have I to consult with these subjects when I am their conscience, mind, and heart?'"

Winthrop's chest rose, indignation leaping like fire from his eyes. But he said nothing.

Roger stopped himself. Though uncertain of what thoughts crisscrossed in his mind, I felt that he now faced a dilemma. If he presented a strong case, he risked alienating the governor and defeating his whole purpose to persuade him to change his announced course of action. If he presented a weaker case, however, he would surely betray both himself and many others who depended on him to defend liberty of conscience.

"I mean you no personal offense." Roger avoided the tone of apology.

The governor, however, pulled up his drawbridge as Roger seemed to wait, hoping the fortress gate would open and the bridge lower.

The fortress spoke. "Pray that we do not reach an impasse. But I must speak plainly, my good friend. You bring dissension to the people." Without offering an explanation, Winthrop folded his arms across his chest.

"John, in England did we not stand side by side to oppose tyranny? I too will speak plainly, giving you the truth as I interpret it. Anyone who presumes to be the conscience of the people plays God."

"Conscience?" Winthrop asked. "Did you and I not speak to one another of *false* conscience serving *false* religion? We agreed that like wind in sails, an untutored conscience can drive us willy-nilly onto dangerous reefs. Without a compass, conscience cannot be our guide." Winthrop picked up the Bible and waved it in the air. "Behold our compass!"

"Tell me this, John. Am I right or am I wrong to charge straight off that you propose to punish every private and public error in religion as a crime against the state?"

"Private sin!" Winthrop shook the Bible close to Roger's face. "Do you not yet see that all sins and all errors are public before God?"

"Before God, yes. But before human magistrates? Or do you mean to say that the magistrates now become heaven's eyes on Earth? Do magistrates become all-present and all-knowing through spies? Should we issue every subject a spyglass for informing on his neighbors? Whereas our Lord on Earth went about doing good, should we now turn his followers into finger-waving eavesdroppers and gossip hounds?"

"I warn you, remember that the God of mercy is also the Lord of judgment and wrath. You denounce me unjustly. A magistrate is duty-bound to protect the people from swift and terrible judgment. Do you not see? Sin and error draw heaven's wrath down upon the commonwealth as surely as water draws lightning."

He turned away from Roger and looked at me. Then he planted his elbows on the table, chopped the air with his right hand, and continued to address Roger. "In England I trembled for fear that God's wrath would swiftly fall on the land, given the abominations and every form of wickedness! I believe the plague came as God's punishment. In time, God guided my eyes to reread the inspired account of Abraham in which the father of the chosen people traveled to a land that God had prepared for him. I prayed and . . . ah, this very Bible in my hand became my map; and heaven's sign came to me."

"Do you speak of a sign in the heavens—a rainbow on a clear day or a bird chirping English?" Roger folded his hands on the table.

Seeing the twitch on Winthrop's face, I turned around, pretended to look at the water, and listened to Roger press his argument: "John, I have heard you denounce Anabaptists who profess to hear the voices of angels and archangels. Now you speak of what? When the magistrate has twitches on his skin, rumbles in his belly, or bells in his ears, do you call these heavenly signs?"

Winthrop addressed me as if Roger had left the cabin. "Do you remember, Captain, how the message came to us that day from your friend who spoke of the plague among the Indians?"

"Message?" I asked, still peering at the ocean. "Aye, I remember your observation that so few natives survived the plague."

"In truth, when I heard so few had survived, I knew then it was the sign I had long awaited."

I turned around in bewilderment, half thinking my ears had deceived me. Roger rubbed his palms against his face as if waking himself from a nightmare.

Winthrop continued unperturbed, puncturing the air with his finger. "We, the righteous of England, now possessed God's approval to claim this new land as the Promised Land. God has poured out his wrath upon the red savages, who have defiled the land with their heathen beliefs and practices."

Like a horse running loose and wild, Winthrop could not restrain his speech. The words poured out like hot lava against the heathens who gave themselves to idolatry, unbelief, and religious error. Evidently forgetting our presence, he denounced England one moment and grieved for her in another. As I listened I thought his heart would break with grief. "Oh, England, England, jeweled isle, sick with abominations, fouled by carnal schemes and ten thousand broken covenants, how oft would God have drawn you to himself as a hen gathers her brood under her wings. But you would not."

His earnestness moved me. Serving faithfully as an honest and upright lawyer in England, the man had seen contracts violated without shame and covenants broken without concern. He believed with all his heart that God had made a covenant with the English and that if the covenant were violated, the Supreme Judge of heaven would not fail to punish. More than once I had heard him quote from the last book of the Bible: "And they hid themselves in the dens and the rocks of the mountains and said to the mountains and rocks, 'Fall on us and hide us from him who sits on the throne and from the wrath of the Lamb.'"

He blinked twice and then stared across the table at Roger as if seeing him in a different light. "Listen to me, dear friend. Do you not agree that this land belongs to God? If it pleases him to take it from the unbelieving savages, from the Canaanites of the New World, and give it to the righteous believers, who are we, Roger Williams and John Winthrop, to tell God what to do? It is you who set yourself up as a god to judge God."

Fearing that my two friends might in the next few moments not only cut down the tree of their friendship, but also dig up the roots and hurl them into the fire, I suggested that they part from one another to take the April air into their lungs. This suggestion they accepted, but with sadness. Winthrop went immediately outside and stood with his two men at the ship's stern. I stood looking over the bow. Roger came up beside me. Though he seemed angry, his eyes told me he felt more sadness than anger. He spoke softly in the wind: "Eric, what has happened to my righteous friend John? Has he never looked into the eyes of the native children? If only he had seen Little Snowfeather placing Mary's gift in her bag with other valued objects. If only he had heard Many Tongues patiently instruct me in the Narraganset language."

I could not help remembering the day Roger had introduced me to his friend Miantonomo, roughly Roger's age. Never before had I known a native sachem, and I was struck by the man's reasonableness. Later, Roger told me Miantonomo had taught him much about the forest and its animals. I remembered the little poem Roger had composed about his native friends.

> Boast not, proud English, of thy birth and blood,
> Thy brother Indian is by birth as good.
> Of one blood, God made him and thee and all,
> As wise, as fair, as strong, as personal.

I knew my mission of reconciliation had failed when Winthrop joined us at the bow and said to Roger, "Though we differ regarding the natives, I think you err to trust them as you do. Did Moses trust the Edomites or Canaanites?"

Roger gripped the governor's forearm. "If nature's sons—English or savage—are human, how ill it becomes the born-again righteous to lack humanity!"

At first when Winthrop opened his mouth to speak, nothing came out. Then he tucked his Bible under his arm and turned to face me. "Captain Firebrook, be so kind as to return me to Boston!" Then he faced Roger. Never have I seen such anguish on a mortal face. I thought I saw tears in the governor's eyes.

PLYMOUTH COLONY

August 1631

While spring yielded gradually to summer, John Winthrop's determination yielded to nothing or no one. Using his considerable political skills, he rallied Boston's magistrates against Roger and used them to convince the Salem congregation to withdraw its welcome to their teaching elder, who continued saying that political magistrates should not interfere with religious and church matters. Winthrop quickly effected Roger's release as teacher.

Forty miles south of Salem by water, the Plymouth Colony pilgrims opened their arms to Roger and Mary and invited them to become their pastor's assistant. Although he gladly accepted, he earned his living by farming, Mary working at his side.

He removed his hat and with the back of his forearm wiped the sweat from his brow. He looked up at the hot August sun and remembered the milder weather in England. Feeling shame that Mary had to work so hard in the sandy scrub soil of Plymouth Colony, he shuddered. What would happen to his dear wife if they could not grow enough food in the next ten weeks to last them through the barren months of

New England winter? Before October's killing frosts they must grow and harvest their field peas, potatoes, rye, and *askútasquash*.

Leaning on her hoe, Mary said, "Roger, dear, I will finish planting for the rest of the day if you can catch fish. We will need dried fish for the winter."

"Worry not about fish now. Yesterday, two of the Narragansets told me how to catch cod even though the salt rivers freeze solidly."

Roger remembered the day Plymouth's Governor William Bradford had warned him that violent blizzards and dangerous nor'easters racked Plymouth every winter. Half the people coming to Plymouth had died from various sicknesses and injuries. Virtually none had died of old age.

For the next two hours approaching sunset, Mary and Roger did not talk. They had time for farming and little else. He tried not to grieve over the loss of his position as teacher at the Salem church. Thirteen leagues to the north by water lay Salem and Captain Endecott's comfortable house with Mrs. Endecott's hospitality. How he missed the Endecotts and the vigorous people of the congregation. How he missed fulfilling his dream of a colony where Christians and others could live together in harmony and where individuals could manifest their holiness in kind deeds and a cheerful disposition. How he missed ministering to people in times of trouble and fear. He remembered the gruff fishermen who, though teasingly calling him "Saint Roger," came to him in their times of grief and crises.

Having left his Salem life behind, he was faced with the coming winter months. He indentured himself to the goal of survival.

At sundown Mary and Roger walked wearily to their English wigwam, a small structure they had built with their own hands, modeling it after the native wigwams. When Mary saw her tiny home, she laughed and cried at the absurdity. Her husband had studied day and night at Cambridge to prepare himself. For what? To cross a thousand leagues of water so they could live in a crude dwelling covered with sedge and old mats? So that he could rise daily with the sun to plant field peas?

With his extraordinary talent for bartering, he had taxed his craft to the limit by trading for mats and offering only promises in exchange. When the natives laughed at him, he explained cheerfully without blushing that at least they owed him something for helping them feel superior to still another Englishman.

The wigwam frame looked like a cage with a domed top. The front contained only the hued wooden shape of a doorway because he had found no time to build a door. A large mat hung there to repel the rain and animals. "We shall have a door before the first frost, Mary, dear."

Staring at the wigwam made with small poles fixed to the ground and bowed to fasten at the top and on the sides, she wondered, *In what kind of dwelling will our children grow up?* Her husband and she had of course talked of preparing for the arrival of children. The Narraganset children seemed happy in their wigwams, though not all had survived the bitter winters.

Roger lifted the doorway mat to let her enter first. Since they had no chairs yet, they sat on a large pile of straw. Brushes and straw covered the floor of their one-room abode.

"Do not worry, love. A house will stand on this land before winter." Roger surveyed their surroundings. Privately he sometimes had serious doubts. Working during the nights to build a dwelling would require many bright moons.

He paused at times to visualize the board house he hoped to build. He had already negotiated for posts and beams. With help he would make the walls and chimney of wattle and daub. In addition, he would do the extra work to install two windows so that Mary could enjoy the extra light for sewing and quilting. For the present, the windows would be only oilpaper, not glass. But in time . . . .

Day after day, they toiled in the field from sunrise to sunset. Night after night, they tried not to disturb their distant neighbors as they worked together on the frame for their modest New England cottage.

Toward the end of August, beneath the horned moon's silver light, he laid down his barrowed saw. "I have a confession, Mary. I had plans to build this house with these two hands. We are one flesh with four hands. In all of Scripture, there exists no record of a woman using her hands to build a house."

Though tired and sleepy, she laughed. "In all of Scripture, there is no reference to the winters of New England. If Abraham had moved to this land of extremes, Sarah would of necessity have lifted boards and carried rocks."

He stepped back to admire the cottage frame they had at last completed. "Tomorrow night we will add the boards to the north side."

"Would it not be wiser to start with the south and learn from our mistakes? The north side must be mistake-free." Then she yawned and yawned, inducing Roger to do likewise.

Quickly laying aside their tools, they walked to the nearby spring. Too tired to wash their clothes, they sat down in the stream under the starry sky and let the water flow over them.

He took Mary's hand and kissed it. "Next year will be different. God has given us this test, and we must not fail." His thoughts lifted like vapor and floated away a thousand leagues to England. He thought of Joan Whalley. She would not have left England for the New World. Knowing this, Providence had built an unassailable wall to prevent their marriage.

Roger leaned back to let the gurgling water rush through his hair and over his face. When he could hold his breath no longer, he rose up; and despite all the aches in his bones and the weariness in his flesh, he felt himself a new man. The moonbeams danced off the rippling stream and so reflected in Mary's sapphire eyes that he thought he saw in them another pure stream. He dropped his hand into the cool water and wiped it gently over her face again and again. Then he kissed her lips.

She leaned against his chest and spoke of their dream, which she resolved never to forsake. "Under this bright sky, a new mountain will one day rise up and flourish, and on its peak, a bright torch for all to see."

"And they will call it 'Liberty's Sacred Light,'" Roger added.

Far, far in the distance, a flash of lightning streaked across the sky from east to west.

They walked back to their wigwam. He raised the mat to the doorway for her. She entered and then returned with a large cloth to dry her hair under the stars. "The sun will soon rise. Let us sleep," she whispered.

Inside, after removing their wet clothes, they let the hay cushion their collapse to the ground. Soon after hearing a cow lowing in the field and a faint rumbling of thunder in the heavens, they fell asleep in each other's arms.

BOSTON

August 1631

Affable, jovial Barnabas had watched after my mail, packing it safely away while I traveled around the Bay. Upon returning to Boston from a short trip to Cape Ann, I entered my room at the Blackstone house to find to my pleasure that Lydia had kept everything in order. The only letter of importance Barnabas handed me had arrived from Hammersmith, England.

"Ah! From my good friend Milton." I sat down in the new oak chair Barnabas had made with his own hands. As soon as I leaned back, he grinned triumphantly. Unlike most Puritan chairs of New England, the back to this one tilted slightly and had cushions over the armrests.

"A chair should be a seat of comfort, not of torture." Barnabas beamed.

Roger had once said to me, "Puritans forget their own Protestant theology when they design furniture for punishing the body in atonement for sins rather than for relaxing the body in celebration of life."

After Barnabas left, I leaned back again and read Milton's letter twice, so glad was I to hear from him.

Milton and his father had not settled their disagreement about his becoming a poet. Nevertheless, according to the letter, Milton still had every intention of becoming an Anglican clergyman upon receiving his master's degree from Cambridge. This would please his father immensely. Young Milton had high esteem for the poet-preacher John Donne and at times even fancied himself perhaps his heir. Like Milton's father, Donne had grown up Catholic only to turn Protestant in his early manhood. It grieved me to learn that Donne, the esteemed dean of St. Paul's Cathedral in London, had died, which occasioned Milton's long letter.

I perceived a new and strange maturity in the younger poet's thinking. Perhaps the death of the older poet had given him a new seriousness for life. Like Donne, Milton possessed a keen interest in science, particularly the writings of Copernicus, Kepler, and Galileo. Sixteen years had passed since Galileo's trouble with the Spanish Inquisitors, who demanded that he forsake his scientific explorations unless his conclusions enhanced the opinions of the papal clan in Rome. Ten years had passed since the papal tribe's banning of Johann Kepler's *The Epitome of the Copernican Astronomer*.

Milton had dipped his quill in undiluted venom when he wrote about the inquisitors, calling them the pope's scorpions. To both Donne and Milton, poetry and science needed no police, Catholic or Protestant, looking over their shoulders. While at heart a Puritan, Milton did not lean toward Separatism. His admiration of the Anglican John Donne pulled him away from severing all formal ties with the Church of England.

The new science had shaken Milton and Donne. I confess, it had caused a cloud to drift at times over my North Star. In his letter, Milton included a passage from Donne that expressed our half-spoken apprehensions about the battle between *cosmos* and *chaos*: "A new philosophy calls all in doubt . . . 'Tis all in pieces, all coherence gone." Milton had wondered if Galileo understood the implications of his theories. If everything crumbles into atoms and if the planets and the firmament reduce to mindless atoms swirling without purpose, what lies at the heart of it all? Wherein lies the meaning of the whole? Along with Donne, Milton and I kept asking where the trail ended if everything were relative, all flexible, all pliant?

Milton continued for two pages, contending that the real problem was not whether the Earth or the sun twirled at the center of the universe. The more far-flung problem rose rather as a double mystery, the first questioning whether the universe as a whole manifested a system at all. Were the globes of Earth and stars scattered randomly with no common center? The second mystery questioned whether human societies spewed out willy-nilly like fragments of an explosion having no rational connections. With his unquenchable mind, Milton wondered, "Did any society constitute more than beads flung out with no common thread? Did royalty provide the common thread?"

At Cambridge I had heard secret debates as to whether Henry VIII, Queen Elizabeth, James, and Charles were indeed the Church of England's head and defender of the faith. In one of those debates, Roger had said to Milton, "If royalty threads the beads, then without the beads the royal thread becomes a limp string."

While reading Milton's letter, I realized that for the past intense months one overriding question had haunted me. If no hierarchy prevails among the celestial bodies, then is Earth's hierarchy also a mere will-o'-the-wisp? On this planet, do Winthrop and we all play little games of our own invention while pretending they fly hot off the altar of heaven?

From the whole tone of Milton's letter, I judged that Donne's death had given him a somber turn. On one page, he had drawn a large circle representing the larger cosmos. Inside it the smaller circle represented human history, or as he called it, *the stage across which march human passions, intellect, love of beauty, and proclivity for war.*

An arrow leading to the inner circle carried with it a question: "Wherein lies the plot of Providence, 'the divinity that shapes our ends'?" I myself had begun to wonder about the Great Chain of Being. Did it exist, or was it a changing figure in the clouds—a camel, an arched weasel, a whale—all of my own invention? Had the times ever been in joint?

Milton went on for another page to talk of angels among the atoms. "Are atoms now heaven's messengers replacing the angels? Have all angels suffered the boot, or do atoms serve as mere carriages and sleds for both angels and demons to carry out heaven's designs?"

Two days later while looking out my window, I saw Barnabas hitching the horse to the carriage. I put on a clean linen shirt, picked up my hat, and left for the meeting at Governor Winthrop's house. When I arrived, the aroma of boiled mutton, peas, and corn floated by my nose; but the animated conversation, with John Wilson as its center, turned my head at once.

The Reverend Wilson, pastor of our church in Boston, had recently returned from England. A scholarly man, Wilson wrote poetry and like myself kept copious notes of various events and discourses. Amid his many duties, he found time to write a short history of his own era. In the year that Charles assumed the throne, Wilson composed a grim poem on London's plague.

> The Queen of Cities wont to sit,
> In Chair of highest state,
> Now sat in dust and lowest pit,
> All sad and desolate . . . .

After reading the lengthy poem, no one could justly charge the Puritans slow to look reality in the eye. Like Milton, the good pastor longed to find some way to fit the dread disease into the great coherent scheme.

Winthrop introduced me to the Reverend Wilson's wife. Bidding them to resume their conversation, I revealed my interest in the matters they explored.

Sitting near the east window, an elder gave an account of a voice that had come to him while riding his horse in a thick fog five years earlier in England. "I had lost my way and could tell neither north from south when a voice cried, 'Stop! There is danger.' So compelling was the voice that I pulled hard on the reins and dismounted at once. My body did quake like autumn leaves as I crawled on hands and knees until I reached a steep cliff only ten feet beyond my horse. Had the voice not constrained me, my horse and I would have plunged headlong to our end."

Winthrop gave the elder a stern look that spoke a volume of condemning words.

That did not stop Pastor Wilson from telling about a strange and memorable event having happened to him only four years past. "After outpourings of prayer with utmost fervor and fasting, I saw before me an angel whose face shone like the noonday sun. While his features were those of a beardless man, his shoulders were winged, his garments white and shining, his robes ankle-length. His head was suddenly crowned with splendor, and he wore a belt around his middle that resembled the girdles I have seen from the East. I remember the angel saying to me that the Lord Jesus had sent him to bear a clear answer to the prayers of a certain man in agony who did not know God's holy purpose for him. The angel spoke of this man, prophesying that his works for Christ and the church should be published and that my war with the devil would be not in vain."

Winthrop closed one eye and took aim like a hunter with one eye open. "Pastor, does not the Apostle Paul speak of the devil appearing as an angel of light?"

Pastor Wilson stiffened. "The devil? If all angels appeared as devils, then how can you explain the angel who appeared at Christ's empty tomb? Was he also a devil in disguise?"

To everyone's surprise, the elder's wife professed to have dreamed that she conversed pleasantly with her husband's deceased first wife.

Winthrop shifted as if he had boils on his rear.

"Governor, have you not perchance in a dream conversed with your former wife, now deceased?" The elder's voice sounded meek.

Winthrop cleared his throat twice and spoke no answer, save the stern reply written on his face. I grew increasingly interested in these confessions, in part because I had heard Winthrop say he held in deep suspicion all current accounts of heavenly visitations. Although I know not what suddenly possessed me, I turned to the governor and was on the verge of asking a pricking question when he picked up the Bible and held it for all to see.

"Every revelation I need lies between these covers," he proclaimed.

Though agreeing, some appeared to resent the governor's pontifical manner. I almost asked him, *Are we no longer in need of angels since we have our angelic governor to interpret heaven's ways for us?* This thought gave me considerable discomfort, and I recognized at once that I sounded more like the forthright Mary Williams than myself. I had in truth fraternized with angels no more than had Winthrop; and I remembered Roger had told me he preferred doing the work himself to depending upon the erratic assistance of angels. I almost laughed aloud in Winthrop's parlor upon recalling counsel Roger had given me: *Since devils often pose as angels, I ignore the lot of them and go about my affairs. The Scriptures and common sense are messengers enough for me.*

The elder smiled merrily. "So, Governor, are there no more revelations from heaven?"

"There are no more revelations"

"When did they cease?" the elder asked.

"When there was no more need for them."

The meek elder proved persistent. "When might that have been?"

After taking a long drink of water, Winthrop looked around. I could see in his face that the elder had rankled his pride. The elder tried in vain to conceal the pleasure he received.

Winthrop did not answer, for Pastor Wilson interrupted. "If there be no more revelations—and on that, John, we see eye to eye—then what service have you for angels?"

Holding my tongue, I thought, *Are angels to be locked away in a closet like out-of-season clothing?*

Addressing Wilson's question but speaking to all of us, Winthrop went into a lengthy discourse on ministering angels who on rare occasions assisted horsemen, ship captains, and midwives, but who gave no information except perhaps to goad lazy believers to search the Scriptures more thoroughly. Winthrop's speech grew so long and taxing that no angel would have lingered throughout the ordeal unless he hoped to hear himself flattered. I felt myself more righteous than angels at this moment, for I had resisted every temptation to escape.

Just when I began to weaken, the conversation flared up as if the oven door had opened. Wilson politely asked Winthrop if perhaps he had shackled angels only to give demons license to roam the Earth at their good pleasure. The discussion grew even hotter when Winthrop pronounced angels to be an inferior breed. "What need have I of their assistance when I have the Holy Ghost to guide me to interpret Scripture properly?"

Fortunately, before we saints clawed each other in our dispute about angels, two servants appeared, one announcing the glad tidings of a feast awaiting us at the table. I speculated regarding angels' culinary habits. Would archangels find mutton stew tasty? Or did they dine on ambrosia like the Greek gods?

PLYMOUTH COLONY

August 1631

"Wake up, Roger! Wake up!"

Although he heard the sound of Mary's voice, he thought it part of a dream. Yet when he rolled over, he felt her hands shaking him.

"The wind, Roger! It is strange."

He opened his eyes but saw nothing. The complete lack of light in the wigwam told him he should have hours more to sleep before sunrise.

Mary's tone grew eerie. "Listen, do you not hear it?"

At first he thought he was aboard the *Lyon* on the Atlantic. He could smell the salt in the air. Then he felt the straw and hard ground beneath him.

"I am afraid, Roger. It grows louder."

"Let me think."

"We have little time."

The winds caught the mats that covered the wigwam frame and made them pop. On his knees, he searched frantically for his shoes as the wind rushed inside the wigwam and shook it like a wolf ravishing a helpless rabbit. "Hurry, Mary."

"I cannot see."

"Here are your shoes. Do you have mine?"

The salt in the air grew pungent. He now knew the storm was coming from the coast. Earlier, Governor Bradford of Plymouth had told him that at this time of year, a storm from the coast could mean peril. Although Roger could not explain why he felt as he did, extraordinary fear spread through every muscle of his body. He wished not to alarm his wife, but she was already alarmed, and the rapid increase in the wind's strength signaled danger.

"Listen, Mary. A raging storm will strike land soon. I know not precisely where. Pray we are not in its path."

"Hold my hand. This darkness—"

"Rain. Do you smell it? It could nourish the seeds we planted." *Or undo all our labor.*

"Quickly, Roger. We must gather up everything. But where will we . . . ? The dome mats are working loose in this wind!"

Everything will be ruined unless . . . . "Where is the twine, Mary? Hurry!"

"This darkness! I cannot . . . . Yes, here it is. Where is your hand?"

"Good. Feel our way outdoors. Remember how to tie the mats down?"

"Yes." Mary quickly made her way outside the wigwam.

They both stood up against the howling wind. He cut the twine and placed a piece in her hand.

"You work the top, I the middle!" Mary shouted.

Despite the darkness, they worked patiently, relentlessly, the wind rising, crying now like a panther in the forest. While working, Roger thought ahead. If lightning should come, they would face more peril.

He cut the twine and handed pieces to her. They worked furiously, Roger cutting pieces for himself and weaving the mats firmly to the frame. Time raced as the storm rolled toward them. Yet he tried to avoid alarming Mary.

Just then a tree split and burst into flames scarcely more than a hundred paces to the east.

"Hurry, Roger! It is upon us!"

He felt the wind turn cool. *Hail,* he thought and then prayed it would be all hail and not a torrent of rain that would wash away their weeks of labor.

"I am scared, Roger. It stalks us. Pray!"

"I am. But Scripture says watch and pray. Here, take this twine. Hurry!" He heard the hail strip the leaves overhead. He could smell the storm and taste the salt.

"Did you feel . . . ?" Her question blew away in the wind.

He felt the hail turn to sheets of rain, confirming his deepest fear of a flash flood. An eerie sound came from a distance. "Get inside, Mary!"

"Now? I have not—"

"Now! Take my hand!" Then it came with a force he had not anticipated. "The frame! Hold it down!" Inside the wigwam, he grabbed the bowed poles and clinched his teeth.

Through the spaces, he saw gnarled fingers of lightning. No longer worrying about leaks, he fought to save what he could. The thunder cracked; and the storm hovered like a living creature breathing down upon them, howling in their ears, spewing its malice in their faces, its fangs ripping their tiny wigwam wrathfully.

More terrifying than all was the rising water. At first he could not believe it had come so quickly; and he had not comprehended their plight. In a moment of wild confusion, he shouted vainly, "Do not turn loose, Mary!"

Suddenly he realized how foolish he was to think he could save their only shelter against the howling monster. He wanted to hope that the terror would pass quickly. *Why does it hover? Have we become the prey of chaos?*

"It has found us!" Mary shouted.

Suddenly Roger shook his fists and laughed defiantly, grimly realizing that only a miserable little wigwam stood now between them and the frenzied clouds emptying their fury upon them.

The ceaseless lightning exposed the terror on Mary's face while the mat at the wigwam's opening whipped and popped until the storm ripped it off with one swipe, carrying it away. The water rushed inside, filling his shoes, submerging the small fireplace they had built out of stone.

Mary shouted, but he could not hear her words. The wind's bloodcurdling howl showed no mercy.

All at once, the wigwam shook violently as though two giant claws had clamped against it. Had his prayers disappeared in the wind, rain, and mud? He madly vowed that he would not yield to this wretched, senseless beast of fury that gripped them in its teeth.

Digging his knees into the mud, he clamped his hands around the frame and strained with all his might. His upper arms felt as if they might be torn out of their sockets.

At that instant, a gust of cold wind hit his back. Hearing Mary scream, he turned loose of the feeble frame. Although he had lost the shelter, he would not lose himself or his dear wife! In the darkness, he grabbed for her and called out, "Mary! Mary!" The lightning made everything shockingly clear as the wigwam lifted into the air like a hat off a man's head and vanished from sight. He had, however, no time for anger against the storm's ravings. Thinking only of his beloved wife, he crawled through the mud and in the flashes of lightning saw an image that made his heart leap from its cage. "Mary! I am coming!"

She lay motionless against the stones of the fireplace, the water rising quickly, mingling with her blood and flowing away.

He slipped, cracking his knee. Still he crawled, his hands sinking into the mud. "Mary! Mary!" At last at her side, he reached down to lift her head.

She groaned. "My arm. I think I have cut it."

The lightning flashed, revealing that there was no blood on her head. The relief he felt filled him with new energy. Quickly he pressed the wound on her arm to stop the bleeding.

She pushed him away. "We must hurry. My arm is not serious." Slowly she rose to her feet and shook her head as if to inform the storm that she would not be defeated.

"Roger! The water! The water!"

He felt it rising drastically above their ankles. "The stream! It is overflowing!" He grabbed Mary by the hand, guiding her to a tree and wrapping her arms around it. "Stay here. Never turn loose!"

"The seeds. They will wash away!" Mary shouted.

"I will build a levy with the logs."

"I will go with you."

"No, do not move!" He fought against the mud and rushing waters until he came to a pile of logs. Grabbing the end of one, he pulled it toward the field where they had planted the seeds. His legs ached as he slipped repeatedly but dared not think of the pain.

He dragged five logs one at a time, hoping to build the levy. Yet all his efforts counted for nothing. The rain emptied relentlessly as if from huge, upended barrels. The stream overflowed its banks, carrying the logs with it. He had underestimated the current's power. Every instinct in him turned his face back toward Mary. He should not have left her in this current.

Without warning, a log washed against his ribs, spinning him around. Feeling himself going under, he grabbed frantically for whatever might come his way. He grabbed for another log floating by and clung desperately. To his horror, he felt himself carried now in one direction and then another, spinning like a whirlpool until the log crashed into a tree.

Stunned by the impact, he shook his head and instinctively wrapped his arms and legs around the nearest tree trunk. The splinters pricking his skin meant nothing. Coughing the water out of his lungs, he struggled to catch his breath. "Mary! Where are you?" But he heard only the rushing water, cracking thunder, and wind tearing through the trees.

Frightened that he had lost his orientation and could not find her, he called out for her many times against the exploding thunder, exhorting her to cling for life. He prayed that her strength would hold out. Everything had so turned around that his stomach formed a knot.

"The tree! The tree!" he kept saying aloud as if to give himself a command. He must find the tree.

Immense forks of lightning leaped down from the clouds. A jagged streak lit the sky and struck a tree, the explosion momentarily shattering Roger's mind. *The tree! Oh, merciful God, let it not be Mary's!*

Even though the flood pulled hard at his legs, he kicked against the force that might at any moment pull his feet from under him. With all his strength, he began to scale a tall tree, his feet slipping, his arms scraping against the rough trunk. Still he climbed to escape the rising flood.

"Mary! Where are you? Climb higher!" The booming thunder overpowered his voice, and the wind screamed like a loud whistle. Yet he kept searching for her, calling her name, hoping the clouds would break and dawn would come.

Suspended between the threat of lightning above and swift, treacherous waters below, he commanded himself to think of some way to rescue her. Sensing that his shouts against the storm would soon make his voice too hoarse to reach her ears, he waited to call for her only after each thunderclap had faded. He strained to filter out all sounds but her voice.

Still no cry! No word in response!

At last, the storm ceased. Though it had wreaked its destruction, the roar of the swift water did not relent. *If only daylight would come!*

Come it did, although stingy with its gift. He could see now to climb higher through the branches. He told himself to find the cottage frame they had built. If he could see it, he could orient himself and locate Mary.

Careful, these limbs are slick. Although weak, he inched his way higher up the tree, his muscles quivering. Each inch seemed a mile. Still he did not cease until he had climbed eight or so feet above the flood. No longer heavy, the sky was a welcome light-gray, allowing his eyes to scan the territory.

A surge of panic streaked through his body. *The frame! Where is it?*

The answer came quickly. In the distance, he saw wedged between the trees the twisted cottage frame they had labored to construct, the water having sucked it from its foundation.

Cupping one hand around his mouth, he cried out, "Mary!" No response came above the rushing of the water below. He would not let himself dwell on the possibility that the water had swept her under. She had to be somewhere clinging like himself to a tree. She had to be!

The sun in the east glowed purple, and patches of the sky above turned crystal blue abruptly. Nonetheless, the more light that fell across the bizarre scene below, the more a paralyzing fear rose in him. *Is Mary lost? Am I?*

No landmark seemed familiar. He climbed still higher to the treetop. How clear the morning air suddenly became! Yet he could see nothing but water below. The neighbors' dwelling a half mile to the south had disappeared. Looking farther toward the north, he thought he saw chimney smoke rising from the little town Plymouth, safe on a hill, free from the water's invasion.

Slowly orienting himself, he reasoned that he must search the territory to the east, assuming Mary was still at the tree where he had left her. He longed for a canoe but quickly dismissed the wishful thinking.

"A plan is what I need!" He again shouted toward the east and listened—then to the west. Still no human voice responded.

He told himself that, if cautious, he could walk against the flood's drift. The mud, however, would form a suction that would pull off his shoes. If he lost them, the debris would gash his feet beyond endurance. Removing his shirt, he quickly tore it into strips and tied them around his shoes and feet.

Completing this task, he once more sought to establish landmarks to guide him toward the spot Mary and he had called home.

"Take care!" he ordered himself as he shimmied down the tree. *If I break my leg, I am no use to Mary.* He fought back the rush of panic and scolded himself for giving way to any useless feeling. Everything depended upon self-possession. He knew now what he must do! Fear must be controlled.

As soon as he stepped down to the flowing water, he discovered he had underestimated its swiftness. Ah, a pole wedged in a thicket. If only he could wrap his hand around it, he would have a staff to help him through the muddy current.

His foot sank into the mud. He grasped the branch of another tree and pulled hard. Another branch came into his grip, another, and two more until he had his hand around the pole. He recognized it as part of the frame of their planned cottage. Using it to push his body forward, he dug into the mud, like an oar pulling against water.

It is working. Still he cautioned himself against carelessness. The current would not forgive a serious mistake. Feeling like Noah escaping prematurely from the ark, he shouted, groaned, and trudged inch by inch until he saw an object trapped in debris.

Yes! Yes! Mary's shoe. He strained with all his might as if somehow putting his hand around her shoe could assure him that she remained alive. Another part of his mind formed an image of her far away, floating facedown. "No!" he shouted aloud against the image and forced himself onward.

Above his head, vultures circled. Seagulls called to one another en route to the ocean.

As he moved steadily, stumbling only now and then over logs caught below the surface, he realized that lightning had split a tree trunk straight ahead.

His heart sank. *Could that be the tree?* "No! No! Mary, where are you?"

Then the most beautiful sound wafted across the current.

"Roger! Over here."

Tears rushed down his cheeks, and he laughed with sheer joy. Nothing else mattered. The wigwam, the cottage frame, their possessions, the winter's food—all counted as nothing now.

"Mary, you are alive!" When he saw her, an overwhelming pity came to his heart—and an almost blinding anger at the storm. Instead of nourishing his anger, he gathered up all his might, defied the current, and waded ahead until his legs grew numb. Elation and gratitude strengthened his heart.

"Roger? Is it really you, precious, darling?" Her voice sounded weak, but never had he heard sweeter music.

When he reached the tree, he saw that she straddled a limb and hugged the tree as a rider might the neck of a galloping horse. He put his arms around her and slowly lifted her from the limb. Holding her, he looked down into her sapphire eyes and smiled. "Ah, the jewels still shine."

Roger and Mary did not bother to search for their small farm, the flood having carried away their fall crop.

For a moment, he felt that his own heart had floated away also. *A fine husband I have proved to be. Had Mary spent the rest of her years as a servant in Exeter, she would have enjoyed a more secure and prosperous life.*

Still he kept telling himself that heaven had brought them together. This thought strengthened his sinews and muscles. He tried to look upon the flood as a test for something that required extraordinary patience, fortitude, and perseverance.

Since it could take several days for the water to recede, they elected to strike out through the muddy current toward Plymouth on a modest hill eight miles away.

After an hour of trudging through the mud, she fought to catch her breath. "Please . . . must rest." She pointed ahead to a large maple tree that had survived the storm.

He nodded, too weary to talk. Mary's stride shortened, and her grip on his hand weakened. They had walked less than a mile, he estimated. No longer behind thick clouds, the August sun scorched their bare heads as vapor shimmered off the water's surface.

It was imperative to remain vigilant. When a log floated by, he moved to leap for it but pulled back at the sight of an agitated adder stretched across it.

"Roger, look! A canoe?" She pointed to her left.

He grabbed at his shirt to wave it like a flag only to remember that he had already torn the shirt into strips. He refused to believe that his eyes had played tricks on him. A canoe! It had to be!

He puckered his lips to whistle. But, as if he were a child, nothing came out except an impotent noise. He tried again, only then realizing the full measure of his exhaustion. Mary and he began waving their arms wildly, hoping to attract attention.

"Two natives!" she exclaimed.

Roger saw the canoe slicing its way through the water, two natives effortlessly guiding it toward them. Believing the natives would rescue them, he felt the tension leave his body.

All at once, a ghastly scream erupted from Mary's throat.

Roger jerked his head around. Rushing headlong toward them was an uprooted oak filled with gnarled limbs. For a flash, he braced himself to submerge and let the tree pass overhead. But, no! The underwater branches would drag them downstream!

"Quickly!" he shouted to her. "This way!"

With all their might, they plowed through the water toward the canoe.

"Faster!" He pushed her ahead of him. "Swim! Swim for all you are worth!"

She coughed but kept swimming.

He fought furiously to escape the massive, uprooted oak bearing down on them. It rushed by, its roots reaching out like claws greedy for prey. He saw his beloved's hand extend out of the water and grasp for the canoe. He felt as if he were stretching on her behalf.

Suddenly a savage pain shot up his leg. Without warning he felt his legs go out from under him. He struggled to the surface only to be cut down a second time.

Feeling water rush up his nose, he swung his arms frantically, fighting to return to the surface a third time.

Again his head bobbed up. He gasped for air, fighting against the limb that had snagged his ankle.

Again he felt himself swept under. He struggled, sinking his fingers into the mud in the hope of finding a rock, a stump, anything to give him leverage.

His lungs ached as if they might burst. Fear compelled him to keep his eyes closed lest a tree limb gouge them out of their sockets. His own helplessness in the swift current terrified him. A dreadful thought flashed through him. Had he come face to face with the last moment of his life on Earth? His mind shouted, *No!* Though childhood memories swished before his eyes, he wanted desperately to cry out to encourage Mary to save herself.

Just when he thought he had released his foot, he realized it had been trapped more thoroughly in the gnarled limbs. Despite his trying to roll over, the sharp pain in his knee stopped him. His lungs to the point of collapsing, he doubled over and, using both hands, yanked with all his might. Though the implacable branch still showed no mercy, his shoe came off. He was free!

Rushing to the surface, he felt a throbbing in his head as if it had absorbed more water than it could contain. He blew the water savagely from his nose, shook his head violently, coughed, spit, and fought frantically to fill his lungs with air.

Above all he swam with only one thought—to find Mary! But he could feel his strength leave him and the current grow stronger, threatening to carry him into the river's deep channel. Every muscle from his neck to his toes felt as if it were on fire.

Suddenly the fire seemed as nothing to him. Bliss surged through his whole body at the pure delight of seeing the love of his life escape the jaws of death. There sat his wife safe inside the canoe. Beautiful, beautiful Mary! Shouting his gratitude to the natives, he felt triumphant at being alive.

The natives approached him cautiously. Despite his desperate desire to grab the vessel, he remembered the precariousness of canoes.

One of the natives, speaking English and skillfully keeping the canoe at a distance, called to him. "Englishman! Do not overturn us. When we paddle by, grasp only my paddle."

As the canoe drifted by slowly, the paddle reached out like a kind hand; and Roger took it. The other native lost no time in paddling them all to dry land.

Mary crawled out of the canoe and collapsed on the sandy scrub soil. Roger staggered ashore and fell to his knees at her side. He caressed her to assure himself she was no illusion.

Saying nothing, the two natives paddled away before he could gain the strength to beg them to take at least his wife to Plymouth.

Just when Roger and Mary had oriented themselves and made plans to resume their treacherous journey, the canoe returned. The natives stepped out, and one of them shook with laughter while the other presented Roger with a broken tree limb in which was lodged his lost shoe.

Roger broke out in laughter too, mirthful, rollicking laughter that came from deep inside him, a celebration of being alive to see the humor amid life's absurdities.

The laughing native gave his name as Keplutok and explained in surprisingly clear English that he and his friend Titus belonged to the Wampanoag people.

After Mary and Roger had eaten their fill on the following day and had slept inside the Wampanoag village, Titus took them to Chief Sachem Massasoit. A tall, muscular man of about fifty years, he spoke in his native language, using Titus as both interpreter and advisor.

While in Salem, Roger had learned of Chief Massasoit and his friendship with the Plymouth Governors John Carver and William Bradford. A peace treaty between the Plymouth pilgrims and the Wampanoags had held tenuously for a decade.

Not even proud Massasoit proved immune to Roger's disarming forthrightness. Though still weak from the storm's punishment, he squared his shoulders and addressed the sachem as if they had known one another many years as negotiating merchants.

Massasoit's first question did not disarm Roger, although it might have disarmed a lesser man. "If an Englishman desires to murder his wife, can he find no easier way than building her a home in the path of a flood?"

Smiling sheepishly and scratching his head, Roger ventured no reply.

Massasoit resumed speaking through his interpreter Titus. "The man who lent you the land to grow your peas must have had revenge in his heart. What evil had you done him?"

Roger slowly convinced the sachem that the circumstance arose not from revenge or hatred, but from the ignorant advising the ignorant. "You must understand. A man does not attain this status of ignorance without much study in an English university."

"I see. Then you must have spent many years there at this place you call university."

Again, Roger scratched his head and said that if the Chief Sachem had no objection, he would like to change the subject.

The interpreter and the sachem looked at each other, nodded, and laughed uproariously.

"I have been told," said Massasoit, "that you English stand on what you call a stage and perform lines that make people laugh. You must be England's most accomplished man on stage. Now that you are our guests, we shall perform for you."

Without another word, Massasoit put on a conspicuously English red coat and invited his two guests to sit with him while a dozen or so natives danced and sang. Amid the entertainment, Massasoit explained that an Edward Winslow of Plymouth Colony had given him the coat. The celebration ended with a feast of shellfish, roasted goose, wild plums, and dried berries.

Roger and Mary ate with such enthusiasm that the sachem and his interpreter glanced at each other with raised eyebrows. Roger obviously amused them. Wholly absorbed in feasting, the English couple forgot every line from the many sermons they had heard on the sin of gluttony.

Roger's years with his merchant father had shaped his mind to look for new entrepreneurial opportunities. Desperate to find a way to support himself and his wife, he talked with Titus and other English-speaking natives. Although several plans danced across his mind, none seemed worthy of his full attention.

A little before sundown, however, the dancing sparked fresh plans. He resolved that upon rising on the morrow he would speak to Massasoit about his idea.

Early the next day, he felt someone shaking him. He opened his eyes and saw Mary, who tried to tell him about an incident in another wigwam.

Still halfway in his dream, Roger blinked his eyes and sat up. "What is astir?"

"Do you not hear?"

Though he heard, the ache in his muscles returned his thoughts to the previous morning. He felt terribly confused. *Another storm? Why all the voices?* He rubbed the sleep from his eyes and sprang to his feet, his bones popping like broken sticks.

All at once, the stiffness left his joints when a wild cry pierced his ears. He rushed outside to investigate.

Massasoit's interpreter Titus appeared as if from nowhere, shaking his head and angrily throwing up his arms. When he saw Roger, he rushed to him and quickly pulled him aside. "Listen to me! A wicked thing has happened! One of your white brothers . . . last night . . . . He stole Keplutok's boy!"

Fear raced through Roger. For a moment, he stood speechless, wondering if the natives had made a superstitious connection between his arrival and the disappearance of the child. He looked back at the wigwam where Mary and he had slept. At the same time, he saw what he took to be a small hunting party leaving in a great hurry, iron determination written on their faces.

Titus tightened his grip around Roger's arm. "You must help us!"

"I will, but I must know what . . . . Give me the specifics."

Titus explained that although Keplutok could speak English, he unfortunately could not read it.

"But what has—?"

"Duplicity!" Titus's eyes flashed.

Roger saw genuine fear in the native's eyes and heard the frenzied commotion among the women. "Come, let us talk elsewhere. Give me the story step by step."

As they ran toward a grove of trees nearby, Titus said, "My friend received a bench—"

"Your friend?"

"Keplutok. He received a metal ax and a hunting gun—"

"And a bench?"

"Yes, a bench to sit on."

"From whom?" Roger asked as they reached the copse.

"Rob Greene, an Englishman."

Roger caught his breath. "Where?"

"At Plymouth. This Greene, he required Keplutok to place a mark upon a contract."

Roger could hear a woman wailing and supposed it to be the mother's anguish. "The terms. Give me the terms of the contract."

"If Keplutok fails on payment, Greene recovers the goods."

Roger turned up his palms. "That is English custom. Is it not your custom?"

The veins in Titus's neck swelled like ropes. He grabbed a tree limb overhead and snapped it in twain. "You misunderstand. The Englishman wrote into the contract something so strange . . . ." Titus's words trailed off, and he shook his head as if his eyes saw some horror his heart could not believe.

Saying nothing, Roger gestured to urge the native to tell all.

Bending down on one knee, Titus revealed that Rob Greene had written into the contract the right to carry away Keplutok's youngest male child if Keplutok should delay payment for the goods.

The account so stunned Roger that for a moment he thought he had surely misunderstood. "Are you . . . ? You are certain? Perhaps the child has simply wandered away." He whirled around to scan the forest with his eyes. "Should we not search for him at once?"

"Our best hunters have gone already in pursuit."

"In pursuit? How could one Englishman have overpowered Keplutok?"

"A companion with axe and gun . . . . Greene and his companion captured Keplutok and his little son Swift Deer by surprise."

"Where?"

Titus pointed eastward. "In the forest. I myself found Keplutok tied to a tree and gagged."

"And the boy?"

"Greene and his companion carried him away!"

"How old is Swift Deer?" Roger hoped the boy might have the cleverness to steal away in the forest and find his way back.

"Five winters."

Rage gushed up inside Roger. He clinched his fists and forced himself to think. "Where is Keplutok now?"

"With Massasoit, who will not permit Keplutok to travel with the hunters for fear there would be murder."

Roger ran his fingers through his hair. "Where does this Greene dwell?"

"In Plymouth."

"Will your sachem permit us to talk with Keplutok?"

On the way to see Massasoit, Roger asked Titus, "This villainy happened near sunrise?"

"Scarcely after sunrise, Keplutok saw Greene and his companion carry the boy away. Will you help us?"

"Of course! But you have warriors who—"

"When we capture the villains and take them to the governor, we will need you to witness on our behalf. As an Englishman, you can reason with other Englishmen."

Inside Massasoit's wigwam, Roger and Titus sat with the sachem and Keplutok. Massasoit said that though he desired no bloodshed, he would not rest content until the villain Greene received swift and unbending justice for his stinking deed.

Roger fastened his shoes, determined to travel with the father if Massasoit approved.

Massasoit closed his eyes. "I have knowledge of this Rob Greene, a clever man who knows the ways of hunting and deception."

Listening to Titus translate the sachem's words, Roger felt that the wise leader of his people spoke in contrived vagueness. Might Massasoit have sent his warriors deliberately on a false trail to avoid igniting a war?

Massasoit opened his eyes and looked straight at Roger, Titus quickly translating: "There must be no bloodshed, no violation of the peace treaty!"

Roger began to understand the wise man's intentions and could not help admiring his patience. He lowered his voice to communicate to the sachem that he understood not only the necessity of remaining calm, but also the many political and legal ramifications of the events to follow on this day. "But if we catch Greene before he arrives in Plymouth, will he not fight back? If he dies during the struggle, how will you prove to the Plymouth Court that he stole the child?"

Everyone in the wigwam, including Swift Deer's father, Keplutok, grasped now the necessity for acting in accordance with a well-contrived plan. Wasting little time, Massasoit clarified the position he must take with the governor of Plymouth and the other magistrates among the English.

Roger secretly believed that the sachem had already considered the possibility of permitting the Plymouth authorities to convict and sentence Greene and his accomplice. First, however, the vile Englishmen would have to be captured!

Roger hurried to find Mary. Inside one of the wigwams, he told her what had happened and, trying to subdue his apprehension, concluded, "I think you should return to Plymouth immediately."

"Where would I go? I need another day to recover from my injuries. No, Roger, I will be safe here."

He protested, expressing his fear that the natives might blame her for Swift Deer's disappearance.

She kissed him on the cheek. "You worry needlessly."

He would not listen to her and insisted he could not leave until she had first boarded a canoe for Plymouth.

"They are calling for you, dear. We have no time to argue."

"But, Mary! I cannot—"

"You cannot tell me what I must do. I will make my decision. Now kiss me and promise you will take care."

"Remember, I am your husband."

"Which is not a father. Now go!"

Titus, Keplutok, and Roger stepped into the canoe and pushed away from the bank. Roger looked back, prayed silently, and saw Mary wave good-bye.

The canoe moved swiftly. The natives said little. All the energy and intensity went into their strong arms as the paddles dipped and pulled, dipped and pulled, each native anticipating the other's smooth, rhythmic movements.

After about five minutes, Roger reassured the two natives that the Plymouth Court would quickly return Keplutok's child to him.

Apparently Massasoit had sent some of his young and bold warriors away on a false trail to prevent what he knew would be swift and bloody revenge. Roger conjectured that Massasoit was a man of peace who did not wish to return two mutilated English corpses to Governor Bradford.

Titus and Keplutok assured Roger that they had found the true trail of Greene and his companion. Since the forest path to Plymouth roughly paralleled the river, they could keep track of Swift Deer and the Englishmen who had stolen him.

Three quarters of an hour later, Keplutok quietly eased his paddle out of the water and pointed ahead to a man whose chin seemed to jut off to the right. The face looked as if a fist had rearranged its proportions. Keplutok whispered, "The dog Greene!"

Roger saw a large, burly man sitting on a mare, holding the boy in front of him as they rode, the accomplice following behind on a mule.

Keplutok turned his head to whisper to Titus. "What are the robbers doing?"

"I do not understand the meaning. They veer off course. Why?" Keplutok gripped the side of the canoe and focused all his attention on the two thieves. Then he turned around again. "They have taken the trail to the south."

"The trail leads away from Plymouth," Titus said.

Though Roger wanted to believe that the child-snatchers had in mind to make only a slight detour, the better part of his mind would not indulge him in the delusion.

Titus guided the canoe starboard and paddled toward a large thicket to avoid being seen.

After Keplutok quietly jumped out at the shore and pulled the canoe onto dry land, the two natives, taking a rope and their weapons, followed on foot. Roger kept pace, trotting behind them several paces but never losing sight of them. He had heard that some of the natives could track an animal for half a day.

A quarter of a mile later, Roger saw Keplutok stealthily snatch Greene's accomplice from his mule. Scarcely before Roger could blink, Keplutok's violent blow turned the lanky accomplice into a limp rope.

Roger quickly caught up with Keplutok and took the assignment of tying up the captive and binding him to a tree. Circumstances had changed. The two child-snatchers had taken themselves outside the law in a double sense. Rumors abounded about villains abducting people to work the remote plantations of the Virginia Colony. The more Roger considered that Greene and his accomplice planned to sell the native child, the more he resolved never to rest until the natives and he brought the knaves to justice. *My friend Eric Firebrook fell captive to slave traders when a young man, but with God's help Swift Deer will not become enslaved!*

Titus and Keplutok, fleet-footed and familiar with every twist and turn of the trail, took a shortcut, moving ahead of Greene's mare.

At last the mare made her way around the bend of the trail. Without warning a tree limb bent down across the path, and an arm reached out from it to catch Greene hard across his high, round forehead, knocking him to the ground.

Roger froze, stunned at the swiftness of the fierce blow to Greene's head. The Wampanoags' trap had done its job well. Keplutok leaped down from the tree and caught his son around the waist.

Roaring with pain and rage, Greene leaped to his feet. With unnerving speed, he grabbed his knife from his belt with his huge left hand. "I will kill you, you filthy savage!" He slashed the air with his knife only inches from Keplutok's face.

Keplutok shoved Swift Deer aside. "Run! Hide!"

The crimson-faced Greene raised his huge knife over his head and shook the forest with his murderous roar.

Keplutok hurled a large stone that bounced off Greene's massive chest like a mere pebble. But a second stone brought the knave to his knees.

Still undaunted and with Samson's strength, Greene shook his head and rose to his feet like a towering, wounded bear preparing to kill whatever lay in his path.

Fearless Titus leaped down from a tree, raised his spear, and commanded roguish Greene to surrender.

Filling his lungs and looming like a mountain, Greene gnashed his teeth defiantly and lunged at Titus.

Titus's spear punctured the calf of Greene's leg, blood spurting like a fount. Still the human bear charged, shrieking with agony and murderous rage. He hurled his knife, catching Titus at the shoulder.

Titus staggered.

His teeth flashing, Greene charged toward the fleeing child.

Keplutok lowered his head and drove hard at Greene. But with one swipe, Greene slammed Keplutok against a tree.

Seeing Keplutok's feet fly from under him, Roger breathed righteous fury, forgot his ankle injured in the flood, and hurled his own body like a stone from David's sling, his shoulder colliding with Greene's in full force.

Greene staggered and then fell to one knee. Still strong as a bull, he whirled around and grabbed Roger by the throat, sending him to his knees.

But the fury inside Roger threw off the bridle. The two men rolled downhill like boulders, breathing like wild horses in full gallop. Roger felt a rock cut into his thigh. Ignoring the pain, he shoved the heel of his hand up into Greene's nose and heard a cracking sound. The blood poured out and ran down Roger's arm. With the same arm, he caught the malicious child-snatcher across the mouth.

The bear shook his head and, now on all fours, cried for revenge. His muscles turned to rock as he moved to charge again.

In one formidable effort, Roger raised his uninjured foot and drove his heel savagely into the charging beast's ribs.

Greene's brutal eyes crossed. He grinned maliciously, the blood on his teeth signaling terror.

Keplutok moved into the beast's face and defiantly grabbed him by the throat. The roar came, not from Greene's throat, but from the enraged father's.

Seeing Greene's eyes roll back into his head and fearing that Keplutok would kill him, Roger fought to break the father's iron grip. But when Keplutok seemed oblivious to any opposition, Roger bit hard into the father's arm until the iron grip released.

The beast Greene collapsed to the ground, his breathing frantic.

Roger ripped the shirt from Greene's body. "Keplutok, bring the rope!" he shouted as he rushed to the side of the injured Titus.

The confused Keplutok ran off in search of his son.

Looking over his shoulder, Roger saw that the predator Greene now lay captive of exhaustion. Roger quickly turned his attention back to Titus. But before he could lend assistance, he saw Titus open his eyes, shake his head, and with almost inhuman endurance yank the knife from his own shoulder.

Moving now by raw instinct, Roger hurriedly pressed Greene's shirt against Titus's wound until it scarcely bled. Though tears flowed from Titus's eyes, no sound came from his lips.

Having found Swift Deer, Keplutok returned to bind Greene, who growled and collapsed.

Hearing the villain's accomplice groan, Roger ran to him and tied him firmly across the mule. Then he returned to assist Keplutok.

Roger's heart sank. *Greene's breathing? What is wrong?* "Keplutok! This man . . . he is . . . he is *dying!*"

Stirred to full consciousness, Keplutok whipped Greene across the face with the rope he had brought.

"No!" Roger ordered. "Your sachem wants him alive."

Blood continued to flow from the big Englishman's nose.

Roger fell to his knees and pulled back Greene's eyelid. Keplutok and Roger looked at each other, both speechless. Roger saw Keplutok's face cloud with fear. *Is Keplutok afraid he has disobeyed Massasoit's warning to commit no violations of the peace treaty between the Wampanoags and Plymouth Colony?* Wildness in Keplutok's eyes turned Roger's blood to ice. He saw Keplutok stare murderously at Greene's accomplice. Keplutok had gone temporarily mad. Mingled with the madness was a father's love for his son and a willingness to kill to protect him.

Keplutok began slapping the helpless Greene across the face. Roger tried in vain to pull him away as soon as he realized that tearful Keplutok was slapping Greene as punishment for dying. Roger shouted in Keplutok's ear, "He is not dead!"

Despite Greene's groaning like an old bear emerging from hibernation, Keplutok, now muttering incomprehensibly, could not stop slapping him.

In desperation Roger grabbed the native by the hair with both hands and hurled him in the air and into a thorn bush. Just as Keplutok picked himself up, his child ran up to him and clung to him until the rage subsided. Then the two of them went to the side of the injured Titus.

Roger stood in amazement when Greene growled, hurling invectives against his captors. Then, like a man in a trance, Greene stared at the missing middle finger of his left hand as though it had been severed today instead of years earlier. With a blank expression of incomprehension, he looked up at Roger as if to ask, *Are you not a physician? Restore my finger! What have you done with it?*

Both Roger and Keplutok ignored him. Together they quickly made a rough-hewn sled on which to drag the bound Greene behind the mule.

Titus stood up, shook his head, and found the strength to walk with the boy to the canoe. After helping both his son and Titus into the canoe, Keplutok knelt in the stern and paddled toward Plymouth.

Roger took a deep breath to cleanse the terror from his thoughts. Then, with his two bound captives and their animals, he began his journey to see Governor Bradford.

Sitting behind his official desk and stroking his beard, Governor William Bradford listened without comment to the entire story, including a shortened account of the struggle with the ferocious Greene. Denying all the charges, Greene loudly claimed to be an innocent man attacked by two savages and an English lunatic.

Roger asked Keplutok, "Have you the contract on you?"

The proud native opened his woven pouch and handed the contract to the governor.

"Hmm! Very strange." The governor looked up at Keplutok. "Why would a father sign a document that made *collateral* of his son?"

Titus explained that the written word collateral had meant nothing to Keplutok and that Greene had maliciously deceived him.

The governor raised his left eyebrow.

Roger placed his palms on Bradford's desk and leaned forward. "Keplutok understands spoken English, but not written."

"Then why would he . . . ?"

When Titus nodded his permission, Roger explained, "My Wampanoag friend assumed that making a mark on a contract was an act of courtesy in an English ritual."

Bradford muttered, stroked his thick, wavy beard, stared off into space, and at last turned his hooded eyes toward Greene. "You scoundrel!"

Greene showed no remorse. "You revile me without cause. Scripture itself teaches that those who default on debts may be seized and sold into slavery." Then, after quoting from 2 Kings 4:1 and Nehemiah 5:1-5 to justify himself, he added, "Did not Governor Winthrop himself declare these savages to be Canaanites?"

Bradford's face flushed. "You are not in Massachusetts! Do not speak to me of Canaanites or Edomites."

Feeling contempt for the child-snatcher, Roger pressed the governor for a quick decision: "If Mr. Greene had stolen your child from your home, what penalty would you think fit?"

Though Bradford did not answer, he promised that the court would deliver a just sentence when it convened in early September.

Roger thanked the governor, who again denounced Greene to his face and then disappeared before Roger could inquire about lodging and food.

Feeling embarrassment from having no roof under which to invite his new friends, particularly Titus, whose strength had begun to leave him, Roger took his companions to the home of Pastor Ralph Smith, where he hoped to wash Titus's wound again. In the presence of the Reverend Smith and his wife, he quickly explained that without the help of the two natives and their canoe, he and his Mary might not be alive today.

Though still in pain the next afternoon, Titus enjoyed sufficient stamina to walk about. Apprehensive about having left Mary, Roger suggested they depart at once. He knelt in the canoe's bow; Keplutok knelt in the stern. Despite having never paddled a canoe, he had observed the two natives and felt he now could pull his weight.

They paddled for perhaps two hours, saying scarcely a word. Roger welcomed the time to think about the future. With his scanty farmland still under water and with no goods to trade for food, he entertained several plans. He wasted no time dwelling on what might have been. Two days earlier at the Wampanoag tribal dance, he had seen two natives make an exchange, one using *wampum*, white beads made of small seashells. He had seen the Narragansets use wampum too. Thoughts of the beads now stirred up a hazy idea that might help him earn a living while creating bonds of peace between the English and the natives. No longer satisfied with vagueness, he turned to specifics when Titus interrupted his thoughts with his groans. Keplutok guided the canoe toward a low, grassy bank where they made Titus comfortable. Roger walked around to stretch his stiff legs while Keplutok bathed Titus's fevered brow.

"Keplutok," Roger said, "I wish to ask a question about your debt to Greene."

Though showing no eagerness to pursue the matter, Keplutok made no objection.

"What prevented you from paying your debt?"

Titus called Roger to his side and spoke softly. "To challenge an honest Wampanoag to his face is to humiliate him. Our customs do not permit an honest man to come to his own defense. I, therefore, will come to his defense and tell you that he paid Greene in corn. The Englishman said it was not enough. Keplutok gave him more corn, and that was not enough."

Roger thanked Titus and then faced Keplutok. "Tell me how I can prove my trustworthiness to you, Titus, and Massasoit?"

"You have proved friendship. Is that not enough?"

Roger took the cloth from Keplutok's hand, dipped it into cool water, and laid the cloth gently across Titus's forehead while Keplutok stood to stretch his legs.

Roger smoothed the unruly lock of hair on his temple. "I have need of a friend who will listen to my plan."

As both Keplutok and Titus listened, they grew amused at Roger's ardor and the way he talked with his hands. Above all, they found his ideas amusing, not because of their impracticality, but because of their boldness and novelty.

When he had finished, Titus said, "You must explain all this to Massasoit."

"Will he find me amusing?"

"Massasoit finds all Englishmen amusing but none more than yourself." Titus opened his eyes wide to let them smile.

Roger rubbed his long hands together. "Will he be sympathetic to my plans?" Titus and Keplutok glanced at each other in silence.

Returning to the Wampanoag village, Roger found Mary safe, threw his arms around her, and held his cheek to hers while the natives glanced sheepishly at them. Some smiled when he placed the stem of a white blossom into her hair.

"Where did you find it, dear?"

"From a vine overhanging the river." He held her at arm's length to admire her and to assure himself she was truly safe.

Near sunset, when the animals of the forest ventured to the ponds and brooks before returning to their caves and dens, Roger sat with Chief Sachem Massasoit and his two interpreters. Titus nodded discreetly, signaling Roger to present his plan to the sachem.

Trying to forget that he would be negotiating from desperation, he began: "Your reputation as a sachem of peace and a protector of the English in Plymouth has traveled to the colonies and as far away as England. Your wisdom could benefit us all; for you have taught us that when tribes and nations trade, they have less reason to make war."

When Massasoit made no response, Roger glanced at Titus for a cue. Receiving none, he ventured nevertheless, "I believe you have need of an honest Englishman to serve as mediator of trade and barter between your people and the English. I can help you receive a fair contract and prevent men like Greene from cheating your people. I have learned that according to your custom, a person is forbidden to speak of his own honesty. If I cannot bear witness to my own honesty, then my actions and deeds must be my witness."

Privately, he thought that paper contracts for a people with no written language made little sense. He would speak of that when alone with Titus. "Let me be specific. You have corn, beaver pelts, hides, venison, and deerskin. I can find new buyers who will pay your people. First, we need a common currency." He elaborated on his plan to establish a trading post.

Massasoit sat with his arms folded and his eyes closed for half an hour as Roger talked while trying to read the signs on Massasoit's face the way a native hunter might read signs in the forest. The sachem unfortunately concealed himself behind his mask.

Have I violated some taboo and closed the door to my opportunities? Roger worried.

"You may not wish to translate this, Titus, but is this a soulless statue sitting before me? Has the esteemed sachem embarked on a journey, leaving behind this stone image in his place?"

When Titus translated, Massasoit burst out in laughter. "Which is worse? Talk without thought, or thought without talk?" The expressionless sachem rose to his feet. "Who will protect us from the watchdog?" Then he left with neither explanation nor promise to return.

A quartet of crickets chirped and became a choir. An owl hooted high above. Roger turned to address Titus but saw only his back as both Titus and Keplutok faded into the twilight.

LONG ISLAND

November 1631

On Long Island across from Connecticut, Governor Winthrop waited impatiently for the *Lyon* sailing in from England. Almost two years had passed since he had seen Margaret. He had never laid eyes on their little one, who would be a year and a half. He had of course received news that Ann had been born in good health. Although he had brought books to read while waiting at the dock, thoughts of his family so flooded his mind that he could only nourish his joy and expectation.

On the second day of his waiting, he paced as if to hasten the ship's arrival. From his pocket, he pulled out the last and longest letter from Margaret and read it for the fifth time.

> *Our darling Ann cannot yet speak, but she coos and laughs when we tell her that her father waits to take her in his arms. We may boast of the success of our son John. He has not only sold the estate, but also met all our obligations. He is a precious son of whom you can be infinitely proud . . .*

The anticipated reunion brought bittersweet memories since Henry would not join them. Winthrop found some comfort in having recovered his son's body and in having given him a proper burial. The governor tried not to think of Henry; for he had to consider his wife, his other children, and all the people of the colony who looked to him for guidance.

Just before sunset, gray sails loomed on the eastern horizon. His heart raced. One part of him rejoiced while the other prayed that every member of his family would arrive in good health. In the past two years, he had known many families to lose loved ones aboard ship. He forbade himself to dwell on the possibility that his Margaret had fallen ill and died. Surely Providence would not let him lose a third wife to the cold fingers of death.

He again pictured each of his seven living children on the ship. His first wife, Mary, had borne him John Jr. and two others. Margaret had borne him Stephen, Adam, Deane, and Ann. He thought of the psalm that pronounced happy the man whose quiver was filled with arrows. The sails bulged, the water parted, the *Lyon* approached the shore, and then it dropped anchor. He could hear children aboard shouting across the waves.

A Dutchman standing beside Winthrop lent him a spyglass. There she stood, his Margaret, waving! One by one, he counted his children. He recognized all six. The seventh, little Ann, he could not spot but assumed she lay sleeping somewhere on deck. His happiness soared. When had he known such gladness?

He turned to the Dutchman, who was also jubilant. Together they celebrated their good fortune. Through the spyglass, Winthrop watched the crew lower the ship's boat and John leave the ship. *Why had the others remained behind?* Winthrop wondered. Then he realized it would be simpler for him to go aboard than for the whole family to come ashore.

As Winthrop watched his son approach, the short distance between ship and shore seemed forever. Winthrop rubbed his hands with glee. His love for John had grown since Henry's death.

When at last John stepped onto the dock, both men embraced. The governor felt that the span of the entire ocean could not contain all his love for his family.

Like his father, the son stood tall with aristocratic elegance. The younger man, however, expressed himself more freely. Winthrop admitted to himself that his son and Roger Williams seemed curiously alike in being without guile. Filled with excitement, he introduced his son to the Dutchman and to everyone waiting on dock. John the younger went almost flawlessly through the form of cordiality, showing only a hint of embarrassment. When Winthrop realized his praise was perhaps lavish, he moderated. Seconds later his heart skipped a beat. *What is this cloud of sadness following my son? What gloom does he conceal from me?*

"Father, there is something . . . ." John took him by the arm. "Father, I . . . I must tell you."

"What is wrong? Your face . . . ."

"One of us did not . . . . The little one . . . ." The son could not say what had to be said.

Winthrop felt everything go gray. "Baby Ann?" For one hideous moment, he pictured the captain lowering her little body into the ocean. Then the sickness of his stomach came. He would never see her smile, never hear her coo or call him "Father." She would never say "Mama." She would never pull at his finger or sit upon his lap.

Winthrop glanced back at the ship and thought of his good wife. Margaret's heart must be broken! He looked up at his son and searched the dark eyes as if they were deep pools of mystery. "How . . . how did she . . . ?"

"Eight days after leaving England, a terrible fever befell her. We never saw her conscious again."

The governor walked with his son to the shadows and wept on his shoulder. When he had finished and had wiped his eyes, he spoke in a shaky voice: "John, when we go aboard, let us . . . let us be cheerful. 'To everything, there is a season, a time to be born and a time to die, a time to weep, and . . . .'" His lips trembled. "'And a time to laugh.'"

Winthrop required no scriptural texts to justify his weeping or laughing. Rather, he gained consolation in believing that all his feelings, sorrows, and joys emerged as nothing new to the Creator, who had foreordained all, even this recent tragedy.

At this sorrowful and confusing moment, Winthrop wanted with all his heart to believe that no ultimate accident, not the fall of a sparrow, occurred in the universe apart from heaven's infallible foreknowledge. He wanted to believe that just as Ann's little body had served the sharks, so her young soul now served heaven.

Winthrop stared pensively into the water. "The worms, sharks, and all creatures of high or lowly birth serve God's will in ways we do not comprehend."

Pride and terror mingled in his heart: *terror* that the Lord God of the universe, acting always according to his unfathomable will, answered to none; *pride* that the Lord God had elected him to play a major part in the divine drama of the ages. He suffered no doubt about his destiny: History would proclaim him an esteemed leader; and one day heaven would welcome him, not only as a sinner saved by grace, but also as a faithful servant who did not look back in doubt. *No man putting his hand to the plough and looking back is fit for the kingdom of God,* Winthrop reflected. *Despite all the trials and tribulations contrived by the powers of darkness to unseat me, I walk among those who know heaven has elected them to endure to the end.* Later that night, Margaret and he wept on each other's shoulder.

BOSTON COLONY

November 1631

The next day, Winthrop sailed with his family from Long Island to Boston.

Captain William Peirce looked through his spyglass. "The whole shore is swarming with people!"

He spoke the truth. I stood ashore with the deputy governor and five or six members of the court to join the festivities. To participate in the noisiest celebration of the year, people flooded in from such plantations and towns as Dedham, Newtown, Dorchester, Watertown, Salem, Plymouth, Wallaston, Roxbury, and elsewhere. Natives brought exotic gifts to honor the governor's wife. The captains of various ships in and around Boston Harbor instructed their companies in arms to fire volleys of shot. Cannons boomed. Cheers greeted Margaret, the governor, their children, and Captain Peirce as they departed the *Lyon* to set foot on Boston Harbor.

For several days thereafter, families stopped by to greet Margaret, some depositing fat hogs, goats, venison, chickens, geese, or partridges, all arriving to manifest love for the governor they believed had guided them through months of near starvation to a time of hope. The bleak months having passed, merriment and thanksgiving now filled the air.

Later that week, though normally not demonstrative, the governor asked in private, "Eric, has ever such joy and love been witnessed in New England?"

I truly believe the goodness of the people surprised Winthrop. Perhaps for the first time, something had overwhelmed him.

A week later, my plan to visit Roger and Mary in Plymouth dissolved when the captain of one of the ships summoned me to his cabin. "Captain Firebrook, I am ill. Will you sail my vessel north to Cape Ann and back?" I sailed it to Cape Ann; and upon returning from my voyage, I docked the ship in Boston Harbor and hurried on foot through the Commons on my way to visit friends.

Upon seeing a man in a pillory, I asked myself, *What heinous deed can this man have done?*

"He looks like my ox in halter," a heckler jeered.

"No, he plays the ass in harness," another heckler retorted.

A third spat on the prisoner, dipped water from a nearby pail, and drenched his head.

When I walked over to see who the unfortunate man might be, he recognized me first. "Away, Captain! I do not wish you to see me in this shameful—"

My stomach sank. "Cease at once!" I shouted at the ruffians and felt hot anger in my bones. "Barnabas, my friend, what have they done to you?"

Ignoring my presence, the ruffians taunted him more, one pulling at Barnabas's ears and looking at them covetously.

I raised my fist and would have struck the first man in range had they not withdrawn. They turned to face me with glaring resentment and flashing, fiery eyes for my having spoiled their sport.

"He is a man, not a beast!" I roared.

They stiffened to hold their ground, their chests swelling as though to charge me. Ironically, when I grabbed a stick and charged at them, they scattered like rodents running for cover. Throwing the stick after them, I turned to Barnabas and felt the heat of his humiliation in my own face. "What have they done to you, my friend?"

"'Tis the doing of our saintly governor. He and his wretched kind."

"Why?"

"I did break their Sabbath as they interpret breaking it."

"For that, they—"

"For more. Two Sabbaths I worshiped among the trees, not at the church. Though a church is built of the wood of trees, the high and mighty governor proclaims I cannot worship among *living* trees if I so choose."

"Have not others done as you and suffered less?"

"I too would have suffered only public reprimand had I groaned with repentance for Sabbath-breaking. For me, all days are God's days and therefore sacred."

Looking at old Barnabas, I fancied I felt more shame than he. My Puritan friends had committed a foul deed that Roger had warned would occur. Anger cut short my thoughts.

"One request, Captain Firebrook. My children! I beg you. Let them not see me again in this mortification, the wood around my neck as a dumb ox to pull a plow. It pains me truly, but the shame I suffered when my little ones saw me has no equal. My face, I could not hide it."

"Your request is my promise."

"And my endless gratitude to you, Captain. Hear me. I speak of shame not for what I have done or not done in the governor's eyes, but for my children seeing my lack of power to stand erect like one created in God's image. The magistrates would reduce me to a lowly beast."

"I will speak to the governor himself."

"The governor, he did charge me with blasphemy."

"I have never heard you blaspheme."

"'Tis not I who blasphemed, but the governor when he promoted himself to the office of deity."

"Barnabas, what did you say to make him brand you a blasphemer?"

He grimaced. I could almost feel stabs of pain leap from his body into mine. He squinted his eyes. "To Winthrop's face, I did charge, 'You, sir, expand the Godhead to four in one: Father, Son, Holy Ghost, and Holy Winthrop.'"

Old Barnabas seemed weary of talking, his voice now weak. "I will go at once to the governor on your behalf," I promised. Turning to leave, I heard his feeble voice say, "I thirst."

I remembered that another accused of blasphemy had once said, "I thirst." From a nearby pail, I poured water into my cupped hand while he lapped it up like a dog.

Less than an hour later, the governor received me with such uncommon cheerfulness that I did not broach the subject of Barnabas until the opportune time, so I thought. When he chanced to refer to the infinite mercy of heaven, I casually quoted wise Portia's words to Shylock:

> The quality of mercy is not strain'd.
> It droppeth as a gentle rain from [h]eaven
> Upon the place beneath. It is twice blest:
> It blesseth him that gives and him that takes.
> 'Tis mightiest in the mightiest; it becomes
> The throned monarch better than his crown.

Before I completed the quotation, Winthrop's servant entered the room, carrying a bowl of water and a towel. Placing them before the governor, the servant reminded him of another appointment. While the governor washed his hands, he spoke of justice. But when I pictured Barnabas locked in the wooden harness like an ox, I spoke of justice and mercy, quoting my favorite poet.

> Though justice be thy plea, consider this,
> That in the course of justice, none of us
> Should see salvation. We do pray for mercy,
> And that same prayer doth teach us all to render
> The deeds of mercy.

A judge's gavel coming down with a bang could have hit me no harder than the governor's stern, implacable frown. He washed his hands, dismissed thoughts of old Barnabas, and left for his appointment.

I went at once to the Blackstone house, where I told Lydia of Barnabas's wish not to have his children witness his humiliation.

"I told them of their beloved father's wish, but they have minds of their own."

"If you desire me to speak to them like a Dutch uncle—"

"They will heed your word, Captain. Though they meant no harm, I doubt they will return, the shock having cured them. Besides, I have sent them away to spare them more humiliation."

On my way back to the pillory, I kept hearing Lydia's soft-spoken words regarding our governor: "If you are not a piece on Winthrop's chessboard, you count for little."

Upon arriving at the pillory, I covered Barnabas's back with blankets and quilts and shooed away the human pests who swarmed about to torment a man whose shoes they were unworthy to touch.

PLYMOUTH COLONY

November 1631

Roger rolled over on the straw mattress in the small cottage they had rented.

"Mary, love, you are shivering!"

"Hug me tighter."

With the wind howling at their heels, he kissed her neck and sensed that she felt more like a pursued animal than a human being.

She shivered. "The wind grows worse."

He knew that she had not been warm in two weeks, and the whole winter lay before them. "Tomorrow I will trade for another animal skin."

"How can you talk about tomorrow? Since coming to Plymouth, every tomorrow has been more defeating than the day before. You once said God might be testing us. That makes no sense. Does God not know the outcome already? So he tests us for what?"

Roger had never heard her speak in this way or seen her lose heart.

"Sometimes, Mary, I feel I have deceived you grievously."

"Deceived me? How so?"

"By asking you to marry me and sail to this New England. The picture I painted had more bright colors than a more honest painting would. I mean the harsh particulars—"

"You painted only what appeared in your mind then. How could you have known?"

He, of course, could not have anticipated so bleak a future. Mary and he had both lost weight, and their plans for supporting themselves through the winter had crumbled.

She rubbed his shoulder. "If only Massasoit had trusted you to mediate commerce between his people and our friends in Salem."

"It would have worked for everyone's benefit, but it is pointless to blame him." Roger could not rid his mind of Massasoit's blunt response: *How can you represent us fairly in commerce when you failed to gain justice for us in the Plymouth Court?*

Roger had in effect served as prosecutor in the case against Greene, the child-snatcher. He had implored the Plymouth Court to show good faith to the Wampanoags by punishing Greene severely. Instead of sentencing him to hard labor among the natives for a year, which Massasoit had demanded and which Roger had seconded in the name of humaneness and decency, the court had placed Greene in wooden stocks for less than a week after fining him a mere twenty shillings.

Massasoit had said to Roger, "The Plymouth Court thinks very little of us. In the summer, it fined one of our people the equivalent of twenty shillings for stealing a *chicken*. Does the governor value a fowl more than he values a Wampanoag child?"

Despite the intercession of both Titus and Keplutok, the Chief Sachem would not trust Roger to serve as agent. "Assuming your plan had merit," Massasoit had said, turning his eyes away, "a plan without trust is seed without soil."

Roger could taste the bile of his resentment toward the malevolent Greene and the callous magistrates of Plymouth. Had they so soured Massasoit against all the English that trust and trade would never thrive among them? Had Roger's dream of establishing a trading post in their midst sunk like a reef-torn ship?

Keplutok had said he would never blame him for the Plymouth Court's decision. "You risked your life to help me rescue Swift Deer. I will always trust you as I would a brother."

Roger longed for dawn. In the frigid, gloomy darkness, he could neither sleep nor work. Crawling out of the animal skin, he laid another log on the small fireplace. Then he slipped back under the cover. Shivering from head to foot, he wished he were with his friends in Salem. He could almost smell the cooking aromas and feel the warm air floating out of Mrs. Endecott's brick oven. He remembered Winthrop telling him that if he were not so stubborn and filled with dangerous ideas, he could exert more influence in Massachusetts than the governor himself. He could still see Winthrop shake his head and hear him sadly prophesy, *I fear you will come to a miserable end.*

An hour later, after throwing another log on the fire and quickly dressing, Roger stepped outside to see the soft violet clouds in the east appear like chariots rushing ahead to announce the arrival of the emperor named Sun. Roger thanked God for a clear day. After walking around the house to work the stiffness out of his ankles and knees, he went inside.

Mary dressed, warmed herself by the fire, and quickly folded the covers. Then having slipped into a coat and shoes, she pulled out a thick knife to cut two large slices of hard bread. "The milk will warm shortly." She cheerfully set two bowls of frozen milk near the fire. "Did not God command the ravens to feed Elijah? I do declare: if God should send ravens, I would roast them succulently and make you *rave* with delight."

Dawn had arrived like a tower bell summoning them to work. To earn wages for bare subsistence, Roger had gone into debt to purchase tools: an axe for him to chop wood and a cart to carry the wood to customers; for Mary, cloth, needles, and thread for sewing dresses to sell. She started her sewing; and he, picking up his ax, walked briskly to a neighbor's to rent a mule named Kate.

A mile farther into the forest, Roger tied the mule to a tree, threw the large ax over his shoulder, and walked several feet to a maple he had marked two days earlier. Despite the private talks he gave himself, he could not disperse the nagging emptiness. For Mary's sake, he had tried his best to fight off desperation. Now looking reality in the eye, he could not lie. They had come to their last rainbow. To summon courage, he talked to both heaven and Old Kate, chopped furiously at the tree, and fought back useless thoughts about what might have been had he made different decisions or dreamed different dreams. He told himself that every dream had a price. *If the price for this dream is to walk for a season on the cliff's edge of starvation, so be it!*

He began to relish the rhythm of the ax in his strong arms, the expansion of his lungs taking in the cold air, and the feeling of making progress as he cut into the trunk. His mother had often told him, "Hard work heals a troubled mind." Until mid-afternoon he chopped, stopping only to eat and to pick winter berries for himself and his beloved wife.

Three hours before sundown, he glanced at Old Kate and thought that they had shared a bond, a kind of kinship in labor. For the past few months, he had worked as hard as any mule. He scratched Kate's long neck. "Old Girl, God has not given you the mind to spawn plans and dreams; but neither will you suffer a dream gone sour."

The tall maple swayed precariously in the wind. Throwing the ax over his shoulder, he guided the animal out of harm's way. Then returning to the maple, he chopped with joyful ferocity until the maple toppled with a thunderous crash echoing through the forest.

"Limber up your muscles, Kate. Time to work!" He chopped off the tree limbs while singing an old ballad he had heard on the streets of London in his boyhood.

After cutting the trunk into sections, he tied the lower sections to the mule's pulling halter. "What have we here, Kate?" He walked to a plant whose roots the Wampanoags had recommended as a delicacy. "Mary will like these for supper." With his ax, he dug into the hard earth and pulled out the roots.

He suddenly stiffened. A human hand? No, a gnarled limb? No! Were his eyes and mind playing a trick on each other? He closed his eyes and opened them. Still the object drew him closer.

All at once, his eyes and mind agreed. A withered, bony hand was sticking up from the ground, a thumb and two remaining fingers. *Whose? 'Tis a woman's hand! Oh Lord, the rodents have claimed their portion.* Death had claimed its victim several weeks earlier, perhaps months. Hideous thoughts scurried through his mind like hungry rats in the attic. *The ring! I have seen it before. But where?*

Breaking the eerie spell, he quickly gathered stones and piled them around the hand. Then he rushed to Kate. "Go, Girl! We must bear unholy tidings."

The wind whipped his face while the mule, seeming to sense his urgency, pushed against the gusts until they arrived at the village. Roger leaped to the ground, handed the reins to a man passing by, and dashed to Governor Bradford's house.

The governor listened with wide eyes and gaping mouth. When the blood returned full force to his face, the two men quickly assembled eight other men, telling them to say nothing but to bring their digging tools.

"We will need your wagon," Roger said to one of them.

Minutes later, not wishing to alarm the town, Governor Bradford spoke in a soft but somber voice, telling the men to climb quietly into the wagon and to waste no time. Then he handed two men an unlit torch.

Riding a borrowed horse and carrying a flaming torch in his hand, Roger led the way, the creaking wagon following and the men growing more excited with each passing minute. The night air chilled their bones. Roger's horse snorted, and the sense of horror filled the air. Horse and rider picked their way through the murky, merciless forest.

At last they neared the aberrant grave. The flaming torches flickered, and shadows played mischievously among the trees.

Instinctively taking command, Roger instructed the men to wait until the governor and he found the spot. The two men walked deeper into the forest for perhaps fifty feet when Roger stopped abruptly. Pointing at the pile of stones he had built like a monument over the hand, he gave the torch to Bradford and removed the stones. Then he took the torch and held it close for Bradford to see.

Bradford's eyes grew wide. "The Lord have mercy on us."

"No *four-legged beast* dug this grave." Roger was quite aware of the implication of his whispered statement. A month and a half earlier, Nehemiah Byrd had testified that he saw two bears near his house on the day his wife Martha had vanished.

"What thoughts send you into brooding?" Bradford asked.

He hesitated. "The natives who have spent their lives in these forests have no memory of bears stealing a human body, dead or alive."

"Then what rival hypothesis do you construe, Brother Roger? Do you think Nehemiah Byrd saw bears who were not there?"

Though he kept his conjecture to himself, he stood up as if to communicate that they both had reached the same conclusion.

The governor whispered, "Everything must be done decently and in order."

Roger sent for the men, each of whom took a short turn at digging, the stench growing unbearable, the metal striking the rocks, the sound reverberating through the forest. As they talked in soft voices, the men kept looking around, half expecting calamity.

"The ring! A woman's ring!" exclaimed the oldest man, removing his hat.

Another man elbowed his way to the grave. "Martha Byrd!"

Roger felt his skin crawl.

Primitive terror gripped the men, the fire from the torches flashing in their eyes. For a moment, they looked like a band of ancient tribesmen on the hunt. The silence of their voices spoke of vile horror.

Governor Bradford broke the silence. "We must decide the wisdom of it. Shall we take the shriveled corpse of this good woman to the village to serve up to the vulture Curiosity, or leave her bones here to rest in peace?"

The oldest man among them, Jessie Dane, rubbed his forehead with the tip of his fingers. "A grave so far from the village! What can it mean?"

"She did not bury herself," said Miles Standish, the governor's trusted assistant.

A hoarse, gravelly voice added, "Mischief afoot, I venture."

Old Jessie returned his hat to his head and pulled hard on the brim. "Nehemiah Byrd must learn of this tonight."

The man with the gravelly voice knelt down and ran his finger down a split in Martha Byrd's skull. "And Nehemiah must answer to this!"

The others agreed, at first with dismay and then with righteous anger blazing like the torches.

"With our governor's consent," Roger said, "let us bury these remains, not here in desolation, but quietly in our Plymouth churchyard tonight."

Governor Bradford evidently sensed the mood of the men and gave his consent. "Better to bury her in the churchyard than to leave her for wild hogs to come upon." The governor then added that he would take upon himself to speak to Nehemiah.

Roger appointed two men to load the corpse onto the wagon. The procession back to the village spawned abundant speculations regarding Martha's death and Nehemiah Byrd's part in it.

When the party reached the edge of town, Roger appointed two men to stand guard over the stinking corpse at the churchyard while the others made their way in haste to Nehemiah's house.

Flanked by the men holding their torches high, Roger knocked at the door. He knocked again. On the third knock, when still no one answered, Standish peered through a window.

At that moment, a neighbor stepped out of his cottage, put on his coat, and walked up to the men. "If you search for Nehemiah Byrd—"

Roger felt a churning in his stomach as if to alert him to another wave of trouble. He heard Jessie Dane ask the neighbor, "Has Nehemiah escaped?"

The neighbor scratched his head. "It puzzled me, and I asked Nehemiah, 'What is this? Why do you leave in the night?'"

"What answer did he give?" Roger asked.

"I might have received better reply from the wind. Indeed, he departed like the wind."

Roger ignored the sarcasm. "How long since his departure?"

"Less two hours. He quickly loaded up his wagon and headed west."

The men looked each at the other and murmured skeptical thoughts among themselves, reasoning that they had been west more than two hours earlier. Why then had their paths not crossed with Nehemiah Byrd's?

Roger took the governor aside. "If he rode west, the Wampanoags can find him."

"If he rode north," Bradford said, "friends in Massachusetts will help us find him. Tomorrow, I will send Standish to Boston."

A week passed. At sunset white-haired Jessie Dane came to Roger's tiny cottage. "The governor requests to speak with you."

The silver moon bathed the land while Roger washed his face and tired body as best he could. Why would Bradford call for him after dark? Was Bradford still nursing anger at him for severely criticizing the court's decision regarding Greene?

He dried his face and hurried in the moonlight to the governor's office, which stood Spartan and unpretentious near the center of the village. Candles burned, casting shadows on the wall.

"Please sit down." Bradford pointed to a rough-hewn bench. "I have two matters of urgent business with you. I have heard from Governor Winthrop."

Roger felt an emptiness. Had Winthrop sent a delegation to Plymouth as he had done in Salem, a delegation to rail against him?

"Many rumors about you are astir."

"I have no time for hearsay." He could glean no clues from Bradford's expressions.

"I will speak plainly. When you denounced the court's decision, claiming that our punishment for the child-snatcher insulted the peaceful Wampanoags, I took offense. Now I reverse myself and praise your wisdom."

The fatigue of Roger's body seeped into his mind. Though hearing Bradford's words, he felt they belonged to another conversation with another man.

Bradford added, "Massasoit has sent word that he desires to meet with me."

Roger nodded his head and waited.

"You do not seem surprised," Bradford said. "Did you know?"

"I knew only that Massasoit would not wrap his anger forever in a blanket. The court's decision regarding Rob Greene the child-snatcher weakened the treaty with the Wampanoags. If Massasoit takes the welts like a dog tucking his tail, he will lose face." Even though weary with the day's hard labor, Roger felt indignation boil up inside him. The people of Plymouth were Separatists who professed Christian purity. Yet they had betrayed Christ's Golden Rule, judging Keplutok's son less human than their own children.

"I acknowledge your right to pass judgment on me, Master Williams. Unlike our neighbor Winthrop, I am a governor who makes mistakes. Still, we have reached an impasse with the Wampanoags. Massasoit will not yield in his demand that we give him Greene to use for one year's labor. As you know, English law will not permit a more severe sentence once the less severe has been meted out."

Roger placed the palms of his hands flat on the table and leaned forward into the governor's face. "There is a higher law. Send me to serve the sentence."

The governor's head snapped back. "You confuse me."

"The message from Massasoit may teach us Christians a lesson in forgiving."

"'I too have a conscience,'" Bradford said, quoting Massasoit.

Roger stood up straight and shook his head. "We both have violated Massasoit's conscience and our own!"

Bradford held up both palms. "Go no further! You raise welts on my own conscience."

"Then send me to serve Greene's sentence!"

"It is unjust that one man should—"

"If I voluntarily accept Greene's sentence on myself, it is no injustice to me. Whether Massasoit will accept it, I do not know."

Stammering, the governor stood up to catch his breath. He walked to the window and looked out at the bright stars and the peaceful moon. "Yes, you do truly confuse me. My mind is at sea." Then, as if arguing with himself, the governor muttered, "Too severe! One year of servitude and hard labor!" He whirled around and stared at Roger. "We are both Englishmen, but before heaven, I have never met an Englishman like you. I cannot permit such an injustice. An innocent man! No, I forbid you even to speak of this again!"

He smiled and waited, trusting that Bradford would see the value of his proposal.

The governor sat down slowly behind his table. "I . . . know I cannot forbid you, my good brother." Then he sprang to his feet and gripped Roger by the arm. "Heed my words. If I cannot command you, I will implore you. Of late I have given much thought to you. Be my assistant. Do not go to live with Massasoit and his people, but abide here. I have more need of your skills. Standish will agree I am sure."

"If I serve the sentence that should justly fall upon Greene, how better could I serve both you and these people?" He hoped his voice carried the tone of sweet reason.

He would press the governor no more, but give him time to wrestle with his conscience in his own way.

Bradford studied Roger's face in the candlelight. "According to one rumor, you are a most remarkable yet exceedingly stubborn man. I half believe this rumor. Although a second rumor paints you with horns, a forked tail, and lips that spew dangerous ideas, I see no resemblance between you—the man—and the portrait painted by the gossip hounds. Your plan to become Greene's substitute carries danger. Still it is you and not my people who will face it. For this I call you brave."

"Bravery is in the eye of the beholder, though I thank you for your kind words. More brave is it of my wife to live on this cliff's edge."

Bradford frowned with incomprehension. "If your wife chooses to dwell here among us for the year, she will find work, food, and shelter."

The knock at the door did not seem to surprise Bradford, who frowned.

When Roger opened the door, Miles Standish entered. Roger had heard him described more than once as a man who performed always on stage, and indeed he seemed to perform now as though he expected trumpets to announce his arrival.

Standish closed the door grandly and paused to smooth his moustache. When they all sat down at Bradford's table, Standish revealed nothing until Bradford himself moved to close the shutters.

Bradford returned to his chair. "Miles, tell it from the beginning,"

Standish nodded. "Master Williams, after only two days in Boston, I tracked down the wife-killer Nehemiah Byrd. He was unaware that I had seen him. Moving quickly I made my way to Governor Winthrop's office and laid out our concern. I said, 'Into your fair city has come a man whom Plymouth's governor and many others of sound discernment suspect of murder.'"

Bradford cut in. "Tell him Winthrop's reply."

"He did proceed to paint three halos over the head of Nehemiah Byrd, to which I remarked that another halo would float him off to heaven. I then revealed that we require Byrd's presence in Plymouth. Then Governor Winthrop, who is ill-disposed to his neighbor colony, declared that he would sooner turn innocent babes over to wicked Herod than an innocent man to Plymouth's Court. I did most vehemently protest the slander made against our magistrates. Winthrop made feeble apology but did not yield to our request to return Nehemiah Byrd to the town of his peers."

Roger stood up to pace while thinking. Then he sat back down. "I hear that the younger John Winthrop has recently arrived from England. Can we perhaps speak privately with him on this matter?"

Standish smoothed his mustache, looked at Bradford, and nodded. Bradford said to Roger, "The younger Winthrop intends to sail for Plymouth soon, but not on his father's behalf."

"For what purpose then?" Roger asked.

"To represent a society of merchants who wish to increase trade with Plymouth," Bradford answered.

Roger's heart leaped with excitement. It was now more important than ever to win Massasoit's trust. Without Massasoit, trade between the English and the natives would remain at best a trickle.

Standish asked, "Is it true that you knew this younger Winthrop in England?"

"'Tis true," Roger answered. "I found him a man in whom dwells no duplicity."

"All the more reason you two should negotiate," Bradford explained. "But first you must learn our double interest."

Upon returning to his cottage later that night, Roger told Mary everything that had transpired in Governor Bradford's office.

"Roger, you are as a cat falling from a roof and landing on all fours. I do feel my shame in doubting heaven's Providence."

"When sliding on a roof, doubt is no great sin. But tell me plainly, Mary, will living among the natives sit like green apples on your stomach?"

She inhaled deeply. "When we stood before my father and professed our love, you promised me more adventure than boredom, a promise you have not once broken. I know well of your passion to speak the natives' tongue and talk to them about the gospel."

"What do you think of living among the Wampanoags for a year?"

She swallowed. "A . . . a year? Once as a girl, I went walking with my father in the Scottish Highlands. Suddenly a fog enveloped us, causing us to fear taking another step lest we plunge off a cliff."

Roger held his breath. "You have a similar fear now?"

"Yes. But perhaps the fog will lift. I have one firm request."

"Then I must know it in its naked form."

"'Tis a hard request. On the second weekend of each month, except when the snow and ice disallow, I must return to Plymouth. I have made friends in this short while."

"Do you count Old Kate among those friends?"

"You make sport of me. For what reason?"

He grinned. "Unlike carpet-traveling Persians, you must travel by either your own two feet or another's four. I propose to purchase four-footed Kate for your conveyance."

On the morrow, Governor Bradford and Roger rode west to the primary Wampanoag village. Massasoit received them, using Titus as interpreter. After presenting the sachem with gifts, Bradford confessed to Massasoit that he and the court had wronged Keplutok and the Wampanoag people. Then, with noticeable apprehension, Bradford stepped back to let Roger make his proposal.

After listening intently, Massasoit folded his arms across his chest and peered almost imperiously at the governor. "Who among you invented this strange plan?"

Bradford said nothing but turned his eyes on Roger.

"Why would you do this?" Massasoit asked Roger.

After a pause to collect his thoughts, he looked at his friend Titus and then said to the sachem, "When last we talked, did we not speak of trust between us?"

The thick lids of the sachem's hooded eyes closed as if to concede that they had so spoken.

Roger resumed, "If I work hard among your people, perhaps I will prove my trustworthiness. I confess a burning desire to learn better the language of your people, and I hope my service will strengthen the treaty between you and the English of Plymouth."

Massasoit stood up. "We will talk more of this on the morrow."

He knew that Massasoit would consult with the other sachems to learn whether they regarded his offer as a proper satisfaction of justice. Even though aware that the actions of the astute Massasoit could sometimes be outrageously unpredictable, he felt genuine good will toward the Wampanoag leader.

The next day, the Chief Sachem proved reliably unpredictable by neither accepting nor rejecting the proposal. "I will give you my decision three days hence when I come to Plymouth."

Though not daring to smile, Roger knew at once that he had won favor with the sachems and that Massasoit had elected to use the occasion to generate still another time of festivity, the people of Plymouth serving as hosts and incurring the cost. Titus had once told Roger that Massasoit's main pleasure was to visit other chiefs and to be lauded, provided the praise did not grow wearisome or overflow the banks of propriety.

Only Mary will relish the day more than Massasoit. Roger smiled triumphantly to himself. Mary had eaten peas, hard bread, roots, and milk for months. He envisioned her holding a turkey leg and then sinking her teeth into it.

John Winthrop Jr. arrived in Plymouth on the day of the festivities. Roger had persuaded Bradford to present John with various articles as gifts for the sachem. Roger saw at once that the younger Winthrop grasped the significance of this timely meeting.

As a student of the history of nations, Roger often struggled to discern those forces that beget major change. Like Milton he did not doubt the transitory nature of earthly life at every level. Looking ahead he now pictured Winthrop Jr. not as his father's son, but as a major figure of New England. Then and there, he determined to influence the thinking of this future leader.

While the people celebrated, flirting with the sin of temporary gluttony, Roger talked with Winthrop Jr. Since Roger was not yet six years older than he, they enjoyed many interests in common. He escorted John around the village, introducing him to the saints as well as to the magistrates and showing him various articles and relics the natives had generously given the Pilgrims over the years.

Roger stopped at a tall pole near the gate of the town fort. "Ten years ago in the spring, Miles Standish brought to this village a head belonging to the chief of the Massachusetts tribe." He pointed upward. "There on that pole Standish posted the head as a warning. Since then we have discovered festivities to be more practical than war. I do not relish the thought of one day seeing the head of the chief magistrate of Massachusetts Bay posted in a native camp."

Massasoit gave Roger a fortnight to move himself and his wife to the Wampanoag village to begin his sentence of hard labor.

He had much to accomplish before leaving. Governor Bradford had offered his office for Roger to meet with John Winthrop Jr., Roger's cottage being unsuitable as a place for momentous negotiation. But Roger said to John, "If you have no objection, I would prefer to walk while we discuss a few consequential matters."

"Much has happened since Mary and you departed England," John said as they strolled westward. "My prayers went with you as I stood ashore and watched the *Lyon's* white sails disappear in the distance."

"Now here you are among us. I know your presence fires new hope in your father's heart."

"The loss of Henry wounded him more than he permits us to know. Fortunately our arrival from England has in part healed his wound." John paused, then swallowed, stopped walking, closed his eyes, and took in a slow, deep breath. "I learned recently of your kindness toward my brother before his death. I will ne'er forget your goodness of heart."

"Henry had vowed to go to his father to seek forgiveness and reconciliation," Roger said softly.

John's eyes widened. "You know this in truth?"

"Aye. Henry came to ask me to accompany him to Boston. Would that we had sailed that very day. But Providence had . . . ." He could not finish his thought.

John gripped Roger's hand and shook it. "Amid the clouds of gloom, this is a good tiding! It gives me joy, and I know it will kindle joy in my father's heart too."

"Henry confessed that he had brought much grief to your father."

"All the more reason that this new tiding you have given me will . . . My warm thanks to you! But now, tell me of your plans."

"A part of my heart is in the trading post."

"I will speak to my father of this," John said in sadness. "I know that you and he are presently at odds, but you and I are friends." John seemed to stare far into the future. "Is it not the nature of friendship to give aid and assistance in times of trouble?"

They resumed walking. *Has Providence brought opportunity to my door?* Roger wondered. "I know you came here to Plymouth, John, to expand trade with the English. I have in mind to cultivate the friendship of the Wampanoags for a full year. Soon thereafter, if all goes well, I will found a trading post. Perhaps my plans and yours can link arms."

Although Winthrop Jr. spoke more diplomatically than his father, he came to the point more quickly. "My father has two opinions of you: that you are a godly man, void of infamy, yet a cauldron of divisive doctrines."

Roger guided John to the cemetery behind the church. "Your father did not leave England because Bishop Laud lapped up *his* doctrines as a cat laps milk. To certain

Turks who live by Muhammad's book, *we Christians* are a boiling pot of dangerous doctrines."

"You have keen eyes for the distant horizon. I will speak to the Boston magistrates about your trading post."

They stopped behind the church at a fresh grave, the words carved into the gravestone reading—

Martha Byrd
b. 1581–d. 1631
Loving mother of seven.
Wife of Nehemiah Byrd.
1 Corinthians 13:4-7

Roger studied John's face and saw the blood leave his cheeks. "Your countenance tells me you have heard of Nehemiah Byrd?"

"I have." John still stared at the gravestone.

"Have you heard that when we found the corpse of his good wife, Nehemiah departed like a thief in the night?"

"Before sailing for Plymouth, I talked to Nehemiah. He charges that Governor Bradford levels false accusations against him."

"It is not the governor who accuses him."

"Then who?"

"None that I know, save perhaps his conscience. If a man has a conscience, can he leave it behind the way he would leave a worn shoe?" Roger asked.

"If there is no charge, why did your governor send Miles Standish to bring Nehemiah to you?"

"We have suspicions. Now, after added investigation, our suspicions have doubled. There are questions he must answer."

"Do you have proof?"

He responded to John's question indirectly, giving step by step the account of his discovery of the hand in the grave and the grim events of that baleful night. When Roger told of Nehemiah's claim that two bears had appeared on the day of Martha's disappearance, John inhaled deeply as if to reply. Then his chin dropped, and he stood speechless.

Roger was taken by surprise. "Until now, had you not heard the particulars of the story?"

John shook his head.

Roger now remembered that Byrd had once assisted the daring swordsman Miles Standish in his dishonorable dealings with the natives. *Had Standish withheld particulars that would have cast Nehemiah Byrd in an unfavorable light?*

John cleared his throat and squinted his eyes. "I do not know what to say. If what you claim holds true—and I do not doubt it—then Nehemiah Byrd has reflected falsely on Governor Bradford's character. He has taken pains to cover up the truth."

"If a man will murder his wife and secretly bury her, he will scarcely hesitate to bury the truth about his foul deed."

"This will come as a blow to my father. He has known Nehemiah many years and judges him to be a righteous, truthful man."

"Then let the magistrates of Plymouth journey to Boston and speak with Nehemiah in your father's presence. Bradford and I have unearthed Martha Byrd's body. Now let Nehemiah Byrd help unearth the truth."

"My father will not readily—"

"Had I a good friend who fell under suspicion of murder, I too would come swiftly to his aid. But speak to your father, for he is a lawyer trained well at Gray's Inn. Deliver my two questions to him. First, shall friendship unravel the fabric of just and fair law? Second, if for the sake of friendship we hew down the trees we call the law, then what will protect us and all our beloved from the fierce winds of anarchy?"

Titus and Keplutok joined Roger and John, not by coincidence, but by Roger's invitation to meet him near the graveyard. Having talked with the two Wampanoags earlier in their role as interpreters for the chief sachem, John now conversed with them about native families and customs.

Roger held back, listening with pleasure and hoping that his plan would take its natural course. He observed that the younger Winthrop appeared at first too elemental, asking questions as if speaking to children rather than to grown men.

After about an hour, Titus and Keplutok returned to the festivities. Roger began to carry out his plan. "John, what do you think of the two 'Canaanites'?"

Although a serious frown formed on his face, John nodded agreeably.

Judging that John was of two minds about the natives, Roger quoted from chapter 17 of Joshua. "And it came to pass when the children of Israel waxed mighty, they put the Canaanites to slavery . . . Thou shalt drive out the Canaanites."

After the two Christians exchanged meaningful glances, John let his eyes follow Titus and Keplutok until they moved out of sight. Again John opened his mouth to speak; but as if commanded by a second thought, he returned to silence. He then removed his hat and wiped his brow, the heat coming, Roger thought, not from without, but from within.

"What do you think, John?"

"I have heard rumors that you think we English possess this land illegally."

"The king has ne'er produced evidence to demonstrate that the natives gave permission to take their land."

"Is it not God's land?"

"Would I be justified in taking your property on the assumption that heaven has given me title to it? The deed to Massachusetts, which your father holds, bears the signature of Charles, not of God. I know no document by which God has passed this New World into the hands of the English king."

"You call my father a thief?" A note of indignation rang in John's voice.

"We break two commandments given to Moses: *Thou shalt not covet; thou shalt not steal.* We are a gang of thieves, the chief being Charles." Though Roger spoke softly, he had no doubt that his words stung like a wasp. "To justify our thievery, we label our victims Canaanites."

"Would you have us pack our trunks, load our ships, and return to England's Bishop Laud?" John's chest expanded and his face flushed with the challenge.

"As you will learn, the natives would not have us return to England. They do not abhor us!"

"Then what is their demand?"

"What you and I would demand if we lived in their skin. They desire to be justly compensated for use of their land; to be treated as friends, not enemies; to share knowledge; and to live in peace."

"Are all natives in this land peace-loving?"

"Like Spanish kings some would enslave all, though most seem more civil in manners than many Englishmen I have known."

"Roger, I have heard that when the plague decimated the greater portion of the native population around Massachusetts Bay twelve years ago, it was a sign that God had miraculously prepared the way for righteous Puritans to inhabit this land."

He knew John had heard this from his father. "Yes, so I have heard. Some argue that since all land belongs to the Creator, he may take it from whomever he pleases and give it to his righteous ones." Again knowing that the older Winthrop had said those very words, he added, "But I argue to the contrary. According to Scripture, God causes sunshine and rain to fall on the righteous and unrighteous alike. Around the globe, do not the heathen own more land than do the Christians? Yet some Puritans appear to think Christ died more to give us land than to give us salvation."

Again, perplexity formed on John's guileless face. "According to the Gospel of John, an angel came down at certain seasons to trouble the waters. Whoever stepped first into the troubled waters was healed of his disease. In Boston it is said that you trouble the waters, but I do not think they meant *healing* waters. Perhaps they should have. I know only that you trouble my conscience."

The next morning, the sun filtered through gray clouds driven in by northern winds. Whether the coming hours would bring snow or bluer sky, no one could tell. John promised to speak sternly to the magistrates about Nehemiah Byrd. After again pledging his friendship, John returned to Boston, his heart stirred and pulled in many directions.

BOSTON AND
PLYMOUTH COLONY

November 1631

"Captain Firebrook, I cannot take no for an answer," John Winthrop Jr. said as we sat in his parlor. "I implore you to accompany me when I speak to my father of this matter. You are older than I, and he will not take your opinion lightly."

"Review the story that I may have it straight," I said.

John patiently related everything that both Governor Bradford and Roger had told him regarding Nehemiah Byrd.

I then dared to ask the question that John should have asked himself. "Why did your father not return Nehemiah to Plymouth? Was it friendship, or was it . . . ?" I could not finish my question. Somehow I lacked Roger's gift of speaking candidly without implying an insult. Nonetheless, I wanted to ask if Winthrop Sr. refused to cooperate because he secretly wished to undermine the mild Separatism that had taken root in Plymouth Colony.

John frowned. "I understand your implied meaning but have no answer."

"Does the governor himself know the answer?" My boldness surprised me.

"It is possible that he would be among the last to know. Will you go with me?"

I did not wish to turn my friend the governor into an enemy. Though no man in New England carried the weight of his influence and power, I gave my word to his son because I knew that it was a matter of justice and because I did not wish to fail Roger.

Since Governor Winthrop had yet to return from Newtown, I went to my room. From my window, I saw Barnabas mending a fence. I went to tell him that I might need a horse and carriage for a land trip to Plymouth on the following day. He bade me give his regards to Master Williams. I did not intend to speak to Barnabas about Nehemiah; but to my surprise, I discovered he had gleaned some truth and some falsehood from someone who had served Miles Standish during his visit to Boston.

"Barnabas, if you were the governor of Massachusetts, would you send Nehemiah Byrd to Plymouth to face questions?"

"If I were the governor, I would bathe three times daily in the Charles. Then I would send Byrd to Plymouth without a second thought. Instead Governor Winthrop prefers to place me in stocks for not attending his church while he leaves an accused wife-murderer to strut freely among us."

Later that afternoon, when John and I stepped into Governor Winthrop's office, he greeted us merrily and with his pipe in hand motioned us to sit down. "Why the somber faces?"

"Somber business," his son replied.

"Too somber for a cup of broth? Doctor Zerobable Endecott sent it to me."

"John Endecott's son?" asked John.

"Yes. He recommends a little wine for the stomach's sake, a little broth for the aching throat."

While we sipped broth, John Jr. began. "Father, I talked with Governor Bradford and the other Plymouth magistrates." John glanced at me as if to reassure me that he would take my advice to refrain from mentioning Roger Williams. "Governor Bradford sends his warm regards as do they all."

"The last we talked, Bradford's words came more hot than warm." Governor Winthrop peered at us over the cup near his lips.

"'Tis a question of the law," John said. "If for friendship, we cut down the law, then what will protect us and those we love from the icy winds of anarchy?"

The governor set his cup down and disappeared momentarily into his thoughts. Then his eyes searched his son's face to find someone he recognized, the words about the law seeming to have disarmed the older Winthrop.

"I think we are duty-bound to return Nehemiah to the king's colony where English law prevails no less than here," John said to his father.

The governor shifted in his chair and ran his tongue against his cheek. Then his knuckles crossed over the end of his nose, and he cleared his throat. Pursing his lips, he tapped them with the tip of his pipe. I saw in a flash that the skillful lawyer Winthrop had been upstaged by his own son. The younger man had learned well his father's art and had turned it on him.

The governor also saw this and with a flush in his cheeks asked, "You talked with the troublemaker?"

John ignored the question. "Let us suppose that enmity begins to flow between our two colonies. What then? The king's most conniving advisors find the enmity to work mischief upon all New England, sending another Bishop Laud to mingle in our affairs. Then what position will our two quarreling governors hold?"

Governor Winthrop turned his eyes to me. "I have heard no opinion from you, Captain. As you know, I value your judgment highly."

Spreading butter on my bread will not win me so easily, I thought. "The king could summon us all back to England, Governor. Better to sail on the smooth waters of the law than create waves that return us swiftly to England's turbulent shores."

Early the next morning, Barnabas handed me the reins. I drove to the jail, where I met John Jr. We went inside to claim our prisoner, who roared for angels from heaven and tongues of fire from hell to smite us.

When the burly man lunged at me, I stepped aside and threw him to the ground. Standing with my foot on Nehemiah's chest, I said, "Listen! I am no judge to declare you guilty or innocent, but I am appointed by the magistrates to carry you safely to Plymouth. Carry you, I will!"

Three men who stood guard bound him, and we all picked the burly man up to set him in the carriage. He roared no more, and neither angels nor flaming tongues restrained us. Handing the reins to John, I promised to relieve him within the hour. Then we drove south toward Plymouth.

Though the sun cast long shadows, we arrived before dark. Bradford and Roger met us. Together we marched Nehemiah to the small jail. Roger gave him blankets and a deerskin. The governor posted a guard, who remained shivering in the cold until he heard the prisoner snore.

Just as the guard started to leave, a woman about twenty years old stepped from the shadows. Though saying nothing, she kept wringing her hands.

"Who are you?" the guard asked.

"His youngest daughter," she whispered.

"Come back tomorrow morning."

"You do not understand! I . . . I . . . must see for myself that this Beelzebub cannot escape!"

When morning came, Governor Bradford and five other magistrates, including Edward Winslow and Miles Standish, sat at a table to question Nehemiah Byrd. John Winthrop Jr., Roger, and I, along with a dozen more men, served as their audience.

Standish stood up to greet me with a handshake. "Captain Firebrook, welcome to our humble colony."

As soon as I shook hands with all the others in the room, Standish took the floor and fired the first question at Nehemiah. "When the bears came on the day of your wife's disappearance, were you alone in your house?"

"I was not in my house."

"Where were you?" Standish asked.

"In sight of the house."

"You were alone?"

"Yes. Why are you asking me this? Do you accuse me of lying?"

Gangly Edward Winslow cut in. "We charge nothing against you. But I have a question. When you saw the bears, was perchance any human in your sight?"

"No, I was absolutely alone."

The oldest Plymouth magistrate Jessie Dane asked, "Do you agree that only a human could have buried your wife in the shallow grave where we found her?"

"I do not have the gift of speculation, but it takes no special gift to know who found her mutilated corpse and buried her. It was the heathens of the forest who do not love our Christian laws and customs."

Governor Bradford nodded at Roger, who stood up and opened the door to the room. Byrd's daughter, Doris, and her husband, Rubin Thomas, entered. From Rubin's hand, Roger took a thick piece of firewood. One end was covered with rust-colored spots. He placed it on the table. Byrd's hands, resting palms down on the table, drew back from it as he might from a sleeping serpent he feared might wake.

Roger eased the firewood across the table and left it only inches from Byrd's belly. Doris and Rubin walked to a bench across from Byrd and sat down. Although the color in Nehemiah's face left him for a flash, I thought the wrathful look he gave his daughter would have pinned two men to the wall.

As for Roger, I had never seen his jaw set so firmly. At this moment, he had a courage foreign to most men I had known, as if he saw some deep, moral corruption in the burly man. Yet I sensed no hatred smoldering in Roger's eyes. His piercing look at Nehemiah said, *You are not another species. We are all of one parent. But you, sir, have dipped your hands in innocent blood; and I will not be a party to your deceit.*

In Nehemiah's face, I saw remorse. Did he understand that Roger would render his pretense transparent? For a moment, Nehemiah's face seemed to plead for simple mercy.

Roger's voice was soft and kind. "Why would your youngest daughter call you Beelzebub?"

Nehemiah opened his mouth as if to answer straight from his heart. Then his whole countenance changed. He shrugged, but it did not fit with the sweat above his lip. "Sometimes the devil overpowers your children." His eyes now held his daughter captive. "The devil can make a good child grow angry and violate God's command to honor her parents."

Sitting next to me, Pastor Ralph Smith shook his head in sorrow. Winthrop Jr. sat gazing as if in disbelief.

Jessie Dane stared down at his wrinkled, folded hands resting on the table. "Brother Roger, what do you say? Can a daughter honor her parent if she breaks the commandment to eschew lying?"

After nodding in respect to the aging Jessie, Roger gestured to Doris, who spoke out to Governor Bradford. "I . . . I . . . witnessed the . . . and now I beg to bear witness among you."

"Speak," Bradford said to the daughter.

Gangly Winslow interrupted with a look of pity and sadness in his gray eyes. "We are your friends, Doris. We all remember your dear, kind mother."

Doris's voice shook, and she seemed unable to tell her story until she turned her eyes away from her father. She took a deep breath. "Against my father's wishes, my mother had come to my house. Rubin had gone hunting for fowl in the nearby forest, leaving Mother and me alone. Since my marriage to Rubin, Father had disowned me and forbidden Mother to see me."

Drawing himself closer to the table in the governor's office, Nehemiah laid his Bible before him and read aloud from the Epistle to the Colossians: "'Children, obey your parents in all things; for this is well pleasing unto the Lord.'" He closed the Bible with a bang. "I hold to Scripture as my supreme authority!" Then he opened his Bible again, this time to the Epistle to the Ephesians. "'Wives, submit yourselves unto your husbands as unto the Lord. For the husband is the head of the wife, even as Christ is the head of the church . . . Therefore, as the church is subject unto Christ, so let the wives be subject to their own husbands in everything.'" Again closing his Bible, Nehemiah leaned back triumphantly in his chair and folded his arms across his chest.

His daughter appeared both frightened and indignant. She looked at her father. "If in all Scripture a passage exhorts a man to kill his wife because of her disobedience, then I have ne'er read it; and I call on Pastor Smith to inform me if there be such a passage."

"There is none such," Smith said.

Governor Bradford fixed his eyes on Doris. "We would hear the whole of your story."

Doris seemed momentarily stricken with palsy. Among the Arabians, I had heard of the *evil eye*. It seemed as if Nehemiah's glare at his daughter had somehow persuaded her that she had fallen under his power. When she turned to look at Roger, the superstitious spell disappeared.

She took in one deep breath. "Father was angry that I had married Rubin instead of the man from Boston he had selected for me. I had naught against the man, but we were like two violins playing different melodies. Father persisted, saying the young man could serve as a ladder on which we all might climb to better positions."

Nehemiah leaned forward and stared at her. "She does twist my words! Such invention! I spoke not of a ladder, but of a bottomless well in which she would plummet if she should marry Rubin Thomas." He stretched out his arms. "My prophecy has been fulfilled. Now in revenge, she invents another tale." Suddenly Nehemiah stopped speaking and looked around as if expecting someone to come to his aid.

Doris wiped the tears from her eyes and accepted a cup of water from kind Jessie. Then she resumed, but her trembling voice dropped so low that the governor instructed her to speak up. "While my mother and I talked alone in my house, the door flew open. My father stepped inside."

Standish gestured with an upturned palm. "Do not hesitate. You are among friends."

"I closed the door and heard Father speak to Mother as though she were his *mule*. Reverend Williams, did not the Apostle Paul command husbands to love their wives as Christ loved the church?"

Roger nodded.

"Please, continue," Standish said.

From the fright on Doris's face and the way she spoke, I speculated that she fought an internal battle, one part struggling to open the curtain that concealed her memory, the other struggling to keep it closed.

Doris resumed. "Father hurled Scripture at Mother and called her Jezebel."

Leaping to his feet, Nehemiah pointed his finger at his daughter. "She is a curse upon my family! From childhood, she lied to get her way. She honored neither mother nor father, and she dishonors both today with these abominable lies. The Lord in heaven knows that I have been patient with her over these many years, but she is a viper among doves."

"Sit down!" Standish commanded.

Doris looked at Roger and then at Bradford. Receiving their nod of encouragement, she resumed. "Father's eyes lit up like bonfires. Then he came at my mother, but she backed away as she always did. He snorted like a bull . . . and . . . . It is true, Father. You struck her . . . struck her hard across the mouth, knocking her down. But she . . . she rose again and slapped you. I remember how she slapped you across the ear as you had slapped her. I had never seen her . . . so . . . . Again and again, she slapped you. That is when you slipped down on one knee, filling yourself with double fury." For the first time during the meeting, Doris looked her father straight in the eye. "You know I speak the truth!"

Nehemiah slapped his big palms on the table and would have risen in protest had not Old Jessie grabbed one shoulder and Pastor Smith the other.

Doris accepted a drink of water from Roger and inhaled a deep breath of air. Pastor Smith's nod of approval gave her strength to continue. "But then . . . then he grabbed . . . he grabbed that piece of firewood and . . . and raised it with a rage I have never before seen in him." Doris buried her face in her hands and shook her head like a child denying a horror that her eyes had revealed. "Oh, Mother! Oh, Savior in heaven! If Mother is among the cloud of unseen witnesses looking down . . . ."

All at once, her voice dropped low, an organ in minor key, sounding like that of another being. Her hands fell to her side as she stared knives of unspeakable hatred at her father. "Oh, Son of Perdition! Oh, black-hearted Lucifer, cloven-foot Archfiend! I have never loved you. When I was a girl and confessed to God my hatred for your foulness, I did not repent. Before the Host of heaven, I do swear that if you were in the flames of hell and I had a cool cup of water for your tongue, I would pour it upon the ground."

"Damnable ingratitude!" Nehemiah clutched his chest. "Thankless child; you poison a father's heart with your venom!"

"Oh, hellish man!" Doris hissed like an asp. "I curse the day you were born. Wherever you are, there hell will ever be! Wretched, wretched man who clawed at my frailty! You think me not a human being in heaven's image, but a stringed lyre for your daunting fingers to pluck and play your tunes. If I were of the seed of wicked Ahab, I would count myself less cursed than having you as my father."

Although Rubin grabbed Doris by the arm to pull her beside him on the bench, she shook him off and pointed her finger at her father. "Would that Providence had seen fit to give me premonitions of that sad day when my sweet mother crumpled under your cruel blow. Then heaven be my witness, I, like Ehud of old, would have plunged the dagger into your unholy bowels!"

All at once, one of the magistrates leaped to his feet and raised both hands over his head. "Patricide! Patricide! Harken to me! The devil's wiles snared Eve in the garden. How much more will they snare this daughter of Eve? I smell hot revenge spewing from this ungrateful daughter. Beware, lest by careless questioning we falsely accuse a worthy father!"

The same agitated magistrate then picked up the piece of firewood and pointed to the bloodstains on it. "Whose blood? Do we know that is the mother's? Who wielded the weapon? What proof have we that Nehemiah Byrd entered his daughter's home on that fateful day? Assuming he did, whose word and witness have we? Only this daughter's against his. By her admission, her husband was not present." The magistrate's voice grew husky, and it boomed like a cannon as he pointed an accusing finger at Doris. "The account we have heard comes from one mouth only. I ask you, have we not heard a tale spun from the vain imagination of Eve's daughter?"

Evidently infuriated by the magistrate's insults, Rubin clamored for the governor's recognition. Before he stated his opinion, however, Nehemiah interrupted, shaking his fist in the air.

Doris's low, minor key rose eerily above all their voices, like the sound of some strange creature sweeping through the forest. "Slander! Wicked slander! 'Tis enough that my father slew my mother before these eyes, but now I suffer double crucifixion on a cross of false witness."

Nehemiah stood up, spread his arms out like a cross, and cried tears that flowed down his cheeks. "Oh, female Judas! Ehud's knife had not the steel of your spiteful tongue."

Although poor Rubin struggled to gain a part in the tempestuous drama, he proved no match for Hamlet and Cleopatra on this mad stage. In the presence of father and daughter, Rubin sounded like a braying donkey. When suddenly all others grew quiet, Rubin flushed crimson. Though his lips moved, his words caught in his throat. Stunned by his own ineffectiveness, he sat down like a player who had forgotten his lines.

Doris dropped to her knees and looked up to heaven. "Angels above, bear witness to my innocent heart. If my father hangs upon a cross, call him Barabbas, the thief who hung guiltily beside our innocent Lord and mocked him. Yea, this man who now mocks me is a murderer more vile than a den of rakes and thieves!"

Roger took Doris by the arm, gently lifted her from her kneeling position, and guided her back to the table. "Please sit down. In this colony, the magistrates, not angels, pass judgment. Trim the wick of your halo lest its light blind us to the truth." After that, he laid his left hand gently on the father's shoulder and held it there. With his right hand, he picked up the piece of bloodstained firewood and handed it to Nehemiah. "If this blood is your good Martha's, it cries out and begs for truth. Look at this weapon and read the message. Be not inventive. Tell step by step what you will reveal when you face your Creator on judgment day."

Suddenly speechless, Nehemiah laid the wood on the table and wiped his hand on his coat.

Roger took Nehemiah's hand and looked at it. "If these hands are covered with Martha's blood, what lye or lie will wash it away?"

The room grew quiet as Roger took the wood, stepped over to the daughter, raised her hand, and placed the wood against her palm. She proved unable to hold it with one hand because of its thickness. Still no one spoke as Roger, carrying the wood with him, placed it in Nehemiah's right hand and raised it high as a weapon.

All glared at Nehemiah who, frozen like a statue, moved only his eyes. Then, as if seeing the terrible light of heaven on judgment day, he wept bitter tears of remorse. The curtain dropped, and hot tears washed away the paint from the actor's guilty face. "Lord, have mercy upon me, a sinner," he said hoarsely.

When the governor handed Roger quill and ink, Nehemiah nodded *Yes* when Roger asked if he had killed his wife Martha Byrd just as his daughter had testified.

On the following morning, Mary, Roger, and the mule Kate left for the Wampanoag village.

BOSTON AND PLYMOUTH COLONY

December 1631

Three weeks after the trial, Winthrop Jr. came to my Boston quarters, waved a letter in front of my nose, and said in confidence, "Your friend Roger invites us to join him again in Plymouth to celebrate their special day of thanksgiving."

"Will the Wampanoag sachem permit Roger to return to Plymouth?" I asked in surprise.

"For the celebration. Here, Captain Firebrook, read for yourself."

"We agreed, John, that you would call me by my given name."

"So we did, Eric. Shall we sail together for Plymouth?"

Upon reading Roger's letter, I smiled inside for two reasons. He knew of the older Wampanoag sachem's weakness for feast and celebration. Undoubtedly the younger sachem Massasoit had used Roger to gain an invitation to "the big feast" in Plymouth. I smiled also because I remembered Roger telling me of his intention to influence Winthrop Sr. through Winthrop Jr. He believed the son possessed greater courage of mind than did the governor.

I tweaked John's mind with my question. "You wish to visit the prophet Roger who has troubled the waters of Massachusetts? Do you intend to inform your father of your journey?"

"He has been informed." John winced, looked away, and offered no explanation.

Sensing that they had argued, I probed no further. "When do we depart?" I was eager to learn how Mary had fared among the Wampanoags.

A celebration with my friends would provide me excuse enough to wear my new shoes and jacket, but I elected to leave behind my new hat lest the stricter brethren perceive me as ostentatious. I suspected that the younger Winthrop had a serious purpose in returning to Plymouth. Had he come under the spell of Roger's good will? Did he wish now to probe Roger's fertile mind?

Ten years earlier, the Pilgrims had lost nearly half their population in their first winter at Plymouth. New hope had grown in the summer and fall of that year, leading Bradford and the others to pronounce December 13 as their special day of thanksgiving to revel henceforth in their survival.

With much persuasion on my part, John agreed to wear my new hat. I knew that both Lydia and Barnabas had need of new scenery and, above all, new faces. I said to Barnabas, "A time to weep; a time to laugh." After I convinced Barnabas that Winthrop Jr. was not the governor's shadow, he agreed that he and Lydia would be my guests.

The four of us arrived in Plymouth at the best possible hour. Upon departing from the ship, we whiffed the aroma of roasted meat on spits and rods, and we saw happy children turning the meat before the open fires. We saw youngsters everywhere, some helping their parents, others skipping rope, and still others playing chase with the Wampanoag children.

Bringing wild turkeys and venison, a party of natives mingled with the Plymouth Pilgrims. No sooner had we arrived than some began to sing in our honor. Forthwith we all turned to eating. Although the air was cold, the open fires and the hot food kept us warm. Boiled and roasted foods were spread out on long tables. We tasted each other's delicacies, smacked our lips, and closed our eyes to shut out all other senses save taste. Today Epicurus reigned in the village of Plymouth as the English, Wampanoags, and Narragansets celebrated merrily together.

"You must stay close to my side," I implored Barnabas and Lydia. "Around these stewed blackberries swimming on crusty scones, I am a weak, weak man."

Although Lydia laughed, Barnabas seemed not to hear me, having set his eyes on more scones with juicy pear, plums, and apples. We watched two families carry huge containers of green-currant and Marlborough pudding as if delivering frankincense to the Christ-child in the manger.

As John sank his teeth into a large, succulent cherry scone, I whispered Martin Luther's joke, "If you sin, sin boldly."

As might a child, John laughed merrily through his nose and let his dark, shiny eyes follow the scones served on platters decorated with columns and other architectural designs. Through Roger I had learned something from the natives that I wished some Puritans could learn, namely, the art of harmless, joyful celebration. To be sure, most Puritans could celebrate; but some had grown too stingy with their jubilation.

I called the raisin scone the devil's dish because of its power to seduce. I turned my head and walked by the raisin scones quickly, considering myself a candidate for sainthood. Yet my stomach made war with my feet, the latter winning only a temporary battle.

The best celebration for me, however, came when I saw Roger and Mary. He carried a native child on his shoulders and an English child in his arms, which told me that he had thrived well among Massasoit's people. Mary waved. Barnabas and I waved back.

"Hard labor has done Roger no injury," I said to Winthrop Jr. "But I think by living among the Wampanoags, Mary shows more courage than her husband. She was raised to be not so wild, having grown up in the home of an Anglican clergyman."

"You met her father?" John asked.

"A proper vicar. Served his parishioners faithfully day after day. In Essex Mary worked hard from childhood, but without the grind and precariousness of her two years with Roger."

Barnabas overheard our conversation. "I would never take my wife to live among the natives, knowing not what to expect of Lydia. She might ignite a war with the natives."

Lydia laughed. "If I were captured, you would come to my rescue like Don Quixote on his ass."

I watched Roger set the two children to the ground, put his arms around Mary, and begin walking toward us. While I had seen this scholar shut himself up with books, I knew also that he relished heaven's raw skies and Earth's humming, flowering abundance. Sometimes his infectious cheer in the face of adversity puzzled me, for I would quickly lose my cheer if I were serving another man's sentence.

Still laughing, Barnabas and Lydia made their way to meet the Wampanoag Sachem Massasoit. Roger and Mary greeted John and me warmly. Soon we four became engrossed in conversation, going off excitedly in all directions until Governor Bradford exclaimed, "The two Narraganset sachems have arrived!"

Mary and Roger left with the governor to greet the sachems.

All this time, John Winthrop Jr. seemed to have traveled to another world.

"John, you carry on a private conversation," I said.

While he looked at me, I wondered if he truly saw me. At last he said, "More like a private battle. My suspicion crosses swords with fascination. I ask you. Do you not agree that Roger is an entangling enigma?"

"So you have set your private thoughts to resolving this—"

"I have questions I intend to ask."

"Questions for Roger?"

"Yes. Arguments, too," John proclaimed resolutely.

As soon as Roger returned, the three of us huddled around the hot coals of one of the big fires and fell into a deep conversation. Without warning, John looked Roger in the eye. "When you refer to the power of church and state, you play Machiavelli's flute."

Though I winced, Roger replied without blinking, "Machiavelli did not go far enough."

When John stiffened, Roger cajoled him. "Reason with me. Do you not agree that if Machiavelli had lived long enough to read history more exactly, his naiveté might have shrunk to fit the trousers of reality?"

John stared at him as one might peer at clouds changing their shapes. I thought that if Roger intended to influence Governor Winthrop through his son John, he must speak more circumspectly.

As if reading my thoughts, Roger added, "Machiavelli advised magistrates to wed themselves to the clerics if they wished to unify Italy. Machiavelli, however, underestimated the clergy's cunning. Bishops and magistrates will always flash their teeth at one another unless they find a common enemy to divert their animosity. Machiavelli weighed too heavily the prince's cleverness but too lightly the pope's shrewdness and the bishops' ancient skill of manipulation."

John filled his cheeks with air, exhaled hard and filled them again, calming the inner sea. "One rumor portrays you as an unruly anarchist with no regard for government or law. I do not believe the anarchist hat fits you."

"How so?" Roger seemed grateful for John's willingness to understand.

"Far from being the anarchist, you proved more zealous than us all to bring Nehemiah Byrd to justice before the magistrates, all strictly according to the law."

It pleased me to hear John say this, for I myself had never discerned precisely where Roger would draw the line on the authority of magistrates.

Roger paused. "John, your face sends a strong message, saying you think me inconsistent."

"My face does not deceive you. I confess, I see before me one man with two faces. You say magistrates have authority under law, yet you say they have none."

Roger suggested we step inside the meetinghouse and find a warm corner for ourselves. He wanted no distractions. Since he could not live in Massachusetts to present his own views directly, he would have to depend upon men like Winthrop Jr. to represent him fairly and accurately. It was, therefore, imperative to dispel all confusion about his cherished doctrine of church and state and to lay it out for John to see. Finding benches near the front of the meetinghouse, we sat down.

"John," Roger began, "why complicate the simple? Magistrates have *limited* authority. They exist to protect men, women, and children."

"Protect from what?" John asked.

"From thievery, slavery, and violent aggression, including rape."

John's eyes grew wide in obvious expectation of a much longer list. "Have the magistrates no charge to protect us from false teaching and heretical doctrine?"

"No!" Roger placed the tip of his finger to his temple. "God gave each of us a brain for judging false teaching."

I cut in, "Did you not once tell me the courts may enforce contracts?"

"Legal contracts. But if the parties do not enter *freely*, there is no contract."

"What of evil deeds? Shall they go unpunished?" John seemed astonished and deeply disappointed in Roger's failure to speak of righteousness. "Have you no dream or vision of a righteous society on Earth?"

Roger trembled inside and burned with impatience, feeling he had a right to expect better insight from John. *Why presume I have no moral vision because it is not your father's? The governor may dream for you, John, but not for me.* Afraid such private thoughts might escape from his lips and afraid more of their tone, Roger stepped to the window and placed his hands against the cold pane. He welcomed the coldness. Sensing his own hot self-righteousness, he reminded himself that men and women were never more vulnerable and dangerous than when imagining themselves soaring in perpetual virtue far above others.

Looking through the window, he saw Lydia and Barnabas talking with Keplutok's son, who like his father spoke English. Roger still faced the window. "John, though I too dream of a righteous people who do good deeds and truly worship, let it be done *freely*! I know we agree that hypocrisy adds nothing to the righteousness of a people."

"Aye, it adds to unrighteousness."

It gave me pleasure to hear them quickly agree that for good reason our Lord denounced hypocrisy most severely. So I added, "Hypocrisy causes unbelievers to scorn our Christian faith when they see hypocrisy in our churches."

"By its very nature, hypocrisy is a double sin," John added.

Roger turned away from the window to face us. "If we attend church only because the magistrates require our presence, wherein lies righteousness? When magistrates compel the outward show of religion, they reduce the sum of right-eousness."

"How so?" I asked.

"By using force against the conscience of men and women of peace and by spreading hypocrisy throughout the commonwealth."

"Do you fancy that you disguise your meaning?" John seemed surprisingly sarcastic. "I know you speak of my father."

Roger pulled rein on himself, knowing his habit of following the argument wherever it led him. For that he had no apology. Nevertheless, to influence both father and son, he must not always fire off his thoughts point-blank. He spoke in soft tones. "Let us reason together. I do not doubt the governor's noble intention. He has harvested much goodness among the people and saved many lives in the face of famine. I hold him in high regard and respect. But worship him, I do not."

"Nor do I." John bristled. "Still you impugn his motives when you imply that he spreads hypocrisy."

"Not his motives, but his wisdom in this matter. Forced goodness is only outward behavior, not true religion. If pretense of worship is false religion, then in his zeal to spread only the true religion, the governor unwittingly multiplies false religion among us."

Although John winced, he acknowledged that the argument was at least plausible.

Roger pressed for an answer regarding John's father. "Consider another angle. England and Spain crawl with spies like cockroaches everywhere. When rulers and magistrates fancy themselves God's eyes on this planet, they breed more spies to render themselves omnipresent, seeing and knowing everything. Is that not idolatry—the state like Lucifer exalting itself to God's throne?"

John clinched his fist. "I resent your implication! You would portray my father as a monster."

Again Roger pulled rein on his ardor, his voice scarcely above a whisper. "John, I wish to say no more than what we both know. Like us all, the governor is a mortal. He bleeds. He weeps. He speaks sometimes wisdom, at other times foolishness. Why? Because he is a mere man. But the more we feign divinity, the more prone we are to commit hellish deeds."

When John made no answer, Roger took stock, waited and hoped. He cautioned himself against unloading his thoughts too quickly. *Like meals, thoughts are best digested in small servings.*

Still silent and looking down at his boots, John made a clucking sound as though his brain were a horse in full gallop. Smiling, he looked up at Roger and shook his head. "I confess, you slip a knife into a man's ribs and then make him thank you for the twist. First you inflame me . . . and then put out the flame with sweet wine." John laughed. "Here I sit, taking your insults as nourishing manna. I was warned of your bewitching manner, but perhaps you show deep respect by appealing to our reason and our better selves."

"If I have won your trust somewhat," Roger said with controlled enthusiasm, "then indulge me once more."

"I will, but remember this: when his disciples desired to call flames down from heaven to consume the Samaritans, Christ rebuked them. If you have in mind to rain down fire upon me, rebuke yourself."

"Fire?" Roger asked.

"The flame in your eyes, let it not leap out," John said.

Roger again placed his hands on the cold windowpane and glanced outside, giving himself time to formulate his thoughts. He remembered Sir Edward Coke's words. *Arguments delivered as music will gain better reception than arguments hurled like spears.* "I pose a question. Do not answer to me. Have you lusted in the heart? According to our Lord, such lust is adultery, is it not?"

"It is." John looked at me. I nodded that I agreed, remembering the words of Christ in the Gospel of Matthew: *I say unto you, whosoever looks on a woman to lust after her has committed adultery with her already in his heart.*

Roger resumed, "If the magistrates should extend the Law of Moses to execute adulterers of the heart, they would commit still another sin—suicide, executing themselves."

John agreed but added, "Immoral deeds unchecked are like mad dogs turned loose in the streets of London."

"If the magistrates, however, are the stronger dogs and they run unchecked . . . ." Through the window, Roger saw Keplutok's son Swift Deer hurry toward the meeting-house. Turning to face John, Roger asked, "Can you not see that if we should label every immoral deed as illegal, we would wrongly turn Caesar into a god?"

"What!" John exclaimed. "You would give license to evil deeds? I say that unless evil is judged—"

"In due time, my friend, judgment day will expose all sins before God; but magistrates err grievously when they treat each day before the court as judgment day. They judge prematurely and beyond their proper fences, confusing their own finite schedule with heaven's calendar."

Swift Deer entered the meetinghouse, walked down the aisle to Roger, and told him that Massasoit and the others would leave soon.

"Ah," I said. "The paper and ink." I left at once and returned with a wooden chest containing a large supply of writing material for Roger. Enclosed also were four books he had asked me to bring from the collection he had placed with me for safekeeping in Boston.

In turn he gave me a basket containing his most recent notes. "These are more of my observations about the customs and language of the Narragansets and the Wampanoags. I would value your judgment of them."

I knew the importance of these notes and assured him that I would continue to guard them at all cost.

Mary appeared in the doorway to signal her husband that the time of their departure for the Wampanoag village had arrived.

Young John Winthrop saw her and seemed saddened, as if suddenly realizing that months would pass before Roger and he would again face each other in friendship. He shook Roger's hand vigorously and, looking at Mary, said, "Keep him off danger's path. He might prove to be the most useful man among us."

Mary wished John and me Godspeed and begged us to visit again before spring. Then she left with Keplutok's son to meet Mrs. Bradford.

John walked with Roger alone toward the door. "I will speak to my father. I am no bridge builder, but . . . ."

When John could not find the words, Roger said, "Then let us together work to build one bridge. You begin on one shore, and I on the other."

John nodded his agreement and, opening the door for Roger, caught him by the arm. "Save some of that ink to write Eric and me. Today I have had a feast for my stomach but a tastier feast for my mind and heart. If it please you, count me among your true and loyal friends."

"It pleases me beyond measure." Roger's heart felt a strange apprehension at this moment of highest expectation. He did not know the meaning of this extraordinary feeling. "Pray I will prove to be a true and loyal friend in return."

Since I disliked good-byes, I waited inside the meetinghouse. Through the window, I watched Mary and Roger join the Sachem Massasoit and the other natives as they headed west. Silently I wished them well and hoped they would arrive safely at their village before sundown.

On the ship back to Boston the next day, John Winthrop Jr. and I waved to Governor Bradford and white-haired Jessie Dane. The sails swelled with a favorable wind, and the ship took to the waves as would a young seal.

On deck, Barnabas, who had overcome his bellyache, was once again in high spirits. With a pleasant grin and lilting music in his voice, he began relating an incident that had occurred at the Wampanoag village. "The interpreter Keplutok told me this. One morning, the Reverend Roger Williams saw a native child behaving contrary to high English standards. 'Why do you neglect to discipline your child?' he asked the boy's father, who jumped up and, pretending to be an angry English father, picked up a stick to give the boy a sound thrashing. The father explained that he had seen the English and Dutch beat their young ones. Since the boy had never seen his father burst out in anger toward him, and naturally thinking his father was playing a game, he picked up a stick the way his father had. Keplutok said they resembled two crazy Dutch fencers. The father gently permitted the boy to get the better of him."

I interrupted Barnabas to ask if Roger had found the exchange between father and son amusing.

"Keplutok revealed only that the Reverend Williams learned a lesson that we English have yet to learn."

"What lesson?" I asked Barnabas.

"That children learn customs better without benefit of floggings."

"And Barnabas, my dear," said Lydia, "tell the gentlemen what Keplutok said while you were eating your fourth bowl of stewed blackberries."

Barnabas licked his lips as though he wished for a fifth bowl. "Why, 'twas a simple saying that carries much wisdom. Keplutok said, 'We Wampanoags slap mesquites, not children.'" Barnabas looked at his wife as if to gain confirmation that he had reported accurately.

She nodded. "Captain, these Wampanoags say they have no task more important than raising their children."

"'Tis true," Barnabas added. "They build everything around raising their children in their own customs. According to Keplutok, the Reverend Williams gave considerable thought to Keplutok's words and for two days puzzled over how it came to be that the older the native children grew, the more they honored their parents."

With the sails popping in the strong wind, my friends and I talked perhaps an hour on our way to Boston. I was pleased to hear through Lydia that despite the hardness of life among the natives, Roger had gained the Chief Sachem's respect. Above all I was pleased to learn that Roger had won the hearts of the other sachems, who now bargained among themselves for the privilege of helping him learn the native customs and language.

"It seems this Reverend Williams is a most sincere and understanding man willing to listen to someone other than himself." Lydia spoke cryptically while staring at Winthrop Jr. with unforgiving eyes, as if she were staring at his father.

WAMPANOAG VILLAGE AND PLYMOUTH COLONY

October 1633

During the year from November 1631 to October 1632, Roger had served the sentence of the child-snatcher Rob Greene. It had been hard but fruitful labor among the Wampanoags. The disconcerting circumstances had made the servitude a trial by fire. Each morning he had waked with his bones aching. Though he had found the summer months more physically burdensome, they had proved mentally exhilarating, his mind leaping with an unquenchable passion for learning.

The end of his servitude had become a new beginning. Mary and he had agreed to live with the Wampanoags until he could establish the trading post between the natives' village and the town of Plymouth. Massasoit and he had become good friends, which served the interests of both men.

The summer heat of 1633, however, had proved exceedingly difficult for Mary and the child within her. Roger sensed that Mary sometimes longed for the cool breezes of Lincolnshire and Masham Manor. The native women had tried to make her comfortable as the time of her delivery approached. Even so, Roger knew that the ground on which she made her bed inside the wigwam had felt continually harder and that the added burden of carrying a child in her womb had made her wish for the soft, down-filled mattresses of the Old World.

She had, however, taken the native herbs cheerfully, telling him that sometimes they tasted surprisingly pleasant and proved amazingly restorative. The Wampanoags had a saying: *A healthy mother, a healthy baby.* On a hot August morning, Little Mary came noisily into the world and sucked greedily at her mother's breast as well as the breasts of two of the Wampanoag women. The child flourished week after week and seemed to keep several hands busy feeding, cleaning, and walking her. Mary sang to Roger and her daily.

With the coming of autumn, Roger was pleased to see that everything had changed for his wife. The repressive heat gave way to tingling, cool breezes. She relished now the full color of autumn's red maples and enjoyed good health, the old ailments seemingly loaded upon a raft and carried far away. He knew how much she loved the New England fall and that her heart sang all the more as she cradled her little one. The native women often took turns carrying her daughter, giving Mary rest and time to learn more of the native customs.

Sachem Massasoit's growing interest in English customs came as a mixed blessing to Roger. Fancying himself the native version of King Charles, the foremost sachem had freed him from the servitude of some of the physical labor only to deliver him to the more stringent labor of tutoring the lesser Wampanoag sachems. Life as a tutor might have pleased Roger and Mary had not a veiled rivalry sprung up among the sachems, each demanding more and more of Roger's service, Massasoit taking the largest portion.

"Massasoit treats you unfairly." Mary cradled baby Mary in her arms. "Your year in servitude proved less wearisome than this new agreement between you and Massasoit. You now work harder than a galley slave, journeying with him or other sachems wherever they go, trading right and left, then appearing in Plymouth on the eve of the Lord's day to work with Governor Bradford on his history book."

Mary raised her luminous, teasing eyes to the sky. "Heaven and sleepless angels, look down and have pity on this mortal man, Roger Williams. When God did create the whole universe, Roger rested on the seventh day. But does my husband know a day of rest? No, on the Lord's Day he yields to the saints in Plymouth to be their teacher, then back early the following morn to tutor the topmost sachem in our English traditions and customs. Would that heaven's love had created my husband as three men and I had fallen heir to just one of them!"

Roger found himself chained like a willing captive to her words. He was always surprised upon hearing the wisdom of a mature, older woman coming from Mary, whose face looked younger than her years.

"Mary, I confess, some days I am so exhausted I fear I will fall asleep while paddling my canoe. Yet as Massasoit's tutor, I serve a long-term purpose."

"Not even heaven can make the tongue of a corpse speak. Furthermore can you show me from Scripture how the hands of a corpse performed good deeds?"

He held her and the baby close to him and felt the warmth and goodness of his wife's body flow into his. He planted a kiss on her hair and felt her heart beat. Then he took their daughter into his rough hands and ran the tips of his fingers across her nose and cheeks. "Look, Mary. Her toothless smile melts her father's heart!"

Mary laughed mirthfully at Roger's cooing sounds. "You cannot give her milk, but neither can I give her that special sunshine your heart carries wherever you go."

He kissed his wife on the lips. "I have oft tried to paint a poetic portrait of you. If I were John Milton himself, I would fail. You are a living poem, and all words are poor imitations."

She stroked his cheek, and he relished her attention while he gently twisted their daughter's fine hair with his fingers. "Roger, I grasp more than you think. You stand now on Mount Pisgah and peer across the Jordan to the Promised Land. I want to walk with you through the Jordan. Unlike Lot's wife, I will not look back."

Roger smiled with deep gratitude. "Poor Lot. One day, he had a wife. The next day, a pillar of salt."

"Love, you will be salt in my wounds if you do not heed my advice to give yourself more rest from your hard labors."

"Give ear, Mary, and I promise to give you two."

"You have my ear; but if I hear not reason, you shall have my sharp tongue."

"A tongue more fearsome than Jael's tent peg."

She gently pressed her finger to his temple. "Jael punctured Sisera's temple with a tent peg while he slept in her tent. I hope to touch your brain with reason while you are awake."

"I will heed your wisdom, love. Still I require another month as Massasoit's tutor. I am more the student than is he. Through him I learn the deeper meaning of his people's customs and traditions. My journeys with him have clear purpose. From him I learn many subtle ways to trade among his people and with other natives. He clears the pathway to other sachems who will learn to trust me as Massasoit now trusts me."

"I share your vision, and our children will share it too. 'Tis better to bring the hands of the English and natives together in friendly trade and commerce than in war." She pinched his ribs. "Look how thin you grow."

He wondered how such youthful, inquisitive eyes could reach deeply into his conscience like a canoe paddle dipping into a lake, making fresh ripples and swirls.

Kneeling on a blanket inside their Wampanoag wigwam, Mary took their daughter in her arms, gently stroked the child's tiny hand, and placed her in the padded basket that one of the native women had woven. She looked up at her husband and smiled. "When our Little Mary asks about her father, I do not wish to say, 'Dear child, he grew so frail the wind carried him away.'"

A week later, Roger returned to Plymouth. On the first day, he woke up at dawn and quickly dressed in his best clothes. *Today if all goes well and God wills, my dream will descend from the heavens and touch ground.* Outside he whistled at the morning birds and smiled, picturing his dream as a cloud floating down like an angel. He felt wary of all pretensions to divinely given visions and revelations. *God gave us Scripture and with it a world of teeming nature and human society, more than sufficient substance for the brain.*

At the dock, Roger cheerfully greeted the captain of the *Fairweather* that had carried the delegation from Salem to meet with him. "How did you sleep in your sea cradle, Captain?"

"We rocked as peacefully in the waves as a child in a mother's arms. The party is awake and eating. They wish you to come aboard. Have you broken the fast?"

"I slightly bent it."

"Good. Then come join the rest for a hearty meal."

Three-quarters of an hour later, Roger and a party of six men from Salem bade farewell to the captain of the *Fairweather* and began their journey inland.

"The village of the Wampanoags lies near the Tauton River twenty miles west." Roger handed his roughly drawn map to freckled Jeremiah Paynter. "Fortunately the trading post site I propose is only ten miles into the wilderness." Roger then took Captain Endecott aside. "I know you have knees for praying, but have you knees for canoes?"

"I have." Endecott's voice had grown husky with years of salty sea air.

After walking two miles to the canoes, the men sat on the river's sandy bank to study the terrain. Red-haired Jeremiah pointed. "If we make a mule trail for hauling our merchandise, it would better circle the hill than traverse it, do you not agree, Benjamin?"

Stocky Benjamin Cook removed his broad-brimmed hat, squinted against the morning sun, and slowly nodded his approval. "Around is most always better than across."

Roger smiled to himself, observing that Benjamin relished sweeping generalizations, evidently thinking they made him profound.

They eased into the canoes that the natives had left for them and with much groaning made their way upstream, following Roger, who regularly looked over his shoulder to see that no one had straggled behind.

At the front of Roger's canoe, Pastor Samuel Skelton of Salem paddled as best he could. He seemed sluggish. *Has some affliction come upon him?* In Salem, Roger had known his fellow Cambridge scholar as a vigorous man. He now vowed to speak to Skelton about his health at the proper moment.

Unexpectedly Skelton turned around and said in a most earnest tone, "Roger, you are my friend; and I am pleased to say that the good people of Salem send their prayers and best regards to you and Mary."

"How fondly I remember them. Mary and I have spoken often of our longing to see their pleasant faces."

The Reverend Skelton breathed harder now. "At a more convenient time, we must talk. The people of Salem . . . an empty place in their hearts for Mary and you."

A rumble of thunder from the north caught Roger's attention. Looking up he saw puffy gray clouds punctuating the turquoise sky. Remembering the flood in which they lost their home and almost their lives, he felt a shiver streak through his spine. *Three miles and we shall see Titus and Keplutok standing at the riverbank to greet us.*

Skelton called back to Roger, "The pox recently claimed a few of the natives."

"How many?"

"I do not know precisely. It was thirty miles west of Salem."

"Did Chickatabot survive?"

"The Namponsett sachem? The pox took him last week. Pray that it will not become another grievous plague."

The news of Chickatabot's death came like a hard slap. Roger let the canoe drift for a moment. He knew about the earlier scourge that had swept through the native population, destroying entire villages throughout the bay area. He recalled Thomas Dudley's interpretation of the deaths among the natives: *A cleansing of these idolaters from the land to prepare the way for the godly to inherit the land of promise!*

Roger gripped the handle of the canoe paddle and pulled hard against the current. Anger welled up in him as he remembered the words of another Massachusetts magistrate who described the decimation as heaven's way of "taming the cruel hearts of these barbarous Indians."

The tree leaves rustled and the air cooled; but the rain held back, which pleased Roger. He had prepared for this day, and he desired everything to be perfect. He felt his heart race with gladness when he saw short but vigorous Titus on the small beach, waiting for him and his party. Looking back at those following him, he signaled, directing them to land at the beach.

As soon as the canoes touched the soil, Titus's two assistants moved quickly to give aid.

Where are Keplutok and Massasoit? Roger wondered, glancing about.

The Salem men accepted the assistance of swift-moving Titus and his companions as they carried the canoes to a safe place.

After Roger introduced the natives and the Englishmen to one another, he took Titus aside. "Where are Keplutok and Massasoit?"

Titus cut his eyes left and right. "Here and not here."

Roger laughed along with Titus, both men knowing that Massasoit intended to make his theatrical appearance after keeping his audience in wait. Having heard that European kings seldom arrived on time, Massasoit assumed that English custom required inferiors to arrive before their superior. Roger pictured Massasoit and Keplutok hiding behind trees until the sachem chose to make his impressive entrance. Turning to Titus, Roger lowered his voice. "How went Massasoit's counsel with the Narragansets and the Connecticut tribes?"

"The governor in Boston pronounces the Connecticut tribes 'pernicious' since they fail to lie down for Governor Two Faces to walk upon," Titus said.

"Will the Connecticut sachems talk with me?" He studied Titus's face for clues to hidden meaning.

"Aye. Keplutok built a mountain of praise before them and then set you upon the mountain."

"Keplutok and you must stand nearby to catch me when I slide off." Roger smiled, pretending not to see Keplutok's son Swift Deer perched high in a tree. Though only recently having learned to climb trees, the boy obviously fancied himself a spy for his father. Roger longed for news about his wife and newborn, who were still deeper in the forest at the Wampanoag camp. He had not seen them during the several days he had spent with Governor Bradford and the Salem delegation. Titus obviously carried no fresh tidings from the Wampanoag camp; for he had been accompanying Massasoit and Keplutok in their diplomatic expeditions, journeying from tribe to tribe in Connecticut, Aquidneck, and Massachusetts.

Having grown to trust Titus's good judgment, Roger entreated him to mingle with the men from Salem. "You must convince them of the Wampanoags' trustworthiness and acumen."

When Titus left, Roger took the Reverend Skelton by the arm and walked with him down the narrow beach. "How goes your health?"

Though Skelton answered, it was no helpful answer. Roger now knew less about his friend's health than before, save his recently slow gait and weary speech. Though the good minister had doubtless intended to allay apprehension about him, his evasiveness only increased it. Roger mentally rehearsed ways of approaching the subject with more tact and grace, but a tap on his shoulder interrupted his thoughts.

He turned around and heard Titus say quietly, "Massasoit is arriving."

As soon as Keplutok and Massasoit appeared from the thick forest, Keplutok presented himself to the delegates and made an ostentatious speech to introduce the chief sachem. Roger saw that Massasoit relished the introduction, which the sachem had doubtless composed for Keplutok.

Everyone sat down to the venison that Titus and his two assistants had roasted on an open pit. Lanky, freckled Jeremiah Paynter rose to his feet and said he had never eaten such delicious meat. "Today is a day we will all remember!"

Roger indulged the ceremony with tolerant amusement, realizing its necessity. He often referred to it as commerce courtship and compared it to the dance of courting fowl in the green meadows of Essex.

Titus filled the delegates' palates with *askútasquash* swimming with honey. The delegates ate heartily though their taste for exotic food had diminished, long smothered by the fateful mingling of English culinary tradition and Puritan principle.

A wondrous joy rushed over Roger as he listened to the delegates speak in detail of merchandise they planned to export. They seemed cautious, but not too cautious; eager, but not too eager; friendly, but not too friendly. He thought Massasoit had not only mastered the English style of trading, but also learned to tolerate good-naturedly inadvertent comments offensive to Wampanoag traditions.

Roger's improved understanding of the Wampanoag language gave him a new appreciation of Titus as both translator and skillful adaptor of Massasoit's speech to English ears. Privately, Roger kept thinking, *Where mutual aid grows, mutual slaughter diminishes.*

Without warning a dispute arose between Massasoit and the brazen, tactless John Endecott regarding native beads and shells.

Roger glanced at Titus, who picked up the cue and said to the sachem in his native language, "The big captain blows like a whale coming up for air; his spouting has no significance."

Insensitive to his own gaffe, Endecott rushed headlong toward the cliff of insults. Roger quickly cut in, having more than once seen indelicate Endecott make a shamble of peaceful negotiation. He remembered Mary's description of Endecott as a man who had learned to speak by competing with howling wolves.

Pointing to the white and black shells on Titus's wampum belt, Roger explained in detail that their polish and elegance were the work of highly esteemed and deft artisans called *natouwómpitea.* He pronounced the Narraganset words *nquittómpscat, ompscat,* and *puickquat* to indicate the degrees of value among the beads and polished shells that the natives used as currency.

Captain Endecott shrugged as if to obscure his indiscretions. "No matter! We New England men settle on *wampum* and *peage* as the working names for this currency."

Roger clamped his hand down on the big captain's shoulder and discreetly walked him several steps away both to reassure him and to prevent his tossing a verbal beehive into the circle. Then Roger studied the faces of Josiah Preston and Seth Chapman, two men of eminence among Massachusetts merchants. *The negotiations could fall apart before they scarcely begin.* Every word and every tiny gesture appeared to him to be fit into a mosaic. He caught himself holding his breath as if he feared that the entries would slip to the ground before he had secured everything firmly in place.

At the same time, another part of his heart surged with hope that this special day would fulfill all that he had secretly promised for himself and the natives. Feeling like an actor watching others perform, he all at once realized that he had been thrust back upon the stage and that the plot had moved with startling swiftness toward its climax. Stepping up to join Titus and Keplutok, he talked calmly to the proud sachem and before all the others extolled him with such honesty and straightforwardness that Massasoit seemed both caught off guard and pleased beyond measure. Instead of heaping words of flattery upon Massasoit, he told the simple, undiluted truth about the esteemed leader and his success among all the New England natives.

Endecott himself seemed moved, particularly when Roger related the account of the captain's harrowing journey to the New World and his courage in blazing trails for other Englishmen. Before ending his speech, Roger had portrayed this day as a watershed. When he had finished, a period of silence prevailed like a spell that no one dared break. Each man looked into the eyes of the others as if to ask, *Have we come thus far only to turn back? Have we risked so much only to return to the old ways of making war and nursing hostilities?*

As if each moment were now a new painting, the men stepped out of one frame and into another, the new frame containing previously unknown hopes, dreams, and possibilities.

Roger glowed, his bliss soaring when at last the distinguished pioneer among the English, Endecott himself, gripped Massasoit's hand warmly. Roger remembered his father's hope that he would eventually enter the family business. *If only my father were alive to witness this triumphant adventure in negotiating commerce between the natives and the colonists.* Like Milton, he enjoyed a second or wider calling, a ministry of teaching, translating, preaching, and writing. Now he felt himself to be a peacemaker. At this victorious moment, his elation became complete as he envisioned serving as a bridge of understanding and trade to the natives.

As the traders from Salem began to speak of returning to Plymouth, he saw two natives from the Wampanoag village arrive and rush to Keplutok's side. When Keplutok signaled for him to join them, Roger hurried to learn the meaning of the consternation on Keplutok's face.

"Two of my children burn hot with fever," Keplutok said.

His heart sank, thinking at once of his own Little Mary. He looked into Keplutok's eyes. "Your . . . your son Swift Deer—?"

"Swift Deer fairs well as does your firstborn," one of the native messengers answered.

Roger concentrated hard. "Keplutok's two children with fever, have they—?"

"Only one now has the fever," the older messenger said.

"The other?"

"For the girl, the fever has passed."

Roger looked at Keplutok and then at the older messenger. "Marks?" Roger touched his own face.

"On her face and arms."

"She breathes well?"

The native looked at Keplutok. "Her strength returned after the fever passed."

Roger continued thinking of his own daughter and of the boy Swift Deer. "Keplutok, you and I must return to the village at once!"

Titus laid his hand on Keplutok's shoulder. "I will guide the English back to Plymouth."

Roger thanked the messengers and turned to Titus. "Please inform Governor Bradford that I will speak with him later."

Wasting no time, Roger assured the men from Salem that he would arrange another meeting soon. Then he knelt in his birch-bark canoe, followed Keplutok and Massasoit, and paddled quickly away, his strokes taking their rhythm, the blade entering the water with scarcely a sound. In his mind, he worked out what he must tell Mary and Keplutok. If the two children had the dread disease, then Mary must leave at once and the whole village must act swiftly. But how could he prevent the spread of panic? He reminded himself that English children seldom fell prey to *this* pestilence. Still he sensed irrational panic stirring within himself. *Much work must be done before sunset.* He focused now on his plan.

Upon arriving at the village, he let two of the younger men care for the canoe as he rushed toward his wigwam. Though praying for the best, he prepared for the worst. *If Little Mary has the fever at her young age, she might die!* Again he reminded himself that English children seldom fell prey to this disease. This, however, made him fear even more for his wife's health.

As soon as he entered the wigwam, he held Mary at arm's length and looked at her from head to toe. Then embracing her and looking over her shoulder, he breathed relief. He could see that their daughter lay in good health in her little basket, kicking her feet in the air. "Mary," he whispered as he placed the tip of his fingers on their child's brow, "you must pack and leave with our daughter at once! I will ask Old Big Hands to take you to a little cabin near Plymouth. He will do it for my sake."

Fright spread quickly across her face. "Will you not go with us? Oh, Roger, can you not already feel the hot breath of pestilence on this village? I beg you—"

He pressed his finger gently on her lips and looked down with secret foreboding at their Little Mary. Then putting his fear behind him, he turned rapidly and disappeared into the village.

Upon arriving at Keplutok's wigwam, Roger called him out and asked to see the children. The mother brought them to the threshold. The first child who stood before him answered his questions listlessly, revealing that, *yes,* his head ached particularly at the front, *yes,* he had suffered chills, and *yes,* he had vomited frequently. Roger could see the parched lips, indicating past fever. "Where have you suffered pain, child, other than in your forehead?"

The child did not answer but placed his hand behind him at the lower part of his back. The expression on his face disclosed the severity of his pain.

Roger's heart sank. The child's answers and the pimples on his face confirmed the worst. In only a few days, the pimples would enlarge and spread, and the disease would carry from wigwam to wigwam unless . . . . "Come with me, Keplutok."

They walked side by side as Roger revealed everything he knew about the dread disease that the English called *smallpox*. Back in Essex, he had observed the physician John Clarke treating it. "My friend, your children stand on shaky ground. I implore you to send Swift Deer to the little wigwam where he played last summer. Let him live there until perhaps the first snow."

Keplutok protested, saying that a boy so young must not be made to live outside the village. Nevertheless, Roger prevailed upon him, calling attention to Swift Deer's intelligence. "He is fleet of foot, but his mind is swifter."

Acting without further delay, Roger rushed to Massasoit. "Spread out the village. Let fresh air blow between each wigwam."

Massasoit protested; but when Roger reminded him of the decimation that had occurred only three years earlier north of their village, he conceded the wisdom of the Englishman's advice.

"I will do as you say. The English brought this evil to our people, but bearing grudges will do us no good."

The next morning, Roger took two strong native men with him to Plymouth. There he begged fruit, vegetables, and churned milk. Before returning to the Wampanoag village, however, he again sat down with Mary and their baby daughter in the cabin outside Plymouth. He felt extraordinary relief when the child, far from being hot with fever, touched his finger and seemed free of all worldly cares.

Later, the good Pastor Smith walked him to the canoes and gave him comfort. "My wife and I will leave food for Mary and the little one each day at the place that you have designated. They are in our care and heaven's."

Tearing himself away, Roger entered his canoe and with heavy heart said good-bye to friends, who wished him and the natives Godspeed.

Cutting his way up the river, he pondered the impact that the pestilence sometimes worked on those who survived. He recalled Massasoit telling him that the devastation to the north had wreaked much havoc on their *thoughts*. This meant that from far and near, the sachems had no way to explain *why* the disease had left so many deaths. "Some among us invented what you English call superstitions. Others said we displeased our own gods, and a few claimed we displeased the English god."

When Roger arrived at the Wampanoag village, Chief Massasoit appointed men and women to distribute the food. Roger felt pleased as he looked at the wigwams now spaced far apart from each other. *If only Doctor John Clarke could be here to give me better advice.*

Again with Massasoit's permission, Roger spoke movingly to the counsel of men and women. "Double and triple your portions of drinking water each day. Rinse the children's eyes with clean water."

Then, with Keplutok at his side, he hurried, carrying food and drink to the little wigwam where Swift Deer now dwelled. A thousand emotions whirled in Roger's head: fear and hope, guilt and compassion, rage and patience, ambition and humiliation.

All at once, a tremendous flood of pleasure came over him. In the distance, rosy-cheeked Swift Deer chased a squirrel. Roger felt tears well up in his eyes, but he quickly wiped them away lest the natives see him. He had helped deliver Swift Deer from the hands of the child-snatcher Greene. Now he hoped he could help deliver the boy from disease.

Near twilight, Roger sat alone, mentally composing a letter informing King Charles of the smallpox that the English had brought to the natives. He would say that it was neither Christian nor just to take the land of the natives only to give them the pestilence in exchange. *Yes, the king must understand. The land does not belong to the crown and therefore cannot be the crown's to dispose of as he deems fit. The king must acknowledge that this thievery violates both divine law and universal humanity!*

During the same week in England, Doctor John Clarke, an accomplished linguist who had studied medicine at the University of Leyden, reviewed several pages of his collected documents regarding the perils of Separatists and Baptists in England. Two of the pages contained the following entries:

Henry Barrowe: Founded a Separatist congregation in London not long after (precise year unknown) the defeat of the Spanish Armada. Hanged in 1593 for denying the queen's authority in all matters pertaining to the church. In the same year, Parliament passed law imposing severest penalties for all who dared to "impugn Her Majesty's power and authority in causes ecclesiastical."

Thomas Helwys: In 1612, informed James that no mere mortal, king or otherwise, possessed power over other mortal souls or authority to appoint spiritual lords over them. Spent the last two and a half years of life in Newgate Prison. Died there in 1616.

John Lathrop: Successor to Henry Jacob as congregation pastor. Imprisoned 1632 . . . .

John Robinson . . . .

PLYMOUTH AND THE WAMPANOAG VILLAGE

November 1633

Jeremiah Paynter and Benjamin Cook headed northwest from Salem toward trapper Abel Jones's house ten miles from town. Having arrived in New England before most of the settlers, Jones had positioned himself to supply them with beaver pelts and other skins. Of late, a falling tree had left him lame and less capable of providing for his wife, a handsome son, and two pretty daughters who had brought him much joy.

On the second day of November and about a mile before arriving at their destination, lanky Paynter pulled rein on his mule. "Shh, hear that?"

The two men looked around. Sturdy Cook whispered that he too had heard the ghostly howl. Dismounting from their mules, they walked in a crouched position toward a small pond where they saw two deer, one drinking water and the other listening.

"A wolf?" Paynter whispered.

"Could be a wolf calling for the pack."

Through the trees, Paynter caught sight of a curl of smoke in the valley. He smiled to himself and could almost taste Mrs. Jones's savory venison stew. Then a gnawing in his belly told Paynter to look again. He pointed at the smoke and turned to Cook, who stood upright, his chin dropping.

"Is that smoke too thick for a chimney?" Paynter hoped Cook's observation would correct his own.

Cook, however, said nothing, nodded, and then riveted his eyes on the sight. Paynter walked closer to the cliff. Cook joined him and gasped. "Burned to the ground!"

The smoke rose not from the chimney, but from the smoldering cinders of the two cabins. Paynter and Cook ran back to their mules, mounted them, and rode toward the ruins as fast as the beasts would carry them.

"Go! Go!" Paynter shouted at his animal, slapping him hard.

Again they heard the distant howl. "Abel's dog," Cook said.

Paynter let his eyes scan the whole scene, but he saw no human. A cow bellowed on a hillside behind what was once the Jones house. Near a shack stood Abel's dog, howling.

The mules suddenly held back as if in fear for their lives.

Paynter leaped from his mule and ran toward the little smokehouse, praying he would find the trapper and his family safe.

All at once, the dog barked, turning Paynter's head.

"Jehovah in heaven!" Cook ran toward the shack where Jones kept his pelts and skins. But before entering, Cook fell to his knees, shook his head violently, and crawled away, vomiting.

Watching Cook vomit made Paynter sick, but then he felt his own body stiffen. Less than ten feet away from Cook lay a headless body. Paynter knew at once that it was not Abel Jones, but his son Luke. Paynter looked around, half expecting to be attacked by natives. He tried not to raise his voice in alarm. Then he went to help Cook to his feet. Together they walked to the shack and opened the door slowly, anticipating the killers' presence. To their surprise, they saw neither friend nor foe.

Nothing made sense to Paynter. In England he had known a man to go insane and kill his family. But Abel Jones seemed to be a rational, even-tempered man.

Cook lowered his voice and turned around twice in astonishment. "The place is empty."

Paynter quickly glanced over his shoulder. "The hides! Somebody stole Abel's hides. Everything!" Although still alert to attack, Paynter rushed to the body. Looking from close range at the corpse, the top of its head taken off, Paynter felt sick again. His body shook in disbelief. He had known Luke, an honest lad.

While Cook followed the dog, Paynter hunted for other bodies and hoped the children and Mrs. Jones had somehow escaped. He could feel his muscles tighten like those of a soldier entering the battlefield.

"Come here, Jeremiah." Cook stood far away from the smokehouse and beside the howling dog, who seemed oblivious to everything except her loss. Cook jerked his head to the right. "'Tis Jones himself."

Paynter saw it too, the body covered in blood. He knelt down, but the body made no sound. He touched the hand. "Cold! Abel has taken his final leave." Already the insects had arrived for the feast. "The children!" Paynter looked around. He saw in the distance the beginning of the forest and prayed he might find Abel's wife and daughters safe among the trees. He called out, "Mrs. Jones! Mrs. Jones! Jeremiah Paynter here!" He waited, hoping to hear the voices of the woman and her daughters.

The only sounds were of a cow bellowing and the dog whimpering as she lay down near her master's corpse.

Cook took a long tree branch and poked around in the hot cinders. "They escaped the flames," he called to Paynter.

"Search the edge of the forest to the north while I look to the west." Paynter saw a small hill ahead and reasoned that if he could climb it, he might gain new perspective on the terrain. Cupping his hands to his mouth, he shouted again and again: "Mrs. Jones! Mrs. Jones!"

Veering around a small well that stood in his path, Paynter kept asking himself, *Have the women been taken captive?* When he reached the top of the hill, he let his eyes scan the whole macabre scene. No human stirred, save Benjamin Cook. The smoke curled remorselessly, crows circled greedily, the dog lay in grief, and the cow still bellowed.

Paynter strolled away toward the trees and, looking back, saw the dog stand up. As if coming to her senses, she then trotted toward the little well. *The poor cur thirsts.* Paynter walked down the hill to draw water. All the time, his eyes darted from east to west, from north to south. The empty feeling in his stomach told him that natives had captured the women.

At his feet, an object flashed in the sun. *A knife.*

He picked it up, turned it over, and observed that it had no stains of fresh blood. Slipping it behind his belt, he heard the dog bark and saw her run around the well. Then she began scratching frantically at the well.

Paynter gripped his musket. Cautiously he made his way toward the well, pointed the barrel of his musket into it, and then paused with bated breath.

Cook came running and stopped only feet away from the well. "You think one of the natives might be down there?"

"We will soon know." Paynter then shouted into the well. "Come out of there!" The two men waited with their muskets cocked.

"Come out!" Cook ordered.

When no one responded, Cook crept warily on his knees to the well and pointed the barrel into it. Still no sound or movement.

Paynter lifted his eyes toward the sun and, seeing that it was overhead, knew that it would cast light deep into the well.

Suddenly, Cook peered down the well and then jerked his head away. "Somebody . . . somebody."

Paynter called in a loud voice, "Come out now!" The rope to the well moved; but no one surfaced; and no voice emerged from below. Paynter gave one more warning call.

When again no response followed, Cook backed away and shook his head as though saying he had had enough for one day.

Paynter stepped back and debated with himself. Then he returned to the well, lowered the barrel of his musket, and peered down.

"What . . . what is it?" Cook demanded.

With a deep frown Paynter looked at him.

"What did you see, Jeremiah?"

"Look for yourself, and tell me what you see."

Cook leaned over the lip of the well. "Jehovah above! A golden-haired . . . . Abel's daughter. Abel's daughter!"

Paynter too could see the long strands of golden hair catching the sun's rays. The child cringed on a ledge ten feet below. "Deborah, child," he whispered. She was looking up at him, and he could see her lips move. Yet no sound came out. "Hold on, child! You remember me, old Jeremiah Paynter? I will come fetch you . . . Benjamin, when I give you the signal, lower me slowly and then back up when I tell you!" Paynter grabbed hold of the rope, tied it firmly around his waist, and slowly descended until he touched the stone ledge.

"Easy!" he called up to Cook. "Another two feet! Stop!" Resting his foot on the ledge, Paynter leaned over, put his arm around little Deborah, and signaled Cook to pull them up. "Do not worry, child. You are safe now with Old Jeremiah. Brave girl!"

Cook's strong arms moved rhythmically, the muscles quivering, his breathing now heavy.

"Pull! Pull!" Paynter commanded and then felt himself and the child being lifted toward the well's rim. He threw his leg over the rim and handed Deborah to Cook.

"You are safe now, little one," said stocky Cook in a voice of tender care.

After untying the rope, Paynter, with his long, gentle fingers, picked webs from the child's hair and talked to her as if she were his own darling daughter Naomi, whom he had lost two years earlier. "Where are your mother and sister, child?"

Deborah seemed consumed by fear. She stared, more blinded than sighted. It was as if by taking her from the well, the two men had extracted her from a comforting womb and delivered her into a world too horrible to be believed. Paynter realized that she had grown numb and that she perhaps neither saw nor heard anything. He wondered if her brain had mercifully closed its doors and shutters to seal her senses from the fire and blood. The two men looked at each other and tried again to coach her to speak, Paynter getting down on both knees.

Still Deborah's eyes spoke terror, and her lips remained mute. Paynter, who had visited the Jones family several times to buy pelts, remembered Deborah's sweet voice when she had sung English ballads with her mother.

Paynter brushed the hair from the child's eyes. "Where have your mother and sister gone? Point if you know."

Though she did not point, her eyes fixed on the forest where Cook had searched.

"Stay close by this little one," Cook said softly. Without waiting for Paynter's reply, he rushed toward the forest.

Paynter held the child's cheek to his raw-boned chest and remembered the day that his precious Naomi died in his arms. He clutched Deborah closer and vowed that if she were now without father or mother, he would raise her as his own.

After half an hour, Cook returned. He nodded; but to save the child from the news, he remained silent. Paynter understood and whispered only, "Where?"

Cook turned to face southwest. "Quarter of a mile or less into the . . . ." He cut his words short and looked with compassion at the child.

"Draw more water for her and the dog to drink," Paynter said, giving little Deborah to Cook's care. Then he headed toward the woodland. When he reached the scene and saw the bodies, he hurried back, wishing he had not left Deborah's side. He kept thinking of a way to tell her that she no longer had a mother, father, brother, or sister. All had been murdered.

When he returned, he saw that Cook had begun digging four graves. Paynter was sure the child understood that the graves were for her family.

Cook took Paynter aside. "You saw them?"

"Aye."

"Do you think the natives did this foul deed?"

From his belt, Paynter pulled the knife he had found on the ground. "I recognize this blade. Not a native's."

"You know its owner?"

Ignoring the question, Paynter's tone grew dark. "Those with hot blood among us will call for war with the natives. Say nothing when you return to Salem. I will explain. Until then, I need time to think. Remember, say nothing."

"If you take the child with you to Salem, I can remain behind to bury the bodies and mark the graves."

"When you arrive in Salem, Benjamin, go straightway to my house; talk to no one; for we hold dangerous torches in our hands."

Six days later, on November 8, near sunset, Roger arrived from the Wampanoags' village and rode his horse quickly toward the cabin on the western side of Plymouth where Mary and their daughter awaited his arrival. To his surprise, he saw from a distance his Salem friend Jeremiah Paynter in the cold, pacing like a caged animal. Roger sensed at once that trouble had come to Paynter's town of Salem.

When their eyes locked and he saw the terror on Paynter's face, he hurried to meet him. Sensing that his freckled friend had a long story to reveal, he quickly dismounted. "Jeremiah, I must first determine the health of my family. Come indoors."

Jeremiah pointed. "I will wait under the large sycamore."

Roger then entered the cabin to embrace Mary and their child. He searched their faces for signs of trouble or sickness. A wondrous feeling came over him when he saw their clear, unblemished skin. Still, he put his palm on Little Mary's forehead and then on his wife's to test for fever.

Mary asked, "Did you not expect to see us until the resurrection?"

"You make every day afresh for me, Mary. Even at night, you are sunrise in my heart." He kissed her repetitively, pausing to look into her luminous eyes. For a moment, he felt that they were two deep blue lakes filled with the mystery and wonder of life. Then he blinked, remembering his promise to Jeremiah Paynter. "I must hurry, love. I suspect trouble boils forty miles north." Taking one lingering look at their healthy daughter, he disappeared out the door, leaving behind a promise to return shortly.

He hurried to the large sycamore tree and listened while Paynter spoke in a torrent of words and reported what had happened to the Jones family. "The whole town burns with the fever of indignation, and they talk of swift justice against the natives. You must return to Salem."

Roger turned northward toward Salem. "If anyone can quell Salem's storm, my minister friend Samuel Skelton will."

Paynter pointed toward Governor Bradford's house in the far distance. His freckled face turned pale. "Our good pastor came with me but is too weak for such a task.

At this moment, he sits in Governor Bradford's parlor and longs to speak with you about the tinderbox we call *Salem*."

Inside Bradford's parlor, the Reverend Skelton, though weak, stood respectfully when Roger entered. Roger sat quietly to listen to him speak in an urgent voice.

"All the people of Salem still carry an empty room in their hearts for you and Mary. I more than anyone miss your godly conscience and cheerful manner. There is also a heavy sorrow among us and wicked talk of wrathful judgment against the natives." The Reverend Skelton paused to catch his breath. Roger winced, thinking that his Cambridge friend's health had slipped more than expected.

Skelton leaned with his hands on the table and sat down. "I . . . I speak for the people of our congregation and for Captain Endecott. They beg your return forthwith both to teach our congregation and . . . and to negotiate with the native tribes. Their sachems have heard of threats made against them."

Roger tried to disguise his alarm. "Who made the threats?"

"Hot-blooded men who seek . . . who seek revenge and call it justice." Skelton shook his head in apology for his weakness and then turned his sad, gray eyes toward Paynter, who picked up the cue.

"Master Williams, I wanted to lock the grisly particulars inside my memory, but Benjamin Cook broke the lock and spread rumors like fire among the people."

Skelton added, "Jeremiah and I quickly agreed to journey here. Return with us, Roger. Bring Mary and your new baby . . . ." Again Skelton turned to Paynter for assistance.

"You speak the natives' language, Brother Williams, and the sachems hold you in high esteem." Paynter paused as if aware that his voice had begun to ring with passion. He cleared his throat and resumed, "As for your livelihood, we have given much thought to it. We know you wish to establish steady commerce between us and the natives, peaceful commerce that will contribute to harmony and respect."

Roger pointed westward. "But what becomes of the trading post and commerce with the Wampanoags?"

"Both Seth and Josiah will do all in their power to help you fulfill that dream," Paynter said. "They will give Massasoit what he has requested. There will be a trading post west of Plymouth. You have our solemn word. If you come to Salem, your dream will double; for we will help you establish a new trading post west of Salem."

"To sweeten this appeal," said Skelton, "our congregation would implore you to come with us as our teaching elder. Yes, yes, we send out the appeal. It is my personal desire too. Become my ally, Roger . . . minister to the people!"

Conflicting feelings swirled inside Roger. He could almost taste the excitement of the trading posts and feel the strong bonds of peace developing between the natives and the English. Yet he knew that powerful forces opposed his vision. With painful reluctance his thoughts taught him what his heart fought against—sometime after arriving in New England, Winthrop and the General Court turned into a version of Archbishop Laud. Were the people of Salem truly prepared to oppose the Massachusetts General Court?

Other thoughts he could not ignore rushed through his mind, thoughts that Mary would say he could not in good faith hide in a drawer. Would Paynter simply use him to quell fierce passions and then forget the war with the Massachusetts Court, which might unwittingly set itself up as an infant Protestant inquisition? He shivered upon realizing that in less than a decade the infant could grow into a monster.

He had not come to this new land to lie supinely and watch his dream pass like drifting clouds never touching earth. He would not betray the dream of soul liberty. He would not let Winthrop or the General Court blow their frosty breath on his passion for soul liberty and virtue!

As his eyes fell on his friend Samuel Skelton, compassion flowed through him. A deathly feeling of coldness followed. Was he looking not at the man he had once known in all of life's vigor, but at a frail mortal melting too quickly under death's foul breath?

"I know your thoughts, Roger." Skelton's gray eyes reflected the struggle against mortality. "You ask yourself, 'Will the Massachusetts magistrates strike like lightning if I return to Salem?'"

Governor Bradford interrupted. "Permit me a word. I know how fond the people of Salem have grown toward you, Roger. You, nevertheless, must act wisely, for Winthrop does not bear his grudges lightly. His friendship with you grows warmer the wider the space that separates you. If you go back to serve as clergyman in any Massachusetts congregation, he and the General Court will lose face. Do you doubt they will take stern, irrevocable action against you?"

"Do you doubt that the General Court has plans to gobble up Plymouth Colony?" Roger asked. "Do you intend to sit passively while it happens?"

Rather than answer the question, Bradford lowered his voice and leaned forward. "I have recently learned that some on the court talk openly of shipping you back to Laud's England. Remember the fate of Michael Servetus."

Before coming to New England, Roger had heard from sources in Switzerland of John Calvin's treachery toward Servetus. Under the assumed name of William Laye, the Protestant Calvin had written to the Catholic Inquisitor in Lyon, informing him that Servetus had entered his town. The Inquisitor quickly cast Servetus into prison. When the prisoner escaped to Geneva to throw himself on the mercy of Calvin, with whom Servetus hoped to discuss theology, Calvin arrested him and allowed the Geneva magistrates to burn him at the stake because of his beliefs. "In matters of treachery and the murder of dissidents," Roger had often told Mary, "Protestants have swum in the moral sinkhole with papal inquisitors."

He stood at the bank of the Rubicon. Unlike Caesar, who rode across the river to make bloody civil war, he felt that his crossing, as irrevocable as Caesar's, set his face toward liberty and righteousness. He would not initiate war on the magistrates, but neither would he play the puppet on their stage.

Paynter spoke up. "We of Salem have a plan to entice you back to our fold. If you accompany us to Salem and become *unofficial* assistant to the Reverend Skelton, perhaps Winthrop and the court will take no offense."

"Providence," Roger mused aloud, "works sometimes too wondrous for the human eye." Silently, he thought that like Joseph of old, who in Egypt's servitude followed unknowingly the path of Providence, he in servitude among the Wampanoags had perhaps followed Providence unknowingly. The trading post promised to join the hands of the natives with the hands of the colonists.

"I cannot forsake my trading post in this colony. If I leave, will the Wampanoags not perceive me as a frivolous butterfly flitting from blossom to blossom?"

"To the contrary," Skelton said. "Has not Providence made you a mighty tree?"

"Aye, 'tis true," Paynter joined in. "A tree whose roots spread wide from colony to colony! Who knows, Brother Roger, how many pilgrims seeking peace and virtue may take shade under your flourishing branches."

"'And he shall be like a tree planted by the rivers of water, that brings forth fruit in his season; his leaf shall not wither; and whatever he does shall prosper,'" Skelton quoted with a warm smile.

Paynter seemed suddenly to be a new man filled with boldness. "Brother Roger, permit me to reveal the particulars. The Salem men who traveled with me to your trading post west of Plymouth are earnest about building a trading post for Salem. If you should parent both posts, you could raise them as you see fit. Only allow us as men of commerce to be close uncles and partners in mutual profit for both the natives and ourselves."

Roger held out his two hands and looked at them as though weighing his thoughts on scales. He knew no one could make this weighty decision for him. He remembered the disappointment Mary suffered in leaving her friends in Salem. Closing his eyes, he tried in vain to peer into the future.

Interpreting the silence as hesitation, Paynter urgently clamped his long, bony hand around Roger's arm and looked at him with imploring eyes. "I cannot pretend to discern heaven's secret purpose for you, Brother Roger; but the English and the natives agree that you are no ordinary man. These are fearful times in Salem. To speak bluntly, we ask you to join us immediately, for we desperately need a peacemaker. Did not our Lord on the mountain say, 'Blessed are the peacemakers'?"

Roger hesitated. "Salem's Captain Endecott speaks the language of the natives in your colony."

"'Tis true." Paynter stepped closer and lowered his voice almost to a whisper. "But sometimes the captain does not speak the language of humanity. When someone touches his pride, he puffs up too quickly and turns his tongue into a serpent's tooth. This we do not need when we go to the natives."

The Reverend Skelton joined in, giving Roger no opportunity to answer Paynter. "The Salem congregation sorely needs a Cambridge-bred teacher versed in sacred Scripture." Unexpectedly Skelton rose to his feet again and stepped toward Roger. As if to counter the slight unsteadiness in his stride, he touched the wall and quickly raised his chin. "Be so kind, Roger, as to speak with me outside."

Though nodding their consent, the other men seemed puzzled.

Outside, Skelton said, "Salem's congregation is a ship always amid a tempest. I fear the shadow of Winthrop across our people, a cold and chilling shadow; and I have caught its draft."

Roger felt apprehension weaken his knees. He placed his hand on Skelton's shoulder. "What do you mean, my good and constant friend? Do not walk around the subject. Tell me plainly, how fares your health?"

Skelton shook his head. "Adam's curse claims us all, like Shylock's pound. Still I think each day some new part of me journeys to heaven and, finding it a place of supreme delight, does not return to its mortal home of flesh and bones."

At sunrise the next day, November 9, Roger and Jeremiah Paynter headed for the Wampanoag village west of Plymouth. On the way, Roger kept thinking that with their knowledge of native and English languages and customs, Keplutok and Titus could manage the Plymouth and Wampanoag trading post if they chose. *Keplutok has learned rapidly from his mistakes in dealing with the dishonest among Plymouth colonists.*

Upon arriving at the village, Roger and Paynter met with Massasoit and his advisors. The sachem wasted no time before informing them of the toll the pestilence had taken on the tribe. Although many more had survived than expected, one in ten had died.

Facing Keplutok, who now sat firmly among the permanent advisors, Roger hesitated, fearing the worst. Keplutok did not wait for the question, but said, "My son Swift Deer lives to run as his name foretells."

Warmth spread throughout Roger's body; but then he waited; and Keplutok said, "The oldest . . . . She died."

Speechless, Roger fought back tears and shook his head. With his eyes, he asked about the youngest, and Keplutok answered, "She sings and jumps at her mother's side."

Roger and Paynter relished a night around the fire, the dread pestilence having evidently passed. Massasoit did not restrain his gratitude, for he credited Roger's counsel for helping to save many Wampanoags from the disease.

After listening to Titus translate the tales of the tribe's ancient ones, Roger and Paynter each crawled sleepily into their own prepared wigwams and quickly fell off to sleep while the November wind moaned.

The next morning, Roger and Paynter spoke first with Massasoit to show honor and regard for native custom. Then, with Massasoit's blessing, they spoke in depth with Keplutok and Titus, who weighed each portion of their proposal. Roger smiled secretly at Keplutok's manner of anticipating Paynter's thoughts.

When at last they agreed on the particulars, they brought word to Massasoit, who grinned and announced at once a feast to celebrate their new venture and good fortune. Titus and Keplutok, never before so honored by their people, walked with a new air of charming majesty.

When the sun was high overhead, Keplutok and Swift Deer strolled with Roger a half mile into the forest. They talked of many matters, and the two men shared the pleasure of watching Swift Deer climb trees. Keplutok laughed. "I should have named him Jumping Squirrel." Keplutok then grew quite serious. "Your parents should have named you True Friendship. Henceforth when I hear the name Roger Williams, it will mean True Friendship. Twice you have saved my son's life. Always you have a home among my people."

"And, my most excellent tutor, you have twice saved my life." He remembered not only the day he almost drowned in the flood, but also the first winter he spent among the Wampanoags. "Without your patience and your good wife's sisterly care, Mary and I might have perished during those bitterly cold days." Roger handed Keplutok the chest of writing paper he had wanted.

When Keplutok opened the chest, both men broke out in laughter. Roger had donated a self-portrait he had sketched with a quill.

"With your tongue, Roger, you paint beautiful pictures, but with your quill . . . ." They broke out again in laughter and then parted.

Early the next morning, Roger waved goodbye to Jeremiah, who boarded ship for Salem. Pastor Skelton had sailed two days earlier.

Standing on the shore, Mary spoke to her little one about their forthcoming life among dear Salem friends. "Within three days, these little eyes will see a new home called Salem."

BOSTON

November 1633

"Good morrow, Captain Firebrook."

"And good morrow to you, Barnabas."

"Here now, permit me to help you with that."

Together we lifted my trunk to the table. Though I had in mind to read my copy of the manuscript on predestination, Barnabas lingered.

"I sense a turbulent thought squirming in your mind, Barnabas. Let it out."

As we walked outside and in a direction away from his beehives, he asked if I knew a man named Joshua Winsor.

"Aye, Governor Winthrop's servant. Why do you ask?"

"He has scruples about disclosing Winthrop's conversation he has overheard. I have learned to ask for no morsels of information from his tight lips."

"Your point, Barnabas?"

"Tight Lips Joshua made one exception. He overheard Winthrop the older tell his recent dream to John Jr., who strongly disapproved of it. Or so says Tight Lips, whose veracity I rank higher than most mortals I have known. Three nights ago our governor had a dream whose meaning lies on the surface and needs no Joseph or Daniel to discern it. In his dream, the governor saw his wife dressed as a most gracious queen. She sat in her chamber where her children gathered round her. The children wore a most sweet and smiling countenance, and upon their heads sat crowns. Later in the day the governor disclosed his dream to his son, who asked for its interpretation, which he received without hesitation: 'God will crown my offspring as fellow heirs with Christ in God's kingdom.'"

"Is this kingdom to be above the stars?" I asked.

"Here on the Earth, Captain." Barnabas bent down and rubbed the ground with his palm. "Here on this land. Thy kingdom come upon holy Massachusetts. Hail Winthrop the First! But second to Christ, you understand. Winthrop, a most gracious Caesar, would permit Christ to share his dynasty."

"Do you think the governor has set his heart on a dynasty?" I asked, my tone mildly rebuking.

"Heart and soul, this Christian Faust. Faith, hope, and ambition: these three. But the greatest of these for Caesar Winthrop is ambition."

"Barnabas, permit me to caution you to repeat this to no one else."

The sudden storm from Nova Scotia had driven Roger's ship back to Plymouth scarcely before it had left harbor. While waiting inside Pastor Smith's house, he read a letter from Governor Winthrop. Although he felt abiding affection for the governor for attempting in the letter to restore their friendship, deep disappointment resulted. He handed the letter to Mary. "Read this and show me how not to interpret it as a threat to our native friends."

After reading it, she talked privately with him in a corner. "The governor writes two letters in one. With the first, he offers the olive branch, with the other, the bramble bush. He calls you his conscience and then does not heed it. I think he is a man who wishes his own conscience to follow his ambition."

"When he speaks in this letter of Christ's kingdom, I confess I smell fumes from Constantine's cauldron."

"More than once, my father said that Constantine brewed the devil's elixir of mingled politics and religion."

"Aye, Constantine crucified Christ afresh by transmuting the Apostle's heirs into Machiavelli's princes. Christ established no earthly capital, no Constantinople, no Christopolis."

She grinned.

"And no Winthropolis. Tell me, Mary, how you read the governor's comments on Providence and the natives."

"It seems ambiguous. Yet it is a lawyer's calculated ambiguity, a knife cloaked in purple velvet."

He held the letter again and stared at it. "If I hold it like a mirror to my soul, I see a dangerous ambivalence!" He felt deeply troubled. *The tiny teeth of intended ambiguity slowly gnawed with a purpose!*

The time had come for him to write his formal letter to King Charles. He had intended to write it in Salem. He spread out his notes on a small writing table in Pastor Smith's house, where he, Mary, and his daughter were still staying as they waited out the storm. Roger had composed the letter to King Charles repeatedly in his mind, often discussing with Mary both its content and perils. From Sir Edward Coke, he had learned that letters could serve as a hangman's noose. He understood precisely the risks and implications of his actions. The plan he intended to implement glistened with uncompromising clarity.

Before writing the letter, however, he knelt beside his precious daughter and kissed her forehead. For a long time, he studied her face and ran his finger gently down her forearm. Then he picked her up, held her in his arms, and rocked her.

Mary's eyes took on a teasing look. "Dear, I know of your excellence in learning languages, but this new language of cooing . . . ."

He glanced over his shoulder. "Little Mary understands." He placed her into her crib and let his thoughts shoot like stars into the future. Like Mary, he longed for their daughter to live in a country that prized soul liberty and not groveling before tyrants.

As he dipped his quill into the ink, he again felt deep disappointment in Governor Winthrop. Why would he pretend that the natives had no moral and legal existence?

He resolved to state plainly in his letter to King Charles that the charters given to the English governors and their assistants made not one reference to the natives. The ink now flowed, Roger asking King Charles how he or his father could have bestowed the colonists with land that never belonged to the crown. He accused the king of *unjust usurpation upon others' possessions.* Roger argued that if a Chinese lord should declare all England to be *common ground,* the English would find his words fantastical. He concluded that though the king's charters conformed to English law, they disobeyed the moral law. "If we English pay the natives for their land, justice requires us to pay them with more than the pox."

After copying the letter five times, he delivered one to Governor Bradford. He would send Winthrop the second copy along with a conciliatory letter requesting the governor's response and counsel. The third he would deliver to Captain Endecott in Salem.

When I received the fourth copy, I sat down in my room in the Blackstone house, knowing not what to think. My thoughts spewed off in all directions, settling on none. "What madness!" I said aloud. Would Roger with deliberation and forethought send such an emboldened letter to the king of England? Such reckless abandon! You leave the king no choice.

In their note to me, Roger and Mary had said they would soon return to live in Salem. I resolved to set sail for Salem before sundown to warn him of Winthrop's wrath. I had no doubt that the governor, who viewed Roger as a tamed wolf gone wild again, would take stern measures unless Roger refrained from sending the letter to the king.

Roger knew that the royal charter granted staggering powers to the handful of men who comprised the Massachusetts Bay Company. The Massachusetts General Court possessed the authority to make, interpret, and enforce laws for the whole colony. Few governors in Europe could boast of the sweeping power that Winthrop was legally entitled to wield. I trembled for Roger, for I understood that Winthrop and his men held firmly in hand the legal right to place him in stocks or to imprison him.

A darker thought blew in on me. Had not even John Cotton, the honored vicar of England's largest parish church, found it necessary to flee Laud's men under cover of darkness? Would Winthrop's men soon bind Roger hand and foot and ship him back to the archbishop's henchmen?

I folded the letter, tucked it safely on my person, and threw open the window to my room. "Barnabas, the carriage! The carriage!"

As Barnabas and I rode off to the home of John Winthrop Jr., I mentally rehearsed everything I must say. When the carriage stopped at young Winthrop's house, I leaped out and pounded on the door. The servant obeyed my request and returned speedily with young Winthrop.

"We must speak! Please forgive my abruptness. I plead urgency."

"Enter, Eric. Give me your coat and hat."

"'Tis better we converse privately under the trees. They have limbs but not ears," I said, and then turned to ask Barnabas to wait.

Winthrop Jr. guided me to an elm. "If it is about Roger's letter, I have read it. He sent me a copy."

"Then you perhaps can guess my purpose."

"To put out the fire. But how?"

"Come with me to Salem. We must quench the flame."

"A flame rages already here in Boston. My father—"

"Can you not reason with him?"

"Reason? Do you not comprehend? The letter to the king hangs like Damocles' sword over the Boston magistrates' collective neck. 'Twas a deed of madness."

All at once, I understood what had eluded me. It was not madness, but a well-conceived strategy. "The letter is Roger's veiled warning to the Boston magistrates. It does not spring from a reckless impulse, but from a daring shrewdness worthy of Queen Elizabeth herself."

"Eric, I beseech you to speak sternly to Roger. Tell him plainly that the magistrates will not abide his threat."

"The shoe is on the wrong foot," I replied. "The magistrates must not miscalculate, for no uncalculated impulse drove him to compose the letter to King Charles. With cool forethought, he has forged his own weapon and challenged the magistrates to meet him on the battlefield. By sending the epistle not to the king, but first to them, the fox turns on the hounds."

Winthrop Jr. frowned with a puzzled countenance. "My father rails against Roger, calling him a gambler who takes great risk."

"Are the magistrates blind? Yes, he plays high stakes; but he forces the magistrates to place equal money on the table. If the magistrates think to silence his defense of the natives' rights to their own land by cutting out his tongue, then that tongue will resurrect in England and resound throughout the king's court."

"Surely the king will find the letter so offensive that he will—"

"The magistrates would be fools to presume to predict Charles's response. Even if the king should cast Roger's tongue into the flame, he will use his fingers to write more treatises, each a thousand tongues throughout England and New England."

"Eric, even now you do not understand the danger. I beg you to look at this from the magistrates' perspective. If the letter goes to King Charles, there can be no turning back. Roger threatens their whole mission." John pressed his fists against his temples and shook his head. "Oh, Roger, step back from this cliff's edge! Go to him, Eric. Persuade our friend of the enormous risk he takes."

"Do you seriously imagine that we could make an argument that he has not made already to himself? It is the magistrates who fail to consider the danger. They have met their equal in this flaming tongue called Roger Williams. The stew he now boils is their own concoction."

John Winthrop Jr. looked straight into my eyes. "Tell me, what interest have you in this; and have you any part in—"

"Listen to me, John. My interest is yours. Let *the magistrates* now probe the highways and alleys of the king's mind to discover what action His Highness will take toward *them and their charter* if Roger should forward the letter."

Though the wind was cold, I saw sweat form above John's lip. He said softly, "Sometimes I wonder if one part of my father views Roger as the most farsighted of us all."

Though I made no answer, I too sometimes suspected that Roger's thoughts about the natives often haunted the governor and pricked his conscience. I remembered Roger speaking fervently of his Wampanoag and Narraganset friends and what they had taught him. To my knowledge, no Christian harbored more passion for the conversion of the natives, but he had harpooned the plan to convert the natives by force and manipulation. He had labeled it a *monstrous and inhuman conversion*, comparing it to forcing an unwilling spouse to bed. I filtered my thoughts and said, "Mary Williams thinks a second voice named Roger echoes in your father's conscience."

John fell silent and then cleared his throat. "I will speak with my father. I pray my words will quench his hot anger, not feed it."

We parted, and I suddenly recalled a scene on the Black Sea when I was twenty-one. Two mighty ships had collided in the fog, bringing ghastly havoc to passengers and crew alike.

Barnabas drove the carriage to my side. As I climbed in, he said nothing. He had not overheard our conversation, but he saw the gloom of my countenance. As we arrived at Blackstone's house, he asked, "Captain, do you see the sun trying to peek out between the black clouds?"

Although I saw the sun's rays filtering down, I had thoughts thicker than dark clouds. "Barnabas, when you first learned that the Reverend Williams had chosen to live among the natives, what did you think?"

"Why, nothing. I breathed relief, hoping the good Elijah had found asylum from those sons of Ahab."

When I frowned at the word *Ahab*, Barnabas explained, "I mean those who called themselves God's anointed magistrates. Ah, enough of my opinion! I would learn your opinion of Reverend Williams's life with the natives."

"I confess I believe our friend could live happily and permanently with the natives in this vast temple of New England wilderness."

"What? And never again live among us to raise his voice against injustice?" Barnabas's tone disarmed me.

I tried to explain to him that if Roger had found contentment living among the natives, it would have been more than enough accomplishment for ten men. For that alone, I would have erected a bronze statue in his honor. Who among us could write about the native customs without condescension? "I have misjudged the man's iron, Barnabas. He is twice the man I had thought, a heartwarming and gentle man, yet a blacksmith's anvil!"

Suddenly I felt trepidation, picturing Governor Winthrop's massive sledgehammer crashing against the anvil. "Barnabas, I must set sail on the next ship for Salem! I will pack."

"Permit me to offer a warning, Captain. You once befriended me when my quarters were the stocks themselves. Beware lest you exchange parts in this drama. Like wolves that have tasted blood, the magistrates will stalk until they have their lamb. If the Reverend Williams escapes their claws, they will hunt you for compensation."

BOSTON, PLYMOUTH, AND SALEM

November 1633

Jeremiah Paynter and the Reverend Skelton stepped off the ship and brought the good news to the Salem congregation. Roger Williams would return as assistant to the minister. With the hope of appeasing Winthrop and the magistrates, the church leaders made the position unofficial.

All Salem fermented with growing division among the people regarding the murder of Abel Jones and his family. Before Jeremiah and Skelton had sailed from Salem to Plymouth, Benjamin Cook began painting a graphic, detailed picture of the slaughter of the trapper and his family. He wasted no time in spreading his speculation from one end of town to the other that savages had caused the mayhem. One portion of the town embraced this opinion and would not rest content until they had imprisoned two natives. Like Mark Antony on stage, Captain Endecott raised both hands over the crowd and delivered a stirring speech: "It is time to teach the Indians a firm lesson. I say execute the two captives as an example of our swift judgment. Better that two savages die than the whole Indian village. I say this will be our act of mercy, for it will forestall further savagery and the retaliation to follow."

Before the Nova Scotia storm had hit New England's coast, Jeremiah Paynter and the Reverend Skelton had returned from Plymouth to Salem with the news that Roger and Mary would soon arrive. Immediately, each disputing side in town began to claim that the Reverend Williams would support its position in the controversy. As soon as Endecott had concluded his inflamed speech at the town meeting, another townsman stood to speak. "When the Reverend Williams arrives, he will walk arm in arm with our Captain Endecott in this matter. Did not the honest reverend relentlessly pursue the wife-murderer until the Plymouth authorities brought him to justice?"

The Salem colonists on the other side contended fervently that Roger would join them. Seeing a catastrophe building like a thundercloud over Salem, Jeremiah wasted no time in rushing from house to house to remind the people of their new teacher's friendship with the native tribes. Although not a man to make public speeches, he cried out, "Truth, like fish, does not always swim on the surface. Let us learn from the whalers who move with patience, not reckless abandon. No man or woman among you longs for justice more than I. Did I not see the victims' ashes with these eyes? Did I not go to the well myself to fetch the frightened child? If any among you desires justice more than I, let him stand beside me now."

In taking up this role of town mediator, Jeremiah felt himself to be a clanging understudy on stage, moving awkwardly in King Arthur's bulky armor, making gangly gestures and speaking in a voice not fitting his manner. Still he went about his mediation with the hope of staving off disaster until their new teacher arrived. Fearing that those who cried out for swift execution would turn into a mindless herd, he mopped his brow and comforted himself with the thought that Roger would arrive soon.

En route from Plymouth to Salem, the ship that Roger and Mary had boarded anchored near Boston Harbor and waited for new passengers.

"Eric!" both Mary and Roger exclaimed when they saw me step aboard their ship.

Despite the excitement and relief I felt in seeing them again, I cut our greetings short, their frisky child having caught my attention. Holding the little one in my arms and looking into her smooth, sweet face, I thought I saw another Mary. "Providence has blessed you twice," I said to Roger.

He put one arm around his wife and held her close to him.

Has heaven made anything more beautiful than the female face? I asked myself, remembering a journey that Abba and I had taken among the Arabs, who veiled the faces of their women. When I asked why, Abba quickly snatched me aside and answered, "Since some Arab men cannot veil their own passions, they veil their women."

Little Mary's foot moved, knocking the cover away. Roger laughed with almost boyish glee. "Look at her, Eric. Kicks like a little colt." He took the child and rocked her in his arms. "Eric, I hope you have come to say that you will journey with us to Salem."

"Aye. Behold my belongings—or a portion of them. But I burn with urgent news. The letters you sent me . . . . Hot coals swallowed would have been milder. We must talk. Not here though."

Mary quickly guided us to a solitary place on the ship. I lowered my voice. "Have you sent the letter to the king?"

"No," Mary answered. "He promised to wait."

I felt wondrous relief. "Roger, I think I know your strategy. You are like a ship captain I once knew who through heroic efforts bluffed his way against a pirate ship's threats."

"'Tis no bluff," Roger assured me.

"A man who makes a bluff does not glue the label *Bluff* on it," I pointed out. He did not take the bait, which forced me to ask, "Will you give attention while I paint a different picture?"

As our ship moved northward toward Salem, I explained, "Roger, your presumption may be false."

"What presumption?"

"That you play with *rational* men in this game of chance and risk."

His brow furrowed. Knowing I had stung him, I said nothing, choosing instead to let the poison of my sting take its course.

"Suppose they are not rational men," Mary said to her husband.

"At least not rational on this matter," I added.

Sensing that he had already given thought to our objection, I intended to shift my tactic; but he said, "Ask not *who* among us stands as the most rational, but which *position* enjoys greater consistency and practicality." He drew a circle in the air with his finger. "The Boston circle brings us all back to Bishop Laud's port with the bishop gone and Winthrop as the Puritan bishop under another title."

"Roger, I know you have made many friends in Salem. But like a wise captain, do not sail into battle until you have sufficient powder to finish the attack. I have talked with John Jr., who informs me of his father's hot anger."

"The danger in the governor lies not in his hot anger, but in his cold calculation," Mary said and casually ran her finger across Roger's hairline to brush back the little curl falling over his forehead. Her wondrous eyes glistened with a special mystery, warning that her words carried more than one meaning.

He cocked a half-moon eyebrow and then closed one eye as if to gaze across the Atlantic to the king's court. "I sent the warm letter first to the magistrates to give them opportunity to ponder their action. Let the letter hiss a while at their feet. A rattler who warns before striking will strike less often."

"Some have called you a serpent," I said.

Making no reply, Roger turned to the more practical question of how he might accomplish his purpose. As I stood beside him, I felt like one who suddenly discovers himself beside a general surveying the battlefield. Although this general carried no sword and commanded no cannons, I felt the power of his words. Before we dropped the subject, I heard him say almost casually, "When ship captains sail one thousand leagues, do they count each wave that crashes against the bow?"

As our ship rounded Marblehead Neck and sailed into Salem's bay, Roger saw the crowd waving and heard their joyous music waft across the water. The white gulls swooped down to have their noisy say. The ship's captain swelled his chest as if he knew he brought new hope to the crowd of Salem townspeople. They had gathered near the dock in excited anticipation of Roger and Mary's arrival.

Using his elbows to clear a path through the crowd, Endecott rushed up the plank as soon as the ship dropped anchor. He grabbed Roger's hand and pumped it while flooding him with praise and welcome.

Roger saw men edge each other aside in the race to come aboard. He felt overwhelmed at the crowd's spontaneous joy. Warm delight spread inside him at the sight of people he had taught two years earlier.

Evidently trying to give the impression that his influence had induced Roger to Salem, Endecott kept taking him by the arm and waving at the people as if it was their mutual, triumphal entry. Endecott twice whispered into Roger's ear, "I must speak to you alone."

When the crowd wedged in, easing Endecott aside, Roger turned and said, "Eric, is Salem two currents of opinion?"

"I will play the scout."

Mary and their lively daughter went with Mrs. Endecott to the home of Jeremiah and Grace Paynter to see the child Deborah Jones, whom the Paynters had taken as their own. Roger remained at the meetinghouse to receive greetings.

Two hours later, Jeremiah whispered, "Miantonomo awaits you in the woodland two miles west, Roger."

He had now grasped that the town was severely divided regarding the two natives accused of murdering the Jones family.

He joined me behind Jeremiah's house, and the three of us rode west together as Roger probed Jeremiah for recent details. When we arrived at the place where Miantonomo awaited, Roger said to him, "We meet as friends again, but this time under a thick cloud."

"The Algonquins' chief sachem has appointed me to speak on his behalf," Miantonomo said. Though conspicuously glad to see his friend Roger, he spoke in a momentous voice.

Roger arched an eyebrow. "I have heard of the Algonquin sachem's wisdom and restraint. So why would he need a Narraganset from the south to represent him?"

"We are all Algonquins. He is my wife's brother. I came to see him because he is ill. Word of your trustworthiness came to him, and he wished me to lay his main concern before you. Your Captain Endecott cries for the blood of our two brothers who are in captivity."

Roger nodded to Jeremiah, who said, "Tonight, long after the town snuffs its last candle, we could go to the jail. The guards are my friends."

Later, as twilight yielded to darkness, Roger said, "Miantonomo, we will take you to your brothers, and you and I must talk with them. But first let us sleep a while."

Long after sunset, the two prisoners acknowledged to Roger and Miantonomo that they had traded with Abel. After they had answered Roger's questions, he realized that they had been at Abel's not on the day of the murders, but two days earlier. Roger reflected. Did not some townspeople, after buying pelts from the two natives, claim the pelts as evidence that the natives had murdered Abel Jones and his family?

Early the next morning, Mary and Roger carried two bowls of hot mutton stew to the prisoners. Roger had agreed that Miantonomo should camp outside in the woodland lest some Salem zealot see him and try to arrest him.

While the prisoners ate, the tall one looked up at Mary from his position on the floor, said nothing to her, but spoke to the other prisoner in his native language.

Although she could not translate perfectly, she evidently gleaned that the taller man had mentioned the blue silk scarf she had given to Little Snowfeather. With her husband's help, she inquired about the native child and described her memory of watching the mother braid the girl's hair as a reward for good behavior.

Mary seemed stunned by the taller native's response: "Little Snowfeather is my daughter."

Roger thought the native saw a crestfallen look on Mary's face. Knowing that she suffered anguish, he took his wife's hand, squeezed it, and then looked at Little Snowfeather's father. *My mind and heart,* Roger vowed secretly, *will know no ease until the truth about the murdered Jones family is unearthed.* Like a chilling frost, the image of that baleful day at the home of Abel Jones and his wife settled over his mind.

At noon Captain Endecott took his position at the head of the meetinghouse table. Looking up from the table, Roger thought that Endecott felt the full weight of the status he carried among the Massachusetts magistrates. A congregation of the elders and town authorities sat on hard, backless benches before Endecott.

Endecott began in a low, growling voice. "The time has come to bring the terrible sword of divine justice upon these pagans who have sorely violated heaven's order and offended our consciences with deeds so foul that ink could not describe them in a hundred pages. If I had my way, I would quarter these pagans before the whole town and display their parts to their tribe as a warning."

Pastor Skelton stood up and clutched the table to give him equilibrium. "Touch your face. Is it not frail flesh? Your ears, do they not hear imperfectly? Who among us has eyes that see into the hearts of others?" Pastor Skelton began coughing. Though his eyes watered, he stood erect. "Only heaven knows all things at once. The Apostle Paul admonishes patience, not strife."

His voice trembling, Jeremiah urged the men to heed their pastor. As soon as Skelton had finished speaking, other elders entreated their esteemed teacher to address them. Roger waited for Endecott, who had assumed the leadership role; but when Endecott appeared to have deliberately ignored the elders' request, Roger stood up, gently placed his hand on Endecott's shoulder, and addressed those assembled in the meetinghouse. "We never pose more danger to ourselves and to others than when we run hot with righteousness. Good brothers and sisters, let us put our vengeance on a leash lest it turn upon us. If our craving for justice runs so wild that no doubts can restrain it, the innocent with the guilty will fall prey to its cruel claws."

The elders and authorities debated solemnly and relentlessly, neither side yielding ground to the other.

Lanky Jeremiah abruptly rose to his feet. "'Tis a shoddy piece of work if we cannot whittle out a better conclusion than this! I say we best find other material to whack and chop."

Endecott's jowls shook. "Let the trial begin at once!"

Sitting at the table, Pastor Skelton begged the men to send the prisoners to Boston until they could more confidently agree among themselves upon the evidence.

Refusing to relent, Endecott's people gave voice to their leader's insistence that no time be lost in teaching the natives the Christian way of justice.

Jeremiah succeeded, nevertheless, in persuading the people to adjourn in the hope they would mingle thought with their hot passion.

Sensing that they must move quickly to discover the truth about the murders, Roger and Jeremiah left together. "The knife you found near Abel Jones's well—have you brought it?" Roger asked.

Jeremiah patted his hip. "I have."

When they arrived at the dock, eight or nine fishermen greeted them. They all sat on barrel tops to talk. Jeremiah pulled out the knife and handed it to Ezra Welch, who turned pale and quickly gave it to Ned, a jovial fisherman

Ned turned to another fisherman. "Thomas, is this not your blade?"

A harpooner who wore a patch over his blind eye, Thomas Rice pulled out his own knife and flashed it. "Would that it were mine. This old blade here is no sharper than my wit."

Turning up the collar of his coat, Roger dismissed the disturbing image of Little Snowfeather's father struggling to shake the rope from his neck.

Jeremiah asked each man if the knife belonged to him, but no one claimed it.

Thomas Rice pulled his coat tight around his neck, cocked his head to the side, and stared at Jeremiah with the eye not covered by the patch. "You and the Reverend have reason for these questions, Jeremiah?"

"Aye, one solid reason. Find the man who owns this blade, and you will find the man who must own up to murder."

The fishermen looked at one another in astonishment as if to ask, *Could it be one of us?*

Roger and Jeremiah Paynter continued to make inquiry throughout the day, stopping men going to and fro in the town. Unfortunately like a ship marooned with no favorable wind, they made little progress.

At twilight, Roger said, "Eric, I am glad you have returned. I have been waiting for you."

"I bring no hard news. Only rumors unworthy of your time."

Mary came into the meetinghouse and spoke privately to her husband and me. "Endecott spreads more animosity toward the natives. Perhaps it would be wise to send to Boston for help lest this strong wind turn into a violent storm. What think you, Captain?"

"A plan well worth considering. The magistrates themselves, however, are not of one mind regarding the natives."

Mary then asked red-haired Jeremiah, "On this matter, is Endecott in Winthrop's pocket?"

"I know only that Endecott dislikes Winthrop. On this matter, I believe he is more with Winthrop than with Brother Roger."

Roger raised his voice. "Wait, Eric, where go you? Leaving us?"

"I will return later at Jeremiah's house. For now I have more listening to do."

Scarcely had Roger, Mary, and Jeremiah arrived at Jeremiah's home when a woman appeared, saying she would speak to none but the Williams couple. When the three entered a small room, the woman closed the door. "I am Ezra Welch's wife, Pearl. He . . . every night . . . . He wakes and walks through the house with an unlit candle in his hand, muttering unspeakable visions. Oh, Reverend, he speaks so highly of you. I beg you, come to our house tonight. Witness this unnatural happening."

"When did it first come upon him?" Roger asked.

"Only of late. His eyes open to see what I see not. Hearing what I hear not, he also babbles, 'Murder, murder.'"

Roger softened his voice and leaned forward in a calming gesture. "Mary and I will sit at your side tonight."

"Oh, Reverend, I pray; but my prayers rise not through the ceiling. If only his madness would prove temporary."

In the dark hours of the early morning, Roger and Mary left their daughter in the care of Grace Paynter and departed for Ezra's house. A sliver of moon hung ominously in the November sky. Roger looked up. "The shape of horns."

"Or of a baby's crib." She shivered with the icy wind. "I like not this night, so clear, yet heavy with troublesome clouds in my thoughts. I fear we shall—"

"The house ahead." He pointed to the silhouette of a two-story board house that the carpenter Ezra had completed only two months earlier.

"It has a monster's appearance," Mary whispered. Then she added as if to scold herself, "Mere superstition in silhouette." When they reached the front of the house, she lit the candle according to Pearl's instructions.

The door opened, and Pearl motioned for them to enter quietly. "Ezra sleeps, but he always begins at this hour."

The wind shook the barren trees, and an owl hooted. Roger and Mary sat down quietly on a wooden bench in the parlor. *The sun will rise in two hours*, he estimated.

Suddenly a door upstairs opened. A shadowy image appeared at the top of the stairs. Pearl blew out the candle. Through a window, the moonlight revealed the presence of a man walking slowly down the stairs. In his hand, he held an unlit candle. No words left his lips. Having descended the stairs, he stood facing the observers. The moonlight through the window flashed in his eyes, and Roger thought they looked momentarily like the eyes of a wolf in the forest. Ezra held the candle out before him and walked back up the stairs.

"He said nothing," Mary whispered.

Pearl placed her finger on her lips. "Shh . . . he will return. Behold!"

This time as Ezra walked slowly down the steps, he stopped midway and called out, "Murder! Savage murder!" He turned around and knelt on the steps. "Your blood cries out! Could not the grave contain you? Murder! Savage murder!"

Roger scooted to the edge of the bench and watched Ezra stand and turn around to address the incorporeal vision.

"The grave opens. Ah, unnatural face, bloodless, pale. Oh, Witch of Endor, conjure not again this horror. Bring Samuel or Lazarus, but not this bloodstained Abel. Away! Away! I smell innocent blood. No! No, Abel, I cannot! Who can hide this mountain of wickedness? Revenge? No, Abel, not your avenger. Appeal not to our friendship. Can you not lie in peace in your grave? Fire, fire, consume this unholy scene, consume this misery, consume that day! Let it ne'er return. I heed you not. Go . . . go and return no more!"

Mary whispered into Pearl's ear, "Is it the same each night?"

"Shh . . . there is more."

Ezra slowly descended to the parlor where he paced, still holding the unlit candle as though it guided his way. "A bath in blood. Guilt in the bone and marrow. Double guilt, the doers of the deed and the observer: two hands raised in wickedness; one voice raised not in protest."

Pearl whispered, "Reverend Williams, see how he wipes his right palm down his chest and side?"

Roger nodded, stared intently, but said nothing.

Ezra continued to rub his palm across his chest. "It will not rub off. The sign of Cain! See, they point. But I am not their Cain. I need not go to hell, for hell has come to me."

Ezra turned, walked up the stairs, and disappeared behind his door. Lingering in the hallway were the sounds of his words: "Fiends! Fiends!"

Then the house grew eerily quiet again.

At last Pearl stood up and lit a thin candle. Mary and Roger followed her to the kitchen where they sat down and talked softly.

"When awake, what does he say of the dream?" Roger spoke calmly although he grew extremely anxious for answers.

"He remembers nothing."

Mary patted Pearl's hand. "Have you told him of its contents?"

"I feared it would bring sea monsters from the deep."

"Monsters of our dreams come clothed as for a masquerade," Roger said. "What face have you recognized behind the mask?"

"I would sooner interpret John's book of Revelation than my sleepwalker's conversation. A coldness lingers in this house, more freezing than the chill without."

As the candle burned, Mary used her eyes to tell her husband they must return soon to feed their child.

Soon thereafter he rose from his chair to leave. "Pearl, you did well to bring us here. Tell Ezra I must talk with him before noon and that if harm comes to men falsely accused, he will have their blood on his hands."

"Though oft confused and sometimes weak, my husband is a good man, Reverend."

After sunrise Roger went to the meetinghouse where men and women of the congregation came one by one, usually to welcome him and sometimes to disclose their secrets. When with a woman, he sat always beside a window so that those passing by could see him, a practice he had begun at England's Masham Manor.

"Return on the morrow at nine, and my Mary will talk with you about this matter," Roger said to a married woman whose dialect suggested Shropshire east of Wales. She seemed to carry more than her share of burdens and secrets.

As the woman left, he heard a tapping at the window. When he saw Ezra's face, he motioned for him to enter.

"You look weary and pale, Ezra."

"Perhaps I have seen a ghost, Reverend. Do you believe that we see ghosts?"

"Fevered brains sometimes see trees that walk."

"I concealed these horrid visitations from my wife by feigning crippled memory."

"Horrid visitations?"

"Tell me plainly, Reverend. Do not spare my constitution. Can the devil disguise himself?"

Roger had given some thought to the gentle tactics he would use to coax the truth from Ezra. He remembered that Ezra had once imagined himself to be an exorcist. Believing the man's mind had an insecure hold on reality, he predicted that with Ezra the road to the truth would take many turns. *Patience, gentle patience.* "Ezra, a German clergyman of note once conjectured that the devil disguises himself in a ghost's clothing. He conjectured also that the devil has ghosts and that their ghosts have ghosts."

"But I saw him, bloodstained and speaking as I to you," Ezra insisted.

"From whence did he come?"

"From the grave, Reverend."

"A ghostly grave?"

"I understand not your question."

"If ghosts wear special attire made of ghostly threads, are they buried in and resurrected from ethereal graves?"

"You mock me, Reverend."

"Not I, but your fertile brain."

"My brain has become my own enemy, yet if I am not joined to my brain—"

"Give weight to your brain's skill of self-correction," Roger said gently. "With it, we shall unearth the truth; and it will set you free."

"You know not what you ask."

"If you become too friendly with lies, your brain will bury itself in a grave of its own invention. Speak the truth, Ezra; and we shall scare the devil himself with it."

Ezra hesitated, his eyes moved from corner to corner, and his breathing shifted. Roger waited, letting the silence speak its own eloquence.

"Truth be known, Reverend, I . . . I fear something more than the devil."

"Some*thing* or some*one*?"

"Private revenge. Public disbelief." Ezra looked away as if aware that his answer had been enigmatic.

"Then I presume you fear the townspeople will hold you up to scorn, doubting your report?"

"Doubting and even more, Reverend."

"Falsely accusing you?"

Ezra's big Adam's apple went down. He nodded his head and then closed his eyes tightly as if painfully viewing the scene of the townspeople hurling false accusations at him.

"If you will trust me, Ezra, I will deal with the people and the magistrates. You spoke also of revenge. Now dig up the truth you have buried in your secret coffin. Share this horror with me. Together we will serve both justice and ourselves. Tell me of that day."

Ezra's eyes flew open in astonishment. "Have you the gift?"

"Gift?"

"Why, the gift of discernment, of looking into men's souls and seeing therein—"

Roger shook his head and smiled. "Human souls are not gypsies' crystal balls. Now tell me plainly of that day."

"The day? What . . . day?"

"The truth will set you free. If you trust me to bear the truth with you, Ezra . . . ." He paused and waited. He could see that Ezra's face had become a field where truth and falsehood met for battle.

"I . . . I rode my mule toward Abel's house," Ezra began slowly.

"For what purpose?"

"To trade with him. But . . . but I heard shouting."

"What did you do?"

"Veered back into the woodland."

"To conceal your presence?"

"Aye, and to observe . . . Mayhem as plain as any sight."

"Who were they, Ezra?"

For a moment Ezra's face seemed frozen, his lips moving slowly. "When . . . when they draw their knives, Abel pulls away. Abel Jones and his boy. When they charge down on him, he grabs a hoe. The left shoulder. Abel catches him with the hoe across the left shoulder. No, Abel, behind you! Look behind you!"

Ezra's arms trembled, then his legs, and at last his whole body as though a volcano of secrets rumbled deep within him. His eyes blinked twice, seemingly testing their trustworthiness, and then he stared as if to ask why Roger and he were sitting there.

Roger dared not move. "Ezra, why did you tell Abel to look behind him?"

Ezra's chin dropped. Then his eyes glazed.

"You saw it. How did Abel Jones die?"

"They . . . they held him down . . . cut his throat!"

Roger felt his own breathing shift. Animal fear welled up inside him. "*They*? Who are *they*?"

Ezra gripped his knees hard and shook his head in violent terror as if a third person had suddenly entered the room to threaten disaster. Roger feared that Ezra's mind would come unhinged if he pressed him further. *Patience!*

Ezra seemed to slide into a trance, his face freezing again except for the lips, which emptied grim details of what he had witnessed: the slayings and then the arrival of Jeremiah Paynter and Benjamin Cook. The identity of the murderers, nevertheless, remained imprisoned inside the Bastille that was Ezra's mind.

Like an eagle in the sky, Roger circled round and round, waiting to swoop down upon the truth. But Ezra resisted. *All my coaxing*, Roger thought, *cannot crack the seal of Ezra's superstitious fear.* He remained patient, thinking of Snowfeather's father in jail and vowing to do all in his power to prevent bloody injustice from falling upon the father's neck. "I will stand by your side, Ezra."

To his surprise, his simple, heartfelt words were the key that turned the prison lock. Ezra's lips moved and he spoke of a certain Salem fisherman, describing him in detail but withholding his name. Then he spoke of a second man, again revealing no name.

"No curse will fall upon you if you tell the truth in this matter." While silently running through the details that Ezra had unearthed, Roger all at once guessed the identity of one of the men. *Thomas the fisherman!* As if quite natural to him, Roger began referring to the fisherman as the one with the patch over his blind eye.

Ezra seemed to understand. He too began to circle like an eagle. "The other murderer, the big man with the face and beard of a he-goat. Tangle not with him, Reverend."

"We have done well together, Ezra, you and I. We have put the father of lies to shame. Let us now haunt the ghost with the sunlight, returning him to the grave whence he came."

Ezra's voice shook with a macabre sound. "You will not divulge that I witnessed—"

"No. It is a matter of conscience with me."

"Give me your word, Reverend. Do not mention my name."

"My word you have. By revealing the truth, however, you will set yourself free from the dreams that trouble you. You have delivered the Philistines near to the gate of justice. Do not turn back!"

Ezra seemed to sense that he had unlocked the prison door, captured the first murderer, and indeed delivered him before the gate of justice. He nodded his consent.

Picking up his cue, Roger spoke the name: "Thomas Rice."

Ezra repeated the name: "Thomas Rice."

"He will become our bait to trap his accomplice in murder."

"If the townspeople learn that I have given you details, some with wild fancy will pounce upon me, accusing me of being a companion in the murders."

"I have given you my word. I will keep your identity secret."

Remembering Little Snowfeather's father, Roger then rushed to the jail to inform him that the first murderer had been identified.

"If you save us from this fate, your name will spread far and wide among the Algonquins," Snowfeather's father said.

Again wasting no time, Roger left for Captain Endecott's house. Endecott took him to the parlor, where Roger said, "I need your help. For many years in this New World, you have set traps with bait." As he described the second murderer to Endecott and solicited his help in setting a trap, a strange feeling crept over him. He could not shake loose from the feeling that Endecott already knew the murderer's identity.

Roger's heart pounded like drums in a closet. The noise in his head interrupted his thoughts, yet a new thought exploded. *The description fits Endecott!*

Though fighting to look away, his eyes kept fixing on Endecott. Fear rose up in him, fear that Endecott had grasped his suspicion. *Have I blundered irrevocably?* Endecott's dark eyes stared back at him with unnerving penetration.

He told himself to prevent a meeting between Endecott and Thomas. At the same time, he felt it imperative to remain close to one of them at all times. Thomas and Endecott must not be given time to speak to one another alone.

On the way to the dock to find Thomas, Roger and Endecott approached Jeremiah Paynter's home. Roger asked Endecott to wait while he dashed up to the door. When it opened, Roger's chin dropped. "Eric! What—?"

"Looking for you, my friend."

Jeremiah poked his head outside. "Is that not John Endecott?"

Roger saw his frosted breath vanish with the wind. "Yes, Endecott and I have set our purpose to find the assassin at the dock, which occasions my stop here."

"You require my attendance?" Jeremiah asked.

"Urgently! You too, Eric."

Jeremiah grabbed his coat and hat and joined the group heading for the dock. About two hundred feet before reaching the dock, Roger guided gangly Jeremiah ahead to stay at Endecott's side at all costs. Then he drifted back to me. "Eric, I suspect Thomas Rice. He may prove dangerous if cornered. Observe Captain Endecott constantly. Study his face, his eyes."

"What? You suspect Endecott?"

"Mildly."

Endecott approached us and said in an official tone, "I will hurry on ahead to talk alone with Rice first."

"I cannot permit that, Captain." The strength in Roger's voice took me by surprise. It became instantly clear to me that he had come close to backing himself into a corner. He quickly added, "Eric, as a sea captain, could you forgive yourself if harm came to your fellow seaman at the dock?"

Endecott frowned. He seemed to want to avoid offending me, his fellow sea captain. Yet his face suggested that Roger had intruded on some plan he had concocted.

Staying close at Endecott's side, I moved ahead. Roger caught Jeremiah by the arm and held him back. "Listen, Captain Firebrook understands my suspicions of Endecott. I have a scheme." Then he disclosed his plan to Jeremiah.

When they arrived at the dock, Roger lowered his voice. "Eric, step in front of Endecott and hold fast his attention while Jeremiah and I quickly locate Thomas Rice."

When they found Rice, Jeremiah declared before everyone at the dock, "Thomas, I have news that concerns you."

"News? What news?"

While Jeremiah looked around to see that he had everyone's attention, Endecott rushed up to take over.

With his powerful voice, Roger interrupted. "Give ear to Jeremiah Paynter, for he has information concerning us all."

Jeremiah suddenly appeared to realize that boldness was required of him. Although his voice shook, he did not pull back once he had begun. "Men, you know I tend to speak plainly. I will come to the heart of it. Not the natives, but two colonists murdered the trapper and his family. You all knew Abel Jones, a good and honest man. I must speak of him this day; for if I do not, his blood will cry out from the grave against me. Gather round closer, men. Know you that the shoulder of one among us standing here bears the mark of Abel Jones's hoe."

"Abel's hoe! You speak nonsense," a voice cried out.

Jeremiah's eyes bulged. "'Twas poor Abel's only weapon to defend himself against the treacherous murderers.

"You charge that a fisherman committed mayhem?" another voice called out.

Jeremiah raised his voice. "Aye, a fisherman. A stain will cover the lot of you unless he be exposed."

"Then waste no time. Expose him!" cried still another voice.

"What Cain among us will refuse to reveal his shoulders to us all?" Jeremiah asked.

Endecott rushed forward, roaring, "The witness! 'Tis unlawful unless you first bring forth the witness!"

Obviously carried by the current of his new courage, Jeremiah pushed his red hair from his eyes and stepped closer to the fishermen. "You heard Captain Endecott call for a witness. We have a witness here in our midst, do we not, Thomas, as clear a witness as could be summoned?" He turned to look for Roger and saw that he had backed Rice to the dock's edge.

Despite Endecott's protest, the men joined Roger and gripped Rice's arms firmly while Jeremiah unbuttoned his coat and shirt. A groan of male voices filled the air.

"Cain's mark!" Jeremiah shouted triumphantly.

Endecott protested and made loud proclamations that frightened the seagulls.

Roger whirled around, walked up to Endecott, and spoke in a quiet voice. "It is fitting that you, the only magistrate among us, should arrest this man."

Endecott looked back defiantly; but when he saw all other eyes focused on him, his expression changed. In a loud voice, he commanded the fishermen to give assistance in taking Thomas Rice to the jail.

Still, after arriving at the jail with the new prisoner, Endecott behaved so strangely that Roger could not help thinking that Ezra's description of the second murderer fit him precisely. Endecott, however, grew furious at every suggestion that he release the two imprisoned natives.

Before a small group of townspeople, Jeremiah spoke boldly of Cain's mark, the wound that Abel Jones had inflicted on his murderer.

Evidently sensing that the tide had turned against him, Endecott became still more defiant. "Cain's mark, is it? 'Tis more likely a fishing accident as Thomas Rice claims."

Despite Jeremiah's appeal, Endecott reminded those around him that he was the only magistrate available at this crucial time. The two natives therefore remained in prison.

Roger sensed that further exchange of words would only deepen the division. Never had he seen Endecott so implacable. The more entrenched the partisans became, the more righteous each presumed to be. From Sir Edward Coke, he had learned that the more people pictured themselves dwelling among haloed angels, the more they pictured their opponents dwelling among sinister demons. Rarely had he seen angels and demons convene in sweet reasonableness.

Standing now before the crowd, Roger looked each person in the eye until silence reigned. "Let us turn down the wick of passions. Give this matter time. Go home, good friends, and speak mildly among yourselves. A throng has neither brain nor heart. We will meet again when we have gained greater knowledge of the particulars and when our discernment equals the wind of our lungs."

Some in the crowd turned to do their minister's bidding, whereas like a loose wagon rolling recklessly downhill, Endecott filled his lungs and roared above the crowd like a lion: "We tempt the Lord our God when we fail to bring swift judgment against these Amalekites. Did not the prophet Samuel rebuke Saul when he failed to slay the king of Agag and hew him into pieces?"

A voice shouted, "What say ye to that, Reverend Williams?"

Knowing now that Endecott wished to light the fuse, Roger waited for the opportune moment. When it came, he raised his hands to quell the passions. "You have read the account of Christ passing through Samaria. You have read how two disciples implored him to follow the steps of the fiery prophet Elijah. 'Give us leave to command fire to come down from heaven to consume these Samaritans,' the disciples said to him. But do you remember Christ's reply?"

Another voice from the crowd called out, "Christ rebuked them!"

"Aye, and if Christ were here today, would he not rebuke us?"

Just as flush-faced Endecott raised his finger to heaven to speak, he saw that the people had walked away. He opened his mouth as if to roar at them. The lion, however, had no more roar in him. Muttering angrily, he rushed away, vowing that the cause of justice would yet be served.

Making certain no one followed, Roger hurried to search for the carpenter Ezra. He urgently needed to resolve a burning question. *Is Endecott the second murderer?* Despite the compelling description Ezra had given of the second murderer, Roger's heart longed to refute his suspicion of Endecott. He wished to take little Deborah Jones with him to look at Endecott and ask her whether she recognized him as the slayer of her father and mother. Another part of Roger forbade him to subject the child to such torment.

He found Ezra's wife, Pearl, at home. "I need to speak to your husband immediately and privately!"

"Thank heaven you have come, good Reverend!" She threw the door wide open and guided him to a chair in the parlor. "I will send him to you." Saying no more, Pearl disappeared upstairs and returned to the parlor at once with the neighbor's children. "Quickly," she said to them, "let us go to the meetinghouse." Putting on their coats and hats, they followed her into the November air.

Shortly thereafter, Ezra entered the parlor, his hair in disarray, reminding Roger that the carpenter's life was now in disarray because of what he had witnessed in the woods. In a hoarse, weak voice, Ezra said, "Angels have brought you, Brother Roger, to fight the whisper of demons in my ear."

"What do your demons say, Brother Ezra?"

"In unnatural whispers, they command me to drown myself in Martin's Pond."

He realized that if Ezra should drown himself, the two imprisoned natives might suffer execution. "If Pearl commanded you to drown yourself, would you obey?"

Ezra blinked with surprise and stammered, "No! By heaven, no! No wife shall order her husband to—"

"Has a pack of demons in your head more wisdom than your good Pearl?" He hoped to restore Ezra to his right mind.

Blushing, Ezra sat down to listen as Roger reported what had happened at both the dock and the jail.

"The big man with the face of a goat—if it is not Captain Endecott, then tell me." Roger fought against his swelling apprehension.

A loud pounding on the door interrupted them. "Open up! Open up!" a voice cried out.

Ezra jumped to his feet. "'Tis Jeremiah Paynter."

Both went to the door and saw Jeremiah pounding his fists now against his chest in consternation. Ezra threw the door open wide.

Jeremiah began speaking at once. "Endecott has persuaded . . . . He came in from the forest and—"

"Who came from the forest?" Roger demanded.

"The second magistrate. Endecott has persuaded him to call the trial."

"When?" Roger looked at Jeremiah and then cut his eyes toward Ezra.

"On the morrow." Jeremiah closed the door against the cold November wind.

"Tomorrow at this time, two native wives will turn into widows unless some witness stands to speak the truth." Roger walked to the window and looked out, his back to Ezra. *Choose this day, Ezra, whom you will obey: your conscience or the whispering demons of your mind. You are the only witness who can unlock the prison door for the two innocent men.* Roger turned to see Ezra look away from Jeremiah's inquiring eyes. "How fares our Pastor Skelton?" Roger asked Jeremiah.

"The turmoil has taken its toll on the good man. But I did give my word to return upon bringing you the message. Captain Firebrook remains at our pastor's side."

Roger unbuttoned his coat. "I have urgent business here. I will join them soon. Will you be there?"

"Within half an hour," Jeremiah answered and then left without looking back.

Roger stood at the window and watched the people of Salem hurry by. "Ezra, what says your conscience? Can you speak of the second murderer?" He turned around to see Ezra pull at his beardless chin as if thinking of the man with the face and beard of a he-goat.

"The man . . . . He does not live in Salem." Ezra stared at the toe of his boots.

"Not in Salem?" He felt confused. Endecott had been among the first white men to live in Salem.

Ezra put his hands over his face and let his fingers come down slowly. Although raising his head, he seemed lost in fear.

He wanted Ezra's silence to confirm his hope that the murderer had not been Endecott. He let the relief come to his heart even though his mind warned against false hope. Then his thoughts split into two armies. One reasoned that the town would not easily recover if the people believed one of its magistrates had committed so heinous a crime. The other reasoned that even for the sake of harmony the people could not ignore a murder committed by a magistrate. His thoughts dispersed still further into many platoons, each taking him on a different trail, but none successfully leading him incontrovertibly to the identity of the second murderer.

Ezra interrupted. "Tell me again, Brother Roger. You yourself saw the wound on Thomas Rice's shoulder?"

He laid his hand on his own left collarbone. "I saw it. But without the second murderer to confront him, Thomas Rice could walk free . . . leaving the innocent natives to die in his place. Endecott will not budge."

Sweat poured down Ezra's face.

Roger fished for more details. "From what colony came the second man?"

"Ply . . . Plymouth, Reverend."

"A big man. A goat's face. Plymouth." His thoughts converged like several streams flooding into one river. He closed his eyes and saw Endecott's face, but then the image changed to that of another man, a burly man as huge as Endecott. He cut his eyes back to Ezra. "Had this man a crooked chin, like so?" He pushed his own chin to the right.

Ezra bit his lip and nodded confirmation.

He held up his fingers spread apart. "And had the man . . . ?"

Again, Ezra nodded. "His left middle finger."

"Missing?"

"Missing," Ezra whispered.

Roger slapped his forehead. "Rob Greene! The child-stealer turned murderer!" He sprang to his feet. "Ezra, your testimony can free the natives."

A knot of wrinkles formed on Ezra's forehead.

"I have, nevertheless, given you my word and will keep it." Roger began sketching a plan in his mind. When the plan was complete, he was on the verge of leaving when Ezra asked him to sit down.

"I know you will keep your word to me. But do not leave. Does the native have a soul?"

He understood what lay behind the question. "Ezra, you saw the child called Little Snowfeather. Is she an animal like your cows or swine? Would your conscience give you leave to roast her on coals and feed her to your family?"

Ezra buried his face in his hands. "I will be a witness. Go to the magistrates."

He lifted Ezra to his feet. "Abel Jones is dead, but those who murdered him and his family will commit no more mayhem. You and I will see to that." He then left the house and called into the wind, "Wish me Godspeed, Brother Ezra."

He hurried and found Endecott alone. "I have a witness who saw the murder. I beseech you to prevail upon the other magistrates to give me three days to bring the guilty man to Salem."

"No! God's wrath hovers over a city where bloody wickedness goes unpunished."

"Captain, if the blood of innocent men flows through your fingers, do you think heaven will wink at your guilt?"

Endecott protested with such fervent resolution that Roger left to search for the second magistrate, Matthew Grozier, to whom he disclosed all except Ezra's name.

Openmouthed, Matthew Grozier sat stunned in his own house. He raised his eyes toward heaven as if he feared an axe might fall because of some thwarting of justice. Then, vowing to face Endecott, he left without another word.

Two days later in Plymouth, Roger, Endecott, and Jeremiah took their enraged prisoner Rob Greene aboard ship.

"Before we deliver Greene to Salem," Endecott said to Roger and Jeremiah, "leave him alone with me on the lower deck."

To prevent Endecott from using torture, Roger insisted on accompanying him. Still, none of Roger's peaceful efforts extracted a confession from Greene.

Three days later, Rob Greene and Thomas Rice stood trial in Salem. Despite the bitter wind and intermittent sleet, large numbers gathered outside the crowded meetinghouse. At intervals a messenger appeared to deliver the progress of the trials.

Inside, Roger and Ezra had made their way down the aisle. Only the whimper of infants in arms could be heard. Ezra stopped before the magistrates; Roger stood nearby.

The chief magistrate, Captain Endecott himself, announced that Ezra Welch had asked to testify in the witness box. Roger sat down on a bench not far away and held his eyes on Ezra as if to say, *I am here as your friend and minister.* Knitting a cloak for Pastor Skelton, Pearl sat chewing her lip, looking like a squirrel nibbling on an acorn. Now and then, she paused, closing her eyes as if praying for her husband's courage. Standing against the wall with many others, Jeremiah reached down to pick up Deborah Jones.

When Ezra saw the child, the look of pain in his eyes left no doubt in Roger's mind that Ezra remembered seeing Deborah climb into the well. He had confessed his cowardice in failing to rescue the child and had begged Roger to disclose this truth to no one. He sensed the humiliation that Ezra felt in admitting now openly his earlier cowardice.

Ezra faced a new occasion of courage before the magistrates. He spoke in a resolute voice, addressing Jeremiah. "I will tell everything! But first remove the little one. She has suffered more than have we all."

Tears forming in his eyes, lanky Jeremiah turned and carried Deborah from the meetinghouse. While the stern-faced magistrates observed with scarcely a muscle twitching, Ezra spoke slowly and deliberately, giving the excruciating account as though unrolling a scroll of horror before their eyes. Soon Ezra seemed to become invisible, replaced by the graphic images his voice painted. Despite the audible gasps from the spectators, he neither paused nor stammered. The scene of terror he had witnessed appeared to recount itself through his lips as though he were its instrument. The audience sat stunned by the grisly account now snaking its way through their brains. The expression on their faces asked, *Did we not leave England to escape such depravity?*

When Ezra completed the story, Roger thought the man would collapse in exhaustion. Instead Ezra braced himself with his hand and turned to the wily defense lawyer as if to say, *At last, we meet. I stand ready for your assault.*

"He lies! He lies!" Greene shouted at the top of his voice, pointing his finger at Ezra and leaping to his feet.

Although everyone apparently expected Ezra to melt before Greene's hot anger, Roger nodded reassuringly at Ezra, who nodded back as if to say, *Yes, this is no more than what we had expected. The drama has begun.* Instead of melting, Ezra threw his shoulders back as if saying to himself, *I am a new man now, not the coward that my demons wished me to believe. Yes, I am a new man who will no longer listen to their lies.* Indeed he was a new man; for he had stepped into a role so new that he could not have fulfilled it without a new heart.

Though the questions came like driving sleet, Ezra never yielded to the onslaught of the lawyer's sardonic smirk and devious innuendoes. He stood rather like a captain aboard his ship, navigating adroitly through the tempest.

Less than an hour later, Greene came to his feet and pointed. "Here beside me sits the murderer, Thomas Rice. He did it. He committed the foul deed! I . . . I am innocent. There is no blood on my hands."

Rice reached up and pulled Greene down to his chair. "Like Judas," Rice said grimly to Greene, "our end will come at the rope's end. Pray heaven that we do not follow Judas to his own place."

At the hanging hour on the following day, Roger stood beside the father of Little Snowfeather, the Narraganset native Miantonomo, and Ezra. The other native who had suffered false accusation and jail vowed never again to enter Salem.

With the coarse rope around his neck, Rob Greene continued to plead his innocence. None in the town, save his two cousins, professed to believe him.

Having roused the town to the brink of hanging two innocent men and igniting a war with the natives, Benjamin Cook packed his belongings and stole away under cover of darkness to the town of Roxbury south of Boston.

BOSTON AND SALEM

Late November and December 1633

Almost overnight, the hostility that had boiled up in Salem turned into jubilation. Justice had been served, a grim tragedy averted, and new peace established with the neighboring Algonquins. In recognition of their good fortune, Reverend Skelton preached a sermon titled "The Smile of Providence." At its close, his voice grew surprisingly strong: "The good will that Brother Roger helped generate among the Algonquins west of our town and among the Narragansets south of Boston complemented Brother Ezra's courage and Brother Jeremiah's honesty. With the encouragement of many of you and the indispensable assistance of the Narraganset Sachem Miantonomo, Brothers Roger and Jeremiah have established a thriving trading post only twelve miles west of our meetinghouse."

On the next day, Roger and his beloved wrapped themselves in hides that the Algonquins had given them and walked in the cold November air.

"Mary, you and John Milton are alike. He too could walk many miles without tiring."

"When I was only thirteen, my father began taking me on long walks each day."

"Why at thirteen, Mary?"

"At that age, my legs grew longer, and I could keep up with him."

"I know you have dreamed of a house of your own here in Salem." He stopped, put his arm around her, and pointed to four large elm trees. "Could you savor that place?"

"For our house?" She laughed as she scanned the horizon. "How far are we from a river or a brook? I want never again to live within a mile of water that can overflow."

"You can see your house would stand on high ground, a house with glass windows, not oil paper."

As December brought in the cold from farther north, Roger noted that Endecott's jealousy did not wait for spring to blossom. Mary had alerted him: "Dear, when vacillating Endecott observes how people delight in your presence, he seems to feel his own position at the town's center slipping away. The more Pastor Skelton relishes your work among the people and counts your assistance a shining jewel, the more Endecott resents you. Now, behind your back, he calls you the usurper. When others criticize him, he fancies that somehow your machinations lie behind the scene."

During December Roger and Mary, sometimes with Little Mary in her lap, spent several hours a week at the meetinghouse where the congregation came to discuss their hopes, doubts, faith, and fears with their new teacher and his wife. Agnes Barry, who had earlier spoken with Roger at the meetinghouse, complained now bitterly that her husband, Wilfred, had again forced her to bed.

On the next day, he thought it best to talk with Wilfred alone and caught the husband walking from his house to the place where he worked as a carpenter.

"Brother Roger," Wilfred said, "I join the natives and the townspeople to praise you for helping to bring the murderers to justice."

He accepted the praise and then spoke on another matter. "As teacher in our congregation, I have certain obligations and privileges. One of my privileges is to assist members through their conflicts and tribulations. Often I need to receive counsel as well as to give it."

"You come to me for counsel?"

"When I give good advice to others, it proves better advice for myself. In England I knew a vicar who went to a man in his parish and said, 'Since I am your vicar, heaven has appointed me as guardian of your conscience. I, therefore, require you to submit to me as one bearing heaven's authority.'"

"With all due regard to the clergy, I judge the vicar overstepped his bounds. My beliefs and my conscience are my own."

"Then, Wilfred, would you label the vicar's way *soul rape?*"

"Soul rape it is. Many of us left England to escape it."

"Then, Brother Wilfred, is *body rape* less wicked than soul rape?"

Wilfred's brow furrowed, and he squinted with one eye. "I do not follow the question."

"Consider a man who says to his beloved, 'You are my wife, are you not? Therefore, when I, your husband, command you to my bed, you must submit.'"

Wilfred stared dumbfounded. The blood slowly drained from his face. He took four or five steps, stopped, and then returned. "What is a man to do if his wife . . . ?" He flushed crimson. "A gentle and loving woman when we married! Now she is like dough too long in the oven. A loaf harder than granite. What is a man to do, Reverend?"

"Marriage is an alliance for mutual benefit and pleasure, not a war for wreaking havoc upon the enemy."

"But I am a Protestant, not a celibate monk."

"As a good Protestant consider that only at war do men knock down forts and enter to wreak havoc. Knock gently at the door and wait. In marriage let all doors open from the inside only."

"What if the door never opens for me?"

Roger took the hammer from the carpenter and held it up. "I see you share our Savior's profession. Tell me, when you open a window in a house you have built, do you slam the hammer against the pane? Even when you drive large and small nails, do you not tap some gently, all appropriate to the wood's nature and your purpose? Respectful wedlock requires of us the art of gentle finesse." Returning the hammer to Wilfred, he said no more.

Two weeks later, Roger talked again with the carpenter and asked him to supervise the construction of his house.

Wilfred smiled. "You helped me make my house a home. Now I will help give your home a house and contribute a few posts and beams."

In Boston on that same day, Governor Winthrop sent letters to all the magistrates in the towns of the colony. In the afternoon, thick clouds formed over the Atlantic. The citizens from Boston to Salem saw savage chains of lightning drop from the sky. Some preachers spoke of divine wrath.

"She is coming our way!" people shouted to one another as the wind grew high.

"Never have I witnessed such a sight in winter!" a man's voice exclaimed.

Thunder rumbled and crashed. The elements seemed cursed with chaos.

"Lucifer's day!" a woman with a shrill voice cried out, slamming the shutters tight and locking them.

Governor John Winthrop the older, sitting alone in his office, paid little regard to the storm. He suffered an inner tumultuous rage and momentarily wondered if he had been transformed from a self-possessed man to a human volcano. He locked the door and paced in solitude.

"Why, Roger? Why?" He addressed the walls. "A man so filled with the gift of teaching, so commanding of spirit, so winsome and gentle of heart. Has the devil himself stolen into your soul? You insult the king and risk bringing heavy judgment down on us all! Are you the Roger Williams I knew in England, the man who stood at my side for the cause of Christ and righteousness? How oft would I have taken you in as our colony's pride and joy? But you would not have it. Come to your senses, man! How can I stop the forces already at work if you persist? You tie my hands. Ah, such anguish!"

Far into December, the furor over Roger's proposed letter to the king continued.

"Capture Roger and hold him in bonds!" Deputy Governor Thomas Dudley demanded in a hot letter sent out to all the Massachusetts magistrates.

Governor Winthrop sat again in anguish behind his massive desk and removed the pipe from his lips. "Dudley, your letter was unwise. If we imprison Master Williams in our colony, the tumult will only spread. Wherever he goes, he will leave behind a wide path of wildfire."

Dudley shook his head at the very sound of the name *Roger Williams*. "What does the Reverend Cotton say about this troublemaker?"

"You will soon learn."

When Dudley left, Winthrop opened his thick journal and recorded his praise of the Reverend Cotton's service to the congregation. He recorded further, "After confessing their sins upon hearing the Reverend Cotton preach, a number of notorious and evil people have been received warmly into the bosom of the church." Winthrop closed the journal and remembered that in Boston only Cotton equaled him in fame and high regard.

On the next day, a few select magistrates, including Winthrop and Dudley, met informally with John Cotton to consider alternatives for dealing with Roger.

As they talked around the table, Winthrop silently contemplated the ways of Providence and considered that such ways ran deep with irony from a human perspective. *Three years past, Master Williams refused the offer of the Boston church that now stands hard and fast against him.*

Magistrate Simon Bradstreet slapped both hands on the table. "Bind him and send him back to England."

"Hold back! Archbishop Laud would have his talons on him within a month," Cotton protested.

"So be it!" exclaimed Dudley, echoed by others.

Cotton and Winthrop Jr. countered, offering to speak directly and immediately to Roger.

They all agreed that Roger's proposed letter to the king had released a whirlwind whose furor none could predict. They agreed further to bind themselves again in secrecy regarding the threatening letter lest the general population learn of it.

Governor Winthrop hammered the table with the heel of his hand. "Above all we must prevent the news of this letter from escaping to England."

Before the day ended, Roger received a handwritten note from Winthrop Jr. Without second thought, he sent a return message, saying it would please him to meet with Master Cotton and either of the two worthy Winthrops. "Be so kind as to bring my friend Captain Eric Firebrook with you if he be so disposed. I value his counsel."

Roger had given much thought to the possible influence he might have on Cotton if they should meet face to face. Even though Governor Winthrop feared to reason with him, Roger convinced himself that he had made some inroad through his eldest son and that Cotton might become a faithful mediator between the governor and himself.

Before the week ended, he was sitting at his table in the Salem meetinghouse when he heard a carriage roll up. He glanced out the window and recognized the tip of the right eyebrow, which curled up slightly, and the remarkably high forehead. "Jeremiah, do I not see the Reverend John Cotton?"

"Aye, and Captain Firebrook with John Winthrop Jr."

Roger quickly placed his manuscript carefully in a box. In a recent letter, he had told the younger Winthrop of his latest progress toward his book on the natives' language and customs. Despite the knot of apprehension in his stomach and disappointment that the governor had declined to come, he felt a surge of anticipation. Obviously the governor had sought to contain him in a bottle. But if Winthrop refused to respond to his arguments and challenge, then he would broaden the audience. He felt he had no other choice than to use a new method to induce Winthrop to rethink the direction that he had set upon.

It continued to puzzle Roger that a man as intelligent and godly as Winthrop would disregard the natives' claim to the land. It puzzled him also that the governor could not see the long shadow of William Laud falling over him.

Roger knew that even though not a magistrate, Cotton carried far-reaching influence because of his esteem as both scholar and clergyman. Also Winthrop Jr. carried more weight than the magistrates seemed to acknowledge. Looking through the window at Cotton's inquisitive, kind eyes, Roger hoped they forecast a profitable exchange of thought. Knowing that he would soon stand face-to-face with a powerful intellect, he felt apprehension and dared to see in Cotton's high cheekbones the promise of rare understanding as well as keen wit. The Puritan clergyman's white, extended collar reminded him that both Cotton and he were Cambridge men. Startled by the tremor he felt in his lip, he took a deep but shaky breath.

As soon as his three guests entered the meetinghouse, Roger felt elated and walked in a long, robust stride up the aisle to greet them cheerfully. Then he helped Cotton with his coat. "I am deeply honored by your presence."

When Cotton handed him his hat, he could not help noting that the clergyman parted his straight hair in the middle and let it fall neatly to his shoulders like Roger's brother Sydrach.

Winthrop the younger released a smile. "It is good to see you again, Roger. I have given considerable thought to your conversation with Eric and me in Plymouth."

After they had sat down near the front, Cotton said, "On our way to Salem, the three of us agreed to keep this meeting secret."

"We thought it proper to inform Endecott of our intention," Winthrop Jr. added. Jeremiah stood up and, having business to attend to, left the meetinghouse.

When it became clear that the meetinghouse would not provide privacy, Roger suggested going elsewhere. With Cotton at his side, he then guided them toward the nearby parsonage.

John Winthrop Jr. lingered behind. "Eric, do you continue keeping a journal of this New England venture?"

"In considerable detail," I replied.

"Then note well this day when the Reverend Cotton and Master Williams meet face-to-face."

"John, you read my thoughts with one exception. I place you with Roger and Cotton on the Mount Olympus of our New World history. Instead of Odysseus, Hector, and Idomeneus, I see the three of you. Deny not your own place. I confess a deep longing to tell this story. I feel kinship with that ancient Greek minstrel who sang of the wondrous deeds of mighty heroes."

Pastor Skelton met his guests at the parsonage door and guided them to a room for their private conversation. Skelton, like Roger, expressed his pleasure that Cotton and Winthrop Jr. had journeyed to Salem.

As they sat around a table, Winthrop Jr. lost no time in laying before them a copy of Roger's letter addressed to King Charles. "The Reverend Cotton and I come not to contest the content of your letter on this occasion, but to beseech you to weigh the consequences of its arrival in England."

Cotton nodded his agreement.

Roger thought that the Boston magistrates had never given him a fair hearing on this matter. "You have my ear as I trust I have yours."

Winthrop Jr. placed his hand on Roger's shoulder. "You have New England at the precipice, and both continents would feel the devastation of its crash. How can we pull back?"

"If I tell the truth, embrace it. If I err, show me where."

"The letter you fired was aimed at the Massachusetts magistrates. I fear it will hit in London," Cotton said.

Roger rose to his feet. "I reject the comparison. Do you wish that I should compare your sermons to gunpowder? If words were cannons, we would all be ships of battle. I have sent out only missiles of ink and air, drawing no blood and mangling no limbs."

"Do you desire that Archbishop Laud replace our governor and magistrates with his own men?" The younger Winthrop seemed deeply earnest.

Roger returned to his seat but spoke quickly. "No, good friend, we all agree that the archbishop is England's Ahab."

"If you send the letter, Ahab's men will soon thereafter come to govern us; and with them will arrive soldiers to force our complicity," John Winthrop Jr. added.

Cotton stretched forth his hand. "I tremble to think of the consequences, Master Williams. Do you think that Thomas Hooker and I slipped through Laud's fingers only to be snatched up again and brought before his High Commission?"

Roger leaned forward and looked squarely into the other men's eyes. "Laud's High Commission. Winthrop's High Commission. Same substance. Different masks." Though making no reply, Cotton seemed troubled.

John Jr. undoubtedly felt the sting of the comparison of his father with Laud. Nevertheless, he restrained himself admirably. "Roger, I implore you. Do not send the letter to the king. Give our own magistrates time to make restitution to the natives. Is your purpose to preach righteousness only in airy abstractions? If trees of righteousness are to bring forth real fruit, they require time."

"Then let us descend from cloudy abstractions and talk of earthly fruit in particular. I propose that the governor and the sachems come together as equals to negotiate the—"

"Hold!" young Winthrop exclaimed. "What part will you play in these negotiations?"

"The part that the natives ask me to play."

Winthrop Jr. grimaced. "Roger, I know you value our friendship. But I must tell you that more than half the Massachusetts magistrates do not desire your presence at any territorial negotiation with the natives."

Roger studied young Winthrop's face and then Cotton's. "Those magistrates play cat and mouse. If you have come somewhat on their behalf, ask them to picture the Irish sailing today to England and claiming discovery of Essex and Hampshire. In your mind, you hear the Catholic Irish argue, 'Since the English natives lack true religion, God has punished them with the plague as a sign that we Irish should take Essex and Hampshire as our own.'"

"Hold," Winthrop Jr. said. "I see the goal of your winding argument. I concede its logic and morality. Yet the magistrates will wish to speak of particulars."

Cotton nodded, his face revealing hope. "Master Williams, if we here today find agreement on the key particulars, tomorrow the magistrates may prove more amenable to your concern." Cotton spoke in a baritone voice that seemed the essence of reason.

"What will satisfy the natives?" asked Pastor Skelton, who had said little.

Wincing with compassion when he heard the ailing Skelton wheeze, Roger marveled at the man's determination and felt that most men of his frail constitution would take to bed. Before Roger could answer Skelton, a loud pounding at the door startled them. Skelton rose unsteadily and left to see who was there. All in the room heard the door open and the voice of Endecott trumpet his arrival. Roger laughed silently, remembering those Shakespearean plays in which trumpet sounds preceded the entrance of royalty.

Endecott burst into the room, scowled at everyone, and asked why they had convened without him. No one answered, but Skelton urged him to be seated. While Winthrop Jr. politely tried to summarize the progress of the meeting, Endecott cut him short.

"The natives have no claim on me. I brought civilizing English customs to these barbarous heathens and acquainted them with the true Protestant religion!"

Roger felt the heat rush to his face. But he swallowed his anger. Having lived for a short while in the Endecotts' house, he recognized that once the captain began to vent his spleen, his ears could hear no voice but his own.

"I am a magistrate of this colony." Endecott's voice rose like high wind. "I served here at Salem as governor even before your father arrived, young John."

Roger saw gloom settle over young John's countenance.

"I know these Indians," Endecott added, "and I say here and now that if any debt holds between us, it is their debt to me and to all us English."

Cotton raised his rich baritone voice. "You know not what you ask of the natives. Master Williams has pressed upon us a point of conscience. Repentance and restitution are our proper attitudes. If we have stolen their land and in exchange preached the gospel to them, we have besmirched the name of Christ and put the gospel to shame. If the Epistle of James exhorts us to give alms to the needy, logic requires us to forbid stealing from them."

A surge of hope stirred in Roger. All the clergy in Massachusetts held Cotton in high esteem and would heed his counsel. If the clergy were of one accord, the magistrates would give weight to their opinion.

"Restitution!" Endecott said gruffly. "As a practical matter, the Massachusetts Colony has not enough wealth to . . . . We have taken leave of our homeland, weathered the ocean's storms, battled famine and starvation, suffered bitter cold—all this for what? To empty our pockets to the first pack of Indians that appears with an open palm at our door?"

Secretly regarding Endecott as the sort of man who would hear angelic music in the passing of his own wind, Roger looked Endecott in the eye. "A pirate who boards another's ship and pillages his goods cannot be regarded as an alms giver if he returns a pittance of what he has stolen."

Endecott opened his mouth to object, but the Reverend Cotton had already begun to speak. "You know the Indians well, Master Williams. What will they request if the Massachusetts magistrates negotiate with them for land?"

Cotton's question doubled Roger's hope and courage. "Less than perhaps we English would require were we in their position. We English could learn fairness from the Algonquin tribes. First, we must begin by confessing to them our intrusion. Then the natives can say plainly enough for themselves what they require as restitution."

"If my father and the magistrates negotiate with the natives, will you then destroy the letter addressed to the king?" asked young Winthrop

Intending to give no quick answer, Roger tried to read the face of Cotton, who seemed agreeable on the question of fairness to the natives. Could he now take the next step and persuade Cotton to build a restraining hedge separating religious doctrine from government power? Since Cotton resented Laud's encroachment on his religious conscience, perhaps he would understand the necessity of making the hedge grow high and thick.

Cotton seemed to sense Roger's hesitation. "Your letter offends protocol and insults the king. You must forgive my forthrightness, Master Williams."

"I intend no insult to royalty."

"Then was your design to show honor to the king?" Cotton looked askance at him.

"Honor to whom honor is due. Let the king also show honor in return."

"Do you deny that the king is God's anointed?" asked Cotton.

"God anoints a king to serve the people and to assist those who administer civil justice. 'The greatest among you,' said Christ, 'shall be your servant.' No mortal is king of my conscience or of yours. I do not say *Your Worship* to a mere mortal. A crown does not make a god of a man."

Cotton leaned forward and spoke softly. "This is a most indelicate matter, but I think we might pursue it. Give me your version of the point on which you and our governor in Boston most sharply disagree."

Roger needed no time to ponder his answer. "The governor fancies that a nation or a colony makes a covenant with heaven. I state otherwise and wish to be understood on this crucial matter. No king, governor, magistrates, or any other arm of the state represents me or anyone before God. I contend that in this day of grace, covenants are made between God and individuals. I will not yield on this!"

Cotton stiffened in his chair. "What agency then protects the people from the errors of heretics?"

"No agency of the state. No armed gang perpetrating its savagery under the cross of Christ."

"Incredible! How would you prevent the spread of heresy and error?" Cotton asked.

"Oppose them not with the blade of steel, but with the flashing sword of truth in open disputation. Steel does not persuade the *soul and mind*, but only multiplies hypocrisy." Roger felt the joy of at last having the opportunity to state clearly his views to people in positions of influence. He felt that the older Winthrop had never shown him the respect of giving his arguments a fair hearing. "Why cannot the governor and certain magistrates see the simple truth that Almighty God abhors hypocrisy no less than heresy, blasphemy, idolatry, and the like?"

"The governor will not take kindly to such strong words," Cotton said.

Roger had a ready answer, but he held himself in check and made himself stare off in space until his passion cooled. Then he softened his voice and cut his eyes back to Cotton. "I do not speak unkindly either *to* the governor or *of* him. On the point of our contention, however, I claim that the officers of the government have *no authority to enforce true worship or to punish false belief.* The church and the state must not clasp hands as if in wedlock. If we Protestants have justly dismissed the pope, let us not set king, Parliament, or General Court on a papal throne. Idolatry under any name is idolatry."

Cotton studied Roger's face for an inordinately long time. "Is it true that you deny that the English are a chosen people?"

He understood the thrust of the question. "I ask you, if England is the chosen nation, are the Dutch unchosen? Are the Danes chosen but not the English?"

"You answer my question with two of your own."

Roger smiled. "I must speak plainly. Neither Massachusetts nor any other government can justly pose as the anointed to serve as a chosen people."

Endecott remained silent, his face contorting. Roger no longer suffered delusions about him, but perceived him as a man who brooded in a cauldron of anger and jealousy that simmered with poisonous resentment. Revenge had become the secret elixir of his malevolent brew. Calling the whole concoction by the name *divine justice* did not mitigate its malevolence.

BOSTON AND SALEM

December 1633–Spring 1634

Events moved swiftly. In December 1633, the General Court, influenced mostly by Winthrop Sr. and Endecott, summoned Roger to give account of his loyalty to the king. When he, however, appeared in court in January, the Reverends Cotton and Wilson sounded a softer note. They acknowledged before the court that the proposed letter to the king admitted of an interpretation different from Governor Winthrop's and Captain Endecott's. Having recently read several pages from Roger's developing book about the natives, Cotton apparently had begun to see him in a new light.

This surprising turn upset Winthrop Sr. After failing to convince the court to bring the arm of censorship down upon Roger, he complained and stated in his journal that the obscurity of this Separatist's arguments had frustrated all attempts to nail them down. Upon hearing of Winthrop's complaint, Roger could not help smiling at the irony that Winthrop had earlier murmured against the sharpness and plainness of his words.

Though the friction between Endecott and Winthrop Sr. continued to be flint and steel, it had ignited no flame yet. By opposing Roger, they ironically made themselves allies of necessity.

When Mary later learned about some of their attempts to compel her husband to confess publicly the error and danger of his views, she handed him a cup of water. "I once heard of a fox and a weasel who became friends. I know not if it is true. If it is, their names are Winthrop and Endecott."

Unable to come to a firm conclusion, the January court in Boston decided to forgo condemning Roger provided he took an oath of allegiance to the king.

In February an envelope from Boston arrived at the Paynters' home where Mary and Roger lived while waiting for the carpenters to finish their new house. After tearing open the letter addressed to him, he saw that Winthrop Jr. had written the letter on February 10. He read it aloud to Mary.

Dear Friend,

Your years at the side of England's most distinguished judge, Sir Edward Coke, have served you well. Though not a lawyer, you outlawed the lawyers themselves in elucidating your signed oath of allegiance to the crown. Your subtle wording has deeper root in English law than I had at first perceived. I cannot say that I agree with your position, nor can I disagree. Give me time to unpack your barrel of arguments. I am intrigued by your position that the king and magistrates owe more allegiance to their subjects than the subjects owe them. I hear King James turning over in his grave.

As your friend, I nonetheless feel I must warn you that when the members of the General Court untie themselves from the legal ropes with which you have bound them, they will move again and again against you until you become their puppet on a string. Beware Endecott's smiles, for I fear he is drunk with envy.

As for my father, he is now inclined to work out contracts with the natives. I know he thinks well of you and has more than once confessed his anguish of heart at your opinions. My own heart is torn, divided by two loyalties.

Regarding the matter of . . . .

In kindest regards,
John Winthrop Jr.

After they had read the letter, Mary stored it away in a chest of papers. "He tells the truth, dear. You have pressed the court to the wall, I fear."

"I did not fancy that certain members of the court would follow the route I have taken. The majority, nevertheless, will come closer if only Cotton and the younger Winthrop can gain entrance to the governor's mind."

"If you are to enter that guarded citadel, both the governor's son and Cotton must first persuade the governor to lower the drawbridge from inside."

"I know, love, but—"

"Oh, Roger, what does the future hold for us? Five years from hence, will I visit my husband at the prison or . . . or the grave? Or will I perhaps watch them raise a statue in his honor?"

He laughed. "A statue for birds to sit upon and make their comments after I have gone?"

"Ah, sweet husband, you laugh; but in this past month, a full year of seasons has turned inside me."

April now brought the event Roger and Mary had anticipated since arriving in New England. At last they were moving into their new house! On this day of celebration, Little Mary played on the wooden floors and smiled almost perpetually as the church people came to pay their respects. Roger grinned and grinned as he remembered their wigwam days and the harsh winters among the Wampanoags.

The flames in the kitchen fireplace danced for joy. The wind whistled merrily through the trees outside the kitchen window. Mary served her favorite meats and pastries to congregation members and other neighbors and friends. Ezra Welch brought a basket of fresh fish and clams. The bright eyes of a nine-year-old boy grew wide as he peered into the basket and watched some of the fish flap their tails.

Despite declining health, Pastor Skelton came to offer kind wishes and to tease Roger and Mary. "Such scrumptious living will surely deliver you to the stocks."

After everyone gathered in the parlor, Wilfred and Agnes Barry listened to Roger brag of Wilfred's carpentry. Agnes smiled at her carpenter husband. Jeremiah and Grace Paynter sat with their adopted daughter Deborah. Though Jeremiah had rescued her from the well, her love had rescued him from his grief. After jumping off Jeremiah's knee, Deborah ran to Roger and dared him to guess what she held in her hands.

"A horse?"

Deborah looked over her shoulder at Grace and giggled. Then she shook her head.

He guessed again. "A pear?"

Deborah jumped with glee and shook her head.

"A billy goat?"

"No! No!"

He knelt beside her and whispered, "I know. A turkey with a mustache."

She giggled, handed Roger her present, and threw her arms around his neck.

"A present for me?"

"For Little Mary!" Deborah beamed with pride.

He accepted the small metal spoon and held it admiringly in his cupped hand.

"It came from England! From England!" Deborah looked again over her shoulder at her proud new parents.

Roger knew that in this sparse land, a metal spoon was a dear gift. He scooped Deborah up with one arm and took her to see his daughter. As Jeremiah followed them, Roger smiled and shook his head. "So difficult to believe, is it not?"

"Aye." Jeremiah raised his eyebrow inquisitively as Roger lowered Deborah to the floor to let her play.

"Deborah's melancholy has lifted," Roger whispered to Jeremiah. "Through love alone, you and Grace transformed a sad and terrified girl into this happy creature of heaven."

A few minutes later, back in the parlor, Roger kept gazing out the window as if he expected someone. He suddenly felt his own face glow. Little Snowfeather was skipping ahead of her father, who chatted with the Sachem Miantonomo. To Roger's surprise, Titus and Keplutok also appeared. Now his joy was complete.

Mary came from the kitchen to greet them at the door, laughed, and wept until the natives begged her to cry no more.

Just before sunset, Pastor Skelton took Roger aside. "This has been one of the happiest days of my life. How the people love you. You are more than a brother to me.

If only my dear wife could have lived to see this day. With her absence the congregation sorely needs a wise, trustworthy woman like your Mary. Look at her. See how she delights in her new calling."

In May 1634, Endecott dissolved his fragile friendship with Winthrop Sr. when the latter suffered a political defeat in Boston. Charging Winthrop with taking the role of an absolute sovereign, the freemen of Massachusetts dismissed him from office and replaced him with Thomas Dudley, Esquire. Feeling at liberty to oppose Winthrop openly, Endecott now proclaimed that the defeat was richly deserved. Far from diminishing, however, Endecott's animosity toward Roger increased sharply. Both Dudley and Endecott anchored their new friendship in their mutual hostility toward him.

Mary predicted that Winthrop would gain back his full power. "Like a magnificent whale, the man comes up from the deep only to catch his breath." She cautioned her husband against underestimating Winthrop's power.

SALEM AND BOSTON

Summer–November 1634

For Roger, Mary, and the Salem congregation, summer 1634 blossomed with both new trepidation and hope. Some in Salem prophesied thickening mysteries; others predicted the denouement of many plots; a few warned of intrigues while their neighbors whispered of sudden exposure of concealed motives and hidden schemes. Roger, however, talked of new hope and fulfilled dreams amid the ironies and absurdities.

No event proved more absurd than a fruitless controversy that emerged within the Salem church. Four years earlier, the Reverend Skelton had read from the First Epistle to the Corinthians and proclaimed to the congregation his opinion that it was improper for an unveiled woman to pray to God.

Partly because of his respect for his pastor and partly because he, a Protestant, took the Bible as divine revelation, Roger felt obliged to agree that church women should follow the Apostle Paul's advice to wear veils at public assemblies. Yet Roger believed that women outside the church did not come under the Apostle's proclamation.

One hot August day, Mary greeted her husband at the door of their home and gently placed a wooden bucket over his head. "Wear this, and I will wear the veil. Perhaps you and Pastor Skelton and all the other men who advocate the veil can fit together all your brains in this pail." Then she gathered up her daughter and left for a neighbor's house. Having later that night retrieved his wife, he sat with her by candlelight with the Bible opened at 1 Corinthians.

Mary raised her right eyebrow. "Let me read this passage again to you. The Apostle Paul states it as a question, asking whether it is comely or proper that a woman should pray unto God uncovered. He never mentions the veil. For all I know, her hair or her skin is cover enough. Perhaps the Apostle Paul wished all women draped in white sheets and traipsing through graveyards at night."

"Do not speak lightly of the Apostle's inspired words."

"Roger, I love you dearly. But some things regarding the Apostle Paul are not angelic."

"I do not grasp your meaning."

Mary bristled. "You know my meaning quite well. I beg to hear no more of this veiling of my face. When you married me, was my face offensive to you?"

"'Tis a beautiful face."

"Then in heaven's name, why should it offend its Creator? Why should I cover it when I pray? Would angels in heaven flap their wings and stir up heaven's dust upon seeing my face? Pray tell, what strange wine had the Apostle sipped for his stomach's sake?"

Later that summer, after the veil controversy had faded, Pastor Skelton's mortal frame gave up the ghost. At the burial, Roger spoke to the people of their pastor's many kind deeds. The congregation buried him beside his wife in the church cemetery. Having lost their pastor, the grieving congregation turned to Roger increasingly for guidance, instruction, and counsel. Mary's wisdom and favor so grew among the people that her work resembled that of her father, the kindly vicar in Lincolnshire.

A momentous event took place in Boston in September. A tall, stately woman named Anne Hutchinson and her family arrived. Although the ground did not shake when Anne set foot in the New World, some in the church saw her as an instrument of the special gift of the Holy Ghost. Others soon labeled her "The Antinomian Cyclone."

In November sparks from Endecott's flint and Winthrop's steel ignited at last into roaring flames. Endecott stood before an audience in Salem, held up an English flag for all to see, cut out the cross, and declared it a papal X on Christendom's face. Learning of Endecott's actions against the flag, Winthrop instantly charged that Roger had secretly instigated it all. Winthrop later said to only a handful in Boston, "Endecott lacks the brains to invent such a scheme on his own." A day or two before Endecott's public act, Roger had indeed protested that the British flag with its cross did cynically desecrate the Christian faith. He had in fact held up the flag and said softly but sternly to the Salem congregation, "Under this flag, the royalty of England falsely call themselves the defenders of our Christian faith. I charge that they desecrate our faith when they sponsor slaughter, piracy, pillage, and persecution in the name of the Savior. Under this flag, they have mockingly portrayed the Lamb of God as a wolf among other wolves."

Though no longer governor, Winthrop exerted influence in Boston as an outspoken magistrate. He so vented his hot wrath against Roger that other magistrates trembled. One who called himself Roger's friend wrote him a letter to warn him of further intrigues: "Thomas Dudley has vowed publicly to rid Salem of your presence, calling you that 'seditious arsonist who spreads fires of heresy and dissension wherever he journeys.'" Some of the magistrates, however, advised caution, one going so far as to charge that if Williams is the flame, Winthrop and Dudley are "the wind carrying it from town to town."

Roger heard discordant sounds of irony in all of this. He had set out to influence Cotton and Winthrop Jr. directly, thereby hoping to sway the older Winthrop and the other magistrates. Despite having never set out to influence Endecott, he now found himself accused of exerting excessive influence on him and igniting his attack on the king's colors. Irony resounded throughout Massachusetts as Endecott unwittingly provoked events so harmful to Roger that a calculated attack would have been more bearable.

In truth Endecott and Roger had quite different reasons for objecting to the cross in a nation's flag. Endecott contended that it carried popish odor. Roger, on the other hand, contended that the symbol belonged to the Christians alone, not to the governments of Europe, which had perverted the symbol by making it a banner to justify both violence and lust for power.

SALEM AND BOSTON

January–Spring 1635

In early January 1635, a ship from England sailed through icy waters to Salem. It carried a letter from Sydrach Williams to his brother Roger. Alone when he opened the letter, he read the words more chilling than Nova Scotia's icy waters: "Our dear mother is dead."

His knees turning to water and a numbness spreading throughout his body, he sat down and continued to read Sydrach's words: "On the day she drew her last breath, our angelic mother said to me, 'Tell my beloved Roger that no son could warm his mother's heart more than has he. Tell him that no memory do I cherish more than of his boyhood when he befriended the Dutch children when all others of the neighborhood mocked them and cast aspersions upon them.'"

Closing his eyes, he could see his mother's face and see her wave, trying heroically to smile farewell on the day of his departure from England. He remembered thinking then that he might never again see her. *Out brief, gentle candle!*

In trepidation he opened his eyes and read still more of Sydrach's words: "I regret to add that the man who taught you the common law of England and whom you served as a son to a father, Sir Edward Coke, is also dead."

"No! No! It cannot be!" Roger gasped for breath, feeling his heart might crack with doubled grief. Burying his face in his hands, he wept like a child.

The moments seemed like hours as conflicting thoughts tangled with one another like loose twine and whirled through his mind, a hundred regrets tormenting him. Each *if only* tugged at his heart. If only he had stopped at Coke's house on that baleful day of his escape from England . . . . If only he had spent another hour with his mother telling her how much he admired her courage and wisdom . . . . If only . . . if only . . . . His mind entertained possibilities that now perished unfulfilled. He thought of words he might have said, of deeds he might have done, of kindnesses he might have expressed. How brief the gift of life now seemed!

Spring 1635 arrived with the General Court alarmed at events in Salem. Despite the influence of Dudley, Winthrop, John Haynes, and the other magistrates who were hostile to Roger's presence, the Salem congregation grew fonder of Mary and him. With Pastor Skelton now cold in the grave, the people increasingly felt their need for someone to minister to them in their tribulations and to teach them lessons from Scripture and history.

In Boston individual magistrates ran helter-skelter to hold private conferences and to listen to those who deemed the colony in danger because of Salem's growing liberty. Dudley made no secret of his animosity. "This man does not belong among us. I say, let him either confess his error or return to England."

"Is Roger possessed?" one magistrate asked another.

"Has his brain cooked with fever?" still another inquired. "What is the source of his wild notions?"

No magistrate could understand Roger's claim that the government had no right to require an oath in God's name.

The court convened with John Haynes as its newly elected governor. Knowing that Haynes shared his own opinion that Roger posed a danger to the colony, Dudley had met with Haynes to disclose his secret plan against Salem's new pastor.

Holding his broad-brimmed hat in his hand, Roger stood in the Boston Court before the magistrates to hear Governor Haynes list the latest charges against him.

Haynes began in an officious voice. "Master Williams, you are accused of labeling as a sacrilege the oath that all our males of military age stand required to make. I speak of the oath proclaiming loyalty to the governor and to all other elected and appointed officials. How plead you?"

"Such an oath would have the state require unbelievers to take the name of God falsely."

Dudley sucked air through his teeth. "We have no time for this quibbling."

Roger smiled sardonically. "Why call *your* points arguments and *mine* quibbles?"

The newly elected deputy governor shook his finger. "You will not slip around us this time. You must answer the question. Did you call the oath a sacrilege?"

"If as a believing Christian you choose to say *So help me God* when you swear an oath, it is no intrusion on your freedom of conscience. If by the fist of government, however, we require of unbelievers the oath in God's name, we infringe on their conscience and force our religion upon them. Forcing unbelievers to speak such words of worship is to require them to take God's name lightly or in vain."

The deputy clinched his fist and struck the table. "Again I ask you. Is the oath a sacrilege?"

"If in making an oath, Christian believers call on heaven of their own free choice, it is no sacrilege."

Magistrate Winthrop lifted his voice. "Have I not warned each of you in this august body that Mr. Williams would undermine the magistrates' authority?"

Roger cut his eyes to the Reverend Cotton in the hope that the esteemed clergyman would come to his defense. When Cotton said nothing, Roger rose to his own defense. "I undermine no legitimate authority, only its illegitimate extension. Let the magistrates deal with citizens as members of a civil society only. When they dabble in matters of religious doctrine and Christian worship, on the other hand, they become wolves in sheep's clothing."

Known by most of the magistrates as an honest and industrious merchant, Jeremiah Paynter stood up. "I would speak on behalf of Master Williams, who serves us well as our minister and teacher. Above all—"

Haynes lowered the gavel with a bang. "You are present at this assembly only by the good grace of the court members. You have no authority to speak."

"But . . . but our spokesman, Captain Endecott, holds his tongue." Jeremiah shot a reproachful look at the captain.

Endecott sprang to his feet. "I will hold my tongue no longer." With a dramatic flair, he looked around the room. Then a frown formed on his brow as if a new thought had entered his head. "I am Salem's spokesman, and I see before us a path not yet . . . ." Stumbling through his words, he seemed suddenly uncertain of where they would take him.

Before he could resume speaking, Magistrate William Pynchon from Roxbury said in Endecott's ear, "I warn you, do not take liberties with your fellow magistrates. Though no believer can of his own will step outside the circle of God's grace, you may quickly find yourself outside the grace of this court."

Endecott opened his mouth wide and raised his pointed forefinger over his head. Then he closed his mouth, gritted his teeth, and slowly dropped his hand to his side. With an angry but sheepish grin at Roger, he took his seat and said no more.

Another magistrate came to his feet to accuse the Salem church of choosing a minister who held reckless and dangerous opinions displeasing to the majority of the clergy. Although Jeremiah stood again to defend his church minister, Haynes ordered him to sit down lest he be removed.

Roger took the floor and made himself appear as if he were searching for a particular face. "Perhaps during the night, a ship delivered a bishop from England to our shores to tell us how to conduct the affairs of our churches." He glanced at the audience. "If the bishop is present, please signify. Ah, I see no bishop. I hear none. Therefore, no one can play bishop for our church in Salem. Have we not made a covenant among our several congregations that each governs itself without hierarchy?" He turned his right palm down. "Now by a strange sleight of hand, this court transforms itself into a college of bishops."

The first day of the court's session ended in thickening mysteries, new intrigues, and sudden exposure of hidden schemes. The more Dudley and Winthrop called for resolution against Roger, the more the intrigues surfaced.

As soon as Dudley adjourned with the stroke of his gavel, Roger made his way out of the courtroom and toward Captain Endecott, who upon seeing him jumped into a carriage and rode away.

Jeremiah saw what had happened. "Roger, Endecott agreed with your position in Salem on the oaths. His opinions in Boston now flow with the stronger current."

Two days later, Dudley secretly approached Captain Endecott and invited him to walk across the bridge toward Corn Hill where they could talk in private. When they reached a small copse, they stopped. Now pregnant with buds and poised to deliver their blossoms, the trees swayed in the salt air wafting in from the Bay. Geese returning from the south made their way farther north.

Dudley looked around to assure himself that no one could overhear them talk. He squinted his eyes and spoke to Endecott. "Governor Haynes and the other magistrates are not without mercy. Though you have grievously offended the court by defacing the flag, your wisdom in not siding with Roger Williams adds to your credit. The heavier sentence will be dismissed. For the lighter sentence, the court will forbid you from holding office."

"For what period?"

Dudley stretched himself to his full height. "Only a year."

Endecott nodded and smirked. "What will happen to Williams?"

Dudley turned to look behind him. "For the present, his support in the Salem congregation is too strong and would create wide dissension among us. But we are not without equally strong means." A twisted little grin curled on Dudley's lips. He touched Endecott's arm. "Sometimes a castle is better seized from within, eh?"

Only a few days later, the court stated officially that the lightness of Endecott's sentence reflected the court's awareness that he had acted "out of tenderness of conscience, not of any evil intent."

Endecott returned straightway to Salem. He knew he must act quickly. "Sometimes a castle is better seized from within," he mused aloud.

BOSTON AND SALEM

Spring–Summer 1635

The months from spring to summer gave Endecott time to nurture his revenge toward Roger. He rode to the town of Dorchester immediately south of Boston to find Benjamin Cook, who in November 1633 had fled Salem in disgrace. Eventually, Endecott found him living in an abandoned barn. Instead of denouncing him as a rumormonger, he said, "Benjamin, I have need of your service, which will restore your good name before the people of Salem."

Cook dusted the straw from his clothes. "Do not speak of Salem. It is the graveyard of my past."

"But not of your future. Now let us talk, and I will explain."

Cook climbed up into the loft, Endecott following.

Endecott sat down. "Everything is in the timing, do you not agree?"

"So it is."

"Our time has arrived. Marblehead Neck is the place." He proceeded cautiously, recalling that Cook's trustworthiness easily melted under tribulation.

Cook's animal eyes darted back and forth. "I once had some hope for Marblehead Neck."

"More than hope, Benjamin. You have a stake if we seize the moment."

"What action do you propose?"

"Ah, action is the word. I once heard that the moon helps bring the tide. You and I will serve as two moons to bring up the tide of interest in this Marblehead Neck. Come with me to Salem, and I will—"

"Salem is a closed door to me."

"I have the key and the means to bring down the man who proved to be no friend to you."

"Roger Williams?"

"The same. He has swayed the people against their better interest."

"I fear the man's influence and have no wish to fall into his net."

"Fear? Have I misjudged Benjamin Cook? You wish to live your years at the measly table of fear?" Endecott moved to get up.

"Hold! Be not so quick. If you have a plan, lay it out."

Endecott raised his eyes heavenward and inhaled deeply. "'Tis a plan, one in which we hold as a net to catch Roger Williams. Put your head with mine, and we shall direct this drama to the end."

On the next day, Cook appeared in Salem and went at once to the elders of the church to confess his error of the past. With dramatic flair, he proclaimed his intention to restore his good name by bringing news that would benefit the people: "I have reason to conclude that some intend to snatch Marblehead Neck from under your noses and make it a town that will be your twin. Unless you move quickly, this twin will be Jacob the supplanter and you the Esau swindled out of his birthright and blessing."

Jeremiah appeared wary. "What course have you in mind for us to navigate?"

"Why, no course at all. I merely bring you news to use as you will. If you sleep like Saul in your cave, David will come to steal your spear and more. Look across this jeweled bay. Salem on one side; Marblehead Neck on the other. Twin cities. Forlorn Esau here; prosperous Jacob there. Or envision one city only, all Salem thriving and prospering, Salem's children and grandchildren peering back across the bay and calling their fathers blessed."

Day after day, both Cook and Endecott sowed the seeds of aspiration and ambition among the people. Above all, they spread fear, telling the people that they would become Boston's stepchild and Marblehead's shadow unless they moved to take Marblehead Neck as their own. Again and again, Endecott proclaimed, "Marblehead is Salem's birthright."

Day after day, the people peered across the bay as if peering into the future. Their hearts swelled with hope, visions danced before them, and new excitement blew in with warm May breezes.

Early that summer, in Boston, Governor Haynes and Dudley entered Winthrop's large house and accepted his invitation to join him in his study.

After everyone sat down, Governor Haynes scooted to the edge of his chair. "We have news of Salem."

Winthrop stuffed his pipe. "Ill wind?"

"Good and ill," Haynes answered. "The Salem congregation has again voted Roger Williams as their official teaching elder."

Winthrop shook his head. "The monster now has two heads, pastor and teaching elder."

No one needed to explain the role and power of the teaching elder, particularly in Salem. Representing the people's trust, the elder enjoyed the right and opportunity to expound the doctrine and guidelines of the congregation. The elder had no power beyond that of persuasion, but the men in Boston knew that Master Williams required no power beyond that. Secretly they both admired and envied his disarming way of engaging the people in discussion. Winthrop in particular knew that Roger would follow the argument wherever it led, a trait that frustrated some opponents and charmed others.

Frowning, Winthrop laid his pipe in its receptacle and tapped the top of his new desk with his fingers. "Now that the Salem congregation has officially made him both teaching elder and minister, he holds a vice grip on the people."

"'Tis a vice the Salem people will soon regret." Dudley scowled.

Winthrop stood up from behind his desk, walked to the door, and opened it. After looking up and down the hallway, he closed the door and locked it. Sitting down again, he folded his hands on his desk. "We cannot yield to wishful thinking. The hard truth is the people have foolishly placed the key in Roger's pocket!"

Dudley grinned righteously. "Ah, but we hold the string to that key." Winthrop's eyebrows rose sharply as Dudley explained, "Salem's petition for Marblehead Neck has been renewed and carries many signatures. This good wind blows well for our sails. Governor Haynes and I agree. 'Tis time to hoist the sails and ride this good fortune."

"We have in mind to rid ourselves and Salem of the pest Roger Williams," said Haynes.

Concealing all emotion, Winthrop picked up his pipe and lit it. He blew a circle of smoke in the air and leaned back in his chair. "I am listening."

"The great fish Salem has already taken the bait." Dudley smiled as he placed the petition for Marblehead Neck in Winthrop's hand. "We propose to give Salem all the line she needs until we draw her in."

Winthrop pulled open a drawer to his desk. "This petition is like fine wine." He placed the petition in the drawer. "It needs time to age. The Lord was with Gideon because of his patience and diligence in his righteous cause."

Haynes and Dudley looked at one another and nodded their approval as Winthrop dropped the key into his pocket.

At the same time in Salem, the people had united to become like a distance runner gaining velocity, all the body parts working in harmony. Roger and Mary had felt the vibrancy of the town as trading increased and new possibilities sprang up every month. To the west thrived the trading post envisioned by Roger and Jeremiah. To the east across the water lay the Marblehead Neck envisioned by the people as their town's extension. Together they would become as one, a righteous London of the New World. It was a year of hope and dreams.

Mary stood in the kitchen." You must slow down, dear. Now listen to me! I know how much you relish your work as pastor and teaching elder. Yet I have never seen you so burdened with cares. Here, sit at the table and eat."

For both of them, every day seemed busier than the previous. Their firstborn, now twenty-two months, kept them alert and active. Little Mary's curiosity seemed boundless.

Roger laughed. "She is a butterfly, and the whole world is her garden. Look at her dart about, testing everything in her path."

With everyone doting over her, the child Mary smiled freely sometimes from morning until night.

Although certain magistrates had warned him to say no more about the English duties to the natives, about oaths or the limits of the civil magistrates' power, he paid no regard to these men. Who were they to make such demands? The Salem congregation resented what they regarded as the court's intrusion on their autonomy. With the congregation's support, he sent a letter to Governor Haynes.

Honorable Governor,

I hope this short note finds you in good health and that the grace of heaven shines upon you and your family.

Pertaining to your letter demanding my silence on certain topics, I would beg you to consider that civil magistrates are not the guardians of the beliefs and religion of others. In Massachusetts would you marry religion and politics, making them one flesh . . . ?

If you continue with your own premises, the commonwealth and the church will become the same. Do you see the contradiction? The churches in Massachusetts in one accord renounce a bishop's hierarchy in the morning while by night embracing the court's decisions as an archbishop's edict.

The people of Salem's congregation implore you . . . .

With due regard,
Roger Williams

To their mutual dissatisfaction, Haynes and Roger continued to exchange letters. Night after night, Roger walked along the shore because a swarm of ideas in his head rendered him sleepless.

Late in June, a synod of the ministers around Boston gathered to discuss the action to take. Genuine fear gripped some, fear that unless quickly checked, Roger's persuasive power would touch all the churches in Massachusetts. They did not know how to answer him conclusively without raising more doubts and questions about their Puritan way. The Reverend Cotton composed treatises, trying to meet Roger's doctrine point by point.

Deep from inside some ministers, envy surfaced to spray its venom. "The Salem church has grown too powerful," one minister complained bitterly.

Another minister spoke, not from jealousy, but from honest fear. "We must silence the teaching elder before he leads other congregations over the cliff of error and impure doctrine."

The spirit of punishment settled over the whole synod as the elders and ministers called for discipline against Roger and the Salem congregation.

On a hot Wednesday afternoon, young Thomas Angell, tall and uncommonly strong for his age, delivered an envelope to Roger at his house. In London he had attached himself to the Williams family, and Roger had seen to it that the orphan fulfilled his dream of sailing to New England.

Roger broke the seal. "Mary, a long letter from our friend Eric!"

"I know you miss him as much as I. Read it aloud, dear, while I wash our daughter's hair."

After Thomas Angell had left the house, Roger handed her the letter and laughed, patting her stomach. "Give yourself and the wee one in there some rest while I wash Little Mary's hair."

Dear Roger and Mary,

   I hope Little Mary continues to flourish and will enjoy the small present I am sending her separately. Would that I were delivering it in person.

   Until this point, I have felt at liberty to visit you as I pleased free of repercussions. Unfortunately, I must for a while resort to letters to inform you of menacing plots against you. Otherwise, valuable sources would quickly dry up, thus preventing me from being of crucial service to you.

   The first piece of information: the clergy of Massachusetts will meet to pass swift judgment on the Salem claim that each congregation is self-governing. Furthermore a strong rumor (one I half believe) asserts that Winthrop has persuaded many elders from the several churches to consider breaking with the Salem church. In some ways, this move could serve your interests. If I understand the current of your last letter to me, you and some of the Salem congregation plan to cut ties with the other churches because of their perpetual link with the Church of England. (Pertaining to this, I note that our friend Milton has sent sad news of that very link, tyranny and corruption spreading still deeper in the church that mothered us.)

   Now to the second and perhaps more threatening information: I have a friend who, while wishing his identity kept undisclosed, has learned of a secret plot. Some court members intend to delay the decision on the Marblehead Neck petition presented by the Salem merchants and others. The delay serves as a deliberate tactic to induce the Salem authorities to rid their town of your presence. Though in principle the Marblehead Neck territory belongs to the people of Salem, it will never fall officially into their hands so long as you reside in Salem.

   Would that this information were nothing but flimsy rumor. I beg you to take heed, my good and honorable friend. You have unrelenting enemies both on and off the court who fear they cannot counter you in open discourse and debate. They, therefore, plot to use Machiavelli's tools to undermine your position in Massachusetts. I beseech you to accept no honey-coated offer to return you to England, for I am sure some there would feed you to the lion Laud . . . .

Mary stared at the letter. "Oh, my darling, if this plot unfolds, where, pray tell, will we go? What will happen to us when the new baby comes? Dear Lord in heaven, how can these servants of the Prince of Peace make such war upon one another?"

"Mary, you are shivering." He dried his hands, wrapped a summer shawl around her shoulders, and then finished rinsing his daughter's hair and drying it with a cloth.

After singing their daughter to sleep, he walked hand-in-hand with Mary through the house. Like people expecting a storm or even a fire, they looked forlornly at the walls. Might they soon see them no more?

Her eyes lit on the whatnots. "I made a few with these two hands." Fighting back tears, she looked outside her window at the families strolling in the summer air. She saw people whose broken hearts she helped bind, the widow whose husband Roger had buried, a happy couple whose marriage they had celebrated, and two neighbors whose fierce anger Roger had helped turn to deeper friendship. How could she bring herself to vanish from this new life they had woven thread by thread?

He ached with guilt, not for having courageously defended conscience and right-eousness born of liberty, but for having enticed a young woman from her parents in Lincolnshire and drawn her onto a battlefield. Peering at their child sleeping on the pallet Agnes Barry had made for her, he smiled and read aloud the name *Little Mary* stitched in red thread on the pallet.

The court summoned Roger to appear in Boston on July 8. Against his wishes, Mary accompanied him. As they walked across the cobblestones toward the Boston meetinghouse, people lined the way, some calling him a heretic and firebrand, others wishing him heaven's blessing. One magistrate said to another, "See how his damnable doctrine has already divided our people."

Several voices rang out.

"You set us on the path toward anarchy!"

"Do you deny that magistrates have authority from God to protect our souls and minds from dangerous doctrine?"

"There is talk that you permit professing believers to attend or not attend worship according to their choice."

A magistrate in sincere anger shouted, "Do you appoint yourself as the defender of the faith?"

Inside the meetinghouse, Roger listened to the official charges against him. Governor John Haynes conspicuously relished this hour of triumph and apparently thought that by making no pretense at neutrality he demonstrated not only himself more ardent for the cause of righteousness, but also his zeal for order and true doctrine second to none.

While the Reverend Cotton and the rest of the clergy sat at the rear after having counseled at length with the court, Magistrate Winthrop read the charges aloud. As soon as he sat down, three other court members testified heatedly against Roger, who listened in silence but took careful notes.

The whispering throng outside peered eagerly through the windows. Near the rear of the room, a few of the ill-mannered groaned and hissed as though on cue.

Roger eventually looked at Haynes. *If only he would call for order!* When Haynes instead turned his eyes away, Roger addressed the hecklers. "I have not come to parlay with mooing cows and hissing serpents." When the noise continued, he looked sternly at Haynes. "If the moderator has turned into a pillar of salt, perhaps the court should find another."

Haynes flushed crimson, struck the table with his wooden gavel, and waved it at the hecklers. "If you have come to hiss, then take your leave. We have somber business to pursue." Haynes then glared at Roger. Silence came at last.

Knowing that most magistrates and clergy stood with Winthrop Sr., Roger decided to address John Cotton, who though not a member of the court had strong appeal to the clergy and to the people of Boston. Focusing his eyes on Cotton, he began in a low, quiet voice.

Cotton moved to a table and picked up the quill to take notes.

Feeling encouraged, Roger spoke with precision, clarifying his view regarding reli-gious conscience and doctrine. After speaking for half an hour, he paused to collect his thoughts. To reduce the misunderstanding of his meaning, he quickly summarized his position. "First, the state's legitimate duty is not to protect *beliefs* from criticism, but to protect *people* from thieves and aggressors, to protect physical life and property. Second, governments lack both the art and the moral right to attempt to protect the soul or mind. Third, each church or congregation is free to establish its own standards for its members, and each adult should enjoy the freedom to decide which congregation to join or not join. Fourth, compelled belief is no belief at all. Forced worship, a mere act upon a stage, both insults the actor and disgraces the faith." He again faced John Cotton and said with slow deliberation. "If you choose not to join the church in which I hold membership, you must be free to find your own congregation or no congrega-tion and to live your own life so long as you keep the civil peace and do not infringe on your neighbor's life, limb, or property. The state owes you first and foremost *hands off.* It owes you no pure doctrine, but rather the liberty to *seek* it for yourself. It owes you no livelihood, but rather the liberty to *earn* it for yourself. It owes you no happiness, but rather the liberty to *pursue* it for yourself with those who bond with you in mutual freedom."

When the group from Salem standing outside the window heard these words, they clapped their hands. Thomas Angell was the first to throw his hat in the air. Jeremiah beamed as if he had made the speech himself. Winthrop sat somber-faced, yet Roger saw Cotton nod his head vigorously and write as fast as his fingers would move.

From the corner of his eye, Roger saw Mary squeezing her hands. Feeling every eye glued on him, he sensed that many magistrates still hoped he would live up to their description of him as a wild man.

The crowd inside and outside the meetinghouse erupted with cries and shouts, some in anger, others in exaltation. Governor Haynes, the moderator, sprang to his feet and hammered hard, demanding order.

Joining him, Roger waved his hand over the crowd to quell their passions. Looking over his shoulder, he saw Jeremiah Paynter attempt to hold back angry men shaking their fists in the air. Winthrop Jr. was shaking his head in despair at the unruly crowd. When the soldiers entered, Roger prayed that no blood would flow.

After Haynes had restored a measure of tranquility, Roger expected the whole court ordeal to end, and indeed Haynes exclaimed, "Enough! Enough!" and hammered his gavel. Roger sat down.

The moderator had quieted the crowd, however, not to end the interrogation and replies, but to advance more charges. He stared knives at Roger. "Why do you evade the charge of the wider circle of the libertine? This perversion, this . . . . Master Williams, you must address the wider-circle charge."

Winthrop Sr. pointed his finger. "Answer! Answer! Would you embrace all, even the dung heap itself?"

Dudley could contain himself no longer. "Master Williams, do not conceal the seductive libertine coiled within you serpent-like. Do not deny that you embrace all manner of heresy and false belief. Enough of your evasion! I charge you to address the charges!"

He stared at his feet and told himself to wait patiently until Dudley's rage had subsided. Sweat broke out on his forehead, his knees weakened, and a knot formed at the center of his belly. Hoping his weakness had not appeared conspicuous, he placed one hand on the table to brace himself. Then he caught a glance of Mary, whose smile cooled his forehead like a refreshing breeze.

The raging storm inside Dudley played itself out. When Roger saw the magistrate William Pynchon lean over and whisper into Winthrop's ear, he suddenly recalled something Pynchon had told the colonists. Roger then spoke for all to hear. "Many of us felt our hearts moved by the story of Mr. Pynchon's grandfather, who left his home in Europe because the town magistrates sought to make their Catholic religion the gateway to gainful employment. Only Catholics could enter the universities. Sadly we all know of many similar histories. In Europe bitter feuds have survived the generations, each party demanding that all other citizens embrace its religion before enjoying access to honest employment. Turks have required neighbors to be Muslims, Romans to be Catholics, and Geneva's populace to be Protestant of a special mold."

He caught sight of a sea captain standing outside the window. "When you sail from port to port, do you demand that your captain have Calvin's doctrine in his heart or Muhammad's faith? No, you demand that he possess the art and skill of navigation and that he demonstrate elementary regard for human life and property necessary for peaceful commerce. You do not ask the mason whether he lays Hebrew stones, the fisherman whether he sells Lutheran fish, or the tailor whether he sews Arminian cloaks. Let there be no further misunderstanding of my meaning. In Salem or any other town, we must all learn to live together and conduct commerce even though we part on various matters of religion."

He paused to look directly at Winthrop and then at Haynes. "I expect a magistrate to have regard not for my religion, but for my *soul liberty* and my right to embrace the religion that meets the standard of my conscience!"

Haynes interrupted. "You have had your say. The court, nonetheless, grants you a minute to conclude."

"I thank you for your indulgence." He wiped cold sweat from his face. With all his heart, he hoped he had persuaded the scholarly John Cotton. Knowing he had only a moment left, he quickly launched his final appeal. "For those of us who profess to follow Christ, the issue distills to this. If, as the Apostle Paul says, the church is the body of Christ, then we sell that body into whoredom when we sanction her sleeping with bloodstained tyrants for the price of land or power!"

He reluctantly sat down. Had his last words persuaded John Cotton? If only he could see some sign on the reverend's countenance!

"Heresy!" one magistrate cried out. Others labeled Roger's views as "fit doctrine for Philistines," as "Jezebel's milk," and as "Herod's meat."

The magistrates fired a volley of questions, and Roger responded with short answers. When the volleys ceased, Haynes imperiously instructed him to leave the meetinghouse. "You will receive our decision in due time."

When Roger stood and turned to depart, he looked for Cotton. The clergyman's chair at the table was empty. Walking out on unsteady legs, Roger felt the crowd's enthusiasm ripple through his body. "You are music to my heart," he said softly to those around him.

Jeremiah walked up. "You look pale, Brother Roger. Come with me."

He tried to smile his gratitude, but he kept looking for the Reverend Cotton.

Mary caught up with him and walked with him and Jeremiah to meet the coach that Thomas Angell had borrowed.

"Drive carefully," Roger said softly to Angell. "Remember, my wife is with child."

As soon as they all sat down inside the coach, Jeremiah said, "Captain Firebrook sends word that you may rest at Blackstone's house."

Roger leaned his head back and closed his eyes. The ordeal was over.

Or perhaps it had only begun.

BOSTON AND SALEM

Summer 1635

Upon returning to Salem, Roger began working with Herculean effort among the people. Mary took him by the hand near sunset and led him to their small bedroom. Her large, luminous eyes seemed to say to him that she must speak about something of profound importance. The rich blue of her eyes radiated such warmth that he sat down to relish her gaze.

"I . . . I have hoped and even prayed," she began in her soft but resolute way, "that my husband would find time for rest and even leisure. Instead he finds higher walls to scale."

He shifted his whole body in the sturdy straight-backed chair that the carpenter Wilfred Barry had built for him. Since returning to Salem, Roger had broken two chairs under his extreme energy and vigor.

Mary sat down on their bed and rubbed her knees. "You seek to increase your work to the point of risking illness. Is it possible that my husband secretly counts his excess in work as *penance* for his sins?"

He opened his mouth to speak, but she suffered no interruption. "No, give me time to say all in my heart. If your work is secret penance, then you *preach* the gospel of grace but *practice* the old doctrine of works and penance, which is more Romanist than Rome!"

Roger crossed his right leg over his left knee. He felt the sting of her charge and wished to deny it. Yet the truth of her words caught him with such stunning surprise that he could not speak. He felt anger and pride, anger at the accuracy of her words and pride in the depth of her understanding of the gospel of pure grace. His heart was so moved that soon the anger gave way to a flood of gratitude. "I . . . I will ponder . . . . Yes, yes, Mary . . . . I know not what to say. You puncture, but it is like the puncture of a boil that has too long festered."

He stared into those large, wondrous eyes and saw a woman whose passion for truth was no less than his own. Suddenly her presence and her words gave him a new freedom so that he could now honestly admit his limitations. He could not alone carry out the Herculean work he had attempted in the previous months.

On the following day, he stopped Mary in the parlor. "My body sends messengers of pain. A sane man heeds both his body and his wife."

The congregation had already sent the elders to her to encourage their teaching elder to rest. He now took their counsel to heart. But no sooner had he begun to relax than the people of Salem found themselves embroiled in another controversy with the General Court. They turned to him for help.

During the spring, a number of Salem's leading citizens and deputies had clearly demonstrated that Salem enjoyed *prima facie* claim to Marblehead Neck. They had presented a petition, which the Boston General Court would now on July 12, 1635, either accept or deny.

Standing now with the court's decision in his hands, Governor Haynes read aloud: "Access to the land in Marblehead Neck cannot be authorized by this court at this time. Furthermore the court holds the Salem deputies in contempt of court and denies them a voice in all subsequent court proceedings until Salem's authorities comply with the court's demand to dismiss Roger Williams as their teaching elder and minister."

Upon learning of this decision, the Salem congregation wasted no time in enlisting Roger's help. They immediately composed a letter protesting the intimidation and then sent copies to the other Massachusetts churches. Roger sent Winthrop a copy.

Reading it at his desk at home, Winthrop deeply resented the letter's reference to the action of the court as *a heinous sin*. He also resented Roger's charge that the magistrates' rejection of Salem's petition exemplified nothing nobler than political patronage, corruption with rouge and painted lips. Remembering that Roger had heard him speak more than once of his sailing to the New World to escape England's corruption in high places, Winthrop's conscience felt the thrust of the suggestion that his defense of the magistrates' authority had the ring of King James's defense of royal infallibility. In hot anger and alone in his library, he read the last page for the third time. Impulsively he tore the letter into pieces. Then, becoming aware of his irrational deed and remembering his contempt for Thomas Hooker's hot temper, he rebuked himself for yielding to his own hot temper and uttered a secret prayer to become more patient with those who fall into religious error. Losing not a moment of time, he collaborated with Dudley and Haynes to counter the Salem letter. They organized a group of men who would swiftly carry an urgent message to the elders of the Massachusetts churches.

Each messenger had traveled before sunset to his assigned elder to deliver Winthrop's warning: "We must apply wagon brakes quickly to this usurpation of the court's authority. By concealing the Salem letter from the people of your congregation, you will protect them from dangerous and heretical opinions."

To the surprise and dismay of the churches' elders, when their people throughout the Bay learned that their elders had pocketed the Salem letters, they erupted in hot indignation. With his astounding skill at persuasion, however, Winthrop moved rapidly into action, riding from church to church to justify himself. Arguing that Scripture forbade any show of disrespect toward the magistrates and elders, he quoted a biblical passage that hung on his office wall: "Obey your leaders and submit to them, for they keep watch tirelessly over your souls as those who must render an account to God. If you obey them, they will do their work with joy. But if they do their work with sorrow, it will be harmful to you."

In Salem at the Paynter house, however, Roger and Jeremiah sat at the kitchen table with Samuel Sharpe, another Salem elder. As the nervous flame of the candle cast distorted shadows, Roger felt that all Massachusetts had become a nervous flame casting unruly rumors in the air. Upstairs, all was quiet.

While Roger stared silently at the shadows, Jeremiah, his freckled brow deeply furrowed, again carefully read the letter that the three of them had just composed.

A knock at the door interrupted them.

"Who at such an hour?" Jeremiah whispered, rising from his chair. When he opened the door, he turned around and announced, "It is Wilfred Barry and Thomas Angell."

The carpenter and Angell entered and quickly joined the others around the table. "We arrived only now from Plymouth. Haynes and his pack have traveled there to work mischief against us," Wilfred Barry reported.

"Did they meet with Governor Bradford?" Roger asked quietly.

"Bradford is a godly man. But the pack from Massachusetts did bare their fangs," said Angell.

Elder Sharpe, a prudent man, spoke in a rumbling voice. "Give the particulars."

Addressing Roger, Wilfred answered, "Winthrop, Dudley, Haynes, and three others sternly informed Bradford that the Plymouth village would suffer dearly if they found your footprints on Plymouth soil."

Jeremiah looked at Roger's saddened eyes. "Ancient political corruption from the Old World now at work in the New World."

Roger shook his head. "The Massachusetts magistrates have already severed trade with Plymouth. Now they talk of sending men to England to undermine the Plymouth charter."

He knew that because of him, the Massachusetts magistrates had harassed the Salem deputies and assistants for the past year with the threat of taking over Salem's government. Since Plymouth had its own special charter, Massachusetts would not invade but would use other formidable tactics to force Plymouth's submission.

He could almost hear Mary's words. *Dear husband, I pray that Little Mary and our expected baby will one day live where they can practice religion and love without hypocrisy.*

Have we left kith and kin in England under Laud's shadow only to endure the noxious whims of Winthrop and his ilk?

Roger addressed the men gathered at the Paynter house. "When Elijah faced the four hundred prophets at Baal, he feared that he stood alone. Heaven, however, was with him. In the face of our enemies, we have one another and our friends."

Jeremiah said, "This the magistrates know quite well."

"Which causes them to chip away at our friends and to build up their own battalions," Wilfred Barry added.

"They planned this battle well," Roger conceded. "And I was slow to perceive it."

"With his left hand, Winthrop offers the olive branch to the Plymouth authorities," said Jeremiah. "With his right hand, he offers thorns and thistles for those who do not yield to his fanged threats."

Has Cotton also joined those succumbing to Winthrop's wile? Roger wondered. In this battle for liberty of heart and mind, he saw Cotton as the pivotal general. Where did Cotton stand? In the camp of *soul liberty*? On the hill called *Uncommitted*? Or had he *fallen in with Haynes and Winthrop*? He shivered. Such powerful forces! He felt as if he were looking across the battlefield at the enemy's vast numbers and armor and then looking back at his own ill-clad troops. He wanted to believe that truth itself rode like a mighty giant at his side and would carry the day. He had studied history, however, and knew that the body of truth bore many bruises, scars, and wounds. Truth carried no sword, possessed no cannon but the human voice, held no dagger for defense beyond the quill and ink of those who would wield them amid the smoke and furor of battle.

Elder Sharpe held up the letter that the congregation had commissioned Roger, Jeremiah, and himself to compose. He read it aloud.

> As a sister church to the others of Massachusetts, we of the Salem congregation submit that the elders have no proper authority to suppress an open letter from our people to those of the several churches. If the whole body of one congregation is denied communication, in what sense are the churches associated? The elders who presumed to conceal the letters do not profess to be Separatists. Yet their actions separate us more than do the actions of professed Separatists. We of the Salem church abhor the opinion of some elders that church members are too weak and giddy to enjoy open communication on matters pertaining to their governance.

On the following day, the Salem congregation voted to send the letter to the elders of the Massachusetts churches. Two days thereafter, Winthrop's third letter arrived.

> Your arguments lead straight to anarchy, Master Williams. I beseech you to look ahead at the chaos that you foster. If, as you contend, the civil magistrates have no divine commission to establish the true church, then false teaching and false religions will infest the land. If as you contend the civil magistrates have no authority to reform the church when it deviates from sound doctrine, then Massachusetts is an unweeded garden. Scripture itself gives us the examples of Moses, Joshua, and other judges and kings of Israel who received divine

authority to punish heresy, idolatry, and witchcraft. Regarding freedom of conscience, your views fall into serious error. Conscience owns no freedom outside the circle of truth. A conscience uninformed by true doctrine cannot be free. You confuse liberty with license, and thus . . . .

As the sun filtered through the kitchen window of their house, Mary read and commented on Winthrop's letter. "Dear, each letter from him etches deeper disappointment on your face. You cannot expect this man to turn from east to west in one day. What news from the Reverend Cotton?"

"None. Yet it moved me to see him taking notes at my defense before the General Court. I felt he grasped the principles of my position."

"But will he prevail mightily with the Boston General Court on your behalf?"

"Cotton is my best human hope in this bitter controversy."

"Take heart, true love, and cultivate patience. We pilgrims make our progress step by step. Is it not better to shoot forth letters than to hurl spears and daggers? Remember, love, you yourself arrived at these principles only after abundant labor of mind and heart."

Yes, he recalled the twists and turns of his own journey, the battle in his own heart. He could still recall the faded words of the manuscript that an imprisoned Anabaptist had secretly written using milk because his captors had denied him ink.

Suddenly he shivered with a chill. For a moment, he did not seem himself. His dream from last night haunted him now, and the words played in his head as if from another part of him. He turned to Mary. "Last night, love, there came a dream so sad. I stood as a boy in Old England beside the River Cam. I heard other children singing. As they sang, I thought the voice of thunder came. 'Twas the closing gate of London Tower."

"You fill me with apprehension, Roger. But I must hear the end of this dream."

"'Twas only a dream or rather two. For then it changed. The children no longer sang. Gone were the sweet hosannas. All England mourned. A huge crowd of men and women wailed amid the endless procession. 'Stop!' I cried, 'Who lies in the grave?' A robed bishop with flaming eyes looked down upon me and spoke in a proud voice. 'Liberty, my friend. We have killed liberty at last!'"

She laid her palm on his brow. "You are feverish. Lie down."

He lay down, but then he rose up. "Mary, pray for the time when Boston's General Court will no longer presume to be the conscience of others."

Bathing his face in cool water, she sang softly until he drifted off toward sleep. Soon his eyes opened again, and he spoke as if thinking aloud. "Ah, the cruel presumption, the ancient and hoary habit of powerful men!"

While she gently stroked his cheek, he sank slowly into a troubled sleep. Then she slipped away to the kitchen to take the fresh scones from the hearth. An hour later when she returned to her husband's side, she placed before him a tray of mulberry jam and scones. They ate in ponderous silence until he whispered, "What thoughts bake inside that skull of yours, Mary?"

"The Reverend Cotton. If only you could turn his face to the sun."

He nodded and smiled. "When Cotton speaks or his words appear in print, the whole Puritan world takes note."

"Then let him be your passage to Winthrop and all the others." She seemed strangely sad. "But . . . but one thing puzzles me. *Where is* the Reverend Cotton's voice? Is it with us or against us?"

He too had begun to wonder why Cotton had not yet come to his defense. Since that hot day in Boston before the court, he had heard nothing from him. *Does he not see that here in the New World, human dignity itself hangs by the thread of soul liberty?*

He weighed heavily a possible answer to Winthrop's letters; for in all New England, none possessed more influence than either Winthrop or Cotton. Early in their disputation by correspondence, Roger had enticed Winthrop to show Cotton their letters. In this way, he hoped to counteract Winthrop's influence on the court. Even if he failed to win Winthrop to his cause, perhaps his arguments would sway the learned clergyman. Unable to forgo writing Winthrop again, he picked up his quill.

Late in August, Winthrop and Dudley met in Governor Haynes's office to refine their plot of how best to silence Roger, whom they deemed increasingly threatening to proper authority and order in Massachusetts. Having rejected as unfruitful the plan to imprison him in Boston, they listened to Dudley argue.

"If we crop his ears, then the wounds themselves will become tongues to speak out against us and create turmoil. If we bind his limbs with chains, he will only pull them until they ring like church bells that will arouse the town."

All three collaborators had heard new immigrants tell how in England and Holland Puritans were joining the ranks of the Independents and Separatists. The men did not wish to risk giving Roger a platform from which to proclaim far and wide his Separatist teachings.

A grin formed slowly on Dudley's thick lips. "If Roger were in England, he would soon become the crown's thorn, not ours."

"Then, I say, let us rid ourselves of this crazed fox!" Haynes exclaimed victoriously. "Let the king do the job for us and tie the knot in this fox's tail."

Winthrop nodded vigorously.

Dudley said, "But I would add only that we carry out his capture and deportation discreetly at night."

Winthrop bit the tip of his pipe. "If he sends his letter to the king, we will all sink and our charter with us. Let the General Court deal secretly with him once more. If Williams then repents and recants in public, we will have won him over from Satan's snare and have made a public example of him. If he does not recant, we will bind him hand-and-foot and ship him back to Laud's care."

BOSTON

Summer 1635

To keep his promise to her, Barnabas accompanied Lydia to the church in Boston to hear the Reverend Wilson preach. Approaching the front door, he touched the rim of his new black hat, grinned, rolled his eyes piously toward heaven, and spoke in a soft, quivering voice, evidently to imitate the reverend's holy tones: "Greetings, Captain Firebrook. May heaven's glory shine bounteously upon you."

Seeing Barnabas in his clean shirt and new hat, I lowered my voice. "Lydia, is this Barnabas the sinner or his righteous twin at your side?"

She smiled proudly. "Ah, Captain, 'tis Barnabas the sinner himself; but I prefer his companionship to a dozen saints."

Barnabas's eyes sparkled. "Sit with us, Captain, so that I may be seen in the company of a noted principality of the city."

Lydia led her husband toward a pew near the front. He followed, holding to her as though he were a blind man needing her eyes. For two hours, we sang hymns, listened to the Reverend Wilson preach, and heard one of the other men read from the Scriptures. From the corner of my eye, I saw Barnabas discreetly place a hand over his right eye and then over his left. Afterward he closed one eye and then the other as if to test his vision. This continued for perhaps a minute. In time I came to realize that his actions somewhat mirrored the enormous, staring eye that had been carefully painted on the front of the pulpit for the entire congregation to see.

For Puritans, the painting represented the all-seeing eye of God watching over every deed and secret sin. It represented the Puritan belief that God not only saw the sparrow fall, but also witnessed every hardship suffered by the saints.

During one of the longer prayers, I glanced at the enormous eye staring at me. Quickly I closed my eyes and prayed earnestly.

On the following day, I could find Barnabas nowhere even though I had searched far and wide and had inquired of all the servants. I discovered that others in town had searched in vain for him. Giving up the search, I chanced to pass through the small copse behind the Blackstone house when I heard my name whispered. I turned around to investigate, but saw no one.

Then again the voice whispered, "Captain!"

Again I looked right and left and behind me.

A third time the whisper came: "Captain. Up here."

"Where?"

"Above you in the tree."

I saw Barnabas astride a large limb as if it were a horse. He held a pail from which he took various morsels. He appeared to be enjoying his meal alone.

"You are too old, Barnabas, to perch on tree limbs."

"My limbs are younger than those I sit upon." He gave the maple limb a pat as if it were his horse.

"Men from the town have been searching for you."

"Which is why I'm up this tree. Have they gone, Captain?"

"Aye. Who are they?"

"I know two of them are guards from the jail." Barnabas climbed down.

"This morning your good wife told me that two men searched your quarters and made her swear she did not know where you were."

"Poor Lydia." Barnabas brushed the front of his coat.

Later that same day, I learned that Thomas Dudley and the Reverend Wilson had accused Barnabas of desecrating the place of worship. When I went to the Reverend Wilson to inquire, he took me to the meetinghouse where I had sat beside Barnabas on the Sabbath.

"There!" The Reverend Wilson pointed to the pulpit.

To my astonishment, I saw not the one enormous eye, but now *two*, one opened; the other closed. The whole appearance of the new painting was that of a large face winking at the congregation.

"How can a man read the Scriptures or preach the Word of heaven from behind a winking eye?" Wilson sounded exasperated.

At that moment, three men escorted Barnabas into our presence. "We have the guilty agent of the crime," one of the men said to Pastor Wilson.

Wilson looked at him sternly from head to foot. "You are called Barnabas, are you not?"

"That I am, Pastor. My dear mother gave me the name from Holy Scripture, Barnabas the missionary and companion to the Apostle Paul."

"I see you know the Scriptures," said Wilson.

Barnabas grinned. "Somewhat, for no man can know the sacred treasure in all its fullness. Yet 'tis a treasure chest to which I go daily for some precious gem."

Appearing flustered, Wilson cleared his throat. "You know that sacred Scripture forbids bearing false witness."

"That, I have oft read from the tables of Moses. And didn't our Savior say, 'You shall know the truth, and the truth shall set you free'?"

"He did indeed," Wilson replied. "Now give me the truth from your own mouth, Barnabas. Did you paint the picture of the winking eye on the pulpit?"

"I did, Pastor. Doesn't Scripture forbid us to hide our talents under a bushel?"

"Yes, but—"

"So, good Pastor, my talent is to grow plants and flowers and to paint with these fingers. Didn't the Apostle Paul himself in 1 Corinthians write that the body of Christ is one and that it has many members? 'For the body is not one member, but many . . .

And the eye cannot say unto the hand, I have no need of you, nor again the head to the feet, I have no need of you.'"

"I know the text." Wilson sounded irritable and was about to say more when Barnabas resumed, "So, good Pastor, you're the tongue of this congregation. If I may say, a most eloquent tongue to stir the heart and move the soul. So eloquent indeed was your Sabbath sermon that it moved not only my soul, but these very fingers to paint God's winking eye."

Wilson's forehead formed deep rows of ridges; but Barnabas paused only to breathe. "From this very pulpit, Pastor, you did proclaim that on the forthcoming Sabbath you would preach from the Apostle Paul's sermon delivered on Mars Hill. And at once the text of the winking eye from the Book of Acts came to me as if on wings of inspiration, though of course I know it was not special revelation. Still your eloquent tongue stirred my mind as well as my heart."

"You are a river of words overflowing the banks of reason." Wilson's eye began to twitch, he nodded his head impatiently, and he signaled the jailers to take Barnabas away.

Barnabas, however, had more to add. "The river flows straight down from Mars Hill if only you will heed. I lack your eloquence and wisdom, good Pastor, for heaven has denied me such a gift. But if you'll give ear, I'll point to the very text spoken by the Apostle on Mars Hill. You're a minister of Christ's gospel, and as such you carry on your person the Holy Scriptures as the ancient knight in King Arthur's court once carried his sword. If you would be so kind as to lend me the sword of the Lord, I'll show you the very text that moved my fingers to paint the winking eye on the pulpit."

Though Wilson's patience grew thin, his curiosity evidently became so aroused that he placed his Bible in the hand of Barnabas, who quickly touched his finger to his tongue and flipped the pages. "Ah, here 'tis, Pastor. Acts 17:30. Shall I read it aloud?" He waited for no reply, inhaled deeply, and formed a theatrical expression as if he were standing in saintly robes on Mars Hill. Then he proclaimed with conspicuous relish, "The inspired Apostle said, 'And the times of ignorance God *winked* at; but now He commandeth all men everywhere to repent.'"

Holding the Bible open, Barnabas lay it across his left palm as though he were now an elder expounding the text to the congregation. He smiled at Pastor Wilson. "Knowing that gentle shepherd that you are, you would explain to your flock the meaning of this *winking passage*, I used my humble painting talent to supplement the sermon you proposed to preach on the coming Sabbath."

Before the Reverend Wilson could speak, Barnabas moved closer and whispered, "If I might for a brief moment seek your counsel in secret, Pastor."

The perplexed pastor sighed, rolled his eyes heavenward, begrudgingly granted Barnabas his request, and took him aside. "Do you wish to confess your sins in private?" Pastor Wilson asked.

"Later. The confession will require more time. For the present, I make a proposal."

"I am listening. But hasten."

"These fingers heaven gave me for painting, Pastor. Take them as heaven's gift to supplement each of your Sabbath sermons. Consider this . . . ."

The jailers and I waited patiently while Barnabas and Pastor Wilson talked in low voices.

At last the good pastor walked up to the jailers. "I have spoken with this sinner, and he has agreed to produce the fruit of his repentance. There will be no stocks for him." The kind pastor grinned. "The Lord has delivered him into my hands."

The jailers' expression was that of a pack of hungry dogs deprived of their kill. They, nevertheless, refrained from protesting against Pastor Wilson's withering look.

I walked them out the door of the meetinghouse. On the next Sabbath, I returned to hear Pastor Wilson's sermon. To my surprise, I saw a colorful painting hanging neatly from the pulpit. The painting covered up the winking eye. The canvas, a piece of smooth wood, portrayed the scene of the great shepherd Christ himself standing among sheep. At a distance stood hungry, teeth-bearing wolves staring greedily at the poor sheep.

After the sermon, I heard many favorable comments among the people, all praising Barnabas's painting. Even the children spoke of feeling safe, knowing that Christ with his shepherd's staff stood ready to defend the flock against the wolves.

I walked to the front of the meetinghouse to take a closer look at the work of Barnabas's talented fingers. The face of Christ possessed a look of warmth and kindness, but the long staff in his hand pointed at the wolves and warned them they would regret encroaching on his sheep. Looking closer, I thought I saw a human face painted with a certain delicacy on one of the wolves. I moved closer and squinted. To my amazement, I recognized the human face on the wolf. Without thinking, I exclaimed, "Winthrop!"

I glanced around and then felt relieved that no one had heard me. I left at once, hoping no one but Barnabas and I recognized the wolf's face.

BOSTON

September–October 1635

"I should be nursing you, Mary, not you me."

"Do not talk, Roger. Your voice is too weak. Let the fever take its course. Now lie down again and sleep."

"But you are with child."

Though she smiled, he felt that she looked troubled.

She shrugged. "Bearing a child is no illness. 'Tis a healthy child. I feel it kicking hard."

"Are they the kicks of a boy or of a girl?"

"A girl, I think."

Although he felt himself trying to smile, his head throbbed as if a rope had been tied tightly around it.

She again cooled his forehead with a wet cloth. "Your face is on fire, Roger."

"Boston and Salem rage with fever, and now I fall ill with fever." His thoughts wandered. "Freeborn, Freeborn? Do you like the name?"

Mary pressed her finger over his parched lips. "It is the perfect name. Now close your eyes and spare your voice, which already grows faint."

On the next day, men and women of the church took turns sitting quietly with Roger, whose strength had so left him that he could no longer feed himself.

Grace Paynter took Mary and her daughter under wing and brought them to her house. "You must rest half an hour each afternoon, Mary. Do your knees ache?"

"Only a little."

"Then rest, and later today we will sew."

Mary furrowed her brow. "You will keep me informed of my husband's health?" Grace so promised and added she would see that the church people continued to administer the herbs Mary had begun.

As soon as Grace left the room, Little Mary's inquisitive eyes began examining everything. Mary smiled, remembering that only a few months ago her little one was crawling, testing everything with her mouth. She tried to picture Little Mary growing up, traveling with her father, and perhaps reading his books just as she had read her father's books on cold winter days in Lincolnshire.

An hour later she overheard Jeremiah tell his wife that in Boston the General Court had recently unseated all of Salem's deputies and sent them home stripped of all authority on the General Court.

Jeremiah paced angrily across the parlor. "The court has become a high-handed oligarchy."

"What did our Captain Endecott say to the court's decision?" Grace asked.

"He protested like a squall and sought to defend our rights to send letters to the Bay churches, but the court turned a deaf ear and imprisoned him."

Even though in another room, Mary overheard everything and concluded that Endecott's wavering conscience had pricked him. She believed that regarding Winthrop, Endecott's wind blew in one direction for a season and then in the opposite. Recently the wind had shifted so that now Endecott revived his old resentment against Winthrop. She was sure Endecott had never forgotten that almost six years earlier in England, Winthrop had gone behind Endecott's back to solicit a new charter from the king, a charter reducing Governor Endecott to serve as the new governor's left hand.

At noon two men and a woman came into the Paynters' parlor with news that struck fear in Mary's heart. She overheard only the name of her husband and a few others. The tone of the conversation so frightened her that she gathered Little Mary in her arms and walked into the parlor. "My husband! What is the report of his health?"

Samuel Sharpe's wife, Beatrice, a hefty woman with a smooth, round face, took Mary's hand. "Our beloved Elder Roger grows worse. The fever—"

"I must go to him!"

Beatrice patted Mary's hand lightly. "He is not himself. He speaks to people who live only in his head."

Mary set her face toward the front door.

"Do not forbid her to go to her husband," Grace said. "Here now, Mary, leave your daughter with me. I will watch this little chick while you sit with your beloved."

Mary hurried out the door, scarcely aware that her condition made her walk like a waddling duck. The child inside her had moved and kicked all morning as if the womb had become its prison.

The October wind filled Mary's lungs and gave her strength. *Roger needs me at his side*, she kept muttering. *Do not let him die, dear Lord!*

When she arrived at her house, she saw a gathering of church people and friends.

Near the doorway, Little Snowfeather's father handed Mary a leather pouch. "More herbs for the fever," he said in his deep, husky voice.

She thanked him and disappeared inside the house. When she reached the bedroom, she heard Roger whisper and saw heavy drops of sweat pour from his face.

Two women explained in low voices that while half conscious, their teaching elder kept saying, "Freeborn!"

"Poor darling, *Freeborn* is the name we have elected to give our new child." Mary felt helpless as she watched Roger's lips move in his delirium. Having seen the devastating effects of delirium, she fought back her terror. Her cousin Marcus in England had suffered permanently from a fever. *I cannot go on in this land if my Roger loses his mind to the fever. Give my husband back to me!*

Realizing that she held the pouch of herbs tightly in her hand, she quickly mixed them inside the polished wooden cup as she had done earlier. One of the women picked up a kettle of hot water and filled the cup. Mary then stirred the herbs into the water.

After taking the cup to his bedside, she set it down and talked with him lovingly until at last his eyes opened. While one of the women held the cup, Mary used the spoon to feed the herbs to Roger, placing the half-filled spoon to his lips and urging him to accept and swallow.

For a day and a half, she watched her husband's body turn into a battlefield where the fever fought to overcome him. She fought alongside him, whispering her love into his ear and vowing that she would no longer rest her head until her husband's eyes opened and he was himself again.

As the second day grew longer, she rubbed her eyes. Had she seen what she thought she saw? Having lost sleep and grown weary, she was afraid she had only fancied that her husband had returned from death's door. She pulled on the skin under her eyes in the hope of letting in more light.

Her heart leaped. It was true! Her darling had returned. She saw him look around the room like a boy waking up from a long sleep and not fully grasping the meaning of all those gathered around him. He tugged at his shirt and seemed surprised at its wetness. "Have I been in rain?" He looked out the window and smiled feebly at the sunshine.

She laughed. "You have returned, love!" She embraced him and then looked into his eyes as though looking into life itself. She felt his hand on her cheek and then watched him touch his own arms to see whether he was truly among the living.

"I thought ministering angels came clothed always in white," he said.

A trickle of laughter traveled through the room, and then the other ministering angels who had sat with Mary through the night went into another room to leave her alone with her husband.

She felt him take her hand and bathe it in kisses just as Agnes Barry entered the room. Seeing Roger sitting up, she excitedly rushed out, her green shawl hanging loose and flying behind her. Mary heard the front door swing open and Agnes announce gleefully to the people gathered outside in the cool October air, "Lazarus has returned from the dead!"

The sound of the friendly voices entered Mary's ears like old ballads, lifting her to her feet. Though weary from loss of sleep, she felt her tears as replenishing streams of water. She made her way to the door and declared all the well-wishers to be angels of mercy. "Your teaching elder has regained consciousness, and he wishes me to thank you one and all for your affection and loving care."

Little Snowfeather and Deborah ran up to Mary and begged to see their friend. But their parents pulled them back.

"Master Williams will talk with you soon when his strength has returned," Mary promised, enjoying the children's warm affection.

When she unexpectedly felt her lips tremble, she rushed inside and found a corner in which to hide her face. *The angel of death visited this house; but with heaven's help, we turned him away.* After taking a few minutes to compose herself, she held herself erect and returned to her husband's side. Wondrous joy filled her. The whiteness of Roger's face was now pink like sunrise.

She smoothed the covers for him. "Sleep on, my darling." As if in wonderment, he looked up into her moist eyes. "I was on my journey to heaven. Then I returned, thinking I have heaven on earth with Mary and Little Mary. What news from our Freeborn?"

"She sends signals." Mary laughed, cried, and then looked through the wetness of her lashes. "Oh, love, I am more than pleased heaven has sent you back to us. Our need of you is far more than heaven's."

"My shoes. Where are my shoes?" He glanced around as friends entered the room.

No one heeded his demand. Instead, everyone playfully told him to listen to his wife.

"Remember Pontius Pilate," Jeremiah said. "Had he heeded his wife, he would have been spared the cup of misery."

A few minutes later, everyone but Roger and Mary had left the room. "Ah, how fortunate I am to have such a loving wife and good friends. Where is Little Mary?"

"With Grace Paynter."

He then asked for permission to lay his ear against Mary's belly. When he felt the kick, he laughed and kissed her belly. "There, Freeborn. Your first kiss."

Mary handed him a wet cloth and suggested that he wash.

"Have I the aroma of a man?"

"A he-ass or a he-goat." She handed him a second cloth.

He stopped all his motion and stared at her with evident delight and astonishment. Then he resumed washing his chest and arms. "I am alive!" His voice rang in a melody of his own invention. It was truly heavenly music to Mary's ears. Lazarus had indeed returned from death's cave.

SALEM AND BOSTON

October 1635

Roger's recovery came slowly. Evidently fearing a relapse, Mary begged him to give thought to her earlier suggestion that he had worked with excess as if he intended to do *penance* for sins.

"Mary, it is wrong that a wife should have to beg anything of her husband. Your words persuade me."

Each afternoon, he took a half-hour nap at his wife's side although he kept mentally rehearsing the defense he must make before the General Court. He knew he would require supreme strength to face the hostile magistrates.

Four days prior to his scheduled reappearance before the Boston Court, a letter came from Master John Cotton. Roger could scarcely contain his excitement. The powerful surge of hope that had flowed beneath the surface throughout the entire ordeal in Boston now bubbled up in his chest. *At long last, Cotton, who fled Archbishop Laud's hounds by night, will stand with me in my hour of trial.* His heart pounding with anticipation and his fingers trembling, he tore open the letter from the Reverend Cotton.

"Read it to me." Mary's heart sang with gratitude for the Reverend Cotton's willingness to come to her husband's aid.

He began reading the letter.

"What . . . what is wrong?" Mary asked. "Your face is—"

Although he tried to force the words out, they clung to his throat. Then he handed the letter to Mary, who read it quickly: "If it pleases the Lord to stop your mouth by a dread disease and to strike you near unto death, you would do well to take your fever as heaven's merciful sign. Painfully search your soul. Repent of your rebellion against God's appointed magistrates!"

She let the missive fall to the floor.

Stunned, confused, and humiliated by Cotton's presumption, Roger sat down. The blood left his head.

"I feel numb," she confessed. A long silence followed. Then her nostrils flared. "Who would kick even a mad dog when he is down on his belly?"

Roger felt bitterly betrayed. Above all he agonized with the thought that the esteemed Puritan clergyman had engaged in self-betrayal. *Why did I build my hopes so high on Cotton*! His anger now spewed out at both Cotton and himself. *How could I have been so obtuse?* More painful than his anger was the realization that the John Cotton he thought he knew had never existed. Roger had cast his hopes on a shimmering specter.

He grabbed a sheet of paper and a quill. But he could compose no more than two sentences. What would he say? What could he say? He turned around at the table to face Mary. "Is it possible . . . . No, no, I am only deluding myself."

"Is what possible?"

"That someone forged this letter?"

"Love, you know it is John Cotton's hand."

"Something in me resists this bitter conclusion. How could I have so misjudged the man? I had no ripple of warning that the cruel letter would come." He blinked and held up Cotton's letter. "Mary, will you tell me this came as no surprise to you?"

She shrugged. "Like you, dear, I had looked into Cotton's face. It was no crystal ball. A face may conceal as well as hide the heart's meaning."

"No man's face could speak the cruelty of this letter. But why? Why?"

She brewed some turkey broth. "Better to ask *wherefore* than *why*. What lies in the past is done. Attend to the future."

"But this means . . . . Where is Blackstone's letter?"

"Here." She removed a letter from a wooden chest nearby.

"Read it, Mary. I need your interpretation."

She shook her head. "I have read it. Though Blackstone's words come from a friendly heart, the message is a stern warning. All the Massachusetts Bay clergy will attend the General Court to oppose you!" She then handed the letter to Roger, who carefully read Blackstone's revelation that the Massachusetts Court threatened to take control of not only the Salem church, but also the Salem government unless the people of Salem dismissed Master Williams and ceased their talk of Separatism.

He angrily twisted the unruly lock on his forehead. "What is your interpretation of his passage about Marblehead Neck?"

"It means that the price for Marblehead Neck is my husband's neck, his dismissal from Salem."

"The past is done. The future . . . ." He picked up Cotton's letter, looked at it again, and shook his head in dismay. He could almost feel the breeze of Damocles' blade swinging over his head. Much was at stake. The wrong moves, the wrong ploys could severely affect the lives of the natives, the survival of the trading post, the future of Little Mary and Freeborn. He let his eyes study the ceiling, floor, and decorated walls. Will Mary lose this house, which bears the fine touches of her tender care? He closed his eyes at the dreary thought of her living again in a windowless wigwam. Where would they go? He had heard more than one rumor that some among the Boston magistrates had a scheme to ship him back to England where the king and the archbishop would gladly lock him in the Tower.

Still one shaft of sunlight shone through all this gloom. He believed that heaven had destined him for a ministry of peace and the Christian gospel. But where? The shaft of light revealed no answer.

On that same day, Governor Haynes went with Winthrop Sr. and Dudley to the jail to speak with Captain Endecott, imprisoned because of his failure to denounce the letter the Salem church had sent to all the other Massachusetts churches.

Governor Haynes spoke plainly to Endecott, "Publicly acknowledge your fault in this matter, and you will find quick favor with both the court and heaven."

"Oppose us," Dudley cut in, "and your name will be Ichabod. You will be as Abraham's slave woman Hagar wandering with mere bread and a skin of water in the wilderness of Beersheba."

Endecott protested.

"Do not raise your voice!" Haynes warned. "We are here to speak in private, not from the housetops."

In his gruff way, Endecott drew in his flaring temper. He sat down. "If you did not come here to torment me like Job's ironic comforters, then—"

"Do not pretend to be suffering Job's sores." Winthrop's jaw was set, his face like flint. "We will open this prison gate for you if you . . . ."

Endecott rose and looked hard into Winthrop's eyes. "Your offers too oft bear the image of an eagle's talons."

"Our suggestion," Haynes said smoothly, "is a tune already in your repertoire."

"Do not fiddle on my strings. Speak plainly."

"We will give you time in this humble inn to contemplate the consequences of Salem's letter," Winthrop said. "We think eventually you will agree with our apprehension that chaos will infect the land if the churches smirk at the magistrates and form their own wild opinions without benefit of God's appointed rulers." Having finished his speech, Winthrop turned to leave, Haynes and Dudley following.

"Hold!" Endecott said. "I fear Roger Williams more than I fear all of you. You, however, do not understand my circumstance."

The men from Boston turned around.

In his smooth way, Haynes said, "Ah, circumstances can make cowards of us all."

Though Winthrop's face was still hard as flint, he listened to the prisoner's explanation and accepted his vow to align himself with the governor. As the four of them walked away from the jail, Endecott said, "We are united now in our goal to uproot the troublesome thistle from our garden."

In Salem on the following day, October 6, a minister named Hugh Peters arrived with a letter from Governor Haynes and other court members. Governor Haynes had already informed Endecott that the Salem deputies would be well advised to give ear to the Reverend Peters lest they be stripped of all their remaining meager authority. Taking their seats in the meetinghouse, the deputies listened to Endecott explain that the Reverend Peters knew well of what he spoke.

"Then let us hear the man." Elder Samuel Sharpe grew impatient with Endecott's evident design to exalt himself before giving way to Hugh Peters.

When Peters stood to speak, interest in his story surged quickly. He told of Archbishop Laud's swift action against him and his church in Holland. "Know this, if the king and archbishop will reach across the English Channel to control a church under the flag of another country, they will surely bring Salem's church and government under the direct control of crown-appointed rulers."

Samuel Sharpe rose to his feet. "What purpose have you in giving this warning? I perceive it comes not as a flash from heaven, but as an ill wind from Boston."

"My purpose is not hidden in a corner." Hugh Peters wagged his finger ominously. "This finger is the thickness of Boston's influence in Salem. If you do not heed this influence, then"—Peters held up his arm and clamped a hand around it—"then the agents from England will come with a thickness of an arm and the weight of a fist hard down upon you."

From his bench, Endecott said, "Be so kind as to translate these images into steps of action for our people."

"The translation will be rough, but it is thus. If you continue both to tolerate Master Williams as your teaching elder and to harbor him in your town, the crown will appoint deputies who have ears only for the powers in England and no ears for the people of Salem." Having finished his remarks, Peters pulled from his pocket a second sheet of paper, looked at it, and pondered it for several seconds. Though seemingly on the verge of revealing its contents, he returned the paper to his pocket, stood rubbing his forefinger across his lower lip, and frowned as if some fierce warning had come to him.

When Samuel Sharpe stood up to urge Peters to speak further, Endecott leaped to his feet and laid his hand on his heart. "Is this not the very truth I have been proclaiming among you all? But you would not heed it. For you I have suffered imprisonment in Boston. For you I have been reviled. Now perhaps you will heed this humble servant. I tell you what you know already. Magistrate John Winthrop devoted more than five years to convince the English crown that the Massachusetts Colony harbored no treason. By that he meant no Separatists and no Separatists' opinions."

A deputy stood up. "'If your right hand offends you, cut it off,' our Lord did command. The time has come to sever Master Williams from us. I say this with all due respect. But I love this land, this New Jerusalem that God has called into being. It is my love and only my love for this land and these people that drives me to say: *sacrifice one limb rather than send a whole body into hell.*"

Upon leaving the meetinghouse, Endecott and Hugh Peters went directly to Roger's house. Mary met them at the door.

Endecott acted as though he had never been a friend to either Mary or Roger. "Please advise your husband that we have urgent business with him."

She looked at Hugh Peters, who introduced himself and added that he had served as minister of an English church in Rotterdam. She invited them into the small parlor and presented Peters to Jeremiah Paynter.

A knock came at the back door. After Roger opened it, Samuel Sharpe gestured for him to step outside. He complied and heard Elder Sharpe whisper, "You will need me as a witness."

"I am glad you are here. Let us enter and see what new intrigue unfolds."

The five men sat in the parlor. Mary joined them, placing Little Mary on a pallet at her side. Endecott looked at Mary and then at Roger as if to say, *This is a meeting for men alone.* She looked back at him as if to say, *You are a guest in my house.*

"What I have to say," Hugh Peters began, "I might have said to the deputies. I, however, owe you the courtesy, Master Williams, of giving you the information first. I extend the courtesy to you too, Captain Endecott."

Roger picked up Little Mary and held her in his lap. "I accept your generosity in the spirit in which it is given. Mr. Paynter and Elder Sharpe often advise me in my position as teaching elder and minister. Whatever you wish to say may be said in their presence."

Endecott again cut his eyes toward Mary.

Roger flushed. "If a woman named Mary could bear our Savior in her womb, then this Mary can bear a message from Boston with ease!"

Endecott cleared his throat and looked to Peters, who said, "I regret bringing ill tidings."

Before Peters could explain, Endecott cut in. "I spoke with Governor Haynes and Magistrate Winthrop yesterday. The sum and substance is that the court plans to govern Salem from Boston if you continue to defy it."

Roger looked at Elder Sharpe, who said to Endecott, "Then the court has presumed powers beyond its proper authority."

Endecott shook his head and grit his teeth. "You understand nothing. Winthrop and other magistrates have accused Master Williams and the Salem deputies of fomenting nothing less than rebellion against England! Do you grasp the seriousness of this accusation?"

Hugh Peters laid a firm hand on Endecott. "What my friend intends to communicate is that the court fears the crown will conclude that all New England and all America seek *revolution.* What my friend has not communicated is that a ship called *Griffin* is at this hour in Boston Harbor. Aboard it the king's commission stands ready to act."

"With what powers?" Roger lay Little Mary on her pallet again as he trembled inside but forced himself to study the face of Hugh Peters carefully.

"With powers to revoke the Massachusetts Charter," Peters answered.

Roger felt the blood leave his face and saw grimaces of horror on other faces. He paused, closing his eyes to let the explosion of thoughts settle down. "With powers to revoke the charter?" He wondered if at this moment Winthrop and all the other magistrates of Massachusetts were trembling.

He forced himself to face the bitter truth that if the king so willed, he could charge Winthrop, Haynes, Dudley, himself, and the whole lot of them with treason. The words of King James before Parliament exploded in his mind: "Kings have power to exalt low things and debase high things, and to make of their subjects like men at the chessboard."

Filling his lungs with air, he reminded himself that King Charles had no lower opinion of his powers than had his father James. "Master Peters, what further threat comes our way?"

"The king's threat to assume direct control of all government activities and duties in New England."

As the sun went down that day, panic rose in Salem, for Endecott and Peters wasted no time in spreading the news of the ship *Griffin* anchored in Boston Harbor.

On the next day, Salem tore itself in twain. One side contended that no sane path existed beyond yielding to the General Court's demands. "If the king's agents seize control, our past efforts in leaving England will come to naught."

The other side earnestly counseled liberty of conscience and soul autonomy. "If we submit, how do we differ from the Old England from which we fled? Will we not be the new wine in old wineskins?"

On October 8, amid the turmoil, Roger's ship from Salem anchored near Boston Harbor. In the distance, he could see the mighty *Griffin*, which had sailed from England with the king's special deputy. To Roger it was a fortress menacingly poised to do the special royal deputy's interpretation of the king's stern bidding.

He felt relieved that Mary had consented to remain in Salem. The child Freeborn lay safely in her mother's womb, away from the tumultuous crowd.

After leaving the ship, he went immediately to the Boston meetinghouse where he faced the General Court. The air inside bristled with invisible bolts of lightning, every corner tingling with rapid talk of Roger's dangerous opinions. There was scant time for ceremony, and no one seemed to care for it. Time itself seemed in a rush.

The more he poured his heart passionately and eloquently into his defense, the more the faces on the court turned to stone. Their eyes seemed to glare with the signal *futility!* The Reverend John Cotton, sitting with three other clergymen, listened but took no notes.

Governor Haynes and Dudley listened with the eagerness of watchdogs jealous to protect their territory. A mother's infant began to cry, but critical stares drove the mother and child outside.

When Roger finished his comments, Governor Haynes and the other court members consulted behind closed doors. The silence grew more painful each moment. Roger's eyes chanced to see through the window a handful of English soldiers from the ship *Griffin*. The air grew uncertain with the crosswinds of excitement and dread. Within minutes the court members returned, and Haynes announced that the judgment had been reached.

Roger thought of Mary and wondered if Freeborn had yet come into the world. Unable to bear the thought of forced separation from his family on this bleak day, he tried to muster hope that the court would somehow gain the wisdom to look to the future when the New World would no longer be England's stepchild.

For a moment, Governor Haynes stared with a frown at the court members as though he could not believe the decision they had made. The right side of his mouth twitched. He seemed puzzled. Then an odd little grin formed unexpectedly on his lips and quickly vanished. "Master Williams, the court offers you a month's respite so that you may meet with our esteemed clergyman Thomas Hooker. We of the court are persuaded that the reverend's exceptional learning will draw you back to our position and that we will once again have unity of doctrine among us. We are persuaded that a month with the Reverend Thomas Hooker will both teach you a more excellent way and expose your errors to light."

The audience sighed. On every face, frowns of momentary incomprehension played.

"The court will grant you pause to consider your answer, Master Williams." Haynes peered down from his governor's seat.

A feeling of relief came over Roger. Then came ambivalence when he realized that the court members had made no decision at all. They had merely tipped their hats to the king's agents. Still it had been an act of political deliberation and cold calculation.

He knew that some on the court wished to send him back to England. The majority, however, feared that he would stir up such troubled waters in England that the king would send still more ships to New England's shores, each ship returning to England with still another Massachusetts magistrate in captivity.

Winthrop's eyes locked with his and seemed to say, *Roger, I know you think I have misled the king.*

He yearned to reply, *John, you and I see already how the Massachusetts Puritans drift steadily toward congregationalism despite your own hierarchal declarations. How you do posture for the king, mouthing words that tickle his ear and flatter his archbishop! We know that you secretly long to serve as head of New England's dread Star Chamber. I have found you out, and you know it.*

The majority of the court wanted Roger neither in Massachusetts nor in England. Not knowing what to do with him, they now gave themselves a month to deliberate after the king's ship *Griffin* had sailed out of Boston Harbor for the homeland.

"Master Williams," Governor Haynes said, "the court awaits your reply."

Sensing that he would only play into the court's hands if he allowed them to delay their decision about him, he stood up. "I could ask for no better than my learned friend Thomas Hooker to discuss and debate these crucial matters of church and state with me. But if Master Hooker is willing, I am prepared to bring the dispute between us to light today or tomorrow."

The court members glanced at one another in surprise. He knew their thoughts. They had no real interest in a give-and-take debate. Their interest lay in keeping the king's ship at bay. Roger, on the other hand, stood prepared to take the calculated risk of forcing the issue. He again expressed his desire to meet with the Reverend Hooker face-to-face in open discussion as quickly as possible.

"No! No! This cannot be." The governor addressed the members of the court.

The king's chief representative, a tall, proud-looking man, stood up. His very presence seemed to say that he represented the king in New England just as the king represented England to God. "If it please the court," he said in an official tone, more a warning than a request, "I as Special Royal Deputy desire to hear this exchange between the Reverend Hooker and the Reverend Williams. It is my sworn duty to the throne to return to England with full report of the affairs of this colony."

Winthrop gripped his pipe with such force that it snapped in twain. He cut his eyes toward Haynes and let his eyelids close slowly as if to say, *Steer the royal deputy away. Give him a decoy, but do not let him hear Roger Williams.*

Sitting as a member of the court, Dudley proclaimed loudly that there could be no violation of the court's integrity. "It is a question of English law! We are English! We are English!"

Endecott roared, "English! One and all!"

Amid the commotion, the court and Governor Haynes accepted Roger's challenge to meet the Reverend Hooker on the morrow. The court then adjourned amid such tumult that the royal deputy seemed unaware the meeting had ended.

Instead of waiting for the morrow, however, the learned Thomas Hooker and Salem's teaching elder met by candlelight in Boston to debate the heady matters of church and state. The king's special deputy knew nothing of the meeting. John Cotton had been invited to attend as witness but declined.

Early on the following morning, October 9, before the king's special deputy had broken the fast, Thomas Hooker reported to Governor Haynes and John Winthrop. "I have failed to persuade Master Williams of the error of his views."

"Then we must act with all haste," Winthrop said.

Haynes and Hooker understood this to mean that the court must convene secretly before convening publicly later that morning.

At the secret court meeting, Thomas Dudley, known for his proclivity to flash hot in righteous indignation, flushed in the face and called for the banishment of Roger Williams. The other members, seeing the danger in returning Roger to England, overrode Dudley's proposal and appointed one among them to draft their solemn verdict quickly. Winthrop made it clear that their decision must be presented at the public session and that the session should take place before the king's deputy arrived.

At the court's public session scarcely an hour after sunrise, the bailiff commanded Roger to stand at the lower end of the table. Governor John Haynes read the verdict aloud:

Whereas Mr. Roger Williams, one of the elders of the church of Salem, has broached and divulged new and dangerous opinions against the authority of magistrates and has also written letters defaming both the magistrates and the churches of the colony, and whereas he maintains the same opinion without retraction, it is, therefore, ordered that the said Mr. Williams shall depart from this jurisdiction within six weeks; and if he neglects to perform accordingly, the governor and two magistrates are legally empowered to send him to a place outside the jurisdiction, not to return again without explicit license from the court.

Looking out the window, Winthrop saw the royal deputy step out of a carriage and walk in a long, commanding stride toward the meetinghouse. "Be quick!" Winthrop whispered to Haynes.

Haynes glanced out the window and saw the royal deputy in his red coat and golden epaulets. Haynes spoke rapidly, "The court specifies further that during the six weeks of delay, Mr. Williams must refrain from speaking his opinions publicly to anyone in Massachusetts. Moreover he must neither form nor encourage the formation of any group desiring to propagate his new and dangerous opinions."

At the very moment that the royal deputy stepped into the room, the court gavel came down hard. The decision had been rendered. The adjournment procedure went as a flash. The court members stood up, the people stood up, and Winthrop disappeared through the side door. The king's deputy, dressed in his glistening boots and his formal attire, stood like smoldering coals, little flames flickering in his eyes.

BOSTON

October 1635

The carpenter Wilfred Barry and his wife Agnes had come with Grace and Jeremiah Paynter to encourage Roger in his trial. After judgment was passed, the Elder Samuel Sharpe walked up to them as they stood under a maple tree whose red leaves shimmered in the sun.

"What do you think of the ordeal, Jeremiah?" the elder asked.

"The court members know full well that our teaching elder will not abide by their decision."

"Yes," said Agnes, "they knew it ere they gathered to make the decision. Do you not agree, Captain Firebrook?"

"What you say is true."

Thomas Angell, who had just joined us, said, "A fairer man than Master Williams I have ne'er met in Old or New England."

As I listened to Roger's friends talk about the court's judgment, I could not help thinking that my two friends John Winthrop and Roger Williams stood so far apart that they could scarcely recognize one another. Winthrop resembled the Sunni branch of Islam that pervaded most of the Arabian Peninsula. The Muslims of this branch adhered to the tradition and declared the first four caliphs to be the rightful successors of Muhammad. They wished to use the government to enforce right Islamic belief, doctrine, and overt practice. Roger, by contrast, had engraved in his heart liberty of conscience and the high hedge between church and state.

Upon seeing Winthrop Sr. in the distance, I excused myself and picked up my pace. When at last I stepped up to his side, he said, "Ah, Captain. I saw you at the trial."

"You look like King Richard without his horse," I said.

Winthrop shook his head. "I feel like a surgeon who, having amputated an infectious limb, knows he has done well, but feels no joy in his deed. Oh, grievous day!"

"The decision is made. So now the severed limb will soon be cast aside." I suffered the lawyer's pain with him.

Winthrop closed his eyes like a man resolved to trap the tears behind the floodgates. "Would to heaven this madness in our friend would pass and be gone like a summer storm, but I fear . . . . Oh, Roger, what will become of . . . ?"

Standing near the harbor, I looked over Winthrop's shoulder to see Roger approaching from about a hundred feet away and my landlord Master Blackstone walking with him en route to the harbor. Many men and women stopped to shake Roger's hand. Others pulled back, some doubtless afraid of being seen with him, others afraid of catching the disease of heresy that the court had imputed to him.

Winthrop looked deep into my eyes. "Captain, in all my years, I have never heard a tongue more eloquent than Master Williams's nor known a heart more compassionate. Why? Why has heaven allowed the Prince of Darkness to infect him with this unholy madness?"

When Blackstone and Roger reached us, I spoke politely to them.

Winthrop whirled around and saw Roger. The startled look on Winthrop's face soon turned to a strange mingling of what I took to be deep regret, righteous anger, and melancholy. Underlying all these, however, was the look of unfathomable shame. I had never seen shame on Winthrop's face, and the sight of it chilled my bones.

I ached to think of the pain the man now suffered. I could see in Winthrop's face that special love for Roger a father has for a son. I could see Winthrop almost reach out to embrace him and plead with him. Suddenly the lawyer stiffened, held his shoulders back, and spoke such harshness to Roger that we were all taken aback. "So, today, has your cup of chaos been filled? Do you now relish the pleasure of ripping our society in twain?"

Though Roger blinked and looked puzzled, he made no answer.

I could not help feeling that Winthrop's harshness was an armor to contain his love lest it flow out of his control. Then I recalled something Roger had said to me: "Winthrop has more love than most men, but few men fear their love more than does he."

All at once, Winthrop embraced Roger. "My Henry!"

When Roger returned the embrace, however, Winthrop abruptly pulled back, turned, and hurried silently away.

I could not help recalling an earlier time when Winthrop had said to Roger in gratitude, "Because you ministered to my son Henry, I will see him in heaven."

After walking fifty or so feet, Winthrop stopped and turned around to look at Roger. They stood for what seemed forever as if they knew that on this day one of them would take the New World in one direction while the other man would take it in a different direction. I could almost see in Winthrop a longing to come back, yet he seemed to know there was no coming back.

The pain on Roger's face made me turn away. I could not bear to witness such agony. It was as if he had looked deep into Winthrop's heart and found there in the subterranean caverns a thousand streams of love that would never bubble to the surface.

Roger took off his hat and stood there like an honored general bidding farewell to his rival, an equally honored general, before the noise and smoke of battle began. Each seemed to say to the other, *Had our destinies been different, we would have remained consummate friends to the end.*

ABOARD SHIP AND IN SALEM

October 1635

Aboard the *Lyon*, which had only recently arrived from England, Roger stood on deck to breathe the salt air. His thoughts turned to his wife and daughter. *Soon Freeborn will join us,* he almost said aloud.

Jeremiah stood nearby on deck as if to protect his minister and teaching elder from those who wished to interrupt his private thoughts.

Roger found unexpected peace in the ship sails popping, the busy crew members calling to one another, the seagulls squawking, and the waves slapping the hulk. He could hear now and then the voice of Captain William Peirce giving orders and instructions to the crew. Peirce had not seen him arrive aboard ship, but Roger intended to speak with him later.

In the tingling of his legs, he felt the vessel move out into the sea. He allowed himself to speculate about his reception in Salem. Many would welcome him home and try to give him hope. He felt comforted, remembering that after receiving John Cotton's devastating letter, he had received many notes from friends urging him to fight the good fight.

"Master Williams! Master Williams!" a strong, clear voice rang out.

He turned to see a freckled, broad-shouldered young man of about twenty beaming with delight and grinning rapturously. In his excitement, the youth, running up to greet Roger, brushed against Jeremiah.

"Do you not remember me, sir?" The young man spread his arms out to refresh Roger's memory.

He felt somewhat embarrassed. Every eye on deck seemed drawn to him and the youth.

"It is I, sir. Do you not remember? From Shropshire?"

Roger's mouth flew open. Could it possibly be?

"Timothy Tolland, sir. Now do you remember me? You came to—"

"Timothy!" His heart leaped with surprise and elation. "What are . . . yes, yes, of course. You have grown so . . . . Look at you."

Timothy laughed and laughed, throwing his head back. "Ah, what a day that I should see you at last! But a thousand leagues from England?"

He listened with unmingled delight as Timothy told how he had recently joined Captain Peirce's crew.

"Your dear mother? And your sister Kathy . . . and . . . ?" He stumbled over his words so eager was he to learn of the family whose father and husband had been falsely convicted of murder.

"My mother fares well, Master Williams. If only she could stand here this happy moment." Timothy went on to explain that each member of his family thrived in good health and that he had taken to the high seas to earn money for them. Then he added, "Master Williams, heaven sent you to Shropshire. After your departure, the people of the town took your admonition and each day strove to show their sorrow for the horrible injustice our family had suffered. But, Master Williams, in your kind letter, you urged me to climb out of the ditch of bitterness. Ah, sir . . . well, as you can see, I am well and happy."

Roger grabbed him by the arm and introduced him to Jeremiah. Then he walked with him to find Captain Peirce.

"I came into your life, Timothy, on a day of storm clouds when you were a boy, and now as a man you come into my life to bring sunshine amid a storm. And what a cheerful, welcome sight you are. You must go ashore with me in Salem."

Less than an hour later, the *Lyon* docked at the Salem shores. The trip to Salem had proved too short for young Timothy. But the good Captain Peirce gave him brief leave to go ashore to meet Mrs. Williams.

As soon as Jeremiah left the *Lyon*, he made straight for the home of the fisherman Ezra Welch and his wife, Pearl, to tell them of the court's verdict. Though Salem proved that day and the next to be a city of gloom, Timothy Tolland and Captain Peirce brought happiness to Mary and Roger's house and table.

Three days after the court's decision, Roger tried to remain in Salem and resume his teaching because he felt more concerned for Mary's health than for the court's opinion. He elected to teach inside the walls of his house where his defiance would not likely attract the hawk eyes of the special royal deputy.

No one in Salem seemed surprised that he would defy the court's decision. Previously split in twain, the town now mourned as one, everyone fearing that one day their beloved teaching elder and minister would vanish from their midst.

On October 30, 1635, an infant girl named "Freeborn" came into the world. "Never was a child's birth in New England celebrated more joyously," said the people who waited in and around Mary and Roger's house.

The child's very name signaled to the General Court and to all who presumed to be "gods on Earth" that the torch of freedom would burn brightly in America.

Though sore from giving birth, Mary laughed through her tears while her husband counted aloud the ten fingers and ten toes of their new babe. "Freeborn is hale and whole!" He smiled broadly as he held his new babe in his arms.

BOSTON AND SALEM

October 1635–January 1636

In late October, cold weather hit Massachusetts with shocking severity. The people feared that the snow and wind of 1635 would bring many in the colony close to the edge of starvation. Memories of their first bitter winter in the New World haunted some of them.

Despite these memories, many members of the General Court went to Winthrop to petition him to expel Roger from Massachusetts forthwith.

Winthrop furrowed his brow. "Would you banish a mule or a dog in this bitterly cold winter?"

Those who had come to Winthrop looked at one another. A man said to him, "You spoke too softly. We could not understand your words."

Winthrop sipped his hot broth. "'Twas nothing. Let us turn our attention at least temporarily away from Master Williams and onto the problem of food shortage and rising prices."

Dudley, nonetheless, persisted in his animosity toward Roger. Later, on a bitterly cold November day, the court members met informally and listened to Thomas Dudley vociferously protest any show of mercy toward Master Williams. "We must expel him at once! It is not hatred in my heart, but love of pure doctrine that dictates what I say."

"If you wish to have his blood on your hands . . . ." Winthrop looked around at the stern faces. "Have you no regard for his illness or no concern for his newborn? Let the winter pass, and we shall be rid of him once and for all; or peradventure Providence will intervene and convert him from his false teaching."

All except two of the court members agreed. They sent a note to Roger informing him that he was free to reside in Salem until spring *provided* he refrain from propagating his views or discussing his opinions with any group or individual.

When the letter arrived at his new house in Salem, Roger read it and then took it to the kitchen and handed it to Mary. "We must decide this together, love."

She sat down in her straight-backed chair and folded her hands in her lap. Seeing her struggle to appear brave, he wanted to believe that the court would show leniency.

"I know what you think, dear. If you bow down to the court's requirement, you clamp the prisoner's chains on your own limbs."

He felt gratitude that she so quickly grasped the heart of the matter. She understood that to walk about Salem with his mind cut like a wick until the flame scarcely flickers was no human life.

She stirred the potatoes boiling in the pot. "In England we saw men of the cloth die the death of a thousand compromises."

"Guilt cuts my heart, dear. I am your husband and our children's father."

"'Tis not guilt but the clash of two rights that cannot both have their way. 'Tis grief, not guilt." She walked to the window and asked him to join her. For a full minute, they stood silently watching the people rush about. Upon seeing Roger and Mary in the window, many waved warm greetings.

Mary had to return to test the potatoes. "Does a Christian warrior have courage only when he holds a sword in his hand? I am told that on the battlefield, there is a time to charge and a time to retreat. Do you hear the trumpet call of retreat?"

They returned to the window, and he put his arm around her. "I hear no such trumpet."

"Nor do I." She pointed to the people. "Nor do they."

By January 1636, the freezing winds and snows brought aches to the bones, pain to the muscles, and emptiness to many stomachs. All Massachusetts suffered the misery. Some complained that God had visited wrath upon a disobedient people. Others by contrast allowed that the bitter winter came as heaven's trial to prove the mettle of the faithful. Still others shook their fists at the howling wind as if it were the breath of Satan released upon them.

Despite the cold, the hot wrath of Dudley, Haynes, and others of the General Court sitting at the long table spewed out verbal lava. Each pretended to suffer surprise that Master Williams had ignored their stipulation to restrain from voicing his opinions. They professed to take deep offense and said to one another, "He has brought judgment upon his own head."

"If we tarry further to delay his punishment, heaven's wrath will fall more severely upon our people,"

Dudley rose to his feet to address Winthrop Sr. "Shall we turn blind and pretend that Master Williams has not defied this sacred court?"

"Are we not, as Scripture says, 'gods on earth,' called to administer God's wrath upon the disobedient?" asked another at the table.

"He has both defied this court and defiled the land." Haynes's voice shook and grew loud. "I fear God's wrath will come upon all New England if we do not sever this putrid limb from the Commonwealth."

This theme persisted and gathered momentum. In late November at a meeting with the magistrates, the learned, shrewd Thomas Hooker had stood up, quoted from the Scriptures of the old covenant, and portrayed Roger as wicked Achan in their midst. Then he had read aloud from the Book of Joshua: "Did not Achan the son of Zerah commit a trespass in the devoted matters so that *divine wrath fell upon the whole congregation of Israel?*"

Hooker had oft proved to be a man of supreme eloquence. Having no further need to stand, he sat down confidently at the table with the magistrates and lowered his voice. "I have conferred with the Reverend Cotton regarding this rebellious Achan in the land, and we interpret Scripture eye-to-eye on the matter. Achan did not suffer heaven's wrath alone. We must remove our Achan immediately lest we incur heaven's swift and terrible judgment. I warn you that if we do not act soon against Master Williams, heaven's fiery wrath will visit us with pestilence or famine."

"Already we suffer," the scholarly Reverend Wilson warned gently but firmly. "Our storehouses are scant with food. If we delay our duty to God, we risk severe punishment through ice storms, pestilence, and disease. Look around. Count our number and ask, 'How many of us will suffer death or crippling disease within another month if we do not move at once to remove the dread curse, this Achan, from us?'"

Two days later, Roger opened an urgent letter from Boston. "From Winthrop Sr.," he said to Mary, who sat in a chair rubbing oil on Freeborn's red cheeks. "The time has come, love."

Her lips quivered. "We must leave Salem soon?"

"Winthrop warns that the court's emissaries will arrive within four days. He cannot be more specific about the time. A ship stands ready to return me to England."

Roger took Freeborn in one arm and held Mary close to his shoulder with his other arm while she sobbed softly. He wanted to say comforting words to build up her spirit the way she had built his up so many times. Yet circumstances had left them little room for pretense or wishful thinking.

Mary dried her eyes and laid Freeborn in her cradle.

"Why is Mama crying?" Little Mary asked, tugging at her father's britches.

He knelt down beside her and stroked her hair, fighting back his own tears, trying not to think about the loneliness they would suffer in their separation. He talked to Little Mary softly, tried to explain, and then told her a story of a brave little girl.

"Roger, do not underrate the danger," Mary said. "I am terrified that they will capture you and put you on that ship. Depart without delay! Winthrop might have misled you regarding the time."

Standing up, he looked into his wife's big, moist eyes. He could scarcely bear the thought of turning his back upon them and leaving. "But Mary, you and the children."

"We will be safe here in Salem. If you set foot on that ship, you will . . . . Oh, Roger! I distrust Dudley. He is a dangerous man whose righteousness has the odor of sulfur and brimstone."

He was stunned. "Do you think he would—?"

"Dudley has a heart of rock, but he is no fool. The purpose for putting you aboard ship is not to deliver you to England where many would hear your voice. If you board that ship, your children tonight will have seen their father for the last time. Someone with Dudley's thirty pieces in his purse will shove you overboard."

He held up his hand to stop her. "Say no more, love. God has given me a woman with a double portion of wisdom." Then he read Winthrop's letter aloud again, noting that Winthrop strongly urged him to slip secretly away to Narraganset Bay.

Mary put her arms around him. "To live again among the Narraganset natives?"

"Yes. Or among the Wampanoags nearer Plymouth. But not too near."

Mary's lip trembled. "He is right. If you take a ship from Salem to Plymouth, Dudley's men will be aboard waiting."

"Then my safety lies only among the natives deep in the forest south of Boston."

"Oh, this dead of winter!" A crease seemed to etch itself on her face.

He picked up Little Mary, kissed her, and held her with one arm while Mary and he hurriedly packed his knife and the sundry articles he would need to survive in the forest.

He looked again at his daughters and for a moment forgot his plight, forgot his conflict with the court, forgot the many weeks of tormenting cold in the New England forests that lay before him. His world of Mary, Little Mary, and Freeborn seemed for this sacred moment to be more than enough for him.

Mary looked deeply into his eyes. "You are a good father."

"A father who abandons his children?"

"Better to abandon them for a season than . . . . Go! We will be a family again."

"Would that I had another sane alternative."

"Thank heaven that you have dear friends among the natives. Providence go with you to the Narragansets."

He tried to smile as he placed his finger on her lower lip. "Let a smile overcome the trembling."

She looked away. "Be not anxious about us."

"Do not weep, Mary; for my eyes, too, are springs ready to flow. I will go to the Paynters and a few others to arrange for you and the children. You will be secure and safe."

"What trail will you follow?"

"If I give you none of the details, you may truthfully profess ignorance of my escape." *Escape! Once, I slipped through the fingers of Laud and the High Commission. Now the Massachusetts Court sends its hounds.*

As the lingering purple sun disappeared from the lead-gray sky, Roger put on his coat, kissed wife and babes good-bye, and reached for the door.

Then he heard Mary's voice. "Roger!"

He turned around. "Yes, love?"

She bit her lip and shook her head. For a racking moment, they stared forlornly at each other. "Take care, dear husband."

He saw the little twitch on the left side of her mouth and recognized the terror she had tried to disguise. He pointed his finger heavenward. "Trust in the goodness of Providence." Forcing himself to turn away from her, he gritted his teeth, threw open the door, and left.

With his heart momentarily locked as though in a stone dungeon, he slipped out under cover of darkness and quickly found Paynter, Sharpe, Barry, and four other men with whom he had to speak before fleeing. He spoke hurriedly of his imminent departure, revealing nothing of either Winthrop's letter or his means of escape.

The carpenter Wilfred Barry took him by the arm and guided him to a corner in Jeremiah's house. "No brother could have been more to me than you. You taught me the courage of love and ne'er to be ashamed of it."

Even though Jeremiah's lips moved to speak, the trickle of tears flowing down his freckled cheeks robbed him of words. They spoke, nevertheless, what was in his heart. Roger placed his arm on the man's shoulder. "I will not reveal my precise destination lest the court's soldiers interrogate you. I ask one last favor. Tell William Harris that if all goes well, I will keep my promise to help him befriend the Narragansets and Wampanoags. He must of course journey there without me at his side."

"Harris spoke to me of taking the journey in March or April," Jeremiah said.

"Then spring it is," Roger said. "'Tis better that he not attempt it in winter."

Elder Sharpe laid his hand on Roger's shoulder and spoke in his soft way. "Ne'er will this elder be the same after knowing you. Take these few coins."

"No, friend, you have more need."

Sharpe pressed Roger's hand. "For my sake, take the coins." He smiled. "They are not so heavy as to weigh you down."

The two men embraced and then all quickly sang a hymn as the pale moon kissed the horizon. While clouds played chase with the moon, Roger wrapped himself in a heavy cloak of animal skin and headed south through the wilderness. Picturing a party of Algonquins, he prayed that the hand of Providence would guide him across their path.

"Master Williams," said a voice from behind.

Recognizing Thomas Angell's voice, he waited and then said sharply, "Thomas, you must return."

Angell spoke in a firm voice. "We have been friends since England. Now I will go with you from Salem."

"I have no precise destiny."

"I am hearty and strong. Give me less than a quarter of an hour and I will have—"

"Listen, Thomas. You have suffered no banishment. Be not foolish! In Boston Harbor sits an English ship on which some would plant my feet. Now return to your warm bed."

Angell raised his voice in protest.

He quickly clamped his hand over Angell's mouth. "Hold your tongue lest your cannon voice wake both Salem and Boston!"

His big eyes shining in the moonlight, Angell nodded.

He slowly released his hold on Angell. "If you persist in rejecting my counsel and if you are resolved to become my companion in misery, then give heed. I will head for the first trading post six miles south. Meet me there."

"That post has been abandoned."

"True, but it is shelter. And perhaps I will find signs there of our native friends."

"Can you not wait for me now?"

"No, I must leave at once while I have my courage. Bring a torch. If, after pondering, you elect not to follow me, I will think much the better of you." Saying no more, Roger left, praying that Angell would heed his counsel to remain in Salem. He knew he had spoken harshly to Angell, but solely out of affection for his young friend.

Three miles later, the guiding moonlight gave way to thick, heavy clouds. Roger lit his torch. *Another blanket of snow will fall soon.* Without the moonlight to guide him, he slowed down his pace for fear that he would take a false trail and be swallowed by the forest. It was foolish to travel at night in the Massachusetts winter. Yet Winthrop would not have sent the letter urging him to escape unless Dudley and the others had already set the hounds loose.

Roger could see his frosted breath exploding from his mouth. Momentarily picturing the emissaries from Boston arriving presently in Salem, he wondered if they were now searching from house to house. No sane man, however, would venture out in this howling wind to search for me, he thought, trying to console himself and marking trees with his knife to assist Angell in case he followed.

He heard the flapping of an owl's wings and then the squealing of her nocturnal meal. He prayed that he would not become victim to Boston's Court or England's dread Star Chamber.

Walking for still another mile, he felt snowdrops on his nose, and his knees ached from the cold. A current of fear went through his shoulders, fear that if the snow came too quickly, it would cover the trail to the trading post standing perhaps two miles south.

THE MASSACHUSETTS FOREST

January 1636

Roger tried to estimate the distance he had traveled. *Where is the cabin?* He shivered, not from the cold, but from the thought that he might have taken a wrong trail. Trying to ignore the wind's howl, he stopped, held the torch high over his head, and looked round and round. *Nothing!* He felt terrified that he had turned himself around once too often. If only the clouds would break! Then the stars could serve as his map.

The wind's fierce howling threatened to carry away all his rational thinking. The cold made his teeth hurt. "Think!" he cried out aloud. "Think!"

He could see his footprints behind him but none ahead. Perhaps he would walk a quarter of an hour before turning back. Would that not tell him whether he had taken a false trail? What was that? An open space in this dense wilderness? Though his face felt frozen like a rock, he laughed aloud. Scarcely more than fifteen feet ahead—was it rough-hewn wood? Aye, the trading post shelter! He shook violently in the cold wind.

Must kick this new snow away from the door. Now shove this warped door open and enter! Ah, it would serve to break the wind so he could sleep soon. The three natives who had lived at this meager trading post had abandoned it for the winter and probably forever. The natives had assisted Barry, Thomas Angell, and Roger in building a larger and more serviceable post west of Salem.

Realizing that the snow could thicken at any moment, he reluctantly went back into the wind and gathered firewood. *Angell will need a bright fire to guide his way.*

In the manner the Wampanoags had taught him, Roger arranged the sticks and broken tree limbs. Soon the dry twigs began to burn, and the larger wood gave birth to small blue flames.

As the fire began slowly, he prayed for the safety of his short but wiry young friend. Picturing Angell's thick eyebrows, he hoped the lad's strength would not fail him. Having served Roger's family in London for many years, Thomas Angell had come to New England with Roger's blessing. Roger had not only taught this youth of quick native intelligence to read, but also offered him the fruit of some of his Cambridge education. Angell was a trustworthy youth who could be relied on to speak his mind without flattery or guile.

Standing in the wide clearing and near to the infant fire to protect it against the rising wind, Roger felt fear crawl up his back. If the court's agents had set out to hunt him down, they too might see the glowing flames. His pursuers, however, would not venture into the wilderness without a guide. He smiled to himself, thinking that even if some emissaries were insane enough to embark on a search for him tonight, they would find no guide in Salem who would knowingly lead them in the right direction.

Thinking of possible misfortunes that might have befallen Angell, he felt a sinking sensation in his stomach. *Feed on this dried fish rather than fear.* After tossing a large tree limb into the flames, he watched the sparks fly upward to the now moonless, starless sky. To keep from falling asleep out of weariness, he let himself think of Mary. He had wanted to tell her to thank Winthrop for warning him of the court's intention. He imagined a fanciful conversation between himself and his Mary. He was saying to her, "Winthrop is no longer governor, but if he were now—"

Mary's eyes flashed with fire. "No man or woman in all New England wields more influence than Winthrop. If he had wished to save you from this fate—"

Roger was holding Winthrop's letter. "If perchance you see Winthrop, speak my gratitude and tell him I perceived the good will in his letter."

"Good will? No, Roger, it is ointment for his guilt."

"You speak too harshly of him, love."

Mary was helping him button his woolen shirt. "Winthrop knows that if you returned to England, you would tell the truth about the colony and the magistrates. I feel no gratitude toward him."

"You make a devil of Winthrop, I fear."

"No, I make a Winthrop of Winthrop, and that is close enough to the devil. Though he holds affection for you, he is like those who would behead their own kin to gain the crown."

"If he had wished me harm, would he have urged me to flee south to the Narragansets?"

"He sees you also as his tool."

"All the same, for my sake will you give my gratitude to Winthrop?"

"Yes, but I will also give you this warning. Mark it well, dear husband. When you cut deeper into the wilderness to make peace and build strong friendship with the natives, Winthrop will smile. Behind the smile, however, will be his ploys to take possession and to rule. Mark my word!"

The fire that Roger had built grew large. He could feel its heat. Edging closer to the flames, he removed his socks, rubbed his cold feet, and put on the thick socks Mary had knitted for him. He was glad she had urged him to wear his heavy boots.

What is that?

A cracking sound traveled through the forest. A tree limb breaking in the wind?

He saw two eyes that reflected the flames from the fire. Animal eyes? Or the eyes of an Algonquin? No. A native would never roam among the trees at night in the dead of winter. The Boston emissaries! Could they have followed his footprints all the way from Salem?

He slipped out of the clearing, hid among the trees, and tried to hold his breath; but his pounding heart required more air, not less. The logs on the fire burned bright at the center of the clearing. Had he only imagined the eyes in the forest? Now there were only snow eddies moving about like specters. The trees swayed; he pulled the beaver collar tightly around his throat. When a strong gust of wind almost blew out the flames, his skin crawled. *Someone is calling my name.* Although wanting to answer back, he waited. Had his mind tricked him?

"Master Williams," a voice called out again over the moaning wind.

"Thomas? Thomas Angell?"

"Are you alone, Master Williams?"

Roger closed his eyes to savor the relief. "I am alone, Thomas. Come, warm yourself at the fire."

Angell dashed toward the fire, his entire body trembling as if some powerful, invisible arm had taken him by the shoulders and shaken him. "Never have I been this cold. Never!" He edged so close to the fire that for a moment Roger feared he might step into it.

He pulled Angell back. "You traveled far more quickly than I had expected."

"You left signs easy to follow. Then I saw the fire's red glow." Thomas Angell took a hatchet from his belongings, chopped limbs from a dead tree, and threw them onto the fire. The flames reached out like tongues toward the sky. Sparks flew up to meet the falling snowflakes, turning the scene into a winter dance. "The court's men came looking for you." Angell rubbed his own cheeks and ears until the blood returned.

"Did they speak with you?"

"No. But before escaping unseen into the wilderness, I took quick refuge in Endecott's cellar."

"That was risky."

"Governor Endecott did not know of my presence."

Roger guided Angell indoors. "What did you learn from your hiding place?"

"That Endecott is a revolving weather vane. He said *Sir* to them all a hundred times and flattered them until the air grew putrid."

"Did you bring meat to eat?"

"Enough for two days."

"Did you talk to others before leaving?"

"Only vaguely with William Harris, who owed me money. If you have concern about my departure, put your mind at ease. I faded slowly into the darkness."

At sunrise on the following day, Roger woke Angell and opened the door of the abandoned trading post. "Good tidings! The snow lies scarcely more than a foot deep. Let us make our way southwest through this back country to avoid the coast and towns."

Lacking horses or mules and with the wind to their backs, they struck out on foot, hoping to find berries along their way.

By noon two days later, they felt weary from hunger. Despite all his efforts, Roger could not free his mind of images from his mother's table—Holland cheese, rice and fruit, almonds and honey.

Angell also kept thinking of food. "I can smell the scones from your Mary's hearth."

Roger knelt down on one knee and pointed through the birch trees to a wild turkey in the distance.

"We have no gun," Angell whispered.

"Then let us build a trap." He tried to wipe the blowing snow from his eyes. As the howling wind shook the trees, he wished the old trading post were nearby to offer protection. The wind's fierceness grew stronger with every heartbeat. To his surprise, before they could begin to build a trap, the turkey fell to the ground, flapped her wings three times, and then lay motionless.

Angell jumped with glee. "A miracle! God commanded ravens to feed the prophet Elijah. Now He sends us a turkey. Let us cook and eat it."

"Do not move! To the right beyond the turkey."

"A native!"

Roger cut his eyes to the left. Three other natives appeared as if from nowhere and then four more, all gathering around Angell and Roger. He recognized none of them. Reading hostility in their faces, he braced himself, hoping Angell and he would not join the turkey in becoming these natives' prey. He opened his mouth to shout friendly words.

Before he could speak, a tall native brandishing a long knife stepped from behind a large tree and said in English, "You trespass against us."

Roger stood up on unsteady legs. "We seek only safe passage."

"Passage?" the native shouted.

"Journey," Roger answered against the rising, threatening wind.

"Where does your journey take you?"

"South to the Wampanoags and Narragansets."

The natives moved closer. "Why do you journey in this miserable wind and snow? Can you not wait for the milder season?" the tallest native asked.

With his hand, Roger signaled Angell to say nothing. If the natives wish to curry favor with the Boston magistrates, he reasoned, they might capture Angell and him for a generous reward.

All at once, an earsplitting sound jarred Roger from head to foot. The natives jumped, and Roger whirled around. A towering pine had crashed into a number of smaller trees.

"The wind!" Angell shouted. "It will wreak havoc on us all."

Limbs flew in the air like flocks of birds. Everyone dropped to the ground, digging into the snow. The wind scooped up layers of ice from the ground and flung them without mercy. Roger tried to burrow himself deeper, like a fox. Then he heard the tall native with the knife shout.

Looking up, Roger saw him motion, urging them to follow his men to a nearby dense area of the forest. Although they ran after the natives, a flying limb struck Angell across the arm, knocking him down in the snow. Two natives quickly lifted him to his feet.

Another crack split their ears, and another towering tree fell, then a third and a fourth.

Roger snatched up the dead turkey and ran until reaching the mouth of a cave deeper into the dense forest.

The tall native pointed. "Inside!"

Roger and Angell accepted the invitation and joined the natives around the fire. Handing the turkey to one of the natives, Roger looked into the face of the tall one and thought he saw the earlier hostility leave with the wind.

"This storm will drive your English ships from their anchors," said the tall one.

When Roger tried speaking in the Narraganset tongue, he was pleased to discover that three of the natives understood him.

Watching one of them pluck the feathers from the turkey and roast it over the fire, he felt his mouth water. As soon as one part of the turkey seemed well cooked, the native pulled off a large piece of breast and handed it to him. A second piece went to Angell. Three other turkeys soon began to drip with fat over the fire, which popped and sang as the drippings hit the coals. The meat quelled the hungry lions in Roger's stomach; and the fire soothed his cold, stiff bones.

Soon Angell became his cheerful self. "This cave grows as warm as Mary's hearth."

While feasting with the natives inside the cave, Roger had the odd feeling that today might be the last fresh meat he would eat for many weeks. He heard the other natives refer to the tall one as Chosetox. When Chosetox asked why he had wandered so deep into the forest in the snow season, Roger cautioned himself against giving any information that would disclose his status as a fugitive.

When night came, Roger, Angell, and the natives fell asleep with the wind outside still howling, working its havoc. Now and then, Roger woke at the sound of massive trees splitting under the strain of the wild, relentless wind. He could not help thinking of the ship in Boston Harbor and the special royal deputy. He pondered Mary's warning that Dudley's zeal for righteousness would permit him to hire an executioner to murder him at sea.

At dawn he woke to a shaft of teasing sunlight at the cave's mouth. Not daring to move, he cut his eyes to the right and left. The cave appeared empty except for the presence of Angell, who groaned in his sleep. The fire had burned low, the natives had slipped away, and the wind had departed, leaving behind an eerie quiet. Sitting up, he threw a log onto the fire and rubbed his eyes. It was imperative to go outside to take his bearings.

Seeing the sun in the east, he called on the lessons he had learned from the Wampanoags. He was now certain his journey would carry him to his destination far south of Boston. On the night of his departure, he had led Angell to believe that he had not firmly settled upon his destination. He had done this in case the court's soldiers interrogated Angell.

"Wake up, Angell. The natives have gone, and we must continue our journey."

Angell warmed his boots at the fire. "What route will we take?"

"There is a river west of Plymouth Colony that . . . . But I cannot risk encountering trappers and hunters when we skirt Boston."

"I know of the river, Master Williams. But your face is well known in Boston."

"So either we travel in the back-country, making a wide detour around Boston, or—"

"Be forced back to England, eh?"

In Salem before his forced flight, Roger had agreed to take William Harris and three others to the river in March or April. He had no doubt that they would then make the journey. Not being fugitives like Roger, they were free to travel by ship. He now wished he had refused to meet Harris and the others in the spring. They had virtually pleaded to become a part of his venture among the natives. Although he trusted Angell, he could not free himself from growing suspicions regarding Harris.

More pressing was the long and precarious trek ahead. Angell and Roger departed the cave and headed southwest, taking the food the natives had left for them. For two weeks, they traveled and hunted. While Roger's health improved each day, Angell's seemed to decline.

"Your cough grows worse. I fear another fever will come over you. Now for my sake, head east to Boston. Find Captain Firebrook and—"

"No, my cough will pass. I am—"

"I must send a message to Captain Firebrook. Would you have me risk entering Boston?"

Angell sneezed, coughed, and protested.

"Angell, if you are my friend, you will do this for me." Then he placed his hand on the young man's shoulder. "I would rather meet Thomas Angell south of here within the month than to meet him with the heavenly angels in the next life."

"But did I not promise heaven that I would—?"

"Ah, and you have kept your promise. I beg you, take no thought for my journey. Within two Sabbaths I will come upon friendly natives who will minister to my needs. Now assure me that you will leave my welfare to Providence and then go."

"I so promise." A strange sorrow in Angell's voice revealed reluctance and foreboding. " You have been both uncle and teacher to me, Master Williams. I will do as you ask."

"The word *angel* means messenger. Thus, Angell, secretly give our friend Captain Firebrook the message that within the month I will be among the natives of Narraganset Bay."

After they embraced as would uncle and nephew, Roger watched him walk toward the eastern horizon until he disappeared among the trees. Turning and setting his face steadfastly toward the south, Roger resolved to endure the severe hardships ahead. He had no alternative but to pass through more of Massachusetts territory. With no guide save his own wits and with little food in his possession, he planted his right foot in front of him and began his lonely pilgrimage.

Throughout the following week, he built small fires along his trail to warm his feet against the threat of frostbite. On the coldest night since he had left Salem, he fell into a deep sleep. He dreamed of the seamen he had known in his youth, of horses snorting, of Sir Edward Coke and his former employer Sir William Masham. It was as if his dreams carried him through a long tunnel toward his youth and then on toward his childhood and his mother and father. His whole life seemed to pass before him as if on a stage.

Then Mary appeared, holding Freeborn. In his dream, he lay in his bed, his family around him. *Why am I lying here when my family needs me?* The question haunted him until he heard the clear voice of his first daughter Little Mary. "Rise up, father! You must not sleep forever!"

Next came a strange barking high in a tree overhead. When he opened his eyes, the noise continued. In the gray dawn, he saw two squirrels chasing one another and a third cracking nuts and chattering on a tree limb.

Bolting upright, he rubbed his nose fiercely. "My face is numb!"

The new wind howled contemptuously as though a human mortal's survival meant nothing. "I am alive, Little Mary!" He rubbed his hands until he could feel the heat. Defying the wind, he built a fire inside a circle of rocks he had arranged on the night before. "I could have frozen to death," he said aloud as if to test his chilled jaws and throat for their utility.

After eating hurriedly, he warmed himself in preparation for another day's travel. He vowed to train himself to wake up more frequently lest he die in his sleep.

He faced the bitter cold and the fierce nocturnal wind by telling himself that his trial in the wilderness was only temporary. Somewhere among the Narragansets, he would build a sturdy home for Mary and their two children.

Now as the end of January approached, he could focus on little more than finding shelter and food. With no house save hollow trees or rocky ledges, he fought against the loneliness and found himself taking comfort in the company of squirrels by day and owls by night. At times he heard wolves howling in the distance.

The blustery, hostile winds of late January drove him to the brink. He conducted long conversations with himself day after day, vowing, "The bitterness of this cold will not embitter my soul."

Coming upon a frozen pond, he used a smooth stone to sand the surface until it became a mirror. Kneeling on hands and knees, he gazed at the reflection. "Who is this?" He looked again at the bearded ruffian staring back from the icy mirror. He smiled at himself. "Rather, *what* is this? Man or beast?" At that moment, he turned on his knees and was about to stand up when he saw four feet planted in front of him.

THE MASSACHUSETTS WILDERNESS

January–February 1636

Roger had to think quickly. Would the two natives standing over him consider him crazy, a man talking to his reflection in the ice? Would they regard him as an intruder? He prayed that their curiosity would prevent them from sending a blow to his head.

Still on his hands and knees with his head down and trusting in their curiosity, he spoke in the Wampanoag tongue. "I am a friend of the esteemed Sachem Massasoit. Can you guide me to him?"

They did not answer.

He shifted haltingly to the Narraganset tongue. "I have come in friendship."

Though they listened patiently, they made no move either to help or harm him. He shivered, no longer because he feared the two natives, but because the wind cut him like a knife. Slowly he raised his head and struggled to push himself to his feet. His own weariness surprised him. The hollow log that had been his bed during the night had not treated him kindly.

He stood now, staring into the faces of the two natives, who began talking animatedly with one another and glancing back at him as though he were either an object that amused them or a slave under appraisal. Their deep voices created a strange sensation in him. He wanted to call the men "sons of thunder," the nickname Jesus had given to boisterous James and John.

All at once, the younger of the two natives broke out in uproarious laughter and pointed at Roger. "You are the Englishman who once traveled with the Wampanoag Sachem Massasoit?"

"I am."

The older man's face carried the deep scars of smallpox. One of the fortunate ones. When the older man stared back with squinted eyes, Roger said to him, "Because of Massasoit's friendship, I saw the faces of many Algonquin sachems."

"You are the one called Roger Williams!" the older man shouted in his face as if he might thus better understand their tongue.

Roger removed the fur hat Jeremiah had given him. "I am the man or else a block of ice shaped to resemble him."

"The iced beard . . . like thick moss covering a rock! A winter past, I saw you."

Roger pressed his fist against his own chest. "You saw me?"

"You were not bearded when you appeared among my people." The older man laughed again, throwing his head back and relishing the surprise. "Behind the beard, you are the Englishman who journeyed with Massasoit himself."

"I will gladly trade you this frozen beard for a bit of meat." He felt frightened by the weakness in his legs.

The older, pock-marked native shrugged. "Come with us. We have venison for your English stomach."

As they ate under a rocky ledge filled with smoke and the aroma of venison, he learned that even though his two rescuers spoke the Narraganset language fluently, they belonged to another Algonquin settlement northwest of the Narragansets. To his dismay, he learned also that he had another day of hazardous travel before arriving at the river he sought.

"Your eyes speak of illness," said the older native. "Let the meat strengthen your muscles. Stay with us a day. When you part from us tomorrow, you will be strong again."

With gratitude he accepted their hospitality. The decision proved wise. As he regained his strength and recovered from near frostbite, the younger native patiently taught him the art of making more efficient snowshoes. The older man helped him with the Narraganset vocabulary while they talked about religion and the natives' way of caring for their children and the aged.

"The winter has been cruel," the younger native said. "The English lost many cattle."

The knee-deep new snow had made Roger's journey unbearably slow. The improved snowshoes, however, would lift his body and spirits from the wintry, white surface of the cold journey stretching before him.

After taking leave of the two natives and following their instructions for reaching the Wampanoag village, he threaded his way through the forest and thicket, talking to himself again and working out plans to live among the Narragansets. While learning their language and customs more thoroughly, he would compile his dictionary and eventually complete his book about the people.

Each day his passion to serve as evangel among the natives burned brighter. If he learned from them, he could be of special use to them. He must also overcome the European and English arrogance that presumed the "savages" void of ordinary humanity, morality, and intelligence. If he could not learn from the natives in their own land, what right had he to expect them to learn from him, a foreigner?

A day after his leaving the two Algonquins, the falling snow turned into a driving sleet storm. Even though the cold weather became more severe, the northern wind at his back made his walking easier. Though the wolves howled, they kept their distance. The Wampanoags had told him that wolves would not attack a human unless they approached starvation and could find no other prey. This thought gave Roger no comfort. If the wolves were as hungry as he, they would not long hesitate to devour him.

On the next day, he saw deep scratches on a thick, tall tree. *A bear*, he thought, remembering that the Wampanoags had taught him that in winter bears sometimes lodged in the upper part of hollow trees. Fearing he might famish without the bear meat or freeze without the bearskin's protection against the icy wind, he forced himself to stop. Thoughts emerging from the womb of desperation were prone to suffer many flaws, he cautioned himself. *Take time to think*. How would he kill the bear? If he failed to kill her, the animal would surely overpower him. Had he the physical strength to kill so strong a creature? Perhaps in one powerful thrust. Perhaps.

Taking his hunting knife from his belt, he studied it carefully. The blade was too short. He knew, nevertheless, what he must do. From a nearby tree, he cut off a branch as long as his leg and about two inches thick. Although his fingers cramped with soreness in the sleet and wind, he hurriedly cut off all the twigs and whittled one end of the pole to a long, strong point.

Taking a thick rope that the Algonquins had given him, he used it to bend a thick, low tree limb. Calling on all his strength, he tied the long limb firmly to another tree trunk. He would use this trick only as a last resort to defend himself should the bear charge him. He knotted one end of the rope as a trigger to release the limb.

Taking his time, Roger systematically walked off his escape path, which he hoped he would not need. After resting for a minute and rehearsing his movements, he began climbing the tree wherein slept the bear. He knew that ordinarily one native would arouse the bear while a second and third would shoot it. Having no companion, however, he had only two choices: forsake his plan entirely or carry it out alone flawlessly.

While approaching the sleeping bear, he sensed the animal's power. Roger snapped his head back at the shocking pungency of her breath. With his new spear now firmly in his grip, he carefully studied the creature. He knew he could not allow the bear to swipe him even once with her ferocious paw. One blow could break his English neck or render him unconscious.

Suddenly he felt himself more animal than human. Some inner change came over him as if one part of his mind had yielded to another, giving it extraordinary strength. He secured himself on a thick limb next to the bear. With both hands, he grasped his spear and raised it over his head, his arms fully extended.

Now! He brought his arms down with such force that the spear deeply pierced the thick skin of the bear's chest and hurled Roger from the tree. He hit the snow-covered ground hard, but he quickly sprang to his feet. Without looking back, he ran toward his escape path. He could hear himself gasping for breath. When he passed the thick limb he had tied in suspension, he stopped, looking over his shoulder as he grabbed for the rope's free end.

The bear breathed noisily, gushed with blood, bounded from the tree, and pursued him. Roger's whole body shook with terror as he yanked the rope with all his might. The tied tree limb swung savagely back with bone-crushing force, catching the bear across the mouth and knocking her down.

He saw blood pouring from the deep gash he had made in the magnificent animal. She struggled heroically to rise to her feet, but she could only turn her head back and forth in anguish. The roar from her mouth shocked him. Yet he could not flee. The whole scene held him captive as terror flooded his whole body. He could not move. For one fleeting moment, his terror mingled with undeniable admiration for the wondrous giant of the forest. Then an unexpected, disturbing sense of guilt streaking through him like a bolt, which then succumbed to a more primitive sense of triumph and power. Though he trembled from head to foot at the sight of his bloody deed, he could not help feeling an exhilarating yet sickening domination. He wanted to walk up to the struggling creature and loudly proclaim his superiority.

This too gave way to another feeling that surprised him, an almost irresistible urge to beg the animal's forgiveness. To his complete surprise, he burst into wild, angry weeping that made no sense to him. The tears mingled with a fierce, almost savage gratitude to the animal. "You have saved my life," he cried out to her. Then with deep respect for the dying bear, he watched her red blood drain out to color the sleet and white snow.

When at last the animal stopped breathing, Roger took out his knife and quickly cut the skin according to the Wampanoags' instructions. He recalled the biblical passage: *The life of the flesh is in the blood.* When he had removed the skin and cleansed it as best he could in the snow and sleet, he set it aside to let the stringent odor escape.

He built a fire and cooked a good portion of the meat. It had been months since he had eaten bear meat. His fare had recently consisted of many winterberries and the corn the Algonquins had given him in a pouch he carried around his neck.

He longed for his destination, which he could now feel in his bones. Instead of rushing foolishly ahead, he elected to spend the remainder of the morning at the spot where he had killed the bear. He ate until he could eat no more.

Rested and finding strength he did not know he possessed, he packed his bearskin and some meat. *The rest I leave for my friends the wolves. Better they feast on this fat carcass than on my frame.* Tonight he would relish the warmth under his new bearskin.

THE SEEKONK RIVER

Spring 1636

After living through the remainder of the winter under Chief Massasoit's protection in Sowams west of Plymouth Colony, Roger reached his destination farther west at the Seekonk River. If the Massachusetts Court had intended him to suffer setback, pain, and hardship, they had succeeded. If they had, on the other hand, intended to break his spirit, to confine his thinking to a narrow tunnel, to make him capitulate to their theocracy, they had failed.

Again calling upon his early training as a trader, he acquired tools to become a farmer. The Narragansets and the Wampanoags often laughed with amusement, calling him *Bubbling Brook* and *River of Hope*. But the more cheer he brought to the natives, the more practical assistance they gave him. Now he stood ready for the new adventure in his life and in the lives of his family. The months apart from them had seemed like years. Feeling that he sometimes possessed the energy of a buck and the determination of a mule, he set about putting in a crop and building a house, all the while dreaming of the day Mary and the little ones would join him.

In early April, Thomas Angell arrived safely, bearing joyful news that the Williams family had survived the winter in good health.

Roger, nevertheless, felt less than joyful at the news that William Harris and three others would soon join him in the new territory. Having come in good faith to live among the natives and share with them in a spirit of mutual respect, he could not rid himself of secret doubts about the good will of Harris and some of the others. Though he had no proof of their shady intentions, his suspicions left him no peace. He vowed to look with one eye in hope, the other in caution. When Harris and the others eventually arrived, Roger assisted them just as the natives had come to his rescue. He would never forget the kindness the natives had shown him, and he hoped that the English settlers who followed him to the Narraganset Bay would not forget his kindness.

Through the Reverend John Smith of Plymouth, Roger sent word asking Mary to prepare for her departure. Even though some details remained to be completed, he felt he had made sufficient preparation for his family's safety.

On a bleak April day, Angell rushed up to him in the field where he was at work and pulled him aside. "An English messenger from the governor wishes to speak with you."

"Governor?" Roger's heart sank.

"Plymouth's Governor Winslow." Angell pointed eastward. "He awaits you on yonder side of the knoll."

"Wait here." He stretched his legs to a long, vigorous stride until he reached the knoll where the messenger sat on a horse. Roger thought he surveyed the land too carefully, as though he might have designs on it.

"Master Williams?" The man peered down from his saddle.

"Yes. How may I be of service?"

"I am Mark Redding." The messenger threw his leg over the horse and hurriedly lowered himself to the ground. "Governor Winslow has sent me."

"You must be thirsty and hungry. Come to my abode and—"

"Please, Master Williams, I have unpleasant news. I have heard many good things of you. But I did not meet you in Plymouth, for I arrived from England only after your departure from Salem. Please, sir, permit me to deliver this burdensome message."

"You have my full attention, Master Redding."

"Governor Winslow wishes you to know that he had himself longed to speak with you face-to-face. He gives his word that he will come when his urgent duties permit. The message is that the Massachusetts magistrates contend that by dwelling on the east side of the river, you live inside the boundaries of Plymouth Colony. They have made clear to Governor Winslow that the line of trade and commerce between their colony and ours will be weakened or even cut unless you and your company remove yourselves from Plymouth territory."

Roger gazed over the land he had tilled and the crops he had planted by the sweat of his brow. "I purchased this land from the natives through Massasoit himself."

"Governor Winslow knows of your good faith and of the good will between yourself and the natives. But the ill will that the Massachusetts magistrates bear you threatens to boil over and spill into Plymouth Colony. They have greedy designs on our territory and have already stirred up acrimony toward us in London."

"I understand the risk to peace." Anger formed a knot in Roger's stomach. "Walk with me." He swept his hand over the western horizon. "Tell me what you see."

"Why, I see people working side by side, transforming thickets into fields that will bring forth peas and *askútasquash* and—"

"Who will eat of this—?"

Mark Redding blushed. "To take the fruit of another's labor without permission runs counter to my religion. I know it is not Governor Winslow's will to rob you and these good people." Redding stopped in his tracks and looked back at his horse as if he half expected a better answer to come from a dumb animal.

Roger placed his hand on the young man's shoulder. "If a man steals with a knife in his back, I blame not the knife, but the knife-wielder."

"Master Williams, it is the knife of conscience that cuts me. The Massachusetts magistrates harbor the evil spirit of Ahab when he did steal Naboth's vineyard."

Roger felt no forgiveness for the Massachusetts tyrants. Could they not be satisfied with exiling him from his home and friends? Must they now intimidate the people of Plymouth? *While professing to follow the teachings of Scripture, they wink at the commandment against thievery, placing halos over their envy and drawing wings on their malice.* He tried to smile at Redding, whom he believed had come in good conscience. "When you return to my friends in Plymouth, tell them you saw no horns on my head, only calluses on my hands. And I hope that you perceive no calluses on my heart."

Redding took off his hat and wiped his brow. He shook his head. "If I now stood in the shoes of Roger Williams . . . ." He shook his head again despairingly. "To leave behind these fields, to kiss my labor good-bye, to search for new land and start over . . ." Again sighing, Redding looked at his horse as if the humiliation had grown too much for him and he wished now to ride away. "I know not what more to say. Do not condemn the messenger of this ill tiding."

Aware that he had no choice, Roger resigned himself to starting over. What useful purpose would looking back serve? Or nursing his wounds or cultivating a grudge? He increased his pace and looked up at the hawks circling in the bright blue sky. "I will walk you to your stallion. Be my messenger. Give your kind governor my word that I will remove myself and my companions to the west side of the Seekonk River if the natives find my proposal agreeable."

When Redding prepared to leave, Roger implored him to urge Governor Winslow to send a messenger to Mary in Salem, advising her to delay her departure until she received further word from him.

Five days later after a two-day rain had ceased, Roger and his small company departed, leaving their planted fields and newly-begun shelters. *Would that this were a nightmare from which I would soon awake.*

Three native men accompanied him as he walked toward a long canoe. The canoe's covering was thick moose hides sewn together, the seams pitched with a mixture of balsam and charcoal. How grateful he felt to the natives for teaching him how to make his own canoe!

"The English will not reap your harvest," one of the natives vowed to Roger. "We have given you our help. Now you have given us this land, which you purchased from our sachem."

"It will give me pleasure to know that you and your children will eat the produce of these fields." Roger felt his broad smile linger.

The four remaining Englishmen boarded the canoe, having earlier loaded it with their scant belongings. Roger gripped the paddle, bade farewell to his Wampanoag friends, and dipped the paddle into the river.

He made a mental note that if the journey proved free of mishap, he and his company would reach the other side of the swollen river farther south on April 20. *Providence!* Aye, he would call his new home Providence or New Providence, seeing that his journey had lain always in the hands of Providence despite the winter's bitter cold, sickness, howling wolves, and vindictive Massachusetts magistrates.

The swelling river's current, stronger than he had anticipated, carried them swiftly downstream. With considerable effort, Harris and he paddled the canoe west in the hope of arriving at the new shoreline.

A small band of natives huddled on the west shore and waited. Roger could not determine whether they peered across the water in hostility or from curiosity. Believing them to be Narragansets because of their attire, he called out words of cheer.

Looking over his shoulder, he was struck by the considerable distance he had come by crossing the vast river. In the winter, he had left Massachusetts behind. Now Plymouth Colony lay on the other side of the wide river. Using the hand language he had learned from Titus (the Wampanoag who knew several dialects and languages), he signaled to the natives on the shoreline. He had come in peace and intended to land on the neck of the land around the river's bend.

Appearing to understand, the natives hurried at once to the neck.

Within Roger emerged a strange, awesome feeling. He could not articulate the new sensation and thus tried to force it from his mind. Yet it persisted, coloring all his other thoughts. He knew he should proceed with caution in approaching the shoreline. Not all natives were free of animosity. Still an inexplicable excitement pounded in his temples. How he longed to speak with them about many matters. They had much to learn from one another. A childlike curiosity whirled inside him with such strength that he wanted to jump into the water and dash forth to greet them.

Just as the canoe touched the shore, the natives, seemingly no less enthusiastic than he to begin their encounter, pulled the vessel safely onto the beach. The Englishmen stepped out and stood before the natives in a moment of ambivalence that soon burst into buzzing and entangled conversation. Speaking a strain of the Narraganset tongue, Roger sensed at once that they understood his desire to negotiate for land and to live among them.

Although the natives welcomed him, they explained that it was necessary to meet their esteemed sachem immediately.

"What is his name?" Roger asked.

"Canonicus." Their unmitigated pride was unmistakable

As soon as Roger and his company had left their canoe and supplies with two of the natives, they marched off to see the esteemed Canonicus. Roger possessed a disturbing sense of uneasiness. About Canonicus he had heard various strange reports that fell into no consistent pattern.

Roger knew many Catholic and Reformation missionaries assumed that an entire people could be converted to the Christian faith by converting the chief ruler of the people. He, by contrast, believed that no one could convert on behalf of another. Each man and woman must repent and believe personally.

Aware that he was the first wholly dedicated Reformation missionary in New England, he felt the heavy burden of communicating to the natives the Protestant doctrine of *soul liberty* or *individual responsibility*. He admitted his anger upon first learning that many Protestants in Europe had betrayed their own principles by seeking wholesale conversions or proxy faith through the presumed political rulers. In the past five years, he had come to believe that not even baptism could substitute for faith or turn an infant into a Christian. No ritual or external performance substituted for the individual's own conversion of heart and mind. He had slowly come to believe that such ceremonies served as outward expressions of faith.

As he and his companions approached the busy Narraganset settlement, he saw an old man dressed in the special attire that identified him as the chief sachem. Every wrinkle in the proud, bronzed face seemed to tell a harrowing story. Standing before the esteemed sachem, Roger looked into his eyes and sensed danger. The eyes revealed enigma behind enigma. The look of disgust and even hatred on the old man's face infected all those around him. Why did this Canonicus refuse to speak, his silence seeming designed to belittle them and reduce them to bewilderment and confusion?

Roger at first wanted to present his case as though he stood before an English court. This, however, was neither English territory nor Cambridge University. Knowing neither the rules nor the protocol for the occasion, he waited, hoping that somehow an influential native advocate would step forth on his behalf.

Of special importance, he reminded himself, was the need to give due regard to the sachem's position before his people. He must give no hint of being contentious. At the same time, he did not intend to surrender his dignity to the sachem. Tact, *yes*. Flattery and hypocrisy, *no*.

The old sachem's eyes were half-hooded. "You are English?"

Roger sensed the indignation and rage in the sachem's tone. "We are English."

"You English have killed many of my people with the sickness that you spread among us. I have learned of your English contempt for my people. You excuse the evil of your deed by saying that your god sent the sickness to destroy the lives of my people because, you say, we are more wicked than the English."

He listened patiently in the hope of learning the premises that governed Canonicus's thinking.

"Since you are the leader of the English plot to murder my people with the sickness, I order your death." The sachem rose to his feet

Had he heard correctly? Roger's whole body surged with fear

Angell protested loudly through one of the interpreters, but the sachem ordered him bound and carried away.

Through an interpreter, William Harris insisted, "I . . . I had no knowledge of this man's intention. I agreed to follow him because he said he wished to pay a debt of friendship."

Realizing that he had no human help, save his own wits, Roger tried desperately to think of some plan lest he become Canonicus's scapegoat. He spoke directly to the Chief Sachem in his own language. "There is always time to watch a man die. I ask for an Algonquin, not an Englishman, to speak on my behalf."

Frowning, Canonicus turned to the younger sachem, the one called Miantonomo, who addressed Roger with an air of indifference: "Who among us can come to your defense? Not one among our people knows you."

"The honored sachem and chieftain across the river knows me."

"You speak of Massasoit?" asked the younger sachem.

"Yes. His interpreter and advisor Titus also knows me well. And the Wampanoag called Keplutok can bear witness that I did save his son from the sickness and that—"

"Enough!" Canonicus interrupted. "My nephew and I will confer with our own advisors. I warn you. If the Wampanoags speak evil of you, your death will come with much pain."

On the following day as he struggled privately to calm his quivering muscles, Roger sat crossed-legged on a mat before Canonicus, who sat stoically, his arms folded across his chest. They listened to Miantonomo speak.

"I have met with the three Wampanoags who know you. They value your friendship, claiming that you did risk your own life to save many from the sickness and that you did seek full justice against the evil child-stealer called Greene. But my uncle, the great Chieftain Canonicus, trusts you less than he would trust a starving wolf. He demands that you give account of the terrible sickness that the English inflicted against our people."

Roger looked at Canonicus, whose impassive eyes remained fixed ahead and whose countenance chilled him. Taking a deep breath, he addressed Miantonomo: "If the

Narragansets suffered the sickness because of their wickedness, then the English in their own land suffered even more because of their greater evil." He graphically described the corruption, lying, betrayal, stealing, murder, and greed that cursed the land of his birth. "You do well to distrust many of us Englishmen, for we have sinned grievously against one another as well as against the natives. And grievously have we answered for it. I ask the honored chief, however, to show where I have cheated the natives or where I have practiced deceit or treachery. I have instead endured treachery at the hands of some of my own people. I seek only a place of tranquility where I may feed my family and nurture them in liberty, free of hypocrisy, according to the kindly teaching of heaven."

Canonicus's eyes still seemed impassive and enigmatic. "Tell me of the sickness in your England."

Roger spoke movingly of the plague that had taken its toll on English citizens under Elizabeth, James, and Charles. He spoke also of his own father's death.

Canonicus scowled. "Your father suffered the sickness because of his own wickedness and treachery?"

"My father was an honest man." He tried as best he could to explain why the innocent, including children, fell prey to the sickness and death.

Canonicus leaned forward without warning and placed his hand firmly on Roger's shoulder. "You and I are as one man in our ignorance. All my years, I have sought to understand why often the innocent suffer and the wicked sometimes escape their suffering. When I listen to you, I sense that you too possess no explanation. You have defended the goodness of your father. For that you deserve to live. I have heard that you wish to purchase a place among us. Can you live in peace?"

Having heard of Canonicus's clever ways and of his distrust of English promises, Roger gave himself time to compose his answer. At last he spoke quietly. "I will offer gifts to you and your people. I have no desire to steal the land of others. Only you, however, can judge whether the gifts pay for the land. I offer you also my services for dealing with the English. I speak the Dutch language and will be useful to you in dealing with them. I sailed from England to your land to find a world where treachery does not rule. If in using my services, you discover connivance in me, then take my life according to the custom of your people."

Canonicus folded his arms again and turned to face Miantonomo, who nodded his head.

Canonicus then faced Roger. "The Wampanoags speak well of the trade you created between them and the English. The Dutch have occupied much land to the south. Are they to be trusted?"

He made no answer, for he knew that Canonicus had already formed an opinion of the Dutch.

During the rest of the spring in that eventful year, new settlers from Salem came to live as Roger's neighbors. The Narragansets welcomed them and saw them as allies in dealing with the shrewd and aggressive Dutch.

The most welcomed arrivals for Roger, of course, were Mary and their daughters. As soon as he saw them riding in the open carriage far in the distance, he dropped his hoe and ran toward them, pulling a cloth from his pocket and wiping the dirt from his hands. When he saw Mary wave her blue scarf in the air, he wanted to yell for the horses to gallop faster. He saw the driver crack the whip, and then Little Mary came in clear sight. She too waved both arms over her head and held a little blue scarf like her mother's. The thrill that rushed through him was like a hundred mountain streams pouring into the river. "Mary!" he called out in his strong voice.

The horses' hooves pounded like drums. The wagon wheels spun so fast they seemed motionless. The sun itself gave an extra portion of warmth on this perfect spring day. He stopped running and plucked two white blossoms from a vine.

"Ho!" The driver pulled the reins. "Master Williams!" The joyous ring in his voice sounded as though he alone had brought about this happy reunion.

Rushing to the carriage, Roger held out his arms. Filled with trust and love, Little Mary leaped out. He caught her and would have bathed her in kisses had she not begun kissing his cheek, touching his nose, and throwing her little arms around his neck. She clung to him as if she wished never again to let him out of her sight. He placed the white blossoms in her silky red hair, which she had inherited from his mother.

With his free hand, he took tiny Freeborn while the driver helped Mary to the ground. Roger looked at the infant and then into Mary's blue, luminous eyes, now sparkling with tears. Her bone-white teeth shone as she laughed and cried.

The driver took Little Mary and held her so that Roger could greet his wife.

Mountain streams rushed through him again as he kissed Mary on her soft, moist lips. With Freeborn in one arm, he embraced Mary and pulled her so close that their hearts beat as one.

Two women from the fields came up, wiping their hands on their aprons and begging to hold the children.

Roger looked again at Freeborn's smooth, innocent face and then into Mary's eyes that danced. When had he seen such beauty? It was as if two sunrises had appeared over one horizon.

As soon as the women let Little Mary's feet touch the ground, she instantly chased after a spring azure butterfly until a hummingbird with a ruby throat and emerald feathers caught her attention among the yellow blossoms. The melodic song of the bobolink floated from the nearby forest and was answered by his mate.

Roger too answered his mate, laughing with her laughter, picking her up and swinging her around as if they were children.

The women and the men now coming from the fields laughed, clapping their hands. Rushing up with a fiddle he had earned in Boston, Angell played merrily while the children danced in circles. Staring in amazement and amusement, the natives soon lifted their feet too. No clouds appeared on that day. No bitter snow. No sleet. It was springtime, and heaven knelt down to kiss this blessed corner of Earth.

On the way to the dwelling Roger had built for his family, he kept repeating the word *Freeborn! Freeborn!* as if each utterance blessed all those around him. He could almost hear the first time he had suggested to Mary the name of their second child. "Let us call her Freeborn! Her name will be like a comet moving across this vast, wondrous sky."

AQUIDNECK ISLAND

Late Spring–Summer 1636

While the children lay in their beds and the crickets announced the day's end, Roger sat with Mary on a bench outside the window and under the moon's soft light. He softened his voice, trying not to disturb the children. "Tell me news of the court."

"It has awarded Marblehead Neck to Salem. Better to call it a *re*ward for complying with the court's determination to expel you from Salem and all Massachusetts."

"Though the magistrates and some of the clergy have rejected us, Mary, the natives have warmly accepted us."

"I relished reading your letters, particularly the passages touching the natives' manner of raising their children."

"'Twas not in vain or out of idle curiosity that I inquired about such Narragansets' customs. I do not wish to raise our little ones among a people who treat them harshly." He now knew he had made a good decision. Like the Wampanoags, the Narragansets treated their children with loving care and respect. Roger and Mary's children would run and play among people of kindness and affection.

When he thought of busy Salem and the happy life Mary had enjoyed there, he felt a twinge of regret again. Still, sanity could not nurse regret, which lingered like aching bones.

"Mary, you remember our friend Governor Winslow? He came here to our little village of Providence recently to pay his respects."

"What interpretation did he give of the Boston unrest?"

"He thinks they fear the king might revoke the charter and that they continue to regard me as a threat."

Mary glanced up at the moon. "Have you heard the news about John Winthrop?"

Roger saw the cloud circling the moon. "What news?"

"Early in May, the Massachusetts Freemen elected Henry Vane Jr. as the new governor. Some speak of growing discontent with John Winthrop Sr."

He smiled, shaking his head.

She raised a skeptical eyebrow. "You doubt there is discontentment with Winthrop?"

"Listen, Mary. The Freemen have no axe to grind against him."

"Then why did they decline to reelect him?"

"I understand precisely why they inserted this twenty-three-year-old Henry Vane into the governorship."

Slowly, her lips turned upward. "So, you have this puzzle solved, have you? I see where your thoughts lead. Young Henry's father in England enjoys the king's ear."

Roger nodded.

"And a high position in the king's government." She glided her fingertip across his cheek. "So the game of politics comes to fair Boston, does it? By electing the younger Vane as its governor, do the Massachusetts Freemen hope to court the king's favor?"

"And to appear loyal to the crown despite all rumors." Roger enjoyed the fact that Mary had kept her ears open and the needles of her mind adroitly knitting the long yarn coming in from Boston and Salem. He looked up into the sky and remembered the swooping seagulls he had observed as a boy. His brother Sydrach had told him that under King Charles, the seagulls enjoyed far more freedom than did many of the English.

Mary let her fingers play across his knee. He took her hand and kissed it.

"Do you think the children have now gone to the land of dreams?" He watched the moonbeams shimmer in the blue pools that were Mary's eyes.

"Perhaps, but . . . but we need not be anxious. I have asked an angel to come watch over our children tonight." Mary glanced around.

He stood up, stroking her hair, and whispered into her ear, "Might that angel carry the name *Thomas?*"

She laughed softly. "He will be here shortly."

"I hear a gurgling brook calling us. Do you remember the hot summer when we sat in the brook and let the cool water flow over us?"

She nodded, rolling her big eyes, a gesture that always sent him flying among the stars.

Though the Puritans and many Separatists sharply divided the labor between men and women, Mary could not resign herself to ignoring the politics of New England. The women seemed to excuse her by saying she served as her husband's eyes and ears. This amused Roger, who valued her quick brain and generous heart as much as he relished the children jumping around his feet or sitting on his lap.

Little Mary daily tugged at his sleeve. On many days, she followed him to the fields to help pick the peas and to imitate, as far as her small hands permitted, the art of farming. Mary had made her a wide-brimmed hat and had sewn cloth flowers into it. Some women looked askance at the cloth flowers. Soon, however, all agreed that Little Mary was herself a flower in their midst. It gave Roger extraordinary pleasure when he heard his neighbors say Little Mary possessed her mother's keen, inquisitive eyes and her father's buoyant, cheerful manner.

"She is so free of hatred that even the older children prefer her company," one neighbor had said.

On this first summer near the Narraganset Bay, Roger and his older daughter picked peas until the sun faded into the horizon and their fingers began to swell. While they sat with their hands in cool water, he listened to Little Mary chatter, her words tripping off her tongue, sounding refreshingly like her mother.

He at times still let his thoughts travel to the moment the court in Boston had condemned him and ordered his exile. Today, however, he thought of Henry Vane, who had journeyed to Salem to meet with him secretly after the court's decision. Moved upon remembering Henry's talk of their friendship, Roger felt that despite the ten years difference between his age and Henry's, a profound and lasting friendship had truly formed. *How mysterious and astonishing are the winding paths of Providence.* He was glad he had given their new Narraganset town the name "Providence."

He thought also about friends in Salem: Jeremiah and Grace Paynter, Wilfred and Agnes Barry, Samuel Sharpe, and Ezra and Pearl Welch. He wondered about their welfare and about the health and safety of the many other church members who had called on him for help and to whom he had turned for help.

Coming in from the fields with Little Mary, he stopped in front of the rustic house he had built with the help of his friends. It contained a parlor or fire-room below and a sleeping space above. Little Mary had learned to climb the ladder to the sleeping space. Already the house, forty-six feet long and thirty-six feet wide, served as the first public meeting place. The young Sachem Miantonomo had even requested use of the Williams house for meeting with his Narraganset council of advisors. As spring flowed into summer, Mary found her place among the people and seemed not to resent turning her house into an inn for important guests among both the natives and the colonists.

She came outdoors to stand beside her husband and to watch Little Mary bound with energy despite the summer's heat, and to play with the new puppy Governor Winslow had brought her from Plymouth.

"You miss the beautiful house we had in Salem, do you not?" Roger asked his wife as they stood hand-in-hand under the large oak near the house.

"I do," she confessed. "Yet this house is filled with music."

"I vow to build still another room." He knew their Providence house lacked the workmanship of the one in Salem.

As if reading his thoughts, she walked to the house and rubbed her hand across the rough boards. "There is much love and gentleness in each inch of wood."

He could not hide the sheepish look on his face. "One of the Narragansets who helped me build it pointed to the spaces between the boards and said we could look out through the gaps to see friendly neighbors. I promise that before winter, the spaces will shrink." He began to laugh, seeing his eldest daughter talking vigorously to her puppy Eusebius. It delighted him to hear the child talk as if she were already a woman, her speech clear and direct, her alert eyes free of apology.

Early next morning, he crossed the river and arrived at the largest Wampanoag village. There he conferred with Massasoit and the aging Narraganset Chief Canonicus. After spending five days in the village, he returned home. Finding his house empty, he inquired of his neighbors where his wife and children might be. No one professed to know. Roger at first assured himself that Mary had taken a stroll on the edge of the cooling forest and would soon come back. Since he had work to do, he gave little further thought to her absence until an hour later when Angell returned from Boston, saying, "I have news from Captain Firebrook."

Desiring Mary to hear the news, Roger again inquired earnestly about her. When no one could help, he grew irritated. "I am sure no eagle swept down to carry them off! There has been no flood. Surely someone saw them leave."

A Narraganset native whom Roger recognized but knew not by name pointed south.

"Take me there!" When the native began walking southward, Roger shouted, "Run, man. I will follow hard on your heels."

About half a mile into the forest, he saw his two little ones playing near Mary, who sat on a blanket Keplutok's wife had given her almost three years earlier. Roger watched Little Mary struggle to climb a tree. Unfortunately each time she moved off the ground, she slid down.

The native waited as Roger rushed up to the tree. Just as he was about to speak to his wife, he realized that she was crying. Thinking it odd that the children seemed unconcerned about her crying, he knelt down on the blanket and stroked her hair to comfort her, gently taking his thumb to wipe away the tears. "What sorrow has brought these tears?"

"Sorrow? 'Tis happiness."

He felt his face contort with skepticism. "Tears of happiness? Mary, love, I do not cry when I am happy."

She cried and laughed still louder. "Oh, Roger, you are home!" And she began crying all the more.

He removed his hat, scratched his head, and looked at the native as if to say, *If you have light to throw on this woman's tears, come to my aid.*

All at once, four Narraganset men accompanied by four women appeared and began teasing him with evident delight. He did not care that they amused themselves at the way he doted over Freeborn, picking her up, fluffing her hair in the spring breeze, and kissing the tip of her nose.

Two of the women approached him, one saying, "We have been here with your wife and children."

"But why is she crying?"

"Why are you breathing?"

"Ah, I see." In truth he understood nothing but hoped the women would judge him knowledgeable.

The other two Narraganset women approached, one saying, "It has been a good day. Your wife wishes now to go home."

On that good day, he came to look upon each man and woman as a vast flowing river. Each attempt to know another person, including Mary, was like dipping a hand into the river and catching a few drops at most.

Later, after sunset, they lay side by side. "Roger, love, this is our home, and I am glad. True, we cannot take our children to see our friends and acquaintances in Massachusetts or Plymouth. If our friends visit us, our children will be blessed." Before falling asleep, she added with a melodious sigh, "This day has been among the happiest of my life."

AQUIDNECK ISLAND

Summer 1636

Sitting alone on a flat rock on the newly purchased peninsula that jutted down into the upper regions of Narraganset Bay, Roger inhaled the salt air deeply and imagined Dutch and English ships sailing in from the open sea only thirty miles to the south. More than once during the months of June and July, he had brought his elder daughter to this magnificent spot to watch the tidal waterway and to envision the future.

Knowing that neither Little Mary nor Freeborn would be permitted to study at Cambridge University, he vowed that he would help Mary teach them. Thomas Peters, the new minister of the Salem church, had recently collected money and books to form a small school that he proposed to name Harvard College. Only males would gain entrance to the school, its primary purpose to train men for the clergy. Roger took pride, nevertheless, in knowing that the Narraganset natives had already begun educating Little Mary in subjects unavailable to English and European universities. He visualized completing his book on the natives and having it published for English men, women, and children to read.

During this moment of dreaming, Mary came up from behind him and quietly sat down. They held hands and listened to the waves lap peacefully in the sheltered cove to the west. She reluctantly unfolded the letter that Angell had brought from Boston. "Dear, we should read Eric's letter more carefully. His warning deserves our heeding. Would that he were here to elaborate."

Roger took the letter and read aloud.

My Friends Roger and Mary,

    The months have been too long since last I saw you face-to-face. Mary, I thank you for the drawing you made of your two daughters, although I confess that I would have preferred to see them in person, now that you have bestowed upon me the honored title of adoptive uncle.

    Roger, as you requested, I have sent you a copy of the Reverend Cotton's treatise on your experiment at Aquidneck Island. I confess I do not fully understand the hostility

Cotton harbors for you. I have learned that he is among those who refer to your Aquidneck or Rhode Island as Rogue's Island. In seeking to demean you, he has demeaned himself.

Winthrop seems profoundly torn apart in his affection for you. On the one hand, he praises you as a man of conscience (a description that Cotton will not admit in your particular case). On the other hand, Winthrop has come under Dudley's influence. Some of your friends here in Boston have urged me to communicate to you that Dudley and Endecott mean you considerable harm. Dudley and Cotton seem to vie for the position of denouncing you as a dangerous seducer of minds. Despite Dudley's jealousy of Winthrop, they have evidently sealed a covenant between them to stamp out what they regard as the infection you spread in Salem.

Together they have even persuaded your friend Henry Vane to join the magistrates in denying the Separatists all liberty to form their own congregation of worship and teaching in Salem. I know this news regarding Vane will shock you. I confess, I have no grasp of his motive. I say this because he appears to count his friendship with you as more than gold or fame.

Let me give good tidings. Doubtless you have learned that John Winthrop Jr. has received permission in England to become the leading political figure in a territory called Connecticut. This piece of information, however, I cannot yet confirm to my complete satisfaction.

The letter continued for three more pages about various events in and around Boston. The last page mentioned the July murder of a Massachusetts citizen named John Oldham.

Rumors attribute the murder to the Narraganset natives. Governor Vane has excited himself about the murder. If you have information about the true agents of the crime, do not delay to send a letter or messenger to Governor Vane or to our friend Winthrop. Captain Endecott breathes fire against the natives, and I fear that a war with them could ignite unless some way is found to extinguish it before it begins. If you give much weight to your friendship with Sachem Canonicus . . . .

Seeing that within the hour the sun would set over the cove to the west, Roger stood up to return home. But Mary asked, "When you talk with Canonicus and Miantonomo about the murder—?"

"This territory 'tis a powder chest. They are wise sachems who wish to avoid war, but they believe the Pequots must suffer retribution for harboring the murderers."

Mary looked astonished. "Then you conjecture the Pequots killed John Oldham?"

He lowered his voice. "We must speak to no one about this."

"How long have you known?"

"I know only rags and threads. But I will know more tomorrow when I meet with Canonicus and Massasoit."

"You, nonetheless, suspect that the murderers dwell among the Pequots?"

"Aye. If the Narragansets fail to persuade the Pequot leaders to surrender the murderers, then war will likely erupt throughout New England."

"Are the Massachusetts magistrates preparing to attack the natives?"

"Eric confirms news I received today from Plymouth that Endecott in particular calls loudly for attacking at once." Feeling melancholy, he remained silent as Mary and he headed toward their house. When it came into view, he felt her warm hand slip into his.

"Roger, at Masham Manor, did you not oft tell me that the pagan philosopher Aristotle labeled our species *the rational animal*?"

"I did."

"Then please tell me why this rational species whom we believe is created in God's image has committed innumerable crimes, treacheries, thefts, slaughters, and frauds against one another?"

"I have heard many glib answers to this knotted question. It troubles me that during war, men imagine they receive license to suspend conscience and to commit all manner of crimes oft in the name of God."

"Christ divided the fishes and the loaves to feed the multitudes and taught us to share. Yet in wars, we divide other people's land and share misery and heartache, not loaves and fishes."

"We rarely repent of our wars." He lifted his eyes heavenward to see the first evening star. "We who call ourselves Christians like to imagine that these bitter crimes are the habits of pagans at war each with the other. Yet thousands upon thousands among us professed Christians have slaughtered and tortured each other while the name of Jesus Christ fell from our lips. I have heard that dark clouds of war now thicken over England too."

Mary bit her lip. "Whence came this news?"

"From two men recently arrived from London to confer with Governor Winslow." He noticed that she was staring intently at him. "Is something wrong, love?"

"Your face. You speak of the war clouds, yet your eyes almost glow."

He felt his muscles tingle and his heart race. "We make war, but we create goodness too. I envision ships someday sailing to the shores of Providence and all Narraganset Bay. They will bring people from England, Massachusetts, Germany, and Italy. They will come to a land where they may live in peace. Behold, Mary. Can you envision a new house there by the oak tree, a house where Catholics live adjacent to Anabaptists while across the way, they have Jews for neighbors?"

"And Turks. And Wampanoags, too?"

"Aye. And *no* government or magistrate will require them to profess this or that religion! People will live by their own consciences so long as they respect the civil peace and show regard for the person and property of others. Can you see them, Mary? None will be compelled to pay tax for another's clergy or religion."

"Let this trumpet of freedom sound even up to Boston!"

"And across the ocean waves until heard around this troubled globe! Let them come to our shores, Mary. Let them live among us as free men and women!"

Impulsively he kissed her on the cheek and then danced with her. The neighbors' children, watching from a distance, giggled merrily and ran up to dance, too, until they all turned into silhouettes against twilight's purple sky.

AQUIDNECK ISLAND AND THE CONNECTICUT TERRITORY

October 1636

Throughout August and September, peace in New England walked the cliff's edge. Roger's call for tolerance and patient negotiation seemed scarcely more than a cry in the wilderness. While Dudley and Winthrop sought to brand religious error as conspiracy or treason against the state, Endecott and vociferous members of the court quoted the stories of Joshua from Israel's history to stir up war and retribution against the natives.

With the arrival of October came increased trepidation. Anger, fear, threats, and war talk drove away hope. Some Massachusetts clergymen called for fasting and denounced the people for their many imperfections. "The times are cruel. 'Tis God's wrath against his wayward saints," John Wilson of the Boston church thundered from the pulpit.

During the night of October 8, Roger woke many times from a troubled sleep, his mind whirling like the typhoon he had heard seamen speak about when he was a boy. Fears swirled without relief, and thoughts flew about like loose objects carried by powerful winds. All his ideas seemed disconnected, uprooted, tossed helter-skelter. If only the sun would rise. If only Mary were awake. More than once, her comforting words had helped him calm storms raging in his mind.

He rose at dawn, wrapped a woolen blanket around him, and sat down in a hickory chair. What could he do? It seemed that all New England had become kindling while warmongers with torches stood eager to hurl them in mad fury. He felt a hand and knew Mary had come to his side. He quickly dressed and they stepped quietly outside, taking care not to disturb the children.

"What troubles you, Roger dear?"

"Thoughts of our Narraganset friends Canonicus and Miantonomo."

"When you spoke with them two days ago, what—?"

"Mary, I lack all certainty in the matter. Still I cannot rid myself of the thought that the two sachems hid some political strategy deep in their hearts when they spoke to me about the Pequots."

"I know you regard Canonicus as a fox, cunning and indirect, but—"

"I ask you, Mary, would Canonicus and Miantonomo wish to send their warriors alone against the well-armed Massachusetts soldiers?"

"Of course not."

"Then how could Canonicus and Miantonomo best convince the Massachusetts Court that the Narragansets are innocent of John Oldham's murder? How could the two sachems also convince the Massachusetts Court that the Narragansets wish to avoid war with Massachusetts?"

"Ah, now I see. Canonicus will assure the Massachusetts Court that he will send Narraganset warriors against the Pequots."

He felt his muscles tighten like Pequot bows. "It will all spell war unless the Pequot sachems agree to surrender the murderers to Canonicus's people."

"Assuming the Pequots surrender the murderers to the Narragansets, then what?"

"Then, Mary, 'tis plain that Canonicus would deliver them to the Massachusetts General Court."

"That does not make sense. Why should Canonicus involve the Narragansets in this conflict? Would he not pull back and let the Massachusetts Court and its military deal directly with the hateful Pequots? Why should Canonicus's warriors seek out the murderers among the Pequots?"

"Have you forgotten that Narraganset territory sits between Massachusetts and the Pequots? If Narraganset territory becomes the battleground between the Pequots and the Massachusetts soldiers, then . . ."

Mary's mouth dropped open. "Then a large number of Narragansets would die."

"Aye, and I am sure the wise Canonicus has foreseen this too."

She looked around and lowered her voice to a whisper. "If what you say is true, why would the members of the Massachussets Court send yesterday's urgent secret message to you? Why would they swallow their pride and beg your help?"

Fear rose up in Roger. "What do you imply?"

"Nothing except that Canonicus would doubtless form a secret pact with the Pequots."

"The Narragansets joining with the Pequots against the English?" Roger was astonished that he had not considered this possibility. Now he grasped the full implication of Mary's words. Had he naively trusted Canonicus and Miantonomo? Had they deceived him and used him like a pawn? Feeling a cold chill pass through his body, he sat down on a stump to ponder her words as the gray dawn turned to a lavender sunrise. Then he looked up at her. "Have I played the fool? I must think through this matter again. Today Canonicus and Miantonomo will receive the Pequot representatives. What will Canonicus tell them?"

"Are you certain he will demand that the Pequots release the murderers to him?"

Roger looked penetratingly at her and then sprang to his feet as if a spring had hurled him forward. He rushed silently into the house and hurriedly packed three strips of dried fish and two pieces of bread.

She protested, looking back at her children and lowering her voice. "Consider the peril! If you do not think highly of yourself, then think of our children and me."

He shook his head and was already planning what he must say to the sachems.

"At least give yourself a day to think. Let your mind walk first this path, then another, and another to explore their end. Do not rush blindly."

He held her by the shoulders and looked squarely into her eyes. "I see far down the path that these Pequots have taken us all. I cannot wait!"

Little Mary, climbing down the ladder from the loft, ran to her father. "Take me! Take me!"

"Hush, child." Mary snatched her up into her arms.

He kissed the child. "Heed your mother." He glanced at Freeborn and turned away to leave the house. But before he left, an unnerving thought brought him back. Might he never see them again?

Little Mary cried, "No, do not leave, Father, do not leave!" Then she buried her face in her mother's bosom.

He rushed to Little Mary, kissed her forehead, and then disappeared out the door, his wife calling after him, "Roger, take Angell with you! And do not forget . . ."

He did not hear the rest of her words and knew he could not take Angell. *If I fail to return, Angell must remain alive to help watch after them.*

Roger pulled his hat tightly on his head and hooked the cloak over his shoulders. With the bearskin slung over his shoulder and the dried fish in hand, he ran to his canoe. As the sun scarcely rose over the horizon, he pulled away.

The river carried him swiftly into the choppy bay. Ten leagues of rigorous paddling lay before him. His powerful arms quivered when the waves rolled in with unexpected force. The cold spray drenched his clothes. Still he ordered himself to paddle faster. No time for timidity. In his heart, he knew that the Pequots' emissaries were already gathering around Canonicus's warm fire. Faster! If he were too late . . . . No, he must not be late! An hour passed. Even though his arms felt numb, he could afford no time to rest.

Aware that he could drown, he ordered himself to take no unnecessary risks. He had to consider the safety of his family and that of many others if he failed to confront the Pequots in Canonicus's presence! No, do not drift too closely to the shore. The rocks! Watch for . . . . He shifted his paddle from one side to the other, steering his canoe farther into the bay and around the treacherous shore.

Even though the sun reflected in his eyes, he could see towering trees ahead that told him he had come five leagues. If only his weakening arms could endure the final five. Though the wind from the north chilled him, he could not make use of the bear's skin lest it interfere with his arm strokes.

A nagging thought plagued him. Had the Pequots stationed a watch near the shore in anticipation of his arrival? Faster!

The last league of the journey seemed endless. Then indescribable relief! Two Narraganset warriors stood on a nearby shoreline. Recognizing one, he turned his canoe sharply toward shore. The Narragansets grabbed the bow and, evidently seeing his exhaustion, helped him onto dry ground.

"Quickly," he said in the Narraganset tongue, "take me to Canonicus."

Ten minutes later upon arriving at the campsite, Roger's heart sank. He recognized the tall Pequot representatives sitting around a fire with Canonicus and Miantonomo.

Despite the bright sun, the autumn chill lingered. As Roger approached the fire, he saw the sullen countenance of the Pequots. Making his skin crawl even more was the enigmatic flicker in Canonicus's eyes.

The Pequots stiffened.

Deep inside Roger, a savage cry for blood revenge threatened to erupt. He stood facing the hostile Pequots, who had slaughtered more than one of his countrymen. He swallowed hard, made a fist at his side, and spoke somberly in the Narraganset tongue to Canonicus's advisors.

The younger Narraganset Sachem Miantonomo handed Roger a large leaf on which rested an assortment of meat, cooked *askútasquash*, and corn. They ate in silence. When the meal drew gradually to a close, the older of the Pequots addressed Canonicus. "Our fathers hunted these lands. Their fathers and generations before them . . . ."

Canonicus seemed to listen patiently to the Pequot argue that the intruding English and Dutch should be crushed and made to return to their homes across the great sea. Canonicus then nodded toward Roger.

Patience, he said to himself, knowing that Canonicus detested heated, passionate arguments. More than once, he had argued religion and customs with the honored sachem. He thanked Canonicus for his hospitality and Miantonomo for the many favors he had shown him. Then he faced the Pequots and spoke with a sternness that conspicuously surprised Canonicus and Miantonomo. "Your Pequot fathers did *not* hunt this land! Your fathers' fathers lived afar from here. Like the English and the Dutch, you are at best recently arrived *guests* on this soil. I live on Narraganset land only because I have offered gifts to the sachems, but even the gifts are mere tokens. The Narragansets are a peaceful, generous people. You Pequots, however, are greedy and bloodthirsty. Your hands extend not to create friendship, but to shed blood and steal hunting territory."

The youngest Pequot drew his knife, sprang to his feet, and started to lunge at Roger. But two Narraganset warriors grabbed the Pequot and set him down hard on the ground. Then they took his knife and handed it to the oldest Pequot.

Roger trembled inside with fear and rage. Aware, however, that it would be a mistake to show fear, he glared scornfully at the vigorous young Pequot. At the same time, he took note of the Narraganset's tact in returning the knife to a Pequot, a gesture of conciliation mingled with shrewdness.

Roger had not finished his speech and had no intention of being intimidated. He looked to Canonicus for permission to resume. Canonicus closed his eyes, signaling him to continue. "You speak the truth when you charge many of the English with intrusion." Roger faced the Pequot who was obviously the chief representative. "Your Pequot warriors, nonetheless, are brazen hypocrites no better than the bloodiest, foulest Englishman. I, therefore, charge that you are no friend of the Narragansets. You instead wish only to use them as a hatchet to cut a path for yourselves."

Though he had much more to say, he knew that Canonicus disliked long speeches. The Pequots flashed with hot anger. He had no doubt they would have cut his throat on the spot had they not sat in the Narraganset camp. Despite the Pequots' murderous desires and now the strange look of discomfort on Miantonomo's face, Roger felt he had been wise to speak bluntly.

Canonicus said something that made no sense to Roger, something that caused the Pequots to grin and glance at him with conspicuous contempt. Heat rose in his cheeks, but he held his tongue. The older Pequot answered his charge with such eloquence that Roger felt himself caught up in the images painted with words and gestures.

That night Roger lay awake, wondering if the heated exchange had weakened his case. His feverish mind flew off like sparks in all directions. Not until early morning did he fall asleep.

The second day proved grueling and dismaying. Negotiations seemed to be the last of Canonicus's concerns. Had the negotiation ended? Had the Pequots formed some secret compact with the Narraganset sachems? *Why*, he wondered, *has Canonicus gone off alone with the Pequots, leaving me with his nephew Miantonomo?* Desperate, nevertheless, to make full use of his opportunity, he tried to explain to Miantonomo the many disadvantages that the Narragansets would suffer in forging an alliance with the Pequots.

The third day brought him face-to-face with the Pequots again as they sat before the two sachems.

"The English are like ants," the younger Pequot said. "Once a small army of ants enters your camp, you must stamp it out. You cannot live at peace with ants or the English. They know neither peace nor honor. Every year more Englishmen will invade this territory. If they become firmly entrenched, countless others will follow to possess the land, cut down our trees, and kill off our animals."

Roger felt Canonicus's eyes studying him for what seemed to be a full minute.

Then Canonicus closed his eyes. "Speak, Englishman, but do not let your words soar so far from the ground that I lose sight of their plainer meaning."

Roger drew a deep breath and kept his eyes on the Pequots, especially the young, vigorous one who had pulled his knife. "The Pequot speaks the truth. The English and the Dutch will fill this land. Even if you kill all the English families today, thousands more will arrive to replace them. The Pequots compared the English to ants. Have the Pequots eliminated all ants from their land? No. Neither will they eliminate the English. I urge you to see the English as honeybees, not ants. The wise among us learn to live with bees and take the honey and wax. Is it not better, therefore, to trade with the English?"

For the rest of the morning, Roger spoke to neither Miantonomo nor Canonicus. It had seemed to him that Canonicus had looked with contempt upon his speech about the bees and honey. Though the sachems had left him to wander freely in the village, he could not rid himself of the image of Canonicus's scornful face following him wherever he went.

He forced himself to contemplate the worst. The Pequots would persuade the Narraganset leaders to take arms against the English. He knew the Pequots would not hesitate to kill him and deliver the members of his body to the Boston magistrates. He feared above all else that the Narraganset leaders would permit the Pequots to invade Providence to carry away his wife and daughters. *Has Canonicus made a pact with the Pequots to spill my blood this very day?*

The sun stood directly overhead when at last Canonicus called for him. Roger marched through the village, half thinking he was a condemned man marching to his doom, the other half crying out that his friends Canonicus and Miantonomo would not forsake him.

Without knowing why, he began to sense that the Pequots had left. His heart raced. What did it mean? He tried to take hope. Had they left empty-handed or with a new bond sealed between the Pequots and the Narragansets?

Wondering if he would ever see another autumn day, he let the orange, yellow, red, and green leaves capture his whole attention. All his senses broke their bonds and reached out to embrace the bosom of nature with all her beauty and color. The wind blew and stirred the leaves, sending them into a gentle hail of hues that fell at his feet. As the October sun flashed off the little stream that coursed through the village, the brisk air filled his lungs.

He came abruptly into the presence of Canonicus, who frowned cryptically, his thick eyebrows arching like an owl's outspread wings. Although Roger heard words come from Canonicus's mouth, the lips and the sounds seemed out of harmony. Had he heard the words correctly? Had he heard them at all? Had the ironic frown turned into an even more ironic grin? Yet it was not the grin of contempt. Nor of malice. He remembered that more than once at friendly twilight, Canonicus and he had sat down around the campfire. Yet today he felt like a man watching two scenes simultaneously: one real, the other pretense as on a London stage. But which was the stage? Was Canonicus truly asking him questions, and was he truly answering them? *Is this the trick the mind mercifully plays on itself when facing certain death? Or is it . . . ?*

Roger came to his senses as quickly as he had left them. He realized that Canonicus had been making a little speech and that he had not heard the speech because fear had created an imaginary dialogue between them.

Canonicus was indeed smiling, and it was friendly. He was saying, "I think the Pequots have thrust their hands into a beehive called Roger Williams."

He then felt Old Canonicus take him by the wrist and heard him say, "Your Narraganset tongue is sometimes slow, my son. Yet you are quick to see into the future. I am not so old as to drown in the past. Send messengers to your friends Magistrate Winthrop and Governor Vane. Tell them the Narragansets will become allies with the English, not the Pequots."

Roger felt overwhelmed. Everything now moved so quickly that he could scarcely follow everything the prince of the Narragansets was telling him.

"You must serve as a bridge between the Narragansets and the English in Boston," Canonicus explained solemnly.

Scarcely able to anticipate his own words, he heard himself say that he would send messengers at once to the powers in Boston.

"When you have done that," the great sachem added, "then be a friend to both the Narragansets and the English. Go with my nephew to the smaller tribes deep into these forests and draw them into our circle."

Later that day as Roger and Miantonomo walked toward the shore, Miantonomo said, "Tomorrow before the sun rises above the trees, we will set our canoes toward the Wampanoags. Then we must move swiftly to meet with the other sachems in the forests."

When they reached the shore, Roger stepped into his canoe and dipped his paddle into the blue water. In the sunlight, the spray from the waves sparkled like diamonds. The leagues home would give him time to think about his victory. He knew the blood-thirsty Pequots would fight the English to the last drop of Pequot blood. A deep sorrow filled his heart. He had longed to become an evangel to the Pequots. He of course knew that today he had closed the door and dared not turn his canoe around to offer peace to the quarrelsome Pequots. If he should enter one of their villages in the neighboring Connecticut territory, he would, he knew, never leave alive.

En route to his home in Providence, he fought the tide and relished the battle, which gave him opportunity to cleanse his mind, feel the spray of the salt water against his face, sense the pull of the waves against his paddle, and thrive with the air flowing through his lungs.

Long before sunset, he arrived home wearily. The sight of his family and the unex-pected presence of John Winthrop Jr., however, cheered his heart.

After the two friends spoke briefly of Canonicus's bold move of friendship toward the English, John politely excused himself to visit Angell and the others in the commu-nity. Roger understood that John wished to give him time with his family. Later they would talk about Miantonomo's arrival.

Mary stood in the parlor like a statue. He stood staring at her and wondering if she were asking herself, *Has my husband in truth returned, or is it an apparition?*

He walked up to her and saw an eerie look in her eyes. Gently he took her hand, put it against his cheek, and held it there for what seemed to be a full minute. No words passed between them. He could not embrace her but stood transfixed as if the wonders of nature had at this one moment become incarnate in one mysterious face. He stood in awe as strange thoughts entered his head. He remembered Milton's speak-ing of the vastness of the heavens and their impersonality. Now on this tiny planet stood this wondrous woman. He at last enveloped her in his arms and felt he could never again leave her.

An hour before sunset, Little Mary rode on her father's shoulders and around her favorite tree. She agreed that they should all eat at the table.

"Shall we also invite Eusebius to eat at the table with us?" His words made her giggle as she glanced down at her tail-wagging dog.

John Winthrop Jr. joined the Williams family and Angell at the table where Roger told them everything Canonicus and Miantonomo wished to be delivered to the Massachusetts Court.

Mary passed potato soup around the table. "Providence has sent you, John, for you can become the bearer of the glad tidings that Roger brings from the Narragansets."

"I will happily serve if you so choose." John passed the buttered corn.

Roger felt buoyant. "'Tis most fitting. Go to your good father and tell him all. And to Governor Vane." Then, picking up Mary's cue, he added, "And would you do me a special kindness, John? Deliver a letter to our mutual friend Eric Firebrook."

John agreed most heartily and then, upon Roger's request, disclosed the account of his own trials and progress as the new governor of Connecticut.

Roger passed a bowl of beans to John and a pan of hot bread to Angell.

John dipped the beans onto his plate. "For your negotiations with the Narragansets, I stand in personal gratitude to you, Roger. The Pequots have recently swarmed into the south of Connecticut, creating much fear among us living north of them. You have saved us all by reasoning with the Narragansets."

"Then am I correct to think that you do not share your father's opinions that all natives are deprived of common reason?"

John flushed. "My father is a great man. Yet he wears certain blinders."

"As do we all." Roger tasted the corn and smiled.

John put his fork down. "In truth I do not share my father's opinion about the natives and have told him that his view flies in the face of common reason and Scripture. Already from your example, Roger, I have learned to show regard for the natives, especially the Narragansets since they are our nearest neighbors to the east. You once informed me of their admirable principle of fairness, and I have since seen it for myself."

Mary stood up to serve more hot soup. "My husband relishes their keen wit and their yen for irony."

"They are not without our mortal flaws." Roger reached behind him for an apple, which he handed to Little Mary. "But they negotiate well because they speak clearly what they most desire."

John grinned at Little Mary's dainty way of nibbling on the apple. "I remember well your advice, Roger: 'When negotiating, first establish the prime desires. *Set them out on the table.*'"

John then told of the skirmishes between Endecott and some Pequots. When he spoke movingly of the wigwams Endecott's men had burned in the southern portion of Connecticut and nearby, Roger's attention was piqued. He urged John to eat another serving of cabbage and ham. "Inform Governor Vane and the court that Endecott's practice of taking Pequot children hostage in battle serves no good purpose. Or if he must take them, let the court quickly return them through fair negotiation. We do both our children and the native children wrong to use them as pawns in our wars."

John prodded the cabbage and ham with his fork. "On that we are in full agreement, my friend. The Pequots have taken two of our English youths to Long Island to sell to the Dutch. If we, on the other hand, do not rise above their savagery, then what right have we to call ourselves Christians?"

Early the following morning while Roger and Mary bade farewell to their friend John, they heard him say, "Tell the sachems Canonicus and Miantonomo that I have no doubt the Massachusetts Court will soon welcome their presence with extravagant ceremony in Boston."

Roger smiled. John had doubtless discovered that the Narraganset sachems were second only to the Wampanoag Sachem Massasoit in relishing ceremonies, feasts, and merriment. Roger hoped the Boston Puritans would learn more about celebration and merriment from the natives.

BOSTON

October 1636

"You have been away too long," I told John Winthrop Jr. when he stepped off the ship. He hurriedly handed me the letter from Mary and Roger and promised to call at the Blackstone house within a day or two.

"I have no time to lose, Eric. I will, nevertheless, leave you with good news. Roger has become our negotiator with the Narragansets. Good-bye. I must quickly deliver the good news to my father and the court. You and I must talk later."

Understanding, I watched him take a fast carriage to meet Governor Vane, Winthrop the older, and other members of the court. Captains Underhill and Mason, as well as the ensigns, soon heard the tidings and rejoiced that Roger Williams had succeeded beyond their dreams in turning the Narragansets away from a dire alliance with the Pequots.

In a move to rescind Roger's banishment from the colony, some court members openly praised his highly esteemed service. All agreed that no one among the English and Dutch possessed his special command of the natives' language or equaled him in winning the good will of all the natives—save the belligerent Pequots.

Dudley and Cotton, nonetheless, so fiercely opposed his return to the colony that the other leaders relinquished to them to keep peace. Still fighting within himself the old battle between love and order, Dudley took the lead in opposing Roger. "Satan knows that Massachusetts is the new citadel of our Protestant Reformation. He, therefore, sends us a triple portion of turmoil. The evil one relishes nothing more than to cause our citadel of righteousness to face imminent threat of chaos." Dudley went on to call for building a still thicker and higher wall of order around the colony.

Another magistrate stood up at a later meeting to inquire about rumors regarding women in Boston undermining the pure teaching of God's appointed clergymen.

Winthrop joined Dudley and expressed his apprehension. "No sooner had we rid ourselves of Roger Williams than this Hutchinson woman arrived to spread her Antinomian doctrine." Winthrop's vexation about Anne Hutchinson seemed inexplicable to some. Others whispered that he resented her rising popularity among the people of the Boston church. Winthrop himself explained that she did not know the limitations God had placed upon women. "God does not suffer a woman to have authority over a man," he kept saying. I noted the irony that he never seemed to ask whether Anne wished to have authority over men.

Though few gave him ear, my friend Barnabas had pointed out that there were many kinds of authority. He went about Boston asking, "Authority in what? Authority for what purpose? Winthrop is no authority in milking cows, cutting trees, or a thousand other noble deeds called hard labor."

Before the end of October, Miantonomo came to Boston to celebrate the agreement that Roger had negotiated. To show his strong support of the agreement, Canonicus sent his nephew and two sons. The Boston magistrates' celebration of good will in the meetinghouse proved beyond even Miantonomo's expectations.

In his strong, vibrant voice, Miantonomo addressed the crowd: "We Narragansets profess deep affection for the English and desire always to live together in secure peace. We have no bond with the Pequots. As our friend Roger Williams has said, we Narragansets are a people who prefer trade to war."

Although now officially a Connecticut citizen, John Winthrop Jr. rose to speak solemnly and favorably of both Miantonomo and Canonicus. On the following morning, Governor Vane signed a document of nine articles and presented it for the Narraganset sachems to mark also. "I will take these articles to Master Roger Williams," Miantonomo said through his interpreter to Governor Vane, "for he will translate each clearly to us and interpret their full meaning."

Governor Vane agreed as did the senior Winthrop. After dinner the natives asked to take leave. With considerable show, a platoon of musketeers escorted them through town. Captain Underhill followed by sending them away with good wishes and a volley of shots to celebrate the triumph of peace between the English and the Narragansets.

PROVIDENCE AND BOSTON

October 1636

Aware that too much time had elapsed since I had seen my friends Roger and Mary, I jumped at the opportunity to accompany Miantonomo and a handful of other Narragansets from Boston to Providence to celebrate the new alliance. Soon after arriving, I celebrated privately with Roger, Mary, and their two daughters, giving them a mule they named Hugo. I soon knew not whether 'tis more blessed to give than to receive, for I felt blessed by each minute with Roger and his family.

After the feast, six or seven sachems met on the following day inside the Williams's house. Upon receiving the document that Miantonomo had handed him, Roger read it aloud for Mary and me to hear:

The Articles of the Alliance
1. A firm peace between us and our friends of other plantations (if they consent) and their confederates (if they will observe the articles, etc.) and our posterity.
2. Neither party to make peace with the Pequots without the other's consent.
3. Not to harbor, etc., the Pequots.
4. To put murderers to death or to deliver them, etc.
5. To return our fugitive servants, etc.
6. We to give them notice when we go against the Pequots, and they to send us some guides.
7. Free trade between us.
8. None of them to come near our plantations during the wars with the Pequots without some Englishman or known native.
9. To continue to the posterity of both parties.

Speaking in the tongue of his native friends, he carefully interpreted each article. I felt pleased at what I regarded as Miantonomo's gestures of approval.

Mary came up to my side and whispered, "At long last, the Massachusetts Court members understand how much they need my husband. Still I fear their lust to control other people will not allow them to acknowledge their arrogance in banishing him. I confess that sometimes my husband overwhelms me with his good cheer. He complains quickly and forcefully but then lays his bitterness aside. I, on the other hand, remember, and rightly so."

"That is his secret, Mary. I think that out of gratitude, the court would have urged Roger to return with his family to Boston and live among them. Unfortunately, the senior Winthrop is thoroughly nettled in another dispute, this one over Anne Hutchinson's supposed Antinomianism."

"I have heard various reports about Anne Hutchinson. Is she truly an Antinomian, Eric?"

"I know not. What does Roger think?"

"Since he has the mind of lawyers and theologians who find subtleties they regard as crucial, I will not speak for him except to say he strongly questions a few points of her doctrine. He, nonetheless, holds her in esteem, even sending her and her husband, William, a letter to invite them to live at peace here at Providence should the heat of the Boston clergy and the court grow too intense."

As soon as Miantonomo, the two sons of Canonicus, and the handful of other Narragansets left to return to Canonicus with the Articles of the Alliance, Roger asked about William and Ruth Blackstone, in whose house I had lived since my arrival in Boston.

"They will remain some months in Boston and move into their new home just north of you," I said. "He wishes me to say that his library will always stand open to you."

Placing an inkwell before him and taking up the quill at the table, Roger asked about further developments in the Antinomian controversy in Massachusetts.

"It began when Anne Hutchinson gathered women in her Boston home to repeat and explain the Reverend Cotton's sermons." Aware that sitting before me was Roger Williams the listener, analyzer, and man of many passions, I watched him dip a quill into ink. In what appeared to be calm dispassion, however, he now used shorthand to take down my words the way he had once taken down the words of Sir Edward Coke and members of Parliament. He nodded as if to say, *Keep talking.*

"Because of their duties at home, some women were unable to hear the Reverend Cotton at the time of his sermons and lectures. In her home, Mrs. Hutchinson summarized his sermons for them. Sometimes she gave explications of their fuller meaning."

"What opinion has the Reverend Cotton of Mrs. Hutchinson's explications?" Roger dipped the quill into ink again.

Holding Freeborn on her shoulder, Mary pulled fresh sheets of paper from a wooden chest and laid them on the table.

"Why, I think Cotton delighted in Hutchinson's expositions," I said. "It pleased him, as it would any man, to have his public words repeated. Questions among Hutchinson's small audience began to emerge, as was natural."

Roger cocked an eyebrow. "Questions?"

"Aye, many. Several men of the church soon joined their wives in visiting Anne's house to hear her expositions. I myself went on three occasions though I had no wife to accompany me."

"I hear Anne is a most eloquent speaker," Roger said.

"Aye, and some say she quotes Scripture as well as any clergyman."

"So wherein lies the controversy?" Mary walked back and forth with her child but evidently followed every word we said.

"Rumors eventually spread that Hutchinson did more than explain Cotton's sermons."

Roger looked me in the eye. "More?"

"She added conclusions where Cotton had left the matter swimming in a lake of mystery. Some say he is the wiser, not venturing where the problem offers no clear answer. Others by contrast say he is too cautious and holds back, not wishing to offend his ordained brethren with the full logic of his doctrine."

"Where stands Winthrop on these matters?" Roger put down the quill.

"I hear he set forth his own position in a booklet."

Roger's frown told me he was forming a plan. "Have you seen the booklet?"

"No. I know of no one who has. Perhaps it is yet unfinished."

Mary wiped Freeborn's mouth. "What charge has Winthrop made against Anne Hutchinson?" Roger nodded as if to say that his wife's question required an answer.

"Although he concedes Mrs. Hutchinson has a ready wit and bold spirit, Winthrop charges her with dangerous errors and rebukes her for venturing into doctrines that women do well to avoid."

Roger took Freeborn in his arms. "Why women and not men?"

I shrugged. "You have heard Winthrop expound on women. He now contends that women have no calling to teach any man."

Mary again arched her eyebrows like two drawn bows. "Oh, has God given Anne the *wit* and *spirit* for such matters but denied her the call?"

"So Winthrop seems to think," I answered. "Hutchinson further denies Winthrop's claim that good works count as *conclusive evidence* that an individual has been elected to eternal salvation."

Mary placed Freeborn on a pallet while her husband gripped the quill tightly. "Pause for a moment, Eric. This is the critical point. I wish to be clear. Unless Winthrop has greatly changed, he like all true Protestants holds that good works cannot *earn* heaven's election."

"He has not changed on that."

He cleaned his quill. "Then what is his meaning? The matter is too crucial to be less than precise."

"You are right," I said, "We move now to the heart of the controversy. Winthrop truly holds that sanctification does not earn justification before God. He, nonetheless, contends that once an individual has been elected and justified, good works arise in the believer as *public evidence* of the prior election and justification."

"This places Cotton betwixt and between, does it not?" Roger smoothed the covers for his daughter as she slept on the pallet.

"Some contend that Cotton's raft floats back and forth between Winthrop and Hutchinson."

At this point, I thought Roger might explore the possibility of driving a wedge between Cotton and Winthrop, thereby gaining political leverage. That, however, seemed to be of no interest to him. He inquired instead about Winthrop's second charge against Hutchinson.

"Ah, the plot thickens. He charges her with teaching that the Holy Ghost dwells *personally* within the justified believer."

Mary stood up as if in protest. "How does that spell Antinomianism?"

"For Winthrop it is simple. If the Holy Ghost dwells *personally* within the justified believer as Hutchinson contends, then good works are performed directly by the Holy Ghost and not by human believers. This, Winthrop charges, allows believers to imagine that their deeds are God's deeds and therefore *above the Law of Moses*, hence Antinomian."

Roger's eyes seemed fix on some future scene. "Is it true that Winthrop and his supporters make the additional charge that Hutchinson's Antinomianism is but an excuse for loose living?"

"Aye, he makes the charge. Yet when pressed, he concedes that Anne Hutchinson herself stands upright as a godly woman full of good deeds and righteous living. Despite her neighbors testifying to her good character, many clergymen harbor strong grievance against her."

"Grievance or jealousy?" Seeing that Freeborn was awake, Mary tried to smooth down her baby's fine, unruly hair.

Freeborn's father looked up and laughed. "Mary, you washed her hair earlier today, did you not?"

We laughed too. Each of the hairs on Freeborn's head seemed like tiny feathers floating at will.

Roger opened his arms, and Mary handed Freeborn to him. He kissed her forehead, pronounced her the perfect child, handed her back to Mary, and picked up the quill. Looking down at his notes, he repeated his wife's question, "Grievance or jealousy?"

"I am not one to say," I answered. "Some of the clergy accuse Anne of not knowing a woman's place in the divine scheme of things. They contend that when a woman steps out of her place, she quickly falls into error as did Eve in the garden."

"Her place?" Mary's tone dripped with disdainful pity. "I have heard that men are our leaders because Eve was deceived by the serpent in the garden. According to Scripture, however, Adam learned of Eve's transgression and then willfully repeated the same transgression, evidently learning nothing from experience. This does not speak well of Adam as a leader."

Not knowing how to reply, I turned to Roger, who said with a wry smile, "Mrs. Hutchinson is not the only New England woman with ready wit and bold spirit."

"Who stands as the authority in your family?"

"In some matters, I do. In other matters, Mary does."

"Did not Abraham urge his wife to call him *Lord*?" I teased him.

He shrugged. "Abraham also lied about his wife, practiced bigamy, and treated Hagar and his son Ishmael in a shameless manner. Abraham is not my model."

The expression on Mary's face seemed more than perplexity. "Eric, messengers from Boston arrive at times, reporting events and . . . . What I mean is that my husband considers the rift in Boston severe."

"If you mean the rift between Hutchinson's followers and Winthrop's, I must tell you that the rift is far wider than I had believed possible. The whole town stands divided, and—"

"But do you see peril howling at the door?" Roger pointed his finger at me as if I were in court giving testimony.

"Peril? Yes. It reminds me of when I sailed into what I thought would be a mild rain but almost lost my ship. By misjudging its severity, I very nearly took a watery grave off the coast of Spain."

"Messengers tell me that new winds of fear blow strong in Boston." Roger wrote himself a note in shorthand on a separate sheet of paper.

I easily translated his implication: *The storm in Boston could send floodwaters to Providence.*

"Boston is currently a city of dangerous crosswinds," I said. "The fear that Winthrop's party has of Antinomianism is coupled with fear of Laudism."

Mary cut in. "Roger suspects that Winthrop falsely labels Mrs. Hutchinson."

"Roger, do you not regard her as an apostle of Antinomianism?"

"Do you?" He cocked a half-moon eyebrow.

I gave the question considerable thought. "I think Winthrop believes sincerely that she is an Antinomian. Or to speak precisely, he stands in terror of this woman because he thinks her teaching leads straight to Antinomianism though she knows it not."

"The terror you speak of," Roger said, "comes because Winthrop holds that the Antinomian is but a short step from the libertine swimming in moral chaos."

"You read his thoughts precisely," I said. "But Mrs. Hutchinson turns his argument on him and contends that though he knows it not, his course would lead us back to the old papal covenant of works, not grace."

I had intended to remain a full month with my dear friends in Providence, for I relished the scope and intensity of our discussions. I had also intended to help them build a barn, slaughter swine, and trade with the natives. But when the news came that Captain Peirce had fallen ill and that he wished to see me, I returned to Boston.

Three days later, as temporary captain of the *Lyon*, I sailed for Nova Scotia. Before embarking I sent a letter to Roger and Mary, giving them additional information about Anne Hutchinson and informing them that I would return to Boston in November or early December.

Our letters crossed. In his letter to me, Roger wrote:

Dear Eric,

Thank you again for giving us Eusebius. No other dog could so warm our heart. Seeing the girls play with him is like reading one of Mr. Shakespeare's comedies. Our mule Hugo too plays his part, helping us with our crops.

Regarding the political disease that plagues us, I stand with Winthrop in suspicion of those who claim to receive special revelations from the Holy Spirit, revelations which elevate them to the rank of prophets and apostles; nevertheless I fear more those civil magistrates who fancy themselves the gatekeepers of the human heart and the watchdog of conscience. If Hutchinson's danger is tenfold, Winthrop's, I regret to conclude, is ten-thousandfold. If Winthrop and his followers think they will forcibly eliminate the claims of those boasting of divine revelations, they are no wiser than lunatics who imagine they could capture all the flies and insects of the Earth and contain them in jars. Winthrop and his followers have yet to see that their zeal to eliminate all heresy and error will bring more devastation, chaos, and evil than the human mind can imagine.

In Old England, the king's butchers did sever ears as punishment. Will Winthrop's heirs follow his lead to cut out the tongues of those who in their judgment speak heresy? Will they gouge out the eyes of those who risk gazing upon impurity, or behead those who do not think proper thoughts? Will they search for the human organ wherein harbors false conscience so that they may carve it out? Will their own sons and daughters become their victims? Will they sacrifice my Freeborn on their Molech altar?

BOSTON

March–Early Spring 1637

Upon returning from Nova Scotia, I continued corresponding with Roger, each of us sending the other detailed notes. On a rainy day in March, I organized my notes as well as his and picked up another letter he had sent me.

> Most Worthy Eric,
>
> I am pleased that you have agreed to remain in Boston to make a written account of the reputed Antinomian controversy. The sacrifice was ours, for my family and I had longed to see you here again in Providence before now. In recent months, I have received conflicting reports of the Boston turmoil over Anne Hutchinson and the charges against her. I count on you for accurate information on these matters of utmost concern to us who have chosen the New World for our home.
>
> I will continue to follow your request to supply you with a faithful account of my work with the natives and of my struggles in Providence, for I know of your intention to write a broader narrative of what you call our New England experiment . . . .

Roger and I came to a deeper understanding of every true Puritan's inflamed concern for salvation. We saw some Puritans scale the peaks of joy regarding their salvation or justification before God. We saw others sink into the abyss of despair because they suspected they had been chosen for damnation. Sometimes I thought their agony would have been less had they been thrown upon a Spanish rack of torture.

I occasionally felt as if I were a philosopher deposited amid a magnificent and awesome experiment. The mystery of life I sought to unpack grew more complex each day. From recent correspondence with Milton, I had learned more about Galileo's unyielding curiosity and how the people of Florence spoke of him as a man driven to comprehend the movement of the heavenly bodies. I now drove myself to understand better the *earthly* bodies, minds, and hearts of those around me. I viewed my neighbors at times as human planets and human stars, each possessing several moons and powerful fields of influence that crossed each other with such power as to make my mind quake.

The agony some of my Puritan neighbors suffered regarding their salvation often touched me in a most personal way. From nearby Weymouth, a man whom I knew to be most sensible fell into a fit of despair regarding his salvation. His soul's agony so unhinged his mind that he cried out in the night, "Have you come, Lord Jesus?" Then he leaped out a high window into the snow. Later his grieving widow told me that half-clothed, he ran seven miles, stopping along the way to pray and finally dying on his knees. Whether he died of fever of the body or the soul, I know not.

In late winter, all of Massachusetts became a pot boiling with such religious anguish and controversy that I sometimes expected half the population to go mad in a strange way that I had never before witnessed. Few leaped out of windows or shrieked obscenities. It was instead the madness of acrimony and hostility exploding at every meeting in every town.

One woman of the Boston congregation became distraught about the state of her soul. A gloomy cloud so settled over her that none of her neighbors and friends could comfort her. As though each day vied to give us a horror more shocking than the previous day, she entered her neighbor's house, announced that she had damned herself forever, and then cried out in confession, "I threw my infant into the well!"

At her trial, my spine chilled. Still my heart ached with compassion when the woman proclaimed, "While I was yet in my mother's womb, God chose me for damnation. I know I shall go to hell. But God will not send a baptized infant to hell. I have sent my loving little Martha to heaven. Though I be damned to hell, I have acted from a mother's heart."

Though many clergymen professed to know the cure for the running fever that had spread throughout Massachusetts, they all seemed more like physicians offering stump water to cure the plague.

As if to outdo the clergy, John Winthrop the older saw himself as the physician that heaven had appointed to restore the colony to health and *natural order*. He began to blame the madness on the errors of Anne Hutchinson and her followers, including a woman named Mary Dyer. Charging that they were more sinister than innocent, Deputy Governor Winthrop brooded over the thought that foul demons had begun to possess the minds and bodies of those drawn to Mrs. Hutchinson's opinions. For a while he kept these darker thoughts to himself, disclosing them in his journal only.

In early spring 1637, a group of Boston ministers, including Thomas Shepard and the short-tempered Dudley, approached Cotton in his home and sternly warned him of strange opinions circulating among his parishioners.

"If such opinions exist," said Cotton, "give me their source."

"Could I be looking at the source?" Dudley fired.

Cotton merely gave Dudley a withering stare.

Shepard interjected, "Let us not lay charges against each other when in truth the source would appear to be a woman."

Cotton frowned. "A woman?"

Dudley slapped the table. "Anne Hutchinson, your devoted follower."

Two weeks later, Winthrop, Dudley, and several clergymen met to give thought to ways of curtailing Anne Hutchinson's influence.

Endecott joined them and agreed that they faced dangerous enemies. "The Pequots breathe fire from the south while here in Boston this woman inflames the populace with her wretched teaching."

Dudley's voice roared with more wrath. "A public interrogation of her regarding her theological opinions would serve the cause of righteousness well. Before all the people, we could prove her opinions to be a peril to the commonwealth."

A clergyman protested. "No, no! This will only puff her up with pride and give the populace too much access to her heresy."

Winthrop stood up and paced. "Patience is often the better strategy. We must eventually bring her up for interrogation. Let us first strip away her armor piece by piece."

The clergy listened to the strategy. All agreed that Winthrop's scheme should prevail. Endecott and Dudley looked with approval at one another. A crooked smile curled up on the right side of Endecott's mouth.

PROVIDENCE, RHODE ISLAND

March–April 1637

Roger and Angell struggled to pull their nets out of the cold water of Narraganset Bay. They connected two canoes with poles to serve as a pontoon to reduce the chances of overturning. While the codfish squirmed and flipped in the net, they reached down carefully, cautioning themselves against being stuck with the fins. Keeping the blustery wind to their backs, they worked quickly, relishing their own vigor and the freedom to live by their own labor. When they had caught perhaps two dozen cod, they paddled ashore and cleaned them with their cold, stiff fingers. Then they washed their hands in the waves, hid their canoes, and rode their mules back toward Providence.

When they reached the house, Angell took half the catch and Roger the other half. Inside his house and out of the relentless wind, he laid the fish on a long board. At that moment, a messenger arrived with a letter from Boston. While Mary cut up the fish, Roger opened the letter.

"Who is it from, dear?"

"Eric. Two pages." He began reading aloud.

My friends Roger and Mary,

Tell Little Mary that I have a gift for her, which I will bring upon my next visit . . .

Regarding the controversy over Anne Hutchinson, I must give you the report. Perhaps you have received messengers from Boston already regarding the staggering fine of £40 that fell upon Stephen Greensmith. You may not know him, for he is a man given little to disputation. According to Samuel Sharpe, who has been in Boston for the meeting of the General Court, Winthrop's men dealt severely with Greensmith to set an example. They compelled him also to travel to every congregation of the colony to confess the error of his way.

I must add that the court summoned Mrs. Hutchinson's brother-in-law John Wheelwright on March 9 to charge him with sedition, to which he replied—

"If I am guilty of sedition, you must put me to death according to the law."

The Boston church reflects the division of the town. Its Reverends Wheelwright and Wilson stand at opposite poles regarding Mrs. Hutchinson. The majority of the people favor Pastor Wheelwright and Mrs. Hutchinson, a fact that sticks like bone in Winthrop's throat.

Mary laid down the knife. "Roger, it cannot be that the court would execute this esteemed minister for sedition."

He read more from the letter.

The General Court opened the interrogation of Wheelwright to the public. Behind the scenes, however, Dudley and Endecott had worked faithfully with Winthrop to overcome Governor Vane and the others who favored Wheelwright and Mrs. Hutchinson. Though convicted of sedition and contempt, Wheelwright will not learn the nature of his sentence until a later meeting of the court. Barnabas says, "Better the sentence hang than Wheelwright."

Mary placed the fish in a large skillet. "I see this as the court's way of suspending the sword over Wheelwright in the hope that he will bow the knee before the next court session."

Roger continued to read: "Winthrop's men fought hard to set the court's May meeting across the Charles River in Newtown. Against the protest of many, the court decided on Newtown . . . ."

He looked at Mary. "Do you understand the purpose behind this action?"

"Doubtless to weaken the voices of those following Anne since most of her followers reside in Boston."

He felt a knot in his stomach, ""I fear our young friend Vane will not be governor two months hence."

"Ah, the elections are in May." She turned the cod over in the pan.

"In Newtown, not Boston. Even if Winthrop has lost ground in Boston, he maintains his hold on the other towns."

Before the day ended, Roger sat down at the table and dipped his quill into the ink.

Honorable Governor Vane,

I write in friendship and in concern for the future of our colony. Though having been banished, my heart lies still among the people of Massachusetts. Permit me to suggest counsel. As you know, I do not fully agree with Mrs. Hutchinson's theology, but I agree less with Deputy Governor Winthrop's scheme to strip away her armor by political intrigue.

The court already has succeeded in taking away the helmet Wheelwright and the breastplate Greensmith. I see you as the sword of liberty in our colony because you have spoken of liberty in matters of religious diversity. I pray that you will not permit this sword to be wrested from your grip. Our Lord counseled us to be wise as serpents.

I know you are aware of Winthrop's scheme to take the election from you in May by moving the meeting to Newtown. Would that I could stand at your side and speak on your behalf, but I can offer only a few words of counsel. Like many battles, the winning is in the preparation. Do not neglect to advance a counter-strategy . . .

His jaw set tightly, he let the ink dry. As he put the quill and ink away, he pondered the news he had received. The synod of ministers had discussed a resolution forbidding church members to question ministers in such a way as to cast doubt or aspersion on the doctrines delivered in their sermons. *Protestant popes*, he thought grimly.

NARRAGANSET BAY AND SALEM

April 1637

Shortly after a brief spring shower scarcely a mile from his trading post, Roger kept searching for a trail. Beams from the midday sun filtered through the trees with their fresh buds and leaves. From deeper in the forest came an uncanny cry. At first he took it to be a wild animal. Then he heard a human cry. Throwing his axe over his shoulder and looking right and left, he charged into the woods.

Had a wild boar or some predator come upon a human victim? He was breathing hard and cautioning himself against being taken by surprise.

Keep low. What is that? The sound came again. He recognized it. His heart pounded. Pequots! The bloodcurdling cry of the Pequots! He had no delusions about those fierce natives. Their very name in the Algonquin meant *Destroyer*.

He dropped to his flat belly, eased his breathing, and listened. Hearing no birds sing and seeing no animals, he sensed that the Pequots were nearby.

Patience! He froze, moving only his eyes.

A figure appeared in the shadows. The creature moved closer. Then a shaft of sunlight through the treetops exposed the shape of a bloodstained man. A wounded Pequot?

Gripping his axe handle, he vowed to take the native prisoner. But rushing ahead would risk exposure. Were other warriors nearby? If attacked, would the Pequot bellow for his tribesmen to rescue him?

While Endecott might enjoy torturing prisoners, Roger would not. *Still I must have information from this Pequot.* Sufficient information might reveal a way to divide the Pequots against one another, turning some into allies. He knew that General Endecott and even Captains Underhill and Mason from Massachusetts would laugh at such a thought. Perhaps it was laughable.

He waited, hoping the Pequot would not hear his heart pounding wildly. Yet he knew that the well-trained Pequot warriors could hear the snap of a small twig.

Pulling one knee up under his body and gritting his teeth, he determined to take the Pequot by surprise. Just as he was about to spring forward, he raised his axe to use as a threat. Then he blinked. Before him crawled a young, shirtless Englishman.

Transfixed, Roger followed with his eyes. The howl of distant wolves turned his head momentarily. He cut his eyes to the youthful English soldier crouched in terror. A thought flashed through Roger's mind. Had the wolves smelled the blood? *Forget the wolves!* At this moment, only fear of the Pequots held his mind, fear of their merciless torture of captives. He had seen the results of their ruthless ways—hands severed from their limbs, heads from their trunks.

All at once, he witnessed a small band of fierce Pequots attacking two Englishmen caught in surprise. Then two Narraganset natives entered the fray.

Just when he sprang to his feet to aid the Narragansets and the Englishmen, the Pequots yelled and fled, the enraged Englishmen and Narragansets pursuing them. Roger dropped to the ground, caught his breath, and cut his eyes back to the wounded young soldier who had been stripped of his shirt. The soldier's hand reached out to clutch a tree limb, but he lacked the strength to pull himself to his feet. Watching him collapse, Roger cautiously crawled closer, carrying his axe in one hand. "Do not move, my friend!" he whispered.

When certain that no Pequot eyes were fixed on him, he edged closer and heard the young soldier speak in a weak voice, "My arm . . . like lead."

For a fleeting moment, Roger could think of nothing but the possibility that if he had moved in haste, he might have axed the Englishman, thinking him the enemy. "Lie still, my friend. I will help you."

The soldier seemed unable to cease talking. "I saw him . . . I saw an older . . . my father's age . . . the soldier . . . his feet cut off."

"Where is he? Point."

The young man seemed unable to cease talking wildly. "He picked one up . . . picked up a foot . . . his foot . . . picked it up . . . to put it back on. 'Exchange it!' I shouted, 'Fool, you have the wrong foot!'"

Roger looked directly into the Englishman's eyes. "Does he live?"

"I do not know. He . . . he passed out." The weak, incoherent soldier pointed west and then let his hand drop.

Though Roger shook him, the soldier remained silent. *He seems so familiar. Who?*

Another noise startled Roger. Grabbing the axe handle, he turned his head around. Scarcely thirty feet away stood one of the Narragansets who had chased after the Pequots. Roger signaled to him.

The Narraganset seemed to recognize him and hurried to his side.

"You are Miantonomo's cousin, are you not?" Roger asked.

"Yes, I am called *Tawhitche*."

Roger pointed to the west. "Tawhitche, an English soldier lies in pain."

Miantonomo's cousin gripped Roger's arm once and then hurried westward to give aid to the older soldier whose feet had been severed.

Picking up the incoherent younger soldier, Roger left his axe behind and moved as fast as his legs would carry him through the forest, not stopping until he reached a clear spring where he gently placed the young soldier on the ground and washed the jagged gash in his arm. Then, removing his own shirt, Roger dipped it into the spring and pressed it hard against the gash, holding it until the blood stopped flowing. After binding the wound, he threw the young man over his shoulder and carried him toward Providence.

For perhaps a mile and a half, he threaded his way among the trees, his body taut with alertness, like a deer fearing bobcats at the water hole. He moved swiftly now, but with trepidation, ears vigilant, eyes keen, legs still strong.

A mile from his house, he grew weary, stopped at a cool spring, and carefully laid the wounded young soldier down. After washing a cloth in the spring, he soaked it with water and put it to the soldier's brow.

The young soldier's eyes opened wide. "Where am I? Have I . . . have I not been killed? Who are you?"

"Roger Williams, a friend."

"Have they come for me? Why would they wish to kill me? Where is my sword, my sword? Ah! I flung it at them."

For a quarter of an hour after resuming his trek toward the house, he listened to the half delirious youth babble about being cut off from his fellow soldiers.

As soon as he caught sight of his house, he saw Mary rush out with Freeborn in her arms. Little Mary hurried along, falling to her knees and getting up without a whimper.

"Take him inside," Mary said. In the house, she boiled hot water and cleaned the wound. The soldier groaned and would have lost consciousness again had she not smacked his cheeks. "When have you eaten?"

"I . . . I cannot remember."

"Then I will heat this stew."

While she fed the soldier, Roger questioned him. But soon the delirium rendered the soldier unconscious again.

"This face?" She closed one eye and then the other to study it.

"A familiar face?" Roger sat down at a wooden bowl of stew and a plate of cheese.

"I cannot fit it with a name, but . . . but there is something . . . ." She again put a cool, wet cloth on the fevered brow.

Roger sat down at his wife's side. Little Mary climbed into his lap and begged to hear a story, but he asked his wife, "What do you think of his wound? While he is unconscious . . . . Have you thread and needle?"

"Yes. Perhaps Little Mary should leave."

After taking his older daughter outside to play with the neighbors' children, he returned to hold the soldier's arm while Mary stitched the wound. When she bit the thread upon finishing the task, he dipped the cloth in the boiling water, squeezed it dry, and pressed it to the wound.

Without a word, she took the same cloth from him, dipped it into cold water, and cooled the wound to prevent bleeding. Then she looked at Freeborn, who had begun to cry. "It is time for Freeborn's feeding." She kept her voice calm.

While Mary fed the baby, Little Mary returned from playing just in time to help her father clean his boots outdoors. Knocking the mud from the boot heel, he began telling a story to his older daughter. Afterward, while singing a ballad for her, he kept glancing through the window at the Englishman. One part of Roger's mind seemed to say to another, *We know this young man from somewhere. Can he be from Boston? From Plymouth? Salem?* Scarcely had he finished the ballad when he jumped to his feet and dashed indoors. "Mary, look at him! The chin!"

"John Endecott's chin." Her expression revealed astonishment at her own words.

Roger remembered having helped the boy out of a tree. "John Endecott's son Samuel."

She smiled at the soldier. "He has grown into a man. The last we saw him he was a boy."

Ten days later, while Samuel Endecott recuperated in Mary's care, John Greene from Providence entered Salem on business. A *gentle*man much extolled by his Providence neighbors, Greene sought out Ed Batter, an old friend he had known from his youth in England. On this mild day in Salem, the two old friends talked about buying property and other matters that gave them pleasure.

"Do you intend to return to live here in Salem?" Batter asked Greene.

"I have many Salem friends, but in Providence there is . . . ." Greene hesitated.

"A freer air?" Batter asked.

"'Tis indeed a place where soul and conscience can breathe deeply. I regret that in Salem the lord of conscience has now passed into the hands of the civil authorities."

John Endecott chanced to pass by and overheard Greene's comments. He stopped Batter later on the street and questioned him about the conversation between the two men of business.

On the next day, Endecott found Greene, peered into his gentle eyes, and thundered, "I did not like the insinuation you made to Ed Batter in my presence!"

"Insinuation?" Greene tried to step around his assailant.

Endecott however shifted to stand in his face. "I will tell you the insinuation. You insult this town and its authorities by saying that Salem's air does not have the fragrance of freedom. It has in fact more than sufficient freedom for those who live by heaven's injunctions."

Greene again stepped aside to walk away, wishing no confrontation. Endecott, nonetheless, persisted, denouncing the village of Providence as a cesspool.

Greene had had his fill of Endecott. "In Providence lives a man whose shoes you are unfit to buckle. But in Salem, you persecuted this truly righteous man among us."

"If you mean Roger Williams, we did well to expel him." Then as if some inner explosion moved Endecott, he boomed out to a nearby deputy, "Arrest this man! Massachusetts cannot countenance such blasphemy. To make accusations against God's anointed is to blaspheme God himself."

A heavy fine of £20 fell on Greene, and he would have remained captive in Salem had he not spoken a humiliating retraction of his comments.

When Greene returned to Providence and spoke of his humiliation, Roger sent a letter of protest to Endecott and advised him to find a compass so that he would know which way to walk each week, seeing that he changed his direction at every shift of political wind.

"I admire your courage on the battlefield," Roger added bluntly, "but off the battlefield, your moral courage becomes a sparrow's feather in the wind."

Two days later, John Greene sent his own letter to the Salem authorities to request that his retraction be reversed. In the letter, he added,

> I fear someday the very name Salem will become a term of ridicule whereas the name Roger Williams will fly overhead like a flag of freedom and soul liberty. When I came as a guest to Salem, I found myself treated as an enemy. In Roger Williams's home, by contrast, his enemy's son now receives the care and nurture reserved for friends. Following the example of our Lord, Master Williams practices love of enemies whereas Salem's magistrates would treat friends as foes.

As soon as John Endecott's son had recovered in body and in spirit, Thomas Hooker and Minister John Wilson of the Boston church came for him. Mary fed them at her table and made them tell her of their wives and children. Then she discussed a matter evidently close to her heart. "I had wished that John Endecott himself might have joined you. His son yearns to see him, and I perceive that my husband still longs to restore what was once his good friendship with the general."

Hooker and Wilson blushed, turned their heads, and dared not tell her why Endecott had sent them as his emissaries. Standing in a corner at the opposite end of the parlor, Roger saw the crestfallen expression on her face. He knew she missed her Salem friends and other friends who had sometimes sailed up from Boston. He could not help thinking that Endecott had dealt her a blow of ingratitude from which she could not quickly recover.

Only two days earlier, Roger had received a letter from the Salem magistrates informing him that if any citizen from Providence were found within the territory of Salem, the said person would be required to renounce John Greene's letter. Failure to comply would lead to imprisonment and further censure. Roger recognized Endecott's vindictive spirit behind this order. Having returned home from making war against the Pequots, the general now seemed bent on stirring up old animosities.

The fate of Elder Sharpe, the Paynters, the Barrys, the Welches, and other Salem citizens who had publicly decried his banishment gnawed increasingly at Roger's mind. He could not erase the apprehension that the Massachusetts authorities had greedy designs on little Providence. Having defined Separatism as religious leprosy, the aggressive authorities would not rest content until they had done all in their power to remove it from New England.

He had heard that Anne Hutchinson did not veer toward Separatism. Winthrop and his stalwarts nevertheless had come to see her as yet another disease that could not be tolerated among them. He quivered inside at the ease with which his fellow Christians, by blinking their eyes, as it were, could classify fellow human mortals with roaches and vermin. Would Winthrop now reduce Anne Hutchinson to vermin? If he succeeded in doing so, how long would it be before he convinced other Massachusetts magistrates that the people of Providence were a breeding swamp of vipers to be exterminated?

PROVIDENCE

May 1637

During the first two weeks in May, Mary saw her house and surroundings transformed into the headquarters for military strategy. Since no house in Providence could contain the large number of warriors that accompanied the Sachem Miantonomo, they erected dwellings around her house and covered the structures with mats for the chief warriors to enter. Staring out the window, Mary wondered where her husband would fit in with this throng even though the warriors had summoned him.

Upon taking his place under the canopy of mats, Roger scratched Eusebius's ears and listened to the native leaders address each other solemnly and respectfully. The seriousness of their purpose reflected the belligerence of the Pequots, who, having entered Connecticut, now moved toward Narraganset territory west of Providence. The Pequots' migration from the upper Hudson River area was little more than the march of a conquering army. Their supreme achievement appeared to be that of alienating all their neighbors, red and white.

Earlier, Canonicus had told Roger of his intention to empower Miantonomo to make alliances with the English and to meet regularly with Roger to plan the tactics against the Pequots. All hope of peace had gone up in smoke.

His English neighbors understood the danger. Except for William Harris, they accepted Roger as their true spokesman and trusted him to negotiate for their safety. A man seething with hostility, Harris could not always conceal his envy. Despite having no command of the Narraganset tongue, he appeared to believe he could serve as their chief counselor or leader.

As they smoked their pipes of tobacco and sat in deep silence, the natives gave attention to those leaders who addressed them one by one. Roger understood the significance. The Narragansets could not go to battle without consensus.

The Sachem Miantonomo urged Roger to stand beside him and address them. Taken by surprise, he looked at Miantonomo for a cue. Miantonomo, however, stood stone-faced, acting more like Canonicus than like himself. Realizing that all ceremonies, like dances, had certain expected moves, Roger glanced around for a clue. When nothing struck his fancy, he mentally rehearsed what had just been said. Still with no grasp of what they expected, he spoke in a strong voice, "I appear among you as one to give counsel but also to receive double what I offer. If I have heard aright, then I perceive you intend to join the English in defending yourselves against the Pequots. I regret the Pequot leaders have no regard for their neighbors, have always refused to establish common laws among us, and have approached us with butchery and thievery. I will speak with my friend the Massachusetts governor and tell him of your wishes that the English and the Narragansets stand together as one force in mutual trust."

When he moved to take his seat, Miantonomo urged him to say more. Although he did not know what to say, he felt that the time had come to inspire courage. He did this simply by speaking of their children, wives, and old men and women. He talked of the ancient Narragansets of whom Canonicus had oft spoken. He praised Canonicus and extolled him as a man whom he had learned to trust as he would his father. As soon as Roger saw the warriors look at one another in approval, he knew he had stirred powerful chords in their hearts.

Miantonomo's stone expression transformed into one of brotherly regard. The proud sachem folded his arms across his chest, stepped forward, and announced that the two of them would now draw the battle plan to send to the English in Boston.

When Roger and the tall Narraganset sachem entered the house, Mary directed them to the table and allowed Little Mary to sit down with them. With his quill, Roger drew a crude map as he followed Miantonomo's description of the Mystic River and the Pequot fort located deep in the forest swamp.

With his finger, Miantonomo traced a line indicating the place where the Pequot warriors would likely sleep at night inside their fort.

Roger winced with skepticism. "To attack a fort in a swamp is unwise. The water would quickly turn red with blood."

Miantonomo drew another line on the map. "Here, and no farther."

"But we must entice them out."

Miantonomo threw a stick for Eusebius to catch. "That is the tactic. We must appear on the verge of defeat. Do you not agree?"

"It is a wise plan and will save the lives of many women and children if we can draw the men out. Yet how do we accomplish that?"

Miantonomo bent down and then abruptly rose up, lifting Roger over his powerful shoulder. "Like this," Miantonomo said.

Catching his breath, he understood Miantonomo's meaning. To give the appearance of suffering heavy losses in battle, some of Miantonomo's warriors would carry others over their shoulders.

After Miantonomo let him down, Roger advanced additional tactics to which Miantonomo enthusiastically agreed. He then picked up the quill and drafted a letter to Governor Vane and Deputy Governor Winthrop, telling them of the strategy and tactics. He enclosed the map with added explanations, clarifications, and instructions. Finally, remembering Canonicus's earlier request for a box of sugar, he suggested that the Massachusetts governor send it with Angell.

A moment later, Angell stood before Roger and Miantonomo. Roger handed him the letter and the map. "Conceal this on your person. Then deliver it to Governor Vane. See to it that both he and Deputy Governor Winthrop read it."

"Shall I wait for a reply?"

"Without fail. Regarding the timing of the attack, tell the governor that the Narragansets will attack on May 24 and that we expect Captain Israel Stoughton or one of the officers to meet us on that day or preferably earlier."

Angell pointed to his temple. "I will forget nothing."

Roger, Mary, and Miantonomo stood outside the house and watched Angell disappear on horseback into the forest to the north.

She handed Freeborn to Roger, who looked at her soft skin and fine, unruly hair. He prayed that his children and the children of the natives, whether Pequot or Narraganset, would not be vanquished in the war that lay ahead.

BOSTON

May 1637

On May 16, Deputy Governor Winthrop with Governor Vane at his side accepted the letter and map from Angell's hand. Despite the intense animosity between Vane and himself, Winthrop understood the seriousness of Roger's letter and Miantonomo's commitment.

"Tell Master Williams that on or before the twenty-fourth of this month, Captain Stoughton will arrive in Providence with men and arms," Vane said.

Somberly approving, Winthrop gave Angell four boxes of sugar for Canonicus and further military instructions to deliver to Providence.

Then John Winthrop Sr. abruptly put behind him all thoughts of the approaching Pequot war. The battle with the internal enemy lay before him. To prepare for the inevitable interrogation of Anne Hutchinson, he set about to purge himself of all doubts about his Calvinistic view of the universe. He longed for a clear view of his North Star and had by now convinced himself that no clouds of doubt passed between him and his star.

Still, an unwelcome question nagged at his mind: If Mrs. Hutchinson were one of heaven's elect, how could she become so fatally ensnared in the devil's trap? Like many other Puritans, Winthrop had approached nervous exhaustion with the earlier question of how individuals could know with certainty that God had elected them for salvation.

As if that question were not sufficiently tormenting, the related one of *security* probed like a rusty knife into Puritanism's open wound. Might the Creator elect an individual for salvation only later to revoke his own decree? If God's chosen could slip from the ship of grace and salvation, had they been truly chosen in the first place? Winthrop tried to push these thoughts aside, for he sensed that they cast a shadow not only across the Creator's integrity and stability, but also across the whole doctrine of the believer's *eternal safety*.

Even though Winthrop rarely allowed himself to give outward signs of harboring personal doubt about his place among the elect, the Hutchinson controversy exposed his vulnerable points, raising soul-gouging doubts that he had dared admit to no one, not even his devoted wife. In his private diary, he wrote that if he wished to rid himself of these tormenting doubts, he must somehow rid Boston of the malevolent questions raised by those who listened to Anne Hutchinson's alleged expositions of Scripture. He resolved to banish her disturbing voice even if he had to banish the woman herself.

Winthrop and his followers believed that the recent internal battle, which had smoldered in Boston and now inflamed Puritan against Puritan, had first ignited in the home of Anne Hutchinson, wife of the prominent merchant William. They had charged that she deliberately used her expositions of John Cotton's sermons as a device for propagating her own doctrines.

It irritated Winthrop that his discreet inquiry into the Hutchinson woman's past had failed to find any sinister cause for her doctrines. The more he probed, the more he discovered one simple story. In England, Mrs. Hutchinson and her husband had regularly traveled to hear Cotton expound the Scriptures. Nine months after Cotton's move to Boston, the Hutchinson family arrived there from Lincolnshire. Anne openly told her friends of the joy that filled her heart when her husband had successfully sold their enterprise in Lincolnshire. "I knew then that Providence had made a way for my family and me to sail to America where once again we might hear the Reverend Cotton preach the wondrous covenant of grace."

It also irritated Winthrop that Governor Vane advanced no campaign against Hutchinson. To Winthrop's dismay, Vane and a growing number of others in the prestigious Boston church seemed increasingly intrigued by her teachings. Winthrop accurately concluded that his control over New England's political and religious future would slip from his hands permanently if the Hutchinson woman's influence continued to spread. By way of Anne's friend Henry Vane, a wedge had already slipped into Winthrop's power. He suffered no delusion about the crisis. In a battle for his political life, he congratulated himself on successfully persuading the court to move tomorrow's election to Newtown.

The late afternoon was stormy as Winthrop's carriage pulled up at the Reverend Thomas Shepard's home. Upon entering the house, he took his completed booklet from beneath his cloak and handed it to Shepard. With the storm had come a chill. Sitting by the fireplace, Shepard read the pages that Winthrop had written to refute Anne Hutchinson's theological views. Halfway through the manuscript, Shepard looked up at his friend and shook his head. Then he continued reading. Upon finishing it, he laid it aside, again shaking his head. "She will make sawdust of this." Shepard tapped the manuscript with his fingers.

"What do you mean, sawdust?"

"John, since we are friends, I would spare you public humiliation. She could pick this apart piece by piece. For your sake, I beg you to burn these pages."

Feeling humiliation, Winthrop grew more resentful of Anne Hutchinson. Why should he, the man who had devoted more than anyone to Massachusetts, now be compelled to live in the same community with this woman of strange doctrines?

For the rest of the month, he could not bear the sight of her. Wherever he went, her eyes nonetheless seemed to follow and taunt him: *You were not made to probe deeply into such theological matters, John Winthrop. Attend to your own work.*

He felt the sting of her irony. Had she a right to turn his argument against him? Who was she to imply that he was inferior to her in theological discourse, that he was less equipped, and that his natural ability was no match for her natural wit? Could she not see the conspicuous difference between a man's mind and a woman's in these matters? He abhorred her imperious eyes upon him, treating him as inferior to herself in theological matters. How bitter was the gall in his throat—to hear his friend the Reverend Shepard imply that he, John Winthrop the older, could not demolish her arguments with the ink flowing from his own quill. "The cause of truth and pure doctrine will triumph tomorrow over her corrupting influence," Winthrop told himself aloud as he rode in his coach through the storm toward home.

PROVIDENCE

May 1637

Captain Israel Stoughton and the Reverend John Wilson entered Mary and Roger's home. At her table, she had fed many English, Narraganset, Wampanoag, and Dutch dignitaries.

From the kitchen, Roger carried the turkey that Angell had recently killed and plucked and that she had roasted to a delicate tan. Standing at the table, Roger carved slices of white and dark meat while she dished out the *askútasquash*, succotash, berries, and bread.

A tall, gaunt man with quick movements and clipped speech, Captain Stoughton praised the meal then added, "Roger, the Massachusetts troops will join us before sunset at the spot in the forest north of Providence that you and Miantonomo recommended. Have you spoken with Miantonomo recently?"

"Early this morning. He will arrive shortly. I will accompany you to the spot and lead a platoon—"

"No!" The Reverend Wilson laid his hand on Roger's shoulder. "You are more valuable to us as our translator and negotiator. We cannot permit this. The court and Governor Winthrop sent me specifically to convey their earnest entreaty that you not take the sword in your hand against the bloody Pequots."

Mary nearly dropped a bowl of cabbage. "*Governor* Winthrop? Has Henry Vane been replaced?"

"We leave one battle in Newtown only to join another in these woods and swamps," said Captain Stoughton. "John Winthrop Sr. serves as governor and now general of the forces against the woman in Boston he labels as Antinomian."

Roger sensed that Stoughton's report disturbed Mary but did not surprise her.

Stoughton ignored Wilson. "If our tactics against the Pequots prove as devious and thorough as Winthrop's against Vane and Hutchinson, we will rout the Pequots."

Wilson shook his head. "Let us not feud among ourselves, for I take a different stance regarding John Winthrop and the Hutchinson woman."

Again ignoring Wilson, Stoughton said to Roger and Mary, "The Honorable Henry Vane served us well when he sought to let the theological controversy have its way without political intermingling. Like old King James, Governor Winthrop presumes himself to be the great defender of the Reformation faith."

Wilson cut a bite of meat so hard that the knife scraped the plate. "When Henry Vane lost the election in Newtown, he lost the initiative in the struggle for control of doctrine among the people of Massachusetts."

Mary handed the pan of bread to Wilson. "Has sentence been passed on your fellow pastor John Wheelwright?"

When Wilson seemed reticent to answer, Stoughton spoke up. "Pastor Wheelwright did oft break bread with Pastor Wilson. I remember the last supper they ate together. They broke bread; and on the next day, he turned his friend Wheelwright over to Winthrop, like Judas turning Jesus over to the high priests, but without a Judas kiss on the cheek. I have reason to believe they will banish Wheelwright, which is better than crucifixion, I acknowledge."

Wilson stood up. His cheeks puffed and his veins swelled. Roger thought for a moment that Wilson might take a knife from the table and thrust it into Stoughton's heart.

She broke the tension. "Gentle followers of our Lord Jesus, I have made a berry scone in celebration of your arrival. You would honor me by partaking of it. After that you will enjoy perfect freedom to step outside and dispose of one another."

Though still standing, Wilson replied that he would not dishonor her table and that he would gladly partake of the berry scone, provided he were permitted to eat his share apart from Israel Stoughton.

Roger pushed away from the table, said that he would enjoy the freshness of the air outside, and asked to have the company of one of the men.

Picking up a large scone from his plate, Stoughton glared at Wilson and then stepped out the door.

Looking over his shoulder, Roger saw Wilson sit down at Mary's soothing words. He was sure her berry scone would soon conquer the beast inside the good pastor.

Down by the brook, after eating his scone and washing the plate, Stoughton spread his arms out like a tree. "In Newtown, our friend the Reverend Wilson did climb a tree, like a monkey, and stand upon the limb as a pulpit, shouting over the crowd, calling for the election of Winthrop—"

Roger threw a pebble into the brook and watched Eusebius investigate the ripples. "If Winthrop was elected governor, was a compromise struck with Henry Vane as deputy governor?"

"Our supreme model of tact and discretion, Thomas Dudley himself, was elected deputy governor." Stoughton's bitterness was blatant.

Roger thought, *Winthrop and the clergy have taken away Hutchinson's helmet and breastplate. Now the sword called Henry Vane has been cast to the ground.* No doubt Dudley, Winthrop, and Endecott would unite with the clergy as a force against Anne Hutchinson and, thus, against liberty of conscience. Although saying nothing, Roger resolved to speak to Wilson after the heat of passion had cooled. He would say to him, "My friend, if Anne Hutchinson has advocated Antinomianism, then will those of us who profess to hold the truth do battle with her in debate? Would this not be better than following Winthrop by taking up the sword or threatening to banish her?"

Though the brook flowed with cool water, Stoughton still fumed hot as if new thoughts came like kindling on the flame. "Winthrop brays at length about chaos and the unruly winds of society. Yet I did not hear the ass bray against the pack that howled in opposition to Henry Vane. And when the physical blows fell against the friends of Anne Hutchinson, where was Winthrop to cry out for order? I asked this question of Pastor Wilson, but he had no answer save both to quote the Scripture commanding honor to magistrates and to counsel me against speaking disrespectfully of our governor. I replied to him that Winthrop violated Scripture when he failed to show honor to *Governor* Henry Vane. Winthrop's hypocrisy outstrips that of the infamous Pharisees."

A messenger from Miantonomo appeared at the bubbling brook and said that his sachem wished to meet with them. Roger, Stoughton, and Eusebius returned quickly to the house. Wilson came out, and Miantonomo emerged from one of the temporary wigwams.

Miantonomo's straightened back and the fierce lightning in his eyes told Roger the time for battle had come. After introducing Miantonomo to Stoughton and Wilson, he explained that the two Englishmen had come to bring the court's greeting.

Miantonomo turned his eyes on the Reverend Wilson but said to Roger, "Ask this Christian sachem to pray to his god for victory, for we shall need the favor of your god and ours if we are to see the sunrise tomorrow."

Wilson and Stoughton agreed firmly on one matter. Roger must not join the battle. Wilson again laid his hand on Roger's shoulder. "My friend, after this battle will come a battle of wits and words, of treaties and negotiations. Though there be many disputes between us, we have no disagreement regarding your role in this mad drama."

He stood in front of his house, watching Wilson ride off toward Boston to deliver his report to Winthrop. Then Stoughton and Miantonomo led the warriors toward the forest and Mystic River.

Miantonomo looked back, and Roger waved. *My heart and strength go with you. Return in safety.* He watched them disappear among the trees. The gentle air blowing through his hair, the gulls flying overhead, and the eagle circling far in the distance brought a strange peace to his heart. For a moment, he envisioned the whole land thriving in peace, prosperity, color, beauty, and goodness. Closing his eyes, he envisioned the painting *A Country Wedding* by the Flemish painter Pieter Brueghel. Then streaks of red abruptly spread across the painting as if some madman had vented his spite on beauty.

After Miantonomo and Stoughton rode their horses far into the forest, they came upon the Massachusetts soldiers standing guard.

"Take me to Captain Mason," Stoughton said to a sergeant. "But first, look closely upon this man at my side. This is the great Narraganset Chief Miantonomo. His brave warriors will fight with us against the cruel Pequots."

Moments later, Miantonomo stood face-to-face with Captain John Mason. Each man looked at the other from head to foot as if to gain some quick estimation of the other's sound judgment and valor.

To Mason, Stoughton explained the plan that Roger and Miantonomo had developed, to which Miantonomo added, "My warriors will take what the English call Block Island."

"Block Island is covered with Pequots, like a hill covered with ants," Mason warned.

A tall man, Miantonomo neither raised his voice nor deigned to look down at Mason. "Tomorrow at sunset, I will return with victory."

After bidding Miantonomo good fortune in his battle for the island, Stoughton walked a few paces with him and pointed. "At this very spot tomorrow, we will meet."

Miantonomo held his stallion's reins tightly. "The crafty Sachem Uncas fights with us. If you value my counsel, keep one eye open."

"What do you mean?"

"Uncas has one loyalty and one friend. The friend's name is Uncas."

"I thank you for your counsel," Stoughton said sincerely and returned to Mason.

Captain Underhill joined them. "This Mystic River flows toward the Pequot fort. My men have left their boats behind, but I like not the air's stillness."

Mason nodded. "Silence is a soldier's enemy. These savages can hear a twig breaking a mile away. If only the wind would howl to cover our approach."

After looking around, Stoughton pointed southwest. "If we set our men in separate camps and give each proper directions again, perhaps tomorrow Miantonomo will bring victory from the island."

Underhill removed his armor and shook his head. "Tomorrow and the next will tell the story. If we fail in this venture, the Pequots will not remain content with cutting our throats. They will move against our colony."

Mason groaned bitterly. "These Philistines would capture our children and turn them into riotous pagans and idle worshipers."

Underhill looked at the ground. "I had a chilling dream last night that would have taken my courage had I not been a soldier. I saw the earth open at our feet, and we did disappear. When the earth closed, the beast of the field roamed over us as though we had ne'er existed."

Mason stared hard at his fellow captain. "You did not tell this dream to your men, I trust?"

"Do you take me for a fool? I tell you the dream only to solicit your interpretation."

"My interpretation? Why, 'tis a trick of the demons to rob you of your senses."

"Aye, a man who will let demons take his courage will let his enemy take his powder and blade," Underhill said.

"We fight two enemies—the Pequots and evil spirits that prey upon us in such times as these," Mason said.

Stoughton gestured with a sweep of his hand as if to say, *Enough of this superstitious nonsense.* Then he grabbed Underhill by the wrist. "Rehearse your men lest their imaginations become prey to useless tactics. Instruct them in what they must do, and see that they miss no cue. Miantonomo will finish Act I by the morrow. Then Act II will set the pace for us all. If we fail in it, Act III will go according to our enemy's direction, not our own."

"I like not this silence." Mason shook his head and then left to confer with his men at their camp.

"Post your men in watch of Pequot spies," Stoughton said to Mason's back. "Let us not be surprised while planning surprise." Then Stoughton turned toward Underhill. "Our second enemy is confusion, not demons. I fear that in the confusion, the Narragansets will suffer some deaths from our weapons. Go teach your men again to distinguish Pequots from Narragansets lest we slaughter our allies."

On the next day, Miantonomo returned with fewer warriors but with triumph over his enemies on Block Island. "Together we must now carry out our scheme against the fort," he said to Stoughton and the other two captains. "The Pequots know we will soon advance."

"How would they know that?" Mason asked.

"Their spies can see the restlessness and judge from the fires that we will not remain long in this place. Have any of our warriors died by Pequot stealth?"

Underhill nodded in evident pain. "I found four of my men with knife wounds at dawn. Only one has perished since then and that was through his own misjudgment."

Miantonomo turned his eyes on Mason, who said, "We have lost none in battle. Two have fallen in fever. A third has broken a limb. But the others stand eager to move toward the fort."

Two hours later, after marching still farther down the river, the three captains called a halt to their troops. Miantonomo moved ahead, promising to wait a mile in advance. When the men had been assembled, Mason stood before them and raised his voice so that all could hear it echo among the trees: "We are a chosen few, a company of brothers. Nonetheless, when your names are spoken, they will think of this day. And when they do, the word *bravery* will leap into their minds. Fill your cups with honor. Sharpen your blades with valor. Jehovah has set in the heavens the strategy of all strategies, and we are but a part of the greater scheme. Play your parts well, brothers. Let your swords be another arm. Let your voice cry for justice against these vicious knaves who have murdered our kin, stolen our bread, and threatened our wives and babes. We came here not to be captured, but to capture; not to suffer the steel, but to wield it for the sake of righteousness. When you hear the battle cry, roar like lions; make the savages tremble at your beastly rage!"

A mile later, the Englishmen and the Narraganset warriors met. Miantonomo pointed to the fort high on the distant cliff overlooking the river. "A vast swamp surrounds the fort. The cliff is studded with sharpened stakes to greet us."

Underhill shielded his eyes from the sun and studied the cliff. "What is your counsel, Chief?"

"We must draw the Pequots out according to our plan of feigned retreat." Miantonomo then urged Captain Stoughton to give his counsel.

"Gentlemen, we must play our parts precisely. We cannot assault this fort until we have set the trap. We must find the point of weakness."

"Which is?" asked Underhill.

"The Pequots' arrogance. When you feign the retreat, hobble convincingly across this swampy stage. Let those who are whole men carry others who are whole men pretending to be wounded."

The soldiers and the warriors nodded, each indicating his understanding of the parts to be played in this drama.

Underhill rose. "Men, look convincing!" When the Narragansets who understood English received Miantonomo's approval, they translated Underhill's three words to the warriors.

Knowing that they had taken no one by surprise yet pretending that the attack would catch the Pequots unaware, the Narragansets and the English made their way through the swamps. They took care to spread themselves far apart, giving the appearance of double their number. According to the tactic arranged by Roger and Miantonomo, a third of the men stopped. Another third walked very slowly. The final third moved ahead. All cried out in fierce yells; all splashed in the muddy marsh, throwing logs and waving green tree limbs to look like Birnam Wood approaching Dunsinane.

The Pequots shot their arrows and hurled their spears. Still Birnam Wood moved toward the fort until Stoughton's signal. Then the front men began to fall, not from wounds, but according to the scheme. The men behind them rushed up to throw them over their shoulders and carry them in retreat. Those who had been far behind hurried forward and grabbed up the tree limbs. They charged a few yards and then, upon the command of their captains, retreated in haste.

Captain Stoughton faced the fort and raised his fist. *Take the bait, you savages!* Still nothing happened at the fort. Stoughton stood both quivering with excitement and fearful that the enemy had deciphered their plot. *Take the bait!* He turned to look at his own men fleeing, the gap between the fort and his men widening. Suddenly he realized that he alone stood between them. He cupped his hand to his mouth to call the captains and Miantonomo to tell them to come back. Then he heard piercing yells from the fort.

He whirled around. "The Pequots are descending!" Frozen in his tracks with a strange fascination, he watched as the Pequot warriors poured out of the fort and rushed down the cliff with astonishing speed in fierce pursuit, some clinging to ropes and swinging down, others sliding down on their rumps. More and more warriors came like wild boars, squealing for blood and vowing vengeance. The whole fort had turned into a boiling pot overflowing with warriors. When Stoughton saw the spears splash in the vast bog; he knew that unless he moved at once, he would never move again. He turned his back on the fort and fled for his life, tripping over his saber's sheath. He picked himself up from the swamp, ripped the sheath from his side, and dashed it to the ground.

Stoughton saw Miantonomo ahead directing the English to the escape route. He joined the other captains fighting their way through the mud and water. Upon hitting dry land, the captains glanced over their shoulders and ran until their lungs seemed on the verge of bursting.

Miantonomo's fierce warriors turned to face their enemies. They pulled their bows and sent arrows flying. Their spears followed. Stoughton felt they would have gone to meet them with knives in hand if Miantonomo had not commanded them to return. The retreat into the forest teetered on defeat, the Pequots having proved far swifter than expected.

Let the curtain of night fall swiftly, Stoughton prayed, clinging to a tree and gasping for breath.

But the sun seemed to stand still as if favoring the Pequots. On they came like waves to drown the English and the Narragansets.

The red sun flashed in Stoughton's eyes. He could scarcely see the enemy. "The boats! Where are the boats?" Then he saw them and the men pouring into them at the coast.

Captain Mason cried out, "Hurry, men! Hurry!"

Stoughton could see the boats leave the shore. The last lingered. He fell in the sand, clawed his way to the vessel, and climbed inside with the help of two soldiers. The boat moved away from shore, leaving the Pequots hurling their curses with their spears.

Twilight replaced the sun's brightness. The Pequots, evidently thinking they had vanquished their enemies, hurried toward the fort.

Miantonomo's warriors had already taken boats and circled round, coming up the river to cut the Pequots off from their fort. The colonists, seeing Miantonomo's flaming signal high in the sky, turned their boats around and headed toward shore. The curtain of night lingered still high above, slowly descending.

The Pequots never reached their fort. Before the curtain fell, the blood of the vanquished Pequots colored the swamp red.

Miantonomo led his men to the boats. Without looking back, they rode home to proclaim their victory to Canonicus and the people. Stoughton took another boat with a handful of men to return to Providence. Mason and Underhill, however, breathing righteous wrath and threatening vengeance in the name of Jehovah, led their men to the fort.

With scarcely any opposition save from a few barking dogs and a handful of decrepit warriors, the colonists tore into the Pequot village.

Mason held a torch in his hand and praised heaven for the victory. "We must burn them, for they are a heathen pestilence among us!" He hurled the torch onto the mats covering the wigwams and thanked God for the wind that had come at last.

The wind carried the flames from wigwam to wigwam. Enveloped in flames, women and children ran like human firebrands into the swamp. When the curtain of night at last touched the Earth, only seven Pequots were taken captive. A remnant had escaped.

On the following morning, Mason and Underhill counted 700 men, women, and children roasted to death.

The soldiers seemed more downcast than triumphant. What had they done? They stood dumbfounded, smelling the burnt flesh and beholding a sight abhorrent to honorable eyes.

Captain Underhill filled his lungs with sanctimonious wind and stood on a ladder. "Men, be not faint of heart. There is scriptural guidance for our deed. Did not the prophet Samuel order the slaying of every member of the Amalekites? Did not Joshua obey Jehovah's command to slaughter women and children along with the warriors?"

Mason joined him. "Listen to me, men. Let not your hearts be troubled. Bless the Lord God of Israel, for it pleased God to smite our enemies and to give us this land for our inheritance." Mason threw his head back and laughed. "Scripture teaches that God laughed at his foes and made a footstool of his enemies. 'I will tread them in mine anger,' sayeth the Lord of Hosts, 'and will trample them in my fury, and their blood shall be sprinkled upon my garments.'"

Underhill again raised his voice. "Look about you, men. Are we not alive? Has not heaven spared us? Did not God send us the wind at the precise moment so that these heathens, crowded in this fort, might be exterminated without touching a hair of our heads? Behold, you see a lesson for your hearts, a miniature hell where all pagans go, where go also all unbelieving hearts and the unfaithful, where the flame's rage is never quenched. Take heed that you hold to sound doctrine and have a pure heart lest ye too find your way to hell everlasting!"

Soon Mason and Underhill finished their speeches. Then they washed their hands and sat down to a large meal of roast pork.

PROVIDENCE

August 1637

Three months later, Roger leaned upon his hoe and used his sleeve to wipe the sweat from his brow. "The sun makes these plants grow, Angell. But its heat draws away my energy."

"The sun makes ready for the night. Let us do likewise. Already the crickets serenade us."

"This hoe . . . I can no longer determine where my arm ends and the hoe begins. They have melted into one." Roger laughed and then pointed with his hoe toward Mary and the children approaching. He could see that she carried two letters.

Angell picked up Little Mary by her hands and swung her around. Then he set her down and left for his house.

"Papa, my feet are hot." Little Mary stood on one foot and then on the other.

He stood teasingly on his left foot and then his right. "Listen, I hear the bubbling stream beckon us."

He took Freeborn in his arms, having given his hoe to Mary. The four of them journeyed to the cool stream and sat down on the bank. Little Mary ran through the water, splashing her father. Roger and Mary removed their shoes too and joined her, letting the water tickle their feet.

After Little Mary had sat down in the stream with her mother's permission, Roger dried his hands and took out the letters.

Mary said, "Let us read Eric's first before the sun disappears."

My Four Friends,

Greetings from Tumult City! Would that I were there in Providence with you. I will send more news later but must quickly finish this before the messenger arrives.

The Massachusetts clergymen grow increasingly perturbed and no longer conceal their judgment that Anne Hutchinson has become an insurgent threat. She has stung them with her remark that except for John Cotton and her brother-in-law Wheelwright, the clergy of Massachusetts preach a doctrine of legalism. Even more infuriating to the clergy, she argues that their legalism is the slippery slope that will in time reach the bottom called the papal covenant of works rather than the Reformation's covenant of grace.

The mounting tension and acrimony so disturbed me that I recently resolved to attend Anne Hutchinson's meetings at her home again. This resolve I carried out when you sent me a letter urging me to probe still deeper for information about the conflict. Your letter came at the time that Winthrop not only swiftly organized forces against Anne Hutchinson, but also boldly proclaimed that if the church could not control her, then the state must.

On my way to the Hutchinson house, I spoke to the Reverend Hugh Peters of Salem about his work to found Harvard College. I hear rumors that some wish to change the name Newtown to Cambridge.

Peters asked bluntly, "Captain, do you understand that Anne Hutchinson is a dangerous woman?" Then he took me aside and lowered his voice. "You have a good reputation in both Boston and Salem; and if you will take the advice from a friend who wishes you well, I urge you to have nothing to do with her."

I caught my breath and thanked him for his counsel. He seemed relieved until I added that I desired to explore for myself whether she is a source of harm or help. Upon saying this, I thought I sounded more like Roger Williams than Eric Firebrook.

The Reverend Peters, a persistent man, branded Mrs. Hutchinson a liar and compared her to the serpent in the garden. "She has a perilous subtlety about her. She does pretend to expound in simple language the profundities of her teacher, the Reverend Cotton, whereas in truth she embellishes his message with her own poisonous doctrine."

Not wishing to align with either party of this dispute but to investigate matters further for you as well as for myself, I headed toward the Hutchinson house. Upon arriving, I could not help noticing Winthrop's house nearby. I had heard the rumor, which I had not corroborated, that Winthrop had of late begun to stand at the window to observe the numerous guests entering the Hutchinson house. I noted that while many carriages dotted the area around the Hutchinson house, only one or two stood outside Winthrop's.

This bit of rumor I will pass along though I feed little on Boston's rumors. But I think it is one you need to hear, not because it is true or false, but because so many of Mrs. Hutchinson's followers now believe it.

Mary touched Roger on the arm. "Wait, love, our Mary presumes to be a fish." He held Freeborn in one arm while Mary pulled their elder daughter from the stream and set her upon the bank. "If God had wanted you to swim so much, where are your fins?"

"Mama, I need . . . swim."

"Dear, I will take you to a better place tomorrow. There are too many rocks in this spot, and the water is too shallow. There now, let your feet swim awhile. See how your feet swim, and the little minnows come around?"

Wiggling her toes to make the minnows move, Little Mary became so absorbed that her feet and toes turned into her playmates.

Mary pointed to the letter. "What was the rumor?"

He looked up. "Not a rumor to believe, but here are Eric's words."

According to the rumor widespread among Hutchinson's followers, Winthrop has sunk one leg deep into the quicksand of jealousy. The three of us know that Winthrop seeks power. But is it power for its own sake? I earnestly believe that he seeks it as protection for the purity of the Reformation faith. More than once he has told me that God has called him to keep the commonwealth free of the contagion of crippling heresies. I therefore harbor much reservation regarding the charge of jealousy, which I take to be a serious charge and one that ought not to be believed without strong reason. Our friend Barnabas, who has little regard for Winthrop, says in all sincerity that Massachusetts would be the better if jealousy were the deepest spring of Winthrop's action.

Ah, enough of our friend Winthrop and on to Anne Hutchinson. When I entered her spacious parlor, I observed as many men as women. Originally, only women had attended her meetings; but now husbands and other men come, some asking Anne questions and receiving her answers. A compelling discussion arose around the themes of justification and sanctification. The earnestness of all present would have moved even a heart of stone.

I cannot deny that this woman touches some chord hidden deep within me; and I have vowed not to rest until I probe the enigma to the fullest. Sleep sometimes flees from me as from Macbeth himself. Throughout some nights, my mind prowls like some hungry predator who has yet to find its prey.

Mary shielded her eyes against the blood-red sun sinking in the west. "Who is that?"

Roger stood up and took the hoe that was leaning against a tree. Although Pequots who had either survived or avoided the war had recently been seen ten miles south of Providence, he counted on caution and Miantonomo's warriors for protection. He shielded his eyes. "Can that be Captain Stoughton?"

"Possibly. But who is the second man?" she asked.

"Take the children to the house. Hurry!" He put on his shoes. "Alert the others! Send the mule for me!" Instead of standing in the open, he took the hoe, blended in with the trees and waited, holding his hand out to block the red sun.

The two figures became mere silhouettes. Gripping the hoe handle, he listened to determine whether there were others.

When the two men came to the stream, he recognized Stoughton and called out, "John!"

"Help!"

Roger dashed across the stream. When he saw the wounded Narraganset warrior, his heart sank with agony. "Miantonomo!"

Stoughton laid the tall, muscular sachem out on the bank.

Roger knelt beside him and whispered to his friend in the Narraganset tongue, "Speak to me, Miantonomo. Speak to your friend."

Stoughton shook his head, but Roger would not believe that the life had left the great Narraganset sachem and warrior. He quickly examined the wound in Miantonomo's side and talked to himself. "This is a blade wound. The blood flows too freely."

Stoughton kept looking back and reaching for a sword that was not there. Then he dropped to his knees at Roger's side and stared at Miantonomo.

After scooping up water in the cup of his hand, Roger washed the wound. He tore his shirt in half and dashed it in the water to cleanse it of the day's dirt. Then, to stop the bleeding, he folded the cloth and pressed it on Miantonomo's wound.

Stoughton, talking as if he were a child locked into a nightmare, fell and then struggled to get up. Roger used his left hand to grab him by the collar and hold him to the ground. Stoughton looked half dead too and shook as if awash in an icy sea.

Worried that the brave captain would wander back into the forest, Roger did not relinquish his grip. Though his heart beat in his ears, he ordered himself to think calmly and quickly. He dared not remove his right hand from the wound for fear Miantonomo's blood would flow again.

Stoughton's head rolled to the right and to the left as he babbled, but weariness so overcame him that he struggled no more against Roger's tight grip.

With his left hand and teeth, Roger tore Stoughton's shirt into strips, doused them in water, and then tied them around Miantonomo to hold the compress firmly against the wound.

The beat of horses' hooves! His muscles tightened. He looked up and saw a figure astride a mule in the twilight. "Who is there?"

"Jeremiah Paynter. I have fled Massachusetts as Moses fled Egypt."

"Heaven has sent you. Come quickly!"

The mule stopped at the stream. Jeremiah leaped to the ground. "Stoughton!"

"Help me with Miantonomo." Roger fought back crippling desperation.

Jeremiah knelt down. Together the two Englishmen lifted the chief sachem astride the mule. While Jeremiah steadied the wounded man on the animal, Roger climbed behind Miantonomo. "Jeremiah, stay with Stoughton while I take the chief to Mary. I will send the mule for you."

"Wilfred Barry left with me. He is at your house. Send him back with the mule."

In front of the house, his neighbors and Wilfred Barry the Salem carpenter stood open-mouthed.

"Miantonomo!" Mary exclaimed and grabbed Wilfred by the arm. "Bring the sachem inside. I will make a pallet for him."

With the help of Smith, Harris, and other neighbors, Wilfred lifted Miantonomo from the mule.

"Deal gently with him. He has been sorely wounded." Roger guided Wilfred's hand to the compress. "Hold it firmly lest the clot break."

Inside, the men laid the broad-shouldered chief upon the thick pallet. Wilfred stayed by his side, pressing the wound and talking to him in English as if they had known one another for many years.

Roger stepped inside, took Mary to a corner, and whispered, "I fear he could die before sunrise. Pray heaven that his strength endures."

"Has he spoken?"

"Not a word. Not even with his eyes. He has suffered a head wound too."

"Goodness, does he breathe?"

"Somewhat." His thoughts traveled across the forest to Canonicus and then to the pallet and his friend. His heart ached, but he told himself it was wrong to hurt at this time. It was self-indulgent to feel now. *Time only for acting!*

He turned to Angell, who had just entered the house. "Captain John Stoughton lies a quarter of a mile toward the brook. Jeremiah is with him. Hurry, Angell! Take the mule."

"Is the captain alive?"

"More or less, though, half his mind is elsewhere."

As soon as Angell left, Roger turned to Mary. "I must rush to inform Canonicus."

She held his arm tightly. "But night comes."

"The moon's light will guide me."

"And guide the Pequots to your throat. No, dear, this you cannot do!"

He turned to leave, but she would not turn loose of his arm. "Listen! Are those not your daughters sleeping innocently?" Her tone softened only slightly. "Your heart divides into two streams. You can*not* sail in both directions."

"My wits escape me. My daughters . . . ." Suddenly, as his thoughts turned to his months with the Wampanoags, he remembered the medicinal leaves they used for healing wounds. "Mary, tomorrow I . . . Canonicus must know; but tonight . . . ." Taking a torch, he dashed outdoors and headed for the nearby forest to find the leaves. Although unfamiliar with their name, he felt certain he would recognize their shape.

For half an hour, he searched frantically, hearing strange noises in the forest. He assured himself that the other Pequots from distant camps would not have wandered this close to Providence. Though Miantonomo's approaching crisis kept prickling him, he fought such thoughts fiercely lest they distract from his urgent mission. Again he told himself not to feel. *Think! Search! Act!*

His heart leaped. As if from nowhere, the leaves for which he searched appeared, fluttering in the wind before his eyes. He held the torch higher and plucked a score of leaves. Then, looking above through the nearby clearing, he saw the stars, which guided him home.

As soon as he returned, he said not a word to anyone but quickly ground the leaves as he had seen the Wampanoags do.

Mary understood at once. Already she had boiled the linen and held it on her right palm. Wasting no time, she removed the old compress with her left hand while he sprinkled the finely ground leaves onto the wound.

When he had finished, he nodded. She then carefully placed the linen against the wound. Together they bound it, sealing it with a prayer.

His delirium now waning, Captain Stoughton sat at the table while Wilfred Barry fed him quail broth and berries. "The Pequots," Stoughton said hoarsely as Roger sat down across from him. "They blame Miantonomo for the butchery that our own Captains Mason and Underhill commanded. They lay in wait for him and would have slain him had not other warriors come to his rescue."

Roger spoke harshly. "Why did the warriors not return for their sachem?"

"I think they did not know of his wound and perhaps they too met disaster."

Roger buried his face in his hands "Oh, what butchery have we who preach the Prince of Peace . . . oh, treachery!" He could speak no more. No words could voice his conflicting passions and feelings. The little Pequot children screaming, the terror in their eyes, the quivering lips of the little ones torn from their mother's breasts, Mason's wicked laughter, the scorn on Underhill's face, a scorn that transformed fellow mortals into creatures lower than rodents. For such carnage, a pagan sachem must now bear the blame that should rightly fall on Christian heads. *Oh, Jesus Christ, look down in mercy at this poor benighted species.*

Mary put her arms around her husband. "Go to sleep. I will sit up with Miantonomo."

"No, love, let me stay with him. If my eyes glue together, I will wake you."

"I have tied his hands lest he claw at his wound in the night."

The moonbeams poured through the window where he sat beside his sachem friend. She arranged nearby pallets for Jeremiah and Stoughton. Wilfred elected to sleep in Angell's little house nearby.

Long before midnight, all but Roger slept at peace as if no troubles had descended on that day. Staring out the window at the moon-bathed trees, he could not help comparing this rugged land with Old England. He thought of his London days and of his childhood, of the Dutch children he had played with, and of the English he had befriended at school. He thought of his mother, Sir Edward Coke, and many others who had poured kindness into his life. Despite the guilt and shame that tore at him because of the abominable war he had helped plan, a fountain of gratitude bubbled in his heart. He did not ask why divine Providence had surrounded him with an abundance of loving people from his childhood. Rather, he remembered the passage of Scripture: "Freely you have received; freely give."

Turning his eyes back to Miantonomo, he felt brotherly affection flow out toward the noble Narraganset chieftain. He knew Miantonomo's death would bring overwhelming sorrow to the whole Narraganset people.

How will I tell Canonicus that I let his nephew die in my house? Roger felt both tears in his eyes and Canonicus's grief in his breast. *If Miantonomo dies, Canonicus's great heart will crack.*

The moon rose higher, and the beams fell upon Miantonomo's bronze-hued face. Roger wanted to say, *Rise up, Brother! Rise up!* Yet he knew he had no such powers to conquer the bitter enemy called Death.

Growing weary, he might have succumbed to sleep had not an owl swooped by the window. Watching the winged creature glide majestically, he experienced a strange, unnerving feeling stirring inside him. He whispered only to himself, "The forest teems with life. The field mice, the woodchucks, the spiders—yet my Narraganset brother lies like a stone. Why should a rat, a vulture, a serpent live when Miantonomo lies at the grave's edge?"

Long after midnight, Jeremiah Paynter eased his way to Roger's side and placed his hand on Miantonomo's brow. "Has he waked?"

"He moved and groaned. Nothing more."

"Let me serve as sentinel. Exhaustion knocks at your door."

"I cannot sleep."

Jeremiah pointed at the moon. "Go outside and walk in the moonlit air."

He placed his hand on Jeremiah's shoulder to pull himself to his feet. Scarcely had he stood up when Little Mary rose up on one elbow, rubbed her eyes with her tiny fists, and called to her father.

"I am here," he whispered, lifting her up. As he carried her outside, he felt his bones creak and pop. But the air invigorated him. He saw Venus staring at them. After walking to the bubbling brook, he put her down and let the cool water wash his face, restoring his vigor. He drank deeply from the brook and lay on his back to watch meteors streak across the canopy.

His older daughter seemed enthralled by the same starry heavens. He listened to her talk, babbling like the brook, proud of herself for being awake at such a strange hour.

After a quarter of an hour, satisfied with her new experience, she lay on her side and soon vanished into the land of dreams.

He washed his face a second time and rubbed the cool water across the back of his neck and ears, relishing the peaceful night, wishing that somehow the human race could wash away the violence endemic to its nature. *Would that baptism could restore peace in every village.*

He remembered, however, that Captains Mason and Underhill had been baptized. Those in Boston who had recently sold captive Pequot children into slavery had been baptized. He stood up and stared at the melodic brook. For a horrid moment, it seemed to turn to flowing blood. Then it was the pure stream again. *Wash over my heart*, he thought. *Cleanse away my hatred and my guilt in this violence.*

Was there anything he could do to prevent the enslavement of surviving Pequot children and parents in the other camps? *I will write Winthrop to protest such slavery.* If only he had not been banished from Massachusetts, he could have been there. Why had the clergy remained mute? Some had looked the other way. Others had quoted from the Old Testament to justify enslavement. Had they not read the prophet Micah? "What does the LORD require of you? To act justly and to love mercy and to walk humbly with your God." Had they not listened to the prophet Amos? "Let justice roll on like a river, righteousness like a mighty stream!"

He prayed silently as Little Mary leaned against him and fell asleep. He felt that Miantonomo's restoration now lay solely in the Creator's hands. A mortal could do nothing more except wait and hope.

When he returned with his daughter to the house, he saw his wife standing outside. She took Little Mary from his arms and laid her in her bed. Then under the moonlight, she walked hand in hand with him while the night birds sang.

"The children will sleep soundly," she said. "I fear Miantonomo's strength leaves him. Would that he could wake to take food and drink."

"His body is like a sponge squeezed dry. You must return to your bed, Mary. Tomorrow—"

She placed her hand on her breastbone. "Tomorrow, new hope will come. I feel it."

With the coming of dawn, however, hope for Miantonomo's recovery waned. As Roger left the house, Angell approached and grabbed him by the arm. "Where go you?"

"To Canonicus to tell him—"

"Has Miantonomo returned to life?"

"No, he lies like a breathing stone."

"Then let me go with the news to Canonicus, and . . . . Hear me, Brother Roger. If Miantonomo opens his eyes and does not see his friend at his side . . . . No, you must not go."

"But I have no right to ask you . . . the warring Pequots would—"

"I know the peril but have keen eyes and the step of a cat."

Mary joined them. "Thomas speaks wisely, dear. Canonicus would desire you to stay at his nephew's side." She then gave Thomas Angell the particulars about Miantonomo and bade him go quickly yet cautiously to the ancient Narraganset Sachem Canonicus.

The cock crowed as Angell disappeared into the forest. The swine in the far distance snorted, calves mooed, and donkeys brayed. Wilfred Barry stretched his long arms, pushed his hair back with both hands, and came outdoors to greet the birds. Roger pointed toward the bubbling brook as if to say, *You may wash to start a new day. We will break the fast soon.*

After they had consumed slices of ham, hunks of hot bread with plum preserves, and cups of fresh milk, Roger sat at Miantonomo's side to listen to Jeremiah's report of his recent visit to Boston. Scarcely had Jeremiah begun when Mary interrupted, handing Roger the second letter that had arrived the day before.

He quickly opened it, read the message, and felt the blood leave his face. He looked up at her and then at Wilfred and Jeremiah. "He has left us!"

Jeremiah and Wilfred looked at one another.

"Henry Vane! On August 3, he took ship for England." Then Roger looked into Mary's saddened countenance. "He bids us good health and God's blessing."

She took the letter, read it silently again, and put it away. "Though missed in New England, Henry is doubly needed in Old England."

Roger wondered what Anne Hutchinson would do, now that one of her strongest defenders had departed Boston.

Captain Stoughton stirred in his bed and shouted in his sleep.

Rubbing his eyes and walking over to the east window to look out at the morning sun, Wilfred Barry said grumpily, "I have known some men to talk more sense in sleep than with their eyes open. What did Captain Stoughton say just then, Brother Roger?"

"He merely cried out. I felt I should wake him from some great terror. Yet we should let him sleep. His body works hard to mend itself."

Wilfred grinned as if amused by some irony. "He is a captain. An officer and sleep marry well."

Roger addressed Jeremiah and Wilfred. "Give me your opinion of Anne Hutchinson."

Wilfred stared at the calluses in his carpenter's hands. "We met recently with her."

"Met in her home in late July." Jeremiah gulped down a cup of cool spring water and began giving the detailed account of their visit with her. "When our carriage stopped at the Hutchinson house and we knocked at the door, her husband, William, greeted us. I think he saw perplexity on our faces. Upon inviting us in, he said, 'I am sure you wish to speak to my wife.'"

Wilfred eagerly added, "Soon Mrs. Hutchinson appeared in the spacious parlor. She stood tall, as formidable a woman as e'er I have seen. 'Please, you must sit, gentlemen.' That is what she called us. She jerked her head, signaling to that bright-eyed daughter of hers to serve us broth. She said to us both, 'You have deep concern in your hearts; it is written on your brows.'"

Jeremiah resumed: "We tried to smile pleasantly but could not. I said, 'Mrs. Hutchinson, we have heard of your teaching. We regret the split that widens each day in the colony. Last month Governor Winthrop declared the animosity among us to be more severe than the animosity between some Protestants and papists.' Mrs. Hutchinson pulled her chair closer to us. Ne'er had I seen a woman with such penetrating eyes. In some respects, Brother Roger, she reminded me of your Mary. But of course your Mary has a subtlety not in Mrs. Hutchinson's range."

Wilfred cut his eyes toward the sachem. "Does Miantonomo move yet? I have not heard a groan from him this morning."

Roger could not hide his distress. "Nothing of late. All is now in the hands of Providence."

Jeremiah glanced at Wilfred. "Give Brother Roger your impression of Anne Hutchinson."

Wilfred laced his hands together behind his head and leaned back. "When that tall, impressive woman spoke of the Reverend Cotton, her tone was one of admiration. Regarding Governor Winthrop, however . . . . I do not know the nature of the traffic between them, but something about the governor cuts her like a dull saw. There is no great admiration between them. At the same time, it is far more than disdain. But what . . . ?"

Roger watched the carpenter hold out both hands and move them up and down as if they were scales seeking balance.

Jeremiah interrupted. "Can it be this, Wilfred? If Winthrop saw himself as God's special magistrate appointed to rule over people, the Hutchinson woman looked upon him as a well-paid workman with strict duties to perform."

"And if he failed in his duties, she would have him discharged," agreed Wilfred. "But as I said, she placed the Reverend Cotton high on a pedestal. She urged all those in her house who had come to hear her . . . . Aye, with these ears, I heard her say it was Master Cotton who had the greatest learning among the Massachusetts clergy. A dangerous thing to say, it was. Better to whack a hornet's nest with a stick than to stir up jealousy among the clergy."

Suddenly Roger's heart leaped. Had his sleepless eyes truly seen . . . ? Had Miantonomo's hand risen up to his side? "Miantonomo," he said in a voice scarcely above a whisper. "'Tis I, your friend Roger."

The house grew strangely quiet except for Captain Stoughton's mutterings in his sleep.

Wilfred smiled broadly. "Miantonomo's fingers moved!"

Roger felt his own breathing shift. "Behold, he frowns!"

Miantonomo's head rolled to one side. For a frightening moment, Roger thought the sachem had expired. Then Miantonomo blinked, turned his head, and groaned. He raised his hand. Before it fell back, Roger caught and held it.

"Resurrection morn!" Jeremiah sprang to his feet.

Already standing, Mary began ladling warm broth from the mutton and vegetables simmering in the kettle. She carried the bowl and spoon to Roger, who took them and waited for Wilfred's strong hands to help the broad-shouldered sachem sit up.

Roger carefully placed the spoon of broth to Miantonomo's lips. "Good!" He felt more like a father feeding his child than a friend sitting before a mighty warrior.

"More," Miantonomo uttered in his native tongue.

The thrill of victory traveled through his body as he dipped out spoon after spoon of broth until Miantonomo had drained the bowl.

Miantonomo cut his eyes up toward Mary as if to thank her for the nourishment.

"Still more?" Roger handed the empty bowl to her.

The sachem grunted with a faint smile. For a moment, his eyes seemed enigmatic, so different from those powerful eyes that seemed like surging oceans beneath which swam leviathans and other creatures of the deep.

After Miantonomo had eaten the second bowl of broth, Mary made him lie down again until Roger could wash the wound in the water she had brought from the spring earlier that morning.

He studied the wound and gave the great sachem an accurate, unadorned description of all he saw. Then, with Miantonomo's approval, he sprinkled more of the finely-ground leaves across the wound. "Mary, see how the knitting needles of his skin worked speedily through the night!"

Miantonomo moved to put his feet on the floor. "I must go to my people."

Roger held out a restraining hand. "Canonicus will be here before long. Wait until he arrives. We will abide by his judgment."

Not waiting for Miantonomo's response, she slipped a large bowl of stew into Roger's hand.

Miantonomo smiled. "We are twin stars in the night sky." The wounded chief then gripped his own upper arm firmly. "The strength in these arms and in these shoulders will henceforth be called *Roger Williams*. Wherever I go, my brother will go with me."

BOSTON

August 1637

With my mind in a whirl and at a fevered pitch, I knew I would be fit company for no man or woman. I walked to and fro among the trees near Boston to think alone. Did England not stand on the verge of civil war, threatening to divide herself over theology? Would New England soon follow Old England by serving one another up like sacrificial animals on bloody pagan altars?

Deep within me, the voice of reason stirred with all its fierce passion, for reason is no less a passion than any other. It too comes through human blood, sinew, and the mysterious gray glob we call the brain. In reason I sought an antidote to my mind's fever.

Slowly I dug as best I could to the root that had set me in turmoil. I told myself that I could not take the easy method of cynics who glibly convinced themselves that all theological battles were mere disguise for avarice, greed, power, envy, jealousy, and the like. Though I had always acknowledged that such lowly motives coursed through our veins, I had learned from my venerable Islamic friend and benefactor Abba that human mortals could not survive without their philosophies. "Beavers build dams and live in them because they must. Human mortals build their philosophies and live in them because they have no other choice," Abba had oft told me.

In New England, I thus saw a battle of cosmologies and philosophies forming on the horizon. The theologians served as strategists, the politicians as tacticians, the astronomers as new mappers, and the merchants as suppliers. Some lawyers and rhetoricians served as their consciences and circumstances permitted.

While the voice of reason gained some respectable hearing inside my head, I rode in a carriage to the Reverend Cotton's house on the hill. Cotton's servant guided me to the library. I stood there alone, privately thanking Milton, who had personally packed many books in England to be loaded on the ship that carried Cotton to the New World.

The Reverend Cotton appeared in his library and invited me to be seated. He wore the white collar, which fit with a certain perfection. Though not elegant or ornate, his near-sparkling collar reminded me of the purity to which the Puritans aspire. He moved with regal grace and spoke with commanding resonance that he held in total control. Like Anne Hutchinson, he possessed an aristocratic manner with that special skill of putting a guest at ease. Though I knew Cotton to be a formidable debater, his affable manner in the library came as a pleasant surprise.

Like a ship embarking from the harbor, we did not raise all our sails at once, but glided slowly into our conversation, speaking casually of England, Milton, and Chillingworth in particular.

Cotton's manner seemed so gracious that I wondered how this same clergyman could have spoken so cruelly to and against Roger Williams. I remembered a comment Mary had once made: "Think of Cotton as two men."

As our conversation moved away from the harbor and into the open sea, I said, "I do not wish to presume on your time and good will, Reverend. I, however, have recently grown perplexed over the boiling controversy among us. By traveling through many countries, I learned early that strong disagreement among us mortals is no novelty. Still, why must the disagreement within this righteous colony boil with such fury? Why are so many learned men and keen-witted women whose intelligence I truly respect . . . ? Why do they form two camps and hurl flaming charges, each denouncing the other as traitors of the gospel?"

Cotton stroked his chin and carefully pondered the question. "The answer is simple in some ways, yet not simple at all."

"What is at stake to cause sincere Protestants to fall into such madness?"

Cotton stared thoughtfully into empty space. "At stake?" He inhaled deeply as he traced his finger around the rim of a bowl on the library table. "Picture yourself standing on the wide rim of a volcano, looking down into the infernal lava. A gigantic metal slide leads downward from the rim into the lake of lava. In the lake swim men and women who day and night cry out because of their agony. They know they will never escape. Each day from the volcano's rim, you see thousands of people hurl down the wide and steep slide. The fortunate are mercifully snatched off the slide and carried far away safely from the tormenting lava."

"And the unfortunate?" I looked into his face and thought I had never seen eyes more sincere.

"Ah, the children of perdition." He shook his head slowly and closed his eyes tightly. "They plunge to their fate, the bottomless pit of torment. Picture yourself, Captain. You stand on the rim, looking down. You believe, sir, that someday, you know not when, your time will come. You will find yourself on the great slide. You hear the screams of those already doomed to the lava, and you hear the joyous singing of those who have been rescued for a life of bliss. On the rim, you wonder, 'Will I join the damned below or the elect who are saved?'"

Cotton paused for a full minute, giving me time to think . . . and sweat. My lips became parched and my throat dry as if the heat from the lava had scorched my face. "But, Reverend, I venture that the greater population of New England raises the dread question, 'How may I *know with certainty* that I have been elected for salvation rather than endless damnation and torment?'"

Instead of answering my question, he repeated it as if he too had some secret doubt he dared not reveal from the pulpit. For a moment, I felt that he stood with me on the volcano's rim.

"It is easy for us to ridicule others who suffer despair while we endure only mild discomfort." He seemed to speak to an invisible debater. Then he blinked as if realizing that I too sat in his presence. "Captain, our ridicule would change if we could but step inside the shoes of those whose torment we treat lightly."

Why, I yearned to ask, had he never walked inside Roger's shoes? I said instead, "I came not to ridicule, but to understand."

"Then at least in our imagination, we must step inside the other's world, walk about in it, and feel it as the other feels it. Only then will we begin to understand."

I was tempted to dismiss him as a hypocrite. Then I thought that far from holding some to a different standard from his own, he was captured by a shining ideal to which he could not fully measure up. Curious to gain his explanation of the fierce theological and political battles now raging within Massachusetts, I probed further. "Reverend, do you wear the shoes of the covenant of grace or of the covenant of works?" I, however, did not add that some in Massachusetts had charged him with knowingly wearing one shoe of grace and the other of works.

I had private reasons for asking my question, for I had learned that Governor Winthrop wished the synod of clergymen to assemble to interrogate Cotton himself. So consumed had Winthrop become with Hutchinson's teachings throughout Boston that he would not let his friendship with Cotton stand between him and his move to seal her mouth.

Cotton had already grown cautious with his answers among the ordained brethren. It was as if Winthrop, Dudley, and Endecott had placed many devious feet within the colony, each designed to trip Cotton, Hutchinson, Wheelwright, or anyone else showing signs of hidden Antinomian doctrines.

In answering my question regarding the covenant of works versus the covenant of grace, Cotton weaved and circled like a rabbit chased by a fox. I, nevertheless, could not catch the rabbit. Remembering the request of my friend Roger, I asked bluntly, "Reverend Cotton, has Mrs. Hutchinson sipped the wine of Antinomianism?"

"No! In this fierce controversy, each side takes the other's doctrine in hand as if it were a piece of fruit and squeezes it until it yields more than the sweetness of the juice."

"I do not follow you."

He pointed to a bowl of grapes on a nearby table. "If we squeeze them to a certain point, they yield sweet juice, which in time may ferment to wine. If we know not when to stop, we take the seeds also, grind them up, and throw them into the whole, thus making bitter the fruit of the vine. Each side insists on dumping seeds into the other's doctrine, thus producing what was never intended. When Mrs. Hutchinson speaks of divine grace working in us, she speaks in rhapsody and glowing terms. Like all Protestants, she proclaims the gift of the Holy Spirit in our hearts as nothing less than a gift. It is the nature of a gift that we receive it from another, is it not?"

"Aye, Reverend. I cannot give myself a gift except in the weak sense of the word."

"So Mrs. Hutchinson properly teaches. Some, however, have twisted her words to imply that there is only the Holy Spirit giving the gift with no human heart actively receiving it."

"Ah, I see. It is a matter of emphasis then. She emphasizes the *giving.*"

"Precisely. The others have emphasized the *receiving.*"

"In the current controversy, have they been falsely accused of embracing the covenant of works?"

"They have."

"Has Mrs. Hutchinson herself made this false accusation?"

"This is the point of contention." He shifted in his chair and then walked over to pluck a grape from the bowl. He stared at the grape and rolled it between his fingers. "Captain Firebrook, I fear that the court will step into the controversy. Who can tell what the . . . ?"

I had the strange, almost peculiar feeling that Cotton suddenly realized that if he should continue his thoughts along this path, he would end up in the camp of Roger Williams, who had long contended the court possessed no jurisdiction in theological matters.

Cotton's face turned ashen. The grape fell to the floor. When he saw that I had observed his strange countenance, the red returned to his face with an abrupt flush.

I pretended to ignore the redness. "Reverend Cotton, do the Massachusetts clergy preach, as some have charged, a covenant of works?"

He stooped to pick up the grape. Before his hand touched it, though, a thought seemed to streak through his mind. He froze, bent over. Then he stood up straight, leaving the grape on the floor. A frown came over his face like a dark cloud, and he turned his eyes on me. For a moment, I thought he did not recognize me.

Then he smiled a faint, almost painful smile. His eyes burning with sincerity told a story of their own that had not yet passed through mortal lips. "Captain." His voice rumbled like violent movements deep in the volcano. He stopped himself, cleared his throat, smiled affably, and then sat down. He spoke almost in a whisper as if to tell a secret. "Captain, no clergyman known to me in all New England *lives* by the covenant of works. None believes that he earns justification before God by working or doing good deeds. Yet perhaps Mrs. Hutchinson is correct to contend that some unwittingly *preach* the covenant of works in their zeal to promote righteous works in the community."

Aware of the soul-torture many professing Christians suffered, desperate to know with certainty whether they were elected for heaven or for hell, I leaned forward. "Reverend Cotton, please, I beg you to give a forthright answer. Does not the violent controversy among us spring from a deep source of pain and anguish? Of utter terror! Have we Puritans no right to some clear *evidence* of our having received the gift of eternal justification before God?"

He clamped the arms of his chair. The muscles in his jaws tightened and his fingers turned white. "Captain Firebrook, you do not know the depth of terror some of my people suffer. Yes, they have a desperate craving for such evidence."

"If this is truly so, then pray tell what counts as evidence? If you cannot give the people the answer, will some not go mad? Will they not wander forever in the wilderness of doubt, possessing neither compass nor North Star to guide them?"

My frustration increased as I watched Cotton again stroke his chin. What could be turning inside his mind? Might he too suffer secret anguish? I longed to ask, *How do you, the esteemed Puritan preacher, know with absolute certainty that you have the gift of salvation and are no longer under the curse of eternal damnation?* Did he give credence to some inner feeling, a stirring of the heart, or a holy passion as the sure sign of his election to salvation; or did he regard his good and righteous works not as stepping-stones to salvation, but as *signs* that God had bestowed salvation on him? Though I asked none of these questions, neither did I hear Cotton answer the question regarding those going mad in the wilderness of doubt.

Somewhat to my surprise, I heard a question spring from my lips as if it were a gift from another: "May I assume that good works are the *fruit* of justification?"

"Precisely. Fruit or results, but never the roots."

I struggled to control my fervor. "But Reverend, I have heard Mrs. Hutchinson contend that even the hypocrite can so readily perform such outwardly good works that his neighbors will mistakenly believe him to be among the saved, the justified. I have a twin question to this. Can a person . . . ? No, that is not the way I wish to pose it."

He interrupted. "I think I know your question. No saner one could be asked. You are thinking that if good works can mislead a *neighbor* to think that, say, Mr. Jones possesses true salvation, then can the same good works mislead *Mr. Jones himself* to think he possesses salvation?"

"Aye, it seems that all Boston screams with this and its sister questions."

Cotton grimaced, and he kept talking as if to himself, "*How much* evidence is sufficient? The stakes . . . the stakes, so high."

I ventured to say, "I hear angry controversy regarding who truly possesses the Holy Ghost as evidence or witness. Some charge that their enemies cannot distinguish the Holy Ghost in the heart from either the soul's private palpitations or strange surges in the veins."

"These controversies grieve me. I do not know an easy answer for discerning whether certain inner palpitations of the soul come from God's spirit. Still without the inner witness of God's spirit in the heart, good works become only a religion dead and sterile. When we have totaled all the good we have done and subtracted all our evil, ah, is that not the crux? What is a passing mark when we have been graded? On this dreary path, have we not landed in the sterile lap of the papists, who like morbid bookkeepers of the soul keep bleak records of good deeds, thoughts, gold pieces, earnest intentions, penances, prayers, confessions, knee bends, rosaries? Ah, Captain, what a sorry state it is when religion becomes bookkeeping rather than the spirit dancing."

I shivered, for I saw genuine anguish break out in little red splotches on the minister's face. His lips quivered, and it became clear that some secret horror had surfaced from the depths. A twisted grin curled up on one side of his mouth. "Captain, add up all the month's good deeds, good attitudes, good this and that. And what does the bookkeeping give us at the end of each month? Behold, the evidence! Do you hear? Evidence, I say. Yes, the evidence for this month has, let us say, put our account on the side of credit. Or is it debit? Today heaven, tomorrow the eternal lava."

I sat with my mouth open and felt my own heart so strangely moved that I thought it might leap up and either cry or dance.

Then his voice lowered to an unnatural whisper. "Saved, saved for another month. Saved in January; damned in February; saved in March; damned in April. Dead in April. Hell from April through eternity. Damnable bookkeeping!"

As I listened to Cotton, I thought I heard Roger's cheerful voice singing "Amen" to heaven's grace. I saw clearly why Anne Hutchinson's homilies on heaven's free grace had attracted a multitude. She had boldly renounced the religion of bookkeeping. She had proclaimed that the assured knowledge of justification did not rest on a lawyer's tally of righteous deeds and noble thoughts.

Without thinking, I blurted out, "It was from you, Reverend Cotton, that Anne Hutchinson first learned to deny that our sanctification is a grim bookkeeping of good deeds over bad deeds to prove we have received justification and will enter heaven's bliss! Through your preaching, she first saw clearly that we do good deeds not to earn penance points, but to celebrate two wondrous gifts: life itself and saving grace."

He stared as if thoughts from some distant character of his mind had wandered across the stage.

Soon thereafter I shook his hand and returned to my quarters, realizing that my search had only begun. What solid *evidence* had we earnest Puritans that we belong each to the company of the elect? What unshakable *evidence* had we that we numbered among the justified rather than among the eternally damned? Had Anne Hutchinson courageously sailed beyond Cotton's limits to explore uncharted waters in quest of the answer?

Barnabas greeted me cheerfully at the old Blackstone house in Boston. William and Ruth Blackstone had moved to their new dwelling north of Providence. Barnabas and Lydia had been appointed to repair and sell the Boston house. In her melodious way, Lydia offered to cook a meal for me that would make the French envious. I accepted the gift and called it a touch of grace for the day. After the meal, I sat down and wrote a long letter to my friends in Providence, for I had much to report regarding the politics in the Hutchinson stew over the Boston flame.

PROVIDENCE

Late September 1637

Roger threw his hat in the air, caught it, and opened his arms wide. "Is this Captain Firebrook or a fire brook of the mind, a false creation proceeding from a heat-oppressed brain?"

"It is a portion of me, I think."

He gave me a brotherly embrace that shook my bones. "'Tis the portion we like best. Come, surprise Mary."

"I look like a haggard specter. With this traveling dust on my face, she will think my ghost has preceded me."

As soon as Mary shouted my name, Little Mary leaped into my arms and touched my face with her small fingers.

Roger stroked her hair. "Touch his nose, child. Then tell us if it is really our friend who has come to see us."

"You must stay with us many weeks," Mary said. "How many times have we watched the geese fly north and south since we last saw you?"

Roger picked up Freeborn, pronounced her name with moving ceremony, and placed her in my other arm. The pride on the parents' faces was equaled only by that on the face of Freeborn's older sister.

Little Mary jumped down and, with a look of excitement, pulled at my coat pocket. "Mama says I am sister's in-ter-pre-ter. I teach her Eng-lish." She held up four fingers. "I'm this many, so I am her big sister." Having established her position in the family, Little Mary dashed away to play with children who were happily chasing a brown and white pup, a new member of the community.

I held Freeborn for several minutes while she climbed over my shoulder like an inquisitive raccoon. In a letter, Roger had described how the Narraganset children bonded so closely with many adults that they rarely knew the conflict Europeans suffered when generations turned on one another.

At Mary's suggestion, Roger guided me to the flowing brook, which we followed lazily into the lush woods. While he stood guard, I washed both skin and clothes in the cold, clear water.

"How fare Lydia and Barnabas?" he asked and reminded me of the feast in Plymouth where Winthrop Jr., Barnabas, and Lydia met the Wampanoag Chieftain Massasoit.

"Barnabas only recently finished another visit to the stocks and jail," I answered. "But you know as well as I that he is no thief and has no malicious need to hurt others."

"For what supposed crime then?"

"'Tis not easy to explain. At a meeting, Governor Winthrop expounded on the Law of Moses, whereupon Barnabas interrupted to inquire whether the good governor had recently suspended the commandment prohibiting false witness against neighbors. The governor answered him with a note of scorn, but persistent Barnabas proclaimed for all to hear that the governor himself had born false witness against Mrs. Hutchinson."

"Did the governor deny Barnabas's charge?"

"In a most eloquent way and with even more scorn and contempt. Still Barnabas demanded to know: 'Governor, did you or did you not charge that Mrs. Hutchinson was a lawless libertine who wished to abandon the Christian faith in the service of impulse, mammon, and cravings of the flesh?'"

Giving Roger time to think about Barnabas, I sloshed my clothes in the water, wrung them out, and pulled the towel from the limb I had hung it on. The sun's rays felt good on my back and legs as I dried them.

"Did Winthrop in truth level the charge of lawless libertine against Anne Hutchinson?"

"That and more." I put on the clean clothes I had brought.

"Then Barnabas was right to challenge him on his own territory." Roger seemed pleased that Barnabas had not played the coward. "A magistrate who uses his position to stain the character of a private citizen deserves stern rebuke."

I stood with my back straight, proud of my friendship with Barnabas.

Roger made a clucking noise that reminded me of Milton when he gave himself to new thoughts. "Barnabas has a keen nose for irony," he said.

As we began walking toward the house, I noticed that he seemed downcast. "You have the countenance of brooding King Saul. I fear I lack David's skill at music to lighten your mood."

"Winthrop puzzles me. Does he not see the price he pays to control others?"

I shook my head as we entered the house. "Winthrop pays the price out of the purse of others. Recently Boston's majority turned against him."

Both Roger and Mary stared at me, not in disbelief, but in apparent hope. I could read in their eyes the question, *Is it possible that Boston's tide has begun to turn in favor of liberty of conscience?*

"Roger," I warned, "Boston is at the mercy of the towns that surround her."

"Winthrop knows this, does he not?" He pushed the unruly lock of hair from his forehead.

"Aye, Winthrop has recently learned the art of pitting the other towns against Boston."

Mary looked up from her sewing again. "Why did the people of Boston turn cold toward him?"

"They think he sees himself as the New World Moses making his own laws atop the Mount Sinai of his own mind. Above all they resent his Alien Act."

Roger took Freeborn in his arms and tossed her up. She squealed and then begged to be tossed again.

Mary served us a delectable broth seasoned with peppers. "Before sailing for England, Henry Vane wrote us of the Alien Act and bemoaned the conniving behind it. Pastors Wilson and Stone later gave us their version of the act when they visited us en route from Connecticut to the synod. Yet no one has given us the story behind the public story."

Freeborn reached for me. I put down my cup and took her while explaining that Winthrop had crossed swords with William Hutchinson over the Alien Act.

Roger stirred more pepper into his broth. "I hear that William is a man of mild manner and a merchant of special talent."

"Aye. But Winthrop primed the ire in William, who lashed back and publicly denounced the Alien Act."

Mary raised her forefinger like a lawyer. "On legal grounds?"

"No, William charged that the Massachusetts magistrates deliberately designed it to prevent his own relatives and friends from living in the colony."

Roger frowned. "John Wilson told us nothing about that."

Fire burned in Mary's eyes. "Wilson was too gleeful. For him, the Alien Act is a cannon aimed directly at the people whom Winthrop and the synod of clergy tag as heretics. The Act is in effect a painted sign that reads, 'Keep away, all ye who cannot agree with Pope Winthrop and his self-appointed cardinals.'"

Roger seemed unable to rest until he had explored further intrigue behind the Alien Act. I could see in his face the probing of a mind that had spent years with Sir Edward Coke and English law. He had no need to tell me that his mind begged to plunge below the surface.

I informed him that a number of William and Anne's relatives arrived from England during the summer. "But with the support of the clergy and the magistrates, Winthrop schemed to suspend a sword over their heads. He informed them that Massachusetts would place them on trial within four months to determine whether to ship them back to England. The standard to determine who passes and who fails the test is agreement with their theology."

Roger and Mary looked at one another with pain in their eyes. She shivered. "What sorrow they must feel. I remember those days aboard ship and how we dreamed of new life in a new land. To turn around and leave . . . ."

He turned his palms up. "What will they do? Some doubtless sold their property in England and pulled up roots."

Mary took Freeborn and cuddled her close. "How sad to endure again the hardship of the ocean voyage! And the poor, dear children . . . ."

On the next day, I worked in the fields with Roger and Mary. A Narraganset native would at times wander in to give and receive advice or to bring news from Canonicus and Miantonomo.

I said to Mary as she sat down on a stump to wipe the sweat from her face, "Though this work be hard and my bones stiff, I relish the freedom here. Massachusetts made people increasingly devious. For every one missionary, there are a hundred spies. We grow long ears and divided tongues. Neighbor turns against neighbor."

She sighed. "Eric, sometimes I think envy colors half our theological battles over heresy."

When Roger and Little Mary joined us, Roger seemed preoccupied. His brow kept forming furrows like those at our feet.

I tapped his brow with my finger. "What grows in that garden?" From the corner of my eye I saw a neighbor holding Freeborn on her hip. Mary had told me that the women often exchanged child-tending with one another.

Roger gazed at the sky. "The Reverends Wilson and Stone will arrive before sunset."

Mary looked at me. "You know the Reverend Samuel Stone of Newtown, do you not?"

"Yes. I have observed him more than once knitting an alliance between himself and Winthrop. Friends, I can go hunting in the forest if you need my absence."

"No, Eric, your presence we need," Roger said.

Mary paused. "Yet we do not wish to jeopardize your connections with the Massachusetts leaders. You must live in the colony. To be under a cloud of suspicion would . . . ."

I said to both, "If my presence can assist you, then that is sufficient. Worry not about my status in Boston. Of late I have given some thought to following Blackstone to live near Providence."

Mary clapped her hands. "Oh, Eric, how happy it would make us!"

He rubbed his hands together as if he had already begun to make plans for us.

"Massachusetts has become too unpredictable," I explained. "I dislike the ease with which new heretics are invented from the air. If Separatists were cast out on one day and suspected Antinomians on another—"

Roger could not suppress his passionate thoughts. "'Tis ironic! Winthrop has become more separatist than all the Separatists combined. He would cut off Baptists, Catholics, Jews, Arminians, Lutherans . . . . And tomorrow, who knows? What has happened to our dear friend? Is he the Winthrop we knew in England?"

"I am staunch Church of England with abiding Puritan conviction," I said. "But this practice of carving off other Christians as rotten limbs will kill the tree. I fear already that the party of Endecott, Dudley, and Winthrop has cut at the root of my faith. My secure citadel of neutrality in Massachusetts has of late shrunk drastically."

On the next day, John Winthrop Jr. and the plain-spoken military Captain John Stoughton arrived in good spirits from Connecticut to meet with Roger and the Reverend Stone from Massachusetts. Stoughton quickly stiffened, however, when he saw that the Reverend Wilson had accompanied Stone. If Miantonomo and the lesser sachems among the Narragansets had not arrived then, the sparks between the unyielding Wilson and the flint-hard Stoughton might have sparked unbearable heat.

Mary and her neighbors Jane Verin and Ruth Blackstone had spent the day before preparing for a celebration since the great Wampanoag sachem could have no meeting without a festival. Roger had helped Angell set out long tables behind the house.

For several hours, we talked at length about the remnant of the Pequots, who had scattered into every portion of Connecticut to harass some Narragansets who journeyed through Wampanoag and Connecticut territory. So long as outspoken Stoughton and immovable Wilson kept their focus on their common enemy the Pequots, they gave the appearance of tolerance toward one another.

"These Pequots," Stoughton said, "are like English highwaymen who strike as if from nowhere to rob and pillage whoever happens across their path."

Miantonomo and Stoughton disclosed a plan by which to appoint small bands of the English and Narragansets to search out the Pequot brigands roaming the forests.

Massasoit listened with such intensity that Roger eventually turned to him. "I think you have reservations regarding English and Narraganset bands entering Wampanoag territory in search of Pequots."

"My people cannot permit others to do their own work."

After listening to Massasoit's explanation, Roger said, "Your warriors know best how to patrol your territory. If they can meet upon occasion to exchange information with the Narraganset and English warriors, your mutual cause against the Pequots may be better served."

To this suggestion, Massasoit, Miantonomo, and Captain Stoughton fully agreed.

Roger, however, pressed the matter further. "Without detailed plans, nodding heads and shaking hands do not make a contract."

Later in the day after we had delighted Massasoit with an extended celebration, John Winthrop Jr. took me outside. "Eric, we must knit an even closer friendship with Roger. Though the Massachusetts Court has banished him, we need him now more than ever. If he cannot come to Massachusetts, then Massachusetts will run to him more and more."

I could not help adding, "As will Connecticut."

Winthrop Jr. understood my implication. The new governor of Connecticut was John Haynes, the very man who had led the wolf pack almost two years earlier in banishing Roger.

"Where is Governor Haynes?" I asked. "Why is he not here?"

Winthrop Jr. rubbed the back of his neck and pulled at his ear. "Governor Haynes is a man of extraordinary pride."

I asked no more about the matter, but Winthrop Jr. had apparently drawn me aside for a purpose.

A feeble smile formed on his lips. It had the touch of ambivalence. "Haynes has sent me in his place. Today, I am John the Baptist to Haynes on this mission. My task is to make straight the path between Providence and Hartford."

I laughed to cover my skepticism. "Do you have a plan for creating this friendship? Will Haynes's pride permit him to give way to practical matters?"

Winthrop Jr. pursed his lips and paused a good while. "I think, yes, yes, it would be wise to arrange a meeting between John Haynes and Roger Williams."

"Aye, and let them dine together?" I asked somewhat cynically.

Winthrop Jr. smiled. "I am sure Mary will be glad to boil a humble pudding and watch Haynes eat the whole of it."

"Roger has certainly been forced to eat more humble pudding than has any of us."

When Winthrop Jr. and I returned to the others in the parlor, the Wampanoag Chief Massasoit and his entourage pronounced the meeting a success and left in their boats to cross the river.

The Narraganset Miantonomo rose shortly thereafter to tell the younger Winthrop that he would meet with Winthrop the older in November. Then, with the other Narraganset leaders, Miantonomo left the house. Roger and I accompanied them to the bubbling brook. The natives crossed the brook, and we stood watching them vanish into the forest.

When we returned to the house, Mary showed Roger the basket that Miantonomo's wife had woven for Little Mary.

The heat of conversation rose abruptly. Forthright Captain Stoughton demanded that the Reverend Wilson explain why the synod of clergymen had recently forbidden church members to question them in such a way as to cast serious doubt on the doctrines they delivered in their sermons. "You want parrots repeating your words, not people with brains and hearts of their own."

Evidently thinking he might intervene and prevent the sparks between tactless Stoughton and intransigent Wilson from bursting into unquenchable flame, the Reverend Stone folded his smooth hands and spoke slowly. "You must understand, Captain Stoughton. Our decision did not come at the snap of a finger."

The Reverend Wilson nodded his agreement and tapped his palm impatiently on the table. "Three weeks, three exhausting weeks of debate. Captain Belshazzar, do not therefore pretend that our decision came out of passion and not thought."

"I do not doubt that it came by thought." Stoughton growled through clenched teeth. "Thought indeed, for advancing your positions of authority and control!"

The Reverend Wilson opened his mouth and pointed his finger at Captain Stoughton, but Mary interrupted. "Is it true that the synod's prohibition was a pair of scissors to cut Anne Hutchinson from the community?"

Neither clergyman replied. It was as if, having eaten Mary's food, they had consigned her to another room.

Roger, however, repeated her question and added softly, "Who among the brethren in Massachusetts spread the story that Anne Hutchinson secretly scorned her family ties?"

The Reverends Wilson and Stone looked at one another and then glanced simultaneously at Winthrop Jr.

Roger frowned and seemed puzzled. "John, my friend, I cannot believe such words came from your lips."

John Winthrop Jr. stared at his hands folded on the table. "From my father's, not mine."

"Then your father lied." Stoughton's roar sounded as if he were drawing blood on the battlefield.

Tapping the table now with a faster rhythm, the Reverend Wilson conspicuously attempted to make his voice soft like Roger's. "There are natural duties that belong to the weaker sex. The Hutchinson woman has usurped the role of the pastors and teachers in the churches."

Mary rolled her eyes upward and to the left. "So an army of the clergy unites to stop the mouth of the lion Hutchinson? Such a fierce lion in this den of Daniels!"

Though his eyes turned abruptly cold and hard, the smooth-mannered Reverend Stone sweetly quoted from Scripture: "And if the wives desire to learn anything, let them ask their husbands at home: for it is a disgrace for a woman to speak in the church."

Wilson nodded vigorous consent and spoke with a caustic tongue that cut like a sword. "Anne Hutchinson upends this text of Scripture and says to her husband, *William, if you will learn anything, ask your wife at home.*"

I knew Stone firmly believed that a woman should hold no position of public influence. For him, the word *Eve* meant chaos, and every woman was Eve.

Silver-tongued Stone turned to Winthrop Jr. "I know your father well, and I thank God each day for his faithfulness to the Word. Unlike some in this new land, we of Massachusetts are a colony established to be a holy witness to our Reformation faith. We are not a hotchpotch of rabble."

I glanced at Roger, who although doubtless feeling the piercing of Stone's intended arrow, held his tongue.

Unvarnished Stoughton shook his finger at Stone. "When will you Spaniards bring your victim to the inquisitor's trial?"

Stone turned crimson, and the veins of his neck stood out like ropes.

Wilson cut in. "Your words inflame; but if you mean the trial of the Antinomian heretic Hutchinson, it comes in November."

"The seventh of November." Stone's silvery voice shook. "Between now and then, may God give her the grace and light to see the error of her ways."

In a letter, I had already informed Roger of Winthrop Sr.'s attempt to manipulate the composition of court that would pass judgment on Anne Hutchinson at her forthcoming trial. Winthrop had convinced the magistrates to accept his ruling that no one could serve on the court if deemed unfit.

Quickly seeing through the ploy, Roger had written to me. "By *unfit* the governor means anyone who will not agree to condemn Anne Hutchinson." For the sake of John Winthrop Jr., Roger now guided the conversation toward a more pleasing topic. "John, if we can keep the peace with the Dutch, then Connecticut and points southeast of here might eventually establish shipping docks."

In Boston I had learned that the court planned to dismiss as *unfit* the two Boston representatives: William Aspinwall and John Coggeshall. Winthrop and his colleagues had hoped that dismissing them only a few days before Hutchinson's trial would give her supporters little time to recoup. Once again Winthrop Sr. had demonstrated that Machiavelli might have learned new sly tactics by sitting at his feet. With much reluctance, I admitted privately that Winthrop Sr. had somehow changed. Granted, we had all changed since departing England. Winthrop's transformation, on the other hand, had made us ask, "Where is the man who once composed the wondrous sermon 'A Model of Christian Charity'?" Roger grieved more than us all that the Winthrop we once admired had been replaced by another who radiated more threats than charity.

At her table later in the day, Mary looked the Reverend John Wilson in the eye. "How goes your friendship with the Reverend Cotton?" She knew full well that an uneasy rivalry between them had swelled. Whereas Cotton had tended toward leniency with Anne Hutchinson, Wilson and Stone, along with other clergymen from surrounding towns, combed through Cotton's sermons and lectures to discover whether he had any doctrinal affinity with either Hutchinson or Antinomianism.

Mary waited for Wilson's answer, and I think she relished his squirming.

Wilson cleared his throat twice. Before he could answer, however, Stone said, "In the end, Master Cotton will stand firmly with us."

She looked at me as if to remind me of Barnabas's judgment that Anne Hutchinson had found favor in Cotton's eyes only because she had pronounced him the greatest preacher in England and New England.

All at once, Stone said to Winthrop Jr., "Your father is the wisest man among us. No one understands better than he that to accomplish our holy mission, we must have control of both church and state."

She looked him in the eye. "Is liberty of conscience reduced to agreeing with men like yourselves, men who invent their own version of Old England's infamous Star Chamber?"

Stone ignored her, but Roger repeated her question.

"Liberty of conscience?" Stone answered sternly. "There is no true conscience save in God and God's Law. Liberty and error have no bond between them. No offspring of Adam is freeborn. We have only freedom from error and freedom to embrace the true gospel. Error and false doctrine have no freedom. If you are not with us in the true gospel, your heart is false, thus leaving you no right to liberty."

Roger looked at Mary, who was gently stroking Freeborn's head. I surmised that Mary's compassionate heart had gone out to Anne Hutchinson. He walked to Mary, lifted Freeborn up, and took her outside. I followed and breathed in the free air of Providence.

"Eric, when I listened to these men of the cloth utter tyranny, my heart saddened. I, therefore, renew my vow to heaven! Freeborn, Anne Hutchinson's grandchild, and all other children born in this New World will enjoy a heritage of liberty of conscience."

STUDY HILL AND PROVIDENCE

November 1637

With the help of two Narragansets, Roger and Angell floated a barge south on the channel that led from Providence to Narraganset Bay. Though the wind was cold, Roger felt pleased that it was November rather than January. He would never forget those bitter, lonely January nights of his banishment in which he had felt suspended between life and death.

Though William Blackstone had wanted to travel with them by barge, Roger had persuaded him to wait patiently. The return trip would be difficult, and Blackstone lacked the required strength of arms and shoulders.

After entering the bay, Roger and Angell guided the barge to the north point of the island Chibachuwese to await the ship that would bring Barnabas, who had sold Blackstone's Boston house. As long as the wind was high, Roger dared not take the barge farther into the bay. To capsize in such cold, winter water would be to flirt with death.

"Patience, Angell! The ship from Boston will arrive soon."

"Do we have room for three horses?"

"And more." He smiled grimly, thinking that had Noah embarked on such a vessel, he would never have endured the forty days.

Angell sighed. "We have caught the wind napping."

Roger saw the sails in the distance and felt his skin tingle. "She rounds the island, Angell. The landing will be to our right." He pointed. "Barnabas will unload the horses there, and we will move in after the ship leaves. It is the only port I will trust with this barge."

Slowly the ship cut her way through the waves. Roger could hear the sails popping. The wind roused itself unexpectedly. When a hand went up on the ship's deck, Roger and Angell waved back, patiently waiting until the big ship veered toward the makeshift harbor the men from Providence had built during the summer.

As the snow continued to fall, a shallop lowered slowly down the ship's starboard. Roger recognized Captain Melbourne sitting in it.

"Ahoy!" the captain called to Roger, who watched the oarsmen move their arms backward and forward in the rhythmic movements that guided the shallop to the barge.

He smiled broadly. "Captain Melbourne, I take pleasure in seeing you again."

"The pleasure is mine, sir. Would that I could join you, for we would have much to discuss. But we were late in leaving Boston, and I must arrive in New Amsterdam by two of the clock. Our mutual friend Captain Firebrook sends his greetings."

"Ah, he was here two months past."

"All goes well with him, but he sends this message. He will arrive from Boston two days hence."

"On the twelfth, Captain?"

"Aye, at this hour if all goes well."

He could not rid himself of the feeling that the captain had some other reason for speaking with him, for Barnabas could have delivered the message.

The captain ordered the oarsmen to help him onto the barge. As soon as the captain set foot on it, Roger took him to the farther end and waited. The captain lowered his deep, husky voice. "I count you as a noble and good friend. For that reason, I would counsel you to beware the powers that rule the colony north of you."

"I will not venture to return, for I have been banished."

"I will say this, sir. Some among the magistrates would cut you off. Though you have mediated between them and the natives, they still harbor deep resentment against you. The tumult over the Hutchinson woman has revived the talk about you."

"What warning signs ought I to heed?"

"Beware those from the colony who would buy the natives' land through you. Though they smile, their teeth are iron."

"You have proven to be a friend more than once, Captain Melbourne." He did not disclose that he had recently prevailed upon Canonicus and Miantonomo to sell to Winthrop and himself land from the very island on which he had tied his barge today. He shook Captain Melbourne's hand. "Your friendship I treasure."

The captain stepped back into his shallop. "Ah, I hear our physician friend Dr. John Clarke recently arrived from England. When you see him, pay him my respect. Goodbye, Master Williams. Would to heaven that this land had a hundred more of your mettle."

Across the way, Roger watched as Barnabas and some of the crew unloaded the three horses and the chests that belonged to Blackstone. The sails soon rotated, catching the wind as the men heaved and pulled anchor. Roger stood, watching the mighty ship and Captain Melbourne head south toward Block Island.

As the ship's white sails shrank in the gray horizon, he let himself think of the captain's warning. Then he remembered that Jeremiah had once written to him of Winthrop's contention that Miantonomo had given Block Island to the governor and the magistrates of Massachusetts.

While Barnabas steadied the horses, Roger and Angell guided the barge into the snow-covered harbor. "Tie it well, Angell. The waves drive harder now."

Roger and Barnabas at last greeted one another with a vigorous handshake and cheerful words. Then Roger brushed the snow from the wooden chests. "Angell and I have brought the barge to carry these and the horses back to Providence."

"Has Master Blackstone arrived?" Barnabas asked.

Roger smiled. "Both he and Mrs. Blackstone. Your Lydia sends her love and eagerly awaits your appearance."

Barnabas winked. "Sometimes the appearance 'tis better than the man."

"I think your Lydia loves both equally."

"Brother Roger," said Angell, "these chests—"

Barnabas cut in. "They contain Mrs. Blackstone's possessions and still more of their books."

Roger rested his elbows on his knees, studied the choppy waves, and shook his head. "We brought this barge to carry the horses, but I now think the horses must carry it."

Angell and Barnabas glanced at one another with a puzzled expression.

"'Tis not safe," Roger explained. "I fear these possessions and ourselves might find our way to the bottom of this bay if we . . . . No, we must not tempt God with foolish risks."

Angell shook his head. "But though these horses be strong, they cannot pull this vessel."

"We built the barge. We can unbuild it."

Barnabas and Angell again frowned and squinted their eyes.

"If we make three sledges of the boat, each horse can pull one," Roger explained.

Barnabas removed his fur cap and scratched his head. "In this snow . . . aye, I see."

Angell began at once to dismantle the vessel carefully. Barnabas gave assistance, and soon the three men had turned the barge into three rough-hewn sledges.

Roger motioned with his head to urge Angell to help him with the largest chest. "These runners will serve the purpose over this snow."

The strong horses seemed to understand their duty and made their way across the narrow, precarious ribbon of land that connected the island to the mainland. Once across they headed north toward Providence. Angell led the way with the black stallion. Roger brought up the rear. They traveled steadily until Angell turned around and called back to Master Williams, "Providence is nowhere in sight. But I know this point. If you and Barnabas leave now on this stallion, you can make it home before dark. I can stay here for the night to guard these treasures."

"No, you take Barnabas and the horses. Tell Mary and the Blackstones that I will camp here for the night. Return with the horses at sunrise, and we will deliver these chests in good form."

"I'll stand guard with you," Barnabas insisted. "You'll need help keeping the fire alive through the night."

Angell rode off alone with the horses while Roger and Barnabas gathered wood and built a fire. Then they unloaded the sledges and turned two of them up on their sides to make a barrier against the cold wind. The third would serve as a floor on which to sleep.

As night came, Roger and Barnabas built two more fires and lay between them, using the upturned sledges to shield them from the wind. Throughout much of the night, he listened carefully as Barnabas related in rich detail the events of Anne Hutchinson's trial. The fires roared, the coals burned and glowed red, and Barnabas related not only the account, but also the interpretations that he had gleaned from the citizens of Boston and Newtown.

After talking himself almost hoarse, Barnabas fell asleep on the wooden sledge before dawn.

For Roger, however, neither sleep nor peace of mind came. The more he thought of Anne Hutchinson and her family, the more the fire inside him roared with an intensity that would not have let him sleep had he reclined on the finest down in England. He prayed that his anger would not embitter him. He prayed even more for the Hutchinson family, Wheelwright, Coggeshall, Aspinwall, and all the others caught in the web of intrigue and intimidation. For Winthrop and Cotton, he did not want to pray, but he knew he ought.

He mentally composed a long letter to William and Anne Hutchinson, inviting them again to join him. He imagined sending them a promise that he would speak on their behalf to Canonicus and Miantonomo. He regretted having bought land for the wily Winthrop. If only William and Anne could find a safe harbor where they could earn their living, practice their religion, and speak their interpretations freely to those who chose to listen. On and on, his thoughts spun until the sun rose and Angell eventually appeared with food and well-fed horses.

When at last the three men and the three horses arrived at Roger's house, Lydia rushed out and, slipping in the snow, fell into the arms of her Barnabas.

Always practical and planning ahead, Mary set Roger and Barnabas down at the table and made each of them swallow a bowl of her hot pork stew seasoned with peppers and cabbage. With Ruth Blackstone's assistance, she warmed bricks in the fireplace, wrapped them in towels, and placed them under the feet of the two men who had spent the night under the celestial canopy. They lavishly praised Angell and fed him this and that delectable hot food until he could do little more than lean back and smile contentedly.

William Blackstone sat near the window and quietly read Arminius's *Disputationes publicae* until Roger and Barnabas had devoured enough food for the twelve disciples. Freeborn sat on Barnabas's knee while he told stories. Little Mary and Mrs. Blackstone had soon grown so fond of one another that they became fellow workers at the kitchen hearth, cooking bannock, a native bread of corn meal mixed with water and spread an inch thick on a small board at an incline before the fire. At the same time, they made drop cakes with rye meal, eggs, and milk to supplement the hasty pudding, boiled fish, stewed beans, and cheese.

Mary sat near the window and mended clothing while her husband and Blackstone mended the fishing nets Roger and Angell had washed a week earlier. At the nets, Roger and Blackstone talked about the book by Arminius that Blackstone had almost finished reading.

As Freeborn fell asleep in Barnabas's arms, Mary asked him to tell all he knew about the scoundrel Benjamin Cook, who had moved from Salem to Boston.

Barnabas gently patted Freeborn on her back as he talked. "After Endecott and Cook connived to do Master Williams harm, they in time turned on one another, two serpents baring their fangs and hissing until one crawled away. Cook crawled to Boston to join the other den of vipers, but soon Governor Winthrop found him out and would have no more to do with him."

Ruth Blackstone turned around from the hearth. "Found him out?"

"Cook proved to be a thief. But being a better liar than a thief, he escaped punishment. Still there's one punishment that he'll not escape if Winthrop has his way."

Mary kept knitting. "Give us the whole account, Barnabas."

"It happened on the day after the Lord Brethren passed unyielding judgment upon Mrs. Hutchinson. I'd gone to the governor's office to receive the final seal upon the sale of Master Blackstone's house. The governor paid me a reasonable amount for the use of my brawn to carry a chest from his house to his carriage. We had walked scarcely thirty feet from his house when a woman ran up to him and bowed to her knees. I recognized this woman of misfortune to be Benjamin Cook's wife. I'll tell you plainly what these eyes saw and ears heard: 'I beg of you, kind Governor,' she cried out through her tears, 'spare my dear husband's life.'

"'I cannot. He has broken the Seventh Commandment,' our St. Winthrop said and stepped around her.

"But she caught him by the boot and entreated, 'Did not Christ pardon the woman, and did he not bid her go her way forgiven?'"

"'I am not Christ,' Winthrop confessed. 'Christ was free to suspend the Law; but as his appointed magistrate, I am bound to carry out the Law.'"

"The shivering Mrs. Cook pleaded with such agony in her voice that even the rock that passes as a heart in the governor's breast should have softened. But he set his face against her harder than cruel Goneril's icy glare at her father.

"The dear woman then turned her soft, sheepish eyes on me, moving me to ask him, 'Merciful Governor, does not the Gospel of Matthew itself permit divorce on the ground of adultery?'"

"'It does, indeed,' our governor replied."

"'Then does it perhaps follow that under grace, the Seventh Commandment can in some cases forego punishing by death?' I asked."

"'How so?' our King Arthur responded, peering down at the woman kneeling in the snow."

"'Why, 'tis plain and clear,' I answered. 'If the adulterous husband is put to death, the wife could not sue for divorce as the gospel permits.'"

"'Yes, yes!' Mrs. Cook cried out."

"The governor glared at me as if *I* had committed a crime. But feeling strong in my argument, I pressed the point. 'Do you not see that the woman is free to seek a divorce from her guilty husband only if he remains alive?'"

"Winthrop grit his teeth, and I confess to some pleasure at having cracked his skull with Holy Scripture. I dared hope that through the crack, some light might shine. But when he did not deign to acknowledge the power of Scripture against his stony heart, a fierce anger welled up within me. To cool my anger, I compelled myself to look up into the gray sky, letting the cold snowflakes melt on my face."

"Is there more to this incident you have not disclosed?" William Blackstone asked Barnabas.

"I have given the substance of what I witnessed on that shameful day. I do confess that I then and there stepped to the very edge of revealing to the governor what I had observed while walking through the forest only two months earlier when the birds still sang. On a pleasant September day in the forest only four miles south and east, I had chanced upon one of his kin who, though a married man, lay with a woman not his wife. I recognized her also, not by her cooing and calf-like moaning, but by her profile. I do not believe she saw me, and I made haste to disappear quietly from their steamy meeting. On my return to your house, Master Blackstone, I remembered that our King Arthur and his Knights of the Short Table had recently proclaimed that those convicted of adultery must hang. I'd witnessed the hanging of one such married man brought before the authorities. They charged him with not only seeing another woman, whom heaven had bestowed with outrageous beauty and enticement, but also meeting her behind locked doors. The man boldly attempted to defend himself by claiming that the woman had sore need of his spiritual admonition and counsel and that together they had 'entered the closet' (quoting Scripture) for the sole purpose of ascending to heaven in spirit. To make the story short, I said nothing to the governor about seeing his kin in the throes of adultery on that September day. But on that cold November day, Winthrop grew impatient with Mrs. Cook's pleas. He lifted her to her feet and spoke words colder than the snow at our feet. I do not know what at that moment passed through his heart, but I felt terror pass through mine when I heard him say, 'Your husband has at last confessed his vile sin. God will forgive. All manner of sin, save the sin against the Holy Ghost, will be forgiven. But your husband's forgiveness gains him entrance to heaven, not exemption from execution.'"

"What did the dear woman say to him then?" Ruth Blackstone asked.

"When Mrs. Cook opened her mouth to speak, Winthrop ordered her to leave his presence lest some punishment from heaven fall upon her. But she would not leave. I loaded the chest into the carriage. Winthrop stepped inside and drove away. Even now I hear her crying for mercy."

Upon hearing this account, Blackstone asked Roger, "Had you been in Winthrop's boots, would you have hanged Benjamin Cook?"

He scratched his head. "When King David lay with Bathsheba, wife of Uriah the Hittite, the prophet denounced his sin but lifted no stone against him. Thus the prophet qualified the Law of Moses. Christ later added the quality of *mercy* to the Law."

Freeborn whimpered in her sleep, and he moved to console her, softly rubbing her back. It disturbed him to think that by hanging Benjamin Cook, the magistrates severely punished the widow and her children, leaving them to fend for themselves in the snow. He said to the others in the house, "Mrs. Cook pleaded not only for her husband, but for her children and herself."

Blackstone persisted. "But you have not stated the proper penalty that the state should set."

"Penalty? In the name of justice, will we create a widow and orphans?" Roger knew his anger showed. Still something deeper troubled him. *Why* had such anger against Winthrop boiled up so quickly in him? He tried to separate his anger over Winthrop's treatment of Anne Hutchinson from the account of Mrs. Cook's pleas. He cut his eyes toward Barnabas. "The argument from Scripture that you presented to Winthrop ...."

Barnabas shrugged. "'Twas not the Scripture lesson that Winthrop wished to hear."

All at once, Roger understood his boiling anger. He felt that for Winthrop, Scripture had become more a weapon than a wondrous garden where men and women might gather to pluck the fruit of revelation and share their interpretations. Had Winthrop in his own mind become the holy interpreter for all? Since leaving Cambridge, Roger had come increasingly to believe that God had not given Scripture to make thinking obsolete. Were there not problems for which finite mortals had no perfect answers? Did not the richness of Scripture sometimes *open new problems to explore*, thereby giving believers a larger and richer world? For men like Winthrop, did Scripture serve to shrink the world, to drain the color from human life? In the name of purification, had they cut the veins and drained the blood? To make themselves omniscient, had they reduced knowledge and learning, turning the swift river of life itself into a stagnant swamp, calling it *order*? He looked at Blackstone. "Sometimes Scripture offers no simple answer, but moves us to ask more profound questions that would not otherwise be raised. I, therefore, pose this question as equally worthy, a question that Governor Winthrop swept aside."

"I would hear it," Blackstone said.

"How can justice be two sins committed against one?" Then, raising his head, Roger quoted from Scripture, "For now we see through a glass darkly . . . And now abideth faith, hope, and love, these three: but the greatest of these is love."

PROVIDENCE AND THE
NARRAGANSET VILLAGE

February–March 1638

December and January brought more snow. February's wind hardened the snow, prompting Roger to name it "White Ice." Always in February, Mary's memories returned to England where the winters came less harshly than in New England. She thought of Polonius the cook at Masham Manor. "Ah, love, if only New Englanders had ovens, I would bake you an apple pie like the ones Polonius relished making for you. He gave me his secret recipe."

Little Mary jumped up and down. "Pudding! Mama! Make us some, please!"

"Have we sufficient sugar to carry us through the winter?" Roger asked.

"Enough for some pudding each Sabbath eve." She took the pudding from the hearth.

On the next day, the snow glittered in the sun. The blue sky glistened like a gem. Melting snow slid from the roofs and dripped from the tree limbs. Large chunks sometimes dropped with a splash into the laughing brook.

From his parlor window, Roger saw a ship's sails approach in the clear air. "I will greet the passengers at the channel, Mary." He put on his heavy coat.

Outside in the snow, he thought he heard the brook swell with laughter. Two foxes loped across the meadow as he on his mule Hugo made his way with Eusebius toward the channel.

Upon arriving at the ship, he saw three men, one of whom he recognized as William Coddington, the richest man in Massachusetts and the owner of a full brick house. Roger rode up to the men, dismounted, and welcomed them to Providence. He remembered that Coddington and he had met with Winthrop and many other Puritans at the Earl of Lincoln's Tattershall Castle on that momentous July day in 1629 when they had sketched plans for a better England. He remembered also that the king had sent Coddington along with Earl Theophilus Clinton to London Tower. Mercifully they were eventually released, thanks to the influence of friends in high places.

"We come on urgent matters," Coddington said after introducing Roger to John Coggeshall, a successful silk dealer with a silver beard that looked smooth as silk.

The third man, a prominent merchant of Boston, stepped forward, shook Roger's hand, and introduced himself as William Aspinwall. "We have heard much of your regard for religious forbearance, and we would speak with you at length if you—"

"My house is scarcely half a mile west." He pointed to invite them to be his guests. Hugo the mule stood stoically as the three men from Massachusetts tied their belongings to him. "Is it true that Boston suffers still more turmoil?" Roger asked Coddington, who looked at Coggeshall, the silk mercer.

But soft-spoken Aspinwall answered, "Sixty of us signed a petition on behalf of Anne Hutchinson and her brother-in-law John Wheelwright. Now we sixty are in the stewing pot, and the governor joined the magistrates to throw new logs onto the flames."

Coggeshall gently stroked his silky beard. "When Mr. Aspinwall asked why he was being banished, the court answered in a roundabout way that Hagar and Ishmael were banished for disturbance."

Aspinwall added, "Governor Winthrop then professed to see the devil going about to harden the hearts of brethren against him."

Roger scratched Hugo's ears. "So you have come to find a way out of the boiling pot?"

Hugo moved with disinterest as if their conversation were of no importance and their burdens scarcely a fly on his back.

A man in his early forties, Coggeshall stated their purpose crisply. "We have come to ask you to negotiate for us."

"Negotiate?"

"With the Narragansets for land," Aspinwall explained in his quiet way. "Our children and wives stand in need of refuge."

On the next day, the five Englishmen stood before Canonicus and Miantonomo in the Narraganset village. Roger's heart ached when he saw that his friend Canonicus lay ill. Out of respect for the older man, Roger would have left to talk with Miantonomo; but old Canonicus asked in a weak voice, "Would you take away medicine and herbs from an ailing man?"

Roger smiled gently. "Never."

Canonicus reached out to touch his arm. "Then do not remove your presence from me, my young friend. You are medicine to my spirit."

Sending the other men away to talk with Miantonomo, he remained at Canonicus's side. When they were alone, the old chieftain said, "Sing to me one of your English songs. A sick man might grow well with . . . with—"

"Music." He smiled, knowing that Canonicus had oft been exceedingly amused at his singing. Roger thought of the biblical passage, *A merry heart doeth good like a medicine.* He remembered the day at Masham Manor when Milton came to cheer him out of his fever and the skirmish of words Milton had exchanged with Lady Joan, whom Milton called *Dragon Joan.*

Later, while Canonicus slept soundly, Roger slipped out to talk with Miantonomo and the men from Massachusetts. Roger had explained to the Englishmen the need of bringing gifts. "It is a way of life with the Narragansets. But do not think that it is payment, for they little understand the concept. For them, all of life is payment when it brings them happiness. What you call money, they call a token of celebration. You do not have sufficient money to purchase this land. But you have good will. Mingle works of love and friendship with your good will. Bring these, and the sachems will talk freely."

Roger sat now in Miantonomo's wigwam. "What happiness can I bring to your uncle?"

"Sugar."

Roger blinked.

"Because of this endless snow, we have made no journey to Winthrop's bay to trade for sugar."

Roger made a note to himself that in his trading post, he would store more sugar. "On the morrow, I will return to my house. There is sugar for my friend Canonicus."

For the rest of the day, Miantonomo and the men from Massachusetts exchanged gifts and talked about the sale of the island called *Aquidneck* in the Narraganset Bay. Before dusk descended, Roger and Canonicus discussed the desires of the English to bring their families to Aquidneck.

"Have they no wish to live with their fellow English?" Canonicus's voice grew stronger, his strength seeming to return as he sat up to eat.

Roger broke bread with him. "Though the English have many virtues, they are sometimes flawed, like Narraganset pottery."

Canonicus chuckled. "Did not your god mold these Englishmen? What manner of potter would mold such flawed vessels?"

"You speak too much wisdom for a sick man. We must discuss this later."

Canonicus would not relent, for he relished teasing his friend. "Would your answers make me doubly ill?"

Roger shivered inside, remembering a letter Dudley had sent recently. Might Canonicus and Miantonomo one day fall victim to Roger's fellow Puritans? Dudley's letter still cut like a knife.

Dear Master Williams:

　　We the magistrates, following the example of Israel's obedient warrior Joshua, intend to make slaves of the defeated enemy. We do not lack gratitude for the assistance you gave to this colony in bringing the Narragansets to our support, but we deny your charge that slavery is a sin. Scripture plainly teaches (Genesis 9:25-26) that those who fall under the curse of Canaan shall serve their brethren. Under the permission of Scripture, the magistrates had full right to bring death to the whole people of the Pequots. We, however, have shown Christian charity, electing to enslave many rather than kill all . . . .

When Roger and the Hutchinsons' three friends returned from the Narraganset village, gentle-voiced Aspinwall said, "Mr. Coddington went to Governor Winthrop at his home to learn whether the tide against Anne Hutchinson could be turned."

The wealthy Mr. Coddington explained, "Sometimes in trading, we cut negotiations too short because we fail to hear what the other person says. I, nevertheless, had hoped Winthrop might discover a depth to Mrs. Hutchinson's teaching that he had hitherto missed."

"Winthrop can be a most gracious host at times." Roger remembered the governor's kindness when Mary and he had first arrived in Boston.

"I regret to say that my presence would have been more graciously received had I entered a den of bobcats." Coddington revealed that Governor Haynes and Winthrop came to a parting of the ways because of religious disagreement. Coddington agreed to tell the portion that still burned most vividly in his memory.

"From the very beginning of my arrival in Boston, Winthrop charged that Mrs. Hutchinson had declared herself 'at one with God's spirit.'"

"'But one in what sense?' I asked him. 'Are you and Mrs. Winthrop not joined as one? Yet I perceive that you are two. If a man commits murder, we hang him. But do we hang also his wife even though they are *in some sense one flesh*, as Scripture itself teaches?'"

"Winthrop had no reply to my explanation of what Mrs. Hutchinson meant. Instead he shifted to another charge. 'She professes to receive heaven's revelations as if sacred Scripture were insufficient revelation for her. The woman has made herself into a pope. Massachusetts needs no pope.'"

"At that moment, I did not speak all on my mind. I said prudently, 'At no time has Anne Hutchinson professed to receive *apostolic revelation*. She professes only what you yourself profess, *divine illumination* to interpret Scripture.'"

"I cannot remember all the words that flowed back and forth between Winthrop and me. Yet I thought I detected the flaw at the root of his thinking. He had lost the ability in religious disputes to distinguish between conceivable dangers and actual dangers. When he thought of Mrs. Hutchinson and others of like mind, he no longer permitted himself to distinguish what *might* happen from what *would invariably* happen. If certain supporters of Mrs. Hutchinson *might* fall into the practice of adultery, they would, Winthrop fancied, *necessarily* and *invariably* fall into such a practice. As I listened to the governor's thoughts move back and forth like a spider on the web of its own invention, I saw clearly that he meant to banish anyone who threatened purity of doctrine in his kingdom as he perceived it."

Despite the numerous reports of Winthrop's heavy-handed use of government to entrench his version of sound doctrine and righteousness in Massachusetts and all New England, Roger still believed that the Winthrop he had known in England would return to be the charitable, sensible Christian he had once been. While working in the fields and taking journeys into the forest, he had given much thought to Winthrop.

Mary, seeing the misery on her husband's countenance, challenged him to disclose his thought to Coddington regarding Winthrop. Roger grimaced with conspicuous pain. He turned to Coddington. "Of late I have come to an uncomfortable conjecture regarding my friend Winthrop. Anne Hutchinson has become a mirror image that follows him wherever he goes. He fights too furiously against her image in his mind, and I have been asking myself, 'Why? Does the flaw he fancies to be in her lie instead in himself, a flaw so frightful to him that he fights desperately against it?'"

"Do you know the flaw?" Aspinwall asked in a gentle tone.

"I have only an opinion."

"At least you do not pretend to be quoting the Holy Ghost on the matter. I for one would like to hear your human opinion," said Coddington.

"According to Winthrop, Mrs. Hutchinson believes she receives direct communications from the Holy Spirit, communications that cannot be contested. But it is the governor himself who acts as though he receives direct, indisputable communication by virtue of his being a magistrate. If I am not in error on this, there is a touch of King James in Winthrop."

Coggeshall stroked his silver beard. "How so, Roger?"

"Consider James's speech to Parliament. If we substitute the words *chief magistrate* in the place of *king*, we may better understand Winthrop's image of himself. 'Kings (that is, magistrates) are justly called gods, for they exercise a manner or resemblance of divine power upon Earth.'"

"I have read the very speech," Coggeshall said to everyone in the room. "In it, James said, 'Kings are accountable to none but God only. To the king is due both the affection of the soul and service of the body of his subjects.'"

Aspinwall's eyes grew wide and bright. "Brother Roger, you throw profound light on Governor Winthrop. When he accused Mrs. Hutchinson of violating the Fifth Commandment to honor parents, he like, King James, saw himself as the parent of the people and as deserving their special honor, including obedience."

"It is conspicuous," Mary said. "In him lies a deep, fearful resentment of Mrs. Hutchinson. If he should banish her from Massachusetts, he still will not banish her from his mind. She haunts him by shadowing his thoughts."

"I have a message for you, Brother Roger," Coddington announced. "I think it will surprise you. Joshua Winsor wishes to work for you and Mary and to live in Providence."

The message stunned Mary. "Joshua Winsor, Governor Winthrop's servant?"

"Aye, the same. He has told the governor that it is a scruple of conscience and that he cannot continue serving a household that persecutes other Protestants."

Roger felt numb. So much had happened. "What did the governor say?"

"He will not forbid Winsor to leave," Coddington answered. "There is yet more. Soon there will be eight large families sailing from Boston to Providence to breathe this air of freedom."

Mary made no pretense, saying she could not help feeling vindicated. "If Roger and I cannot return to Boston Bay, then will some of Boston Bay come to Narraganset Bay?"

Eight days later, Mary looked out her window and saw her neighbor Jane Verin walking slowly as though deep in thought. Without speaking to the others in the parlor, Mary hurried outdoors and, though with child, caught up with Jane. "What has befallen you?" She stared at the large bruise on her neighbor's left cheek.   Jane avoided Mary's eyes. "A limb hit me."

"Come with me." She took Jane by the arm and walked her to a maple tree that had not yet begun to shoot forth leaves. Standing under the sprawling tree, Mary put her hand on the lowest limb. "It was not a limb like this that struck you, was it?"

Looking to the ground, Jane shook her head.

Mary remembered that in a recent letter to Roger, Winthrop claimed Jane's husband, Joshua, owed him money, which he requested Roger to collect. As the vicar's daughter in England, Mary had learned well that men who could not pay their debts sometimes beat their wives. "Is it that your Joshua feels less than a man and so behaves like an animal?"

"He is the father of my children."

"You are the mother of his children, but it provides no license for—"

"What you say is true. But . . . ."

Letting silence prevail for a few minutes, Mary wished she could pry open the shell wherein Jane had closed herself. "Remember the clams we harvested from the shores last spring?"

"I remember."

"Has Jane now become a clam?"

She touched the bruise on her cheek. "I deserved this bruise. I did not obey."

"Even when Eusebius disobeys, Roger does not beat him. You have been created in God's image, so do not tell me that you deserve treatment you would not inflict upon a dog!"

After Jane had gone to the spring to bathe her bruise in the cold water, Mary walked toward home. As she approached the house, she came upon William Harris and Joshua Verin. Although they did not see or hear her, she overheard Harris speaking.

"These Narragansets think they do us honor by giving us this land. But who are they, these savages? If I had my way, I would load them all on caged carts and haul them to the Far West. They are no more than field mice who infest the land. Do we receive gifts from mice?"

"If you chip away at the natives' land," Verin warned, "they will soon grow wise to your designs and treat you as they did the Pequots."

"The Pequots were fools." Harris touched his finger to his skull. "They lack what any Englishman takes for granted."

"Do you fancy that Roger Williams will wink and look the other way?"

"The devil take Williams! He means nothing to me."

"And the others?" Verin asked.

"They yap like dogs about liberty of conscience and know nothing about people like me. What care I for this liberty of conscience? If the courts say, 'Pray *this!* I pray this. But if they say, 'Pray *that!* I pray that."

"I fancy I once knew you, William. But I have ne'er heard you talk this way until now," Verin said.

William Harris scooped up a handful of dirt, held it in his hand, and slowly poured it out only to scoop up another. "This is what I want. The land is my religion. Join me, and—"

"And what? What will we do with all this land?"

"Are you blind? In our lifetime, scores, yea, hundreds of ships will come to these shores. People will pour from them. Where will they go? Look at these people, all of them. Do they not want land?" Harris placed the tip of his thumb against his chest. "And if it is in my possession, I will sell it and grow rich. Do not look askance. I see the glint in your eye. You crave riches too though you speak hypocritically, pretending that you love poverty!"

"I have no love of poverty." Verin clenched his fists. "Do you think I relish groveling before Winthrop? Each day I rise, thinking that I owe him money that I do not have."

"But if you had land . . . . Listen to me. I have a scheme that will . . . ."

"What was that?" Verin whirled around and whispered, "Mary Williams! She heard us."

"I think not."

Verin stared incredulously at Harris. "She has ears, and I have eyes. I saw her look at me before she turned away. I will ne'er forget that look."

The next morning, Roger saw Joshua Verin slap Jane across the mouth and shove her to the ground. Without a second thought, he confronted Verin. "Control yourself!"

"Control *myself*? My *wife* wastes her time singing and reading with you Separatists!"

Roger helped Jane to her feet. At that moment, Verin's friend William Arnold rushed up. "Roger, what right have you to interfere? She is not your wife. Does not Scripture command a wife to submit to her husband?"

He ignored Arnold and stared straight into Verin's eyes. "Scripture admonishes a man to love his wife as his own flesh. Would you strike yourself and throw your own body to the ground?"

Verin flushed, his whole face saying, *Get out of my way or I will stomp you into the ground.*

Roger stood firm, cutting his eyes toward Arnold to warn him.

With an angry swipe of his hand in the air, Verin roared at his wife, "Take the children!" He pointed to their house and appeared ready to strike her again but held back, evidently catching sight of the fire in Roger's eyes.

"This is not your concern," Joshua Verin growled fiercely. "It is my liberty of conscience. You preach liberty of conscience, but now you would interfere with mine."

Roger wanted to grab the big man by the collar and throw him against a tree to let him feel the humiliation he had inflicted. "I have seen you show more kindness to your hound than to your wife. Today is not the first time you have violated elementary human decency, Joshua. What has happened to you?"

In the afternoon, Mary heard a pounding at her door. She opened it and quickly caught Jane in her arms.

"You are bleeding!" She pulled Jane to a bed.

No explanation was required. The look of terror on the faces of Jane's children told the story. Joshua Verin had beaten his wife again.

Heavy with child, Mary leaned against the wall and gasped for breath. With the back of her hand, she wiped the hair from her brow and began at once to wash the cut lip and clean the bruises on Jane's face. *Oh, if only Dr. Clarke were here!* she thought, taking gently Jane by the wrist, pulling her arm, and hoping she had set the bone properly.

Jane's children screamed when their mother lay motionless as if life had passed from her.

Mary worked quickly, wrapping the broken arm with a crude splint. After making a sling for the arm, she placed cold, wet cloths on her neighbor's swollen eye. "Little Mary, fetch your father, dear!"

At that moment, Mary heard the voice of Joshua Winsor, formerly Winthrop's servant, coming from the field behind the house. She turned to the oldest Verin child and told her to fetch Mr. Winsor.

While attempting to conceal her horror at the sight of Jane's battered face, Mary rolled up a blanket and put it under her friend's feet to force blood back to her face.

When Winsor and the oldest Verin child entered the house, Mary did not take her eyes off of Jane. "Dr. Clarke is with Miantonomo at the south end of—"

"I know where they have gone. I will take Angell's horse." Winsor then rushed out.

While the sounds of the horses' hooves faded in the distance, Roger entered with Little Mary in his arms. Gasping at the sight of the mother who appeared severely beaten, he felt a sickening rage rise up in him. But the children's eyes, begging him to help their mother, called up a flood of compassion.

"What can I do, Mary?" He gathered Jane's children near him and reassured them with a calming hand on their shoulders.

Mary turned to look at him and opened her mouth to speak. But when she saw the children, she held her tongue. He understood and took his place beside her.

"I have sent for Dr. Clarke," she said.

He found another blanket to cover Jane. As he unfolded the blanket, it occurred to him that the children needed to feel useful. He handed the blanket to the middle child. "Cover your mother," he said softly.

Roger picked up the child who was perhaps five and carried him to his mother's left side. "Here," he said, "take your mother's good arm and rub it. Sing to her. She will hear you."

Though the soft, little voice cracked, the music came out with such tenderness that tears flowed down Mary's cheeks.

Apparently understanding all of today's circumstances, Jane's oldest child took a cloth and wiped Mary's tears lest the other children see them. Mary forced a feeble smile of encouragement.

Roger fought back the fear that Jane would die. Never had he felt so helpless. What could he do? He remembered watching his own father die despite all the work and prayers. The curtain of death had descended so impersonally, so unjustly. Roger now prayed that the Verin children would not lose their mother. Yet he did not know what to do. He could not breathe for her. Longing for her eyes to open, for some part of her to stir, he patted the head of the child who sang heroically.

How could a man savagely attack the mother of his own children? Roger swept away his returning anger. *I must not waste time.* He called two of the other children to the bed and urged each to rub Jane's feet. With all his heart, he believed that few medicines could equal the loving touch of a child's hand. If only he could promise the children that their mother would open her eyes and talk to them. But what he saw made him quake inside.

"Mama, Mama!" the oldest child exclaimed and she looked up into his face. "Did you see her eyes open, Master Williams? I saw them! I saw them!"

Roger nodded. "Kiss her, child. Kiss her cheek and whisper into her ear." Then, aware that he could do no more to prevent their mother from taking leave of this life, he hurried outside to look for Dr. Clarke. If only Miantonomo would come, for he had nurtured many half-dead warriors back to life. Roger felt the desperation in his chest. *Hurry!*

All at once, he saw a horse carrying Miantonomo and Dr. Clarke.

When the horse stopped at the door, Roger quickly took the reins and tied the horse to a post. Both Miantonomo and the doctor hurried inside, Roger following.

The children stiffened as if they had mistaken Dr. Clarke for their father. But when the doctor smiled warmly, they resumed their duties.

After pulling up a chair and sitting beside the patient, Dr. Clarke laid his hand on her forehead. Then he turned around to speak, but the oldest child appeared with the doctor's bag in her hand.

"Thank you, child." Dr. Clarke opened the bag and pulled out a jar. He put some powder between thumb and two fingers and held it at Jane's nostrils. When she did not move, he took more of the powder and rubbed it in his fingers before her nostrils.

The children looked on, their eyes wide with hope *and* fear. With Freeborn in his arms, Roger stood beside the children and comforted them with soft words.

Miantonomo left but soon returned carrying leaves in his hand. Roger and the children watched him roll the leaves in the palm of his hands until they became a little ball. The sachem then handed the ball to the doctor, who placed it near Jane's nostrils.

The children caught their breath when they saw their mother's head move.

Miantonomo folded his arms over his huge chest. The oldest child looked up at him with a smile. Miantonomo smiled back as if to say, *I too have children.*

Mary took the ball of leaves from the doctor and gave it to the oldest Verin child. "Doctor, I think Jane's arm is broken. I tried to set it, but . . . ."

While the oldest child held the ball of leaves near her mother's nose, Dr. Clarke examined the arm. Miantonomo looked to his left and saw a pail of water. He picked it up and set it at the doctor's feet. Mary handed the doctor a cloth, which he dipped into the water and used to bathe the broken arm to counter the fever.

"In time," Dr. Clarke said, "in time."

"Mama!" the middle child exclaimed.

Jane opened her eyes and stared at the ceiling. Her lips parted, and the word *where* came out.

"Mama, we are at Mrs. Williams's house," said the oldest child.

Jane moved her eyes and looked at each child, assuring herself that all were there. Roger and Mary looked at one another as if chains had fallen from their arms. The oldest child tried to smile, but tears appeared instead.

Jane raised her good arm and stroked the child's cheek. The touch seemed to tell her that she was no longer required to be her mother's stoic one. She could be her darling child again.

Roger remembered the touch of his own mother's hand against his face. Though Alice Williams was dead, her kind words and gentle touches had become so much a part of his life that he sometimes felt her to be alive.

All at once, he saw the oldest child looking at him with shame in her beautiful eyes. She seemed to be saying, *Please, do not feel disgust for me because of my father's disgraceful deed.* Roger wanted to tell her that no one held her in disdain because of her father.

Early the next morning, he led a handful of men to Verin's house.

"Joshua!" one of the men shouted. "Come out. We must talk with you at once!"

Unkempt and surly, Verin appeared in the doorway. Leaning against the frame, he shook his head. "You do not know what you ask."

"The time has come to talk, Joshua. Let us speak as men of reason and good will." Roger fought back his own rage. He would have placed the man in stocks or at least before a court, but he knew that English common law gave men more flagrant powers over women than Roman law had given Roman citizens over their slaves. He remembered arguing with Sir Edward Coke, who resisted Roger's claim that all law must be rooted in elementary humaneness. He had quoted to Coke the words of Christ: "The Sabbath was made for man, not man for the Sabbath."

Joshua Verin retorted defiantly, "If our women rise up as our equals, what shall happen to the order of things that heaven has established for us all?"

Roger had tried to set a new example when signing the deed for the territory. He had insisted that Mary's name appear on the deed to give witness to her equality.

Joshua Verin, however, stood among those who regarded women as inferior. More than once, Roger had heard Verin say, "It was Eve, not Adam, who first bit into the forbidden fruit."

With conspicuous contempt, Verin shifted his weight, stooped down to tie his shoe, and again quoted Scripture, portraying himself as the upholder of order against the wiles of the devil.

Taking their cue from Roger, the men let Verin speak at length without suffering rebuke. When at last he could say no more except to repeat himself, Roger sternly cut in. "The devil can quote Scripture, and the hypocrite can hide behind the garb of heaven. Christ has admonished us: *By their fruit, ye shall know them.*"

The other men agreed, urging Verin to repent. The more they talked, however, the more he shook his head insolently. Then he pointed to heaven. "Adam hurled the whole human race into sin when he listened to the woman taken from his ribs."

"You treat your good wife as though she had been taken not from your side, but from your heel," Roger replied. "Christian grace bestows upon no man the authority to strike his wife."

"I will hear no more." Verin then slammed the door shut.

Later that day, Roger and other people of Providence met at Throckmorton's home to decide how to deal with the wife-beater. After a short but intense debate, they proposed denying Verin his right to vote until he showed ample fruit of his repentance and reformation. To this, Roger rose up, his voice shaking. "A man has come near to murdering his wife. He should not be permitted to roam the land. Had he stolen your goods, he would find himself enclosed in stocks before the week's end. Had he beaten your horse to the edge of death, you would have Joshua Verin serving in hard labor for his crime. Have we not agreed that our government exists to protect innocent people from bodily harm?"

"But we are a poor community with no jail. We do not have the means or the jailers to hold this degenerate," John Smith said.

Roger shook his head. "Joshua Verin is no dog, yet he is no less savage than a dog gone mad and dangerous."

John Greene, the man who had angered Endecott in Salem, said, "We cannot extract an eye for an eye in this case. Had he beaten my horse, I would have demanded his horse as compensation. But what can we demand on behalf of the woman?"

"I have no hesitation in my answer," Roger said. "Protection for the woman and children."

"But did Christ not say, 'Turn the other cheek'?" Throckmorton asked.

"This woman has turned a hundred cheeks. 'Tis now time to turn Joshua's cheeks." Roger glanced out the window at Verin's house, wishing he could now enter it and drag the villain to a sturdy jail.

Throckmorton cleared his voice. "I say let us not lock him up but lock him *out.*"

Greene nodded. "Aye, send him out of our midst until he can return in true repentance."

Roger could sense fiery anger flashing in his own eyes. "But this action would only give him freedom and the woman condemnation as though she were the guilty one."

"How so?" asked John Smith, whose hefty wife, Kate, stood at his side.

Roger knew that Kate had once detested Jane. In Massachusetts, she had spread gossip about her. But now Kate said something quite insightful. "The woman's place is with her husband. If you banish Joshua, you unjustly banish her."

"And her children," another voice added.

Roger hoped Kate had repented of her gossip and malice. "Jane has no means to feed herself or her children. If we send Joshua away, do we have a duty to treat her as a widow and her children as orphans? Do we ourselves shelter and feed them until the woman can make a way for herself or until her husband manifests true repentance?"

Some of the women began talking heatedly among themselves. The men waited until one woman stepped forward. "What use is this man Joshua? His children and wife would have fared better had they lived among wolves. We say that it is no marriage between a man and woman, for this Joshua is no man. Give her leave to scrape this carbuncle from her back and the freedom to take a man who has both love and reason."

Joshua's friend William Arnold protested vehemently, pacing before the others, his hands clasped behind him. "It is God's ordinance that wives subject themselves to their husbands. Would you condemn a man who has obeyed this righteous ordinance? If we do not resist this woman's claim on her husband, other wives will pretend to have equal rule of the family!"

John Greene demanded to be heard. "If we play tyrant to our wives in Providence, all the women of New England will justly cry out against us!"

Arnold seemed to fancy himself a lawyer defending an innocent man. "Master Williams plays the hypocrite. He speaks of liberty of conscience, but not for Joshua Verin! I know the reason you have vented your wrath against Mr. Verin. He has not come to hear Master Williams teach, nor has he come to sing hymns. For this, you would persecute him."

"Persecute!" Roger walked up to Arnold. "On which side of Joshua's face do bruises appear? Is *his* arm now in a sling? Is *his* lip cut and swollen? Is *his* eye shut from a blow? A man soaked two weeks in brandy would have stricter logic than yours."

Arnold taunted, "But liberty of conscience—"

Roger's anger erupted. "If for the sake of conscience, Joshua Verin attends no worship, offers no prayers, opens no Bible, then he may freely follow his conscience. But no man is conscience for another man or woman. Heaven gave Joshua one tongue, Jane one tongue; Joshua one brain, Jane one brain."

Arnold threw his arms up in the air. "You do not grasp Joshua's complaint. His wife neglects her duties by praying, reading, and singing too much. When he looks for her, he finds her at the meetings you hold in your house."

"All your charges are according to Joshua's opinion!" one of the women exclaimed angrily. "Does he reason with his wife? Is his fist his tongue?"

"Let us talk with Joshua again," Roger said. "If there is a way to negotiate this matter, it will be to the children's advantage."

"No! No!" Mary stood between her husband and Arnold. "Joshua Verin has lost his power of reason. He will promise, break his promise, promise again, break his promise, bring flowers, and then explode. Do you not see that this man is murderous? He is as vile as a ruthless hog!"

"Amen!" John Greene said.

Adam Morton, with his one leg and one crutch, hobbled forth to stand beside Roger. "I have listened with these two ears, and I say Mary Williams speaks with more wisdom than did Solomon. My left leg lies buried deep in Old England's sod. A wise doctor, seeing the limb corrupt with gangrene, sawed it off lest it kill all of me. I say take the saw to Joshua Gangrene and sever him. If Jane dies by his hand, then her blood be on our hands."

Arnold's young son entered an open door of the house and tugged at Roger's sleeve. Bending over, he listened to the boy whisper that two natives desired to speak with him. Roger stepped outside, and there he met Miantonomo, who leaped from his horse and said, "Two days hence, I will journey to Plymouth for the trial. If my friend Roger Williams would travel with me, I will have justice as my companion."

He understood that Miantonomo referred to the four Englishmen who would stand trial in Plymouth for robbing and murdering a Narraganset native. The flames of anger and passion had already begun to burn high. Some of the English were breathing threats. Although desiring to remain in Throckmorton's house to resolve the decision regarding Joshua Verin, Roger reasoned that he had spoken his heart and mind. The others could render judgment.

He turned to Miantonomo. "What do your people think about the murder? What satisfaction do they demand?"

"The English book says, *Eye for eye, life for life*."

Roger put his hand on Miantonomo's shoulder. "But no more."

The second native clenched his fist. "And no less."

Having followed her husband outside, Mary overheard everything.

Miantonomo placed his huge hand of restraint on the shoulder of the excited Narraganset warrior while he addressed Roger. "If you go to Plymouth on our behalf and on behalf of the English, then those who cry for war must first look you in the eye."

The second native grew calm and looked at Roger. "From your holy book, you read to us, 'Blessed are the peacemakers.' Among our people, you are called the peacemaker."

Miantonomo looked at Mary as if to invite her to join their cause in prevailing upon her husband. "Perhaps your god has sent your husband to us."

Roger shook his head. "My wife is with child. I cannot abandon her at the moment of—"

She placed her hand on her husband's. "Go, love. I will give birth to our child while you give birth to peace. Is it not fitting that a child should grow up in peace and good will?"

He sensed the uneasiness behind her encouragement. He wanted to be at her side. He opened his mouth to speak. But Mary put her finger over his lips and spoke softly. "Did you not tell me that the trial is a chest of powder?"

He again attempted to speak. But Mary pressed her finger harder against his lips. "Let Dr. Clarke do his work. And let my husband do what heaven has given him the gift to do. Go, my love, and carry out this mission for your new child and for all the children in Plymouth."

Like Mary, Roger knew that the cloud of violence hanging over the land was ominous. Her argument had wisdom. If the powder chest exploded, what child, what man or woman would escape the madness?

"You must go," Mary whispered. "Zipporah knows much about childbirth and will give Dr. Clarke good assistance."

Roger looked deeply into her luminous, wise, and compassionate eyes. A cold chill passed through him. *If I should lose my Mary . . . .* With two loyalties tugging at his heart, he said to Miantonomo, "I will not fail you."

Miantonomo turned to face the other native as if to say, *Did I not prophesy that our English friend would join us in search of justice?*

Roger thought that he lacked the wit to discern all of heaven's designs in the quilt of life, but he could not deny that his religion was one of reconciliation. "Miantonomo, if I do not pursue peace, then this face is a mere mask."

Miantonomo laughed. "It is a face that Canonicus delights to behold. He sends his blessing."

On the following day, Roger put on his shirt, stood at the parlor window, and relished the arrival of a rosy dawn.

Suddenly, he exclaimed, "Mary!"

But before she could join him at the window, he dashed outside. "What are you doing, Joshua? I thought you had agreed—"

Joshua pointed one of his muskets at Roger. "Stand back! These are ready to fire."

"Untie her! Jane is not an animal!"

Doors from the neighboring houses flew open, and men rushed out.

Verin called loudly to them all, "This is *my* wife and *my* children. Do not interfere."

Roger turned his eyes on Arnold. "Tell Joshua that what he does is wrong."

"A man has a right to rule his household," Arnold said angrily.

Kate ran out of her house, followed by her husband, who grabbed her arm and said, "No, dear! No!"

"But he has Jane tied! Look at him. He pulls her as though she were a goat!" Kate's plump cheeks grew red with righteous fury.

Throckmorton hurried back into his house and returned with a musket. Roger waved him down and stepped closer to Verin.

Verin raised his musket. "Come closer and I will send you to heaven or hell."

Roger stopped. "Where will you go?"

"To Salem, where the court will give me justice."

If anyone tries to overpower Verin, Roger thought, *more than one of us will die.* "No!" he shouted. "Think of your children."

Greene ran out of his house and raised his pistol.

"Stop!" Roger roared and quickly stationed himself between Greene and Verin, who now had his musket pointed at Jane's skull. "Her blood will be on our hands if he kills her," Roger said gravely. Two thoughts jolted him. If today anyone were killed, the Massachusetts Court would use it as an excuse to send soldiers to destroy the refuge of conscience called Providence. He feared even more that upon turning a deaf ear to the pleas of his children, Verin would shoot Jane and perhaps eventually the children.

Her head bound in white cloths, Jane raised her feeble voice. "I beg you, Joshua. Let no blood be shed."

All at once, Roger's heart leaped. Mary was walking toward Joshua. *What . . . ?*

"Joshua, you may shoot me. I cannot prevent you, but I must speak to Jane." Mary held a large muskmelon in each hand and continued walking toward her friend.

Roger moved to stop Mary, but she held out her arm and shook her head. He understood; and though afraid for her, he admired her courage and compassion. He looked at Verin and raised one palm in peace. "I will do you no harm, Joshua." Then Roger joined Mary, and they walked slowly toward Jane.

The people of Providence stood motionless as if they were bloodless figures in a museum.

Roger and Mary stopped in front of Verin. "Joshua, you know me to be a man of my word," he said in a quiet voice while thinking that Joshua was not a man of his word.

Mary handed a melon to the oldest child. "Take this, dear."

Verin pointed his musket to the ground. His face became that of another man, as though the skin had been removed and a mask given to replace it. The eyes seemed dead, the hatred gone, the love absent, the life drained away.

Mary turned to Jane. "You have won our hearts. We will not forget."

Jane's eyes carried immeasurable sorrow. "Dear, kind friend. The children will always remember Mary Williams."

Mary handed the other melon to Joshua. "When you arrive in Salem, ask for the physician. I wish to look upon Jane's face on another day. Go now. Jane is right. Let there be no bloodshed. God forgive you for your wickedness." Mary then kissed the children, one by one.

The oldest girl threw her arms around Roger but refused to cry.

"Enough of this!" Arnold said gruffly. "The ship will soon arrive."

With all their worldly goods loaded onto the cart pulled by Joshua, the Verin family headed on foot toward the harbor in nearby Narraganset Bay. The forlorn look on Jane's face entered Roger's heart like a cold blade. He shook his head in grief as he watched the children following like little ducklings behind their mother. Their eyes did not look ahead in hope, but stared down at the ground like those of prisoners marching in chains. He felt their humiliation. "Wait, Joshua." Roger rushed to the house and returned with a large piece of cloth and a large pot filled with nuts he had gathered in the forest. Setting the big vessel on the ground, he tore the cloth into squares and scooped out hands full of shelled nuts for each child to tie up in a cloth. "Take them." He gently touched each child on the shoulder. Then suddenly, other men ran to their houses and returned with gifts for the children.

Angell volunteered the services of the mule. "With Hugo's help, you will meet the ship in time."

Joshua Verin put aside his musket, but Mary frowned, doubting that he had put away his wrath.

When the Verins had disappeared over the horizon, Mary hugged Freeborn and Little Mary. "Kate, would you mind tending my children while Roger and I talk privately?"

At the bubbling brook, Mary threw rocks into the water. Never had Roger seen her move her arm so powerfully. Before she could pick up another stone, he took her hand and rubbed it gently. "Love, remember, you are with child."

"And you are with blame! Though you founded Providence as a town of freedom, Jane Verin now serves a life sentence in Joshua's brutal prison falsely called a marriage."

The rocks Mary had thrown in the water now seemed to pound his chest. True, Verin had a weapon and might have killed many if the townsmen had moved to capture him. True, the Massachusetts Court would use the dispute as an excuse to take over Providence. *Yet Mary's charge is properly aimed.* As a minister, he should not have confronted Verin publicly. A man rebuked before his family and friends develops even more rage than a man who cannot pay his debts. *Consider Wilfred Barry, who had forced his wife to bed! A few quiet talks with him had served well his better nature, and now both Providence and Agnes reap the benefits of the carpenter's talents and kindness.*

"Mary, tell me plainly. Do you think Joshua Verin could change into a good husband?"

"Some men twist the gospel to give them control that God never intended them to have. Verin yearns for power too much to listen to reason. I . . . I hurt so deeply for Jane and her children."

They sat silently in each other's arms, watching a red-tailed hawk fly over the bubbling brook. Then Roger looked directly into Mary's luminous blue eyes. "I vow that Providence will be a haven for all law-abiding men and women, even if someday I must sail to England to lobby for a charter to fend off the greedy Boston magistrates. Mary, dear, when the time comes for signing the deed for the Providence territory, you must sign it too. Liberty without means is mere air. You have opened my eyes to this truth. God be my witness. Never will you be without your own means!"

An eagle swooped down and glided over the bubbling brook as hearty chickadees chirped atop a nearby oak tree. Roger sensed hope but recalled the streaks of lightning Mary and he had seen their first year in the New World. Memories of violence merged as if presently before his eyes: Jane and her children in the hands of Joshua; Bartholomew Legate at the burning stake in London; and Sir Walter Raleigh at the guillotine. He remembered Sir Edward Coke's patience and courage in writing the Petition of Right and waiting until the proper time to introduce it. *Yes, patience and courage. But also persistence!* These three Roger vowed he would wield against *tyranny* of every kind.

For the rest of the winter, Providence became the crossroad for news and negotiations among the New England colonies. The home of Roger and Mary became neutral ground where diverse parties and factions could meet in peace, including the Narragansets, the leaders of the new plantation to the west, certain Massachusetts magistrates, the Plymouth delegates, and the enigmatic Mohawks near the Connecticut border.

As winter ended with howling winds and deep snows, Roger fell into deep contemplation. Even when at work at the trading post or in the forest, he would stop, lean on his axe, and disappear into thought. He knew his neighbors jested that when pausing to think, he sometimes turned into an immutable statue. Unconcerned that he appeared ridiculous, he good-naturedly replied to Mary's teasing, "Perhaps I am posing for the day when I become sculpted as a resting station for robins."

Despite all the humor, he knew that those around him understood that his mind, now a center of crosswinds, of necessity spent long hours striving with new thoughts and refining old doctrines.

He had grown exceedingly fond of his and Little Mary's dog Eusebius. As a boy in London, he had seen few dogs, the plague having killed most of them. The chestnut, shaggy-haired Eusebius, larger now than a wolf, followed him lamblike each time he entered the forest. He had become Roger's attentive companion. With his big, brown eyes and alert ears, Eusebius often looked up into his master's face as if to say, *You can talk to me, for we are companions.* Often when they were alone, he talked to the lovable mongrel, whose diverse ancestry complemented the new plurality of Roger's thoughts and Narraganset Bay.

He was pleased of late to observe a tender friendship between Freeborn and Eusebius. The dog seemed to take uncanny pride in serving as her sentinel. Each morning he would wake her with the touch of his nose as if to say, *Freeborn has nothing to fear with Eusebius at her side.*

A letter from John Milton contained such wondrous news that Roger read it again and again.

> My Dear Friend Roger,
>
> Sir Edward Coke's labor bears fruit in England. His work to eliminate all confessions obtained under torture has borne fruit. We in England who cherish liberty have renewed hope. Soon Parliament will vote to stipulate by law that forced confessions will carry no weight and will instead bring swift legal retribution to those who practice extracting confessions by torture or threat of torture . . . .

How fortunate to have known the great English judge! Roger thought, vowing to continue the battle against tyranny. The seeds that Sir Edward Coke had sown, Roger would sow in the New World. And they would take deep root, continuing to produce fruit centuries after his own mortal frame had turned to dust.

www.ingramcontent.com/pod-product-compliance
Lightning Source LLC
Chambersburg PA
CBHW072026020726
47501CB00006B/1979